O9-BTI-937

PYM

PYM

···*A Novel* ···

MAT JOHNSON

SPIEGEL & GRAU
New York
2010

Copyright © 2011 by Mat Johnson

Published in the United States by Spiegel & Grau, an imprint of The Random House Publishing Group, a division of Random House, Inc., New York.

SPIEGEL & GRAU and Design is a registered trademark of Random House, Inc.

LIBRARY OF CONGRESS CATALOGING-IN-PUBLICATION DATA
Johnson, Mat.
Pym: a novel / Mat Johnson.
p. cm.
ISBN 978-0-8129-8158-2
eBook ISBN 978-0-679-60382-5
1. African American college teachers—Fiction. 2. Voyages and travels—Fiction. 3. Arctic regions—Discovery and exploration—Fiction. 4. Poe, Edgar Allan, 1809–1849. Narrative of Arthur Gordon Pym—Fiction. I. Title.
PS3560.O38167P96 2010
813'.6—dc22   2010029331

Printed in the United States of America on acid-free paper

www.spiegelandgrau.com

2 4 6 8 9 7 5 3 1

FIRST EDITION

Book design by Simon M. Sullivan

For Meera

PYM

PREFACE

UPON *my return to the United States a few months ago, after the ex-*
traordinary series of adventures in the South Seas and elsewhere, which
you can read about on the pages that follow, I found myself in the com-
pany of several gentlemen in Richmond, Va., who were deeply interested
in the regions I had visited, and who were constantly urging it upon me,
as a duty, to give my narrative to the public. Yet here our intentions di-
verge (at crossroads travelers may meet, then move on in different, at times
opposing directions). For sociological and historical purposes they
wanted me to tell my story, to enlighten them about my experience. I had
several reasons, however, for declining this request, some of which con-
cerned me alone, others less so. One issue which gave me pause was that,
since I took no pictures or recordings of consequence and barely cracked
my laptop during the greater portion of the time in question, I might not
be able to write solely from memory an account so airtight and accurate
as to leave no doubt of its truth. Another reason was that the incidents to
be retold were admittedly so outrageous that, without having proof (ex-
cept a single corpse who was in life a drunken, two-hundred-year-old
pickle), I could only hope for the trust of my audience, and specifically
those of my past associates who have had reason, over the years, to have
faith in my sincerity. I knew the chances were that the public at large
would regard what I will now attempt to tell as little more than the rant
of a paranoid. Adding to this, I must admit an insecurity in my own abil-
ities as a writer, that this was one of the principal causes that prevented
me from complying with the suggestion of my advisers sooner.

Among those brothers outside of Virginia who expressed the greatest interest in my story, or really the part which related to my experiences in the Antarctic region, was Mr. Johnson, at the time an assistant professor of language and literature at Bard College, a historically white institution, in the town of Annandale, along the Hudson River. He strongly advised me (to the point of discomfort) to prepare at once a full record of what happened, and trust to the shrewdness and common sense of the folks to figure it out. To place it in nonthreatening story form for those who, even if they don't believe my story, would be willing to still take a bite and try to swallow it nonetheless. It was also Mr. Johnson's decision to present these revelations under the guise of fiction, and with this strategy I agree. For one, doing so provides a level of synchronicity with the seminal text that began my journey. Also, it keeps me from being sued by the _____ Cola corporation, and not being sued is always a good thing. And there are more ephemeral motivations as well. In this age when reality is built on big lies, what better place for truth than fiction?

This exposé being made, it will be obvious to those who would compare the few works of Mr. Johnson where his brief assistance in this narrative begins and ends. Regardless, it should be emphasized that I have approved the following manuscript and in thought, intent, and theory I claim it as my own.

C. Jaynes. Philadelphia, January 19, 2009

VOLUME

...I...

CHAPTER I

ALWAYS thought if I didn't get tenure I would shoot myself or strap a bomb to my chest and walk into the faculty cafeteria, but when it happened I just got bourbon drunk and cried a lot and rolled into a ball on my office floor. A couple days of this and I couldn't take it so I ended classes a week early and checked into the Akwaaba Bed and Breakfast in Harlem to be among my own race and party away the pain. But mostly I just found myself back in that same ball some more, still on the floor, just at a more histori-cally resonant address. My buddy Garth Frierson, he'd been laid off about six months before, and was nice enough to drive all the way from Detroit to help a childhood friend. This help mostly con-sisted of him sitting his bus driver ass on my rented bed, busting on me until I had enough shame to get off my own duff and try to make something of myself again.

By then the term was over, graduation done, campus vacant. I didn't want to see anybody. The only things worse than the ones who were happy about my dismissal were the ones that weren't. The sympathy, the condolences. It was all so white. I was the only black male professor on campus. Professor of African American Literature. Professional Negro. Over the years since my original hire I pushed away from that and insisted on teaching American lit-erature in general, following a path toward my passion, toward Edgar Allan Poe. Specifically, I offered the course "Dancing with the Darkies: Whiteness in the Literary Mind" twice a year, regardless of enrollment. In regard to the number of students who chose to attend the seminar, I must say in my defense that the greatest ideas are often presented to empty chairs. However, a different theory on proper class size was cited in my denial letter from the president, and given as a reason to overturn the faculty's approval.

Curing America's racial pathology couldn't be done with good intentions or presidential elections. Like all diseases, it had to be analyzed at a microscopic level. What I discovered during my studies in Poe's and other early Americans' texts was the intellectual source of racial Whiteness. Here, in these pages, was the very fossil record of how this odd and illogical sickness formed. Here was the twisted mythic underpinnings of modern racial thought that could never before be dismantled because we were standing on them. You don't cure an illness by ignoring it or just fighting the symptoms. A Kleenex has never eradicated a cold. I was doing essential work, work affecting domestic policy, foreign policy, the entire social fabric of the most powerful nation of the world. Work that related directly to the way we lived our daily lives and perceived reality itself. Who cared if a bunch of overprivileged nineteen-year-olds with questionable hygiene could be bothered to rise for the 8 A.M. class? Who cared if I chose to not waste even more precious research time attending the toothless Diversity Committee?

"Just get your books, dog. And get out of there. Pack up your place, focus on what you can do. You want, you can come back with me to Detroit. It's cheap, I got a big crib. Ain't no jobs, but still." Garth and I drove up the Taconic in the rain. I was still drunk, and the wet road was like lines on a snake's back and my stomach was going to spill. Even drunk, I knew any escape plan that involved going to Detroit, Michigan, was a harbinger of doom. Garth Frierson was my boy, from when we were boys, from when I lived in a basement apartment in Philly and he lived over the laundromat next door. Garth didn't even ask how many books I had, but he must have suspected.

Because I had books. I had books like a lit professor has books. And then I had more books, finer books. First editions. Rare prints. Copies signed by hands long dead. Angela walked out on me a long time ago and my chance of children walked with her, but I had multiplied in my own way. I'd had shelves built in my office for these books, shelves ten feet tall and completely lining the drywall.

The campus was dead. A vacant compound hidden from the road by darkness and hulking pines. The gravel parking lot was empty, but I made Garth park in the spot that said PRESIDENT— VIOLATORS WILL BE TOWED ON PRINCIPLE. When you get denied tenure at a college like this—intimate, good but not great—your career is over. A decade of job preparation, and no one else will hire you. If you haven't published enough, people assume tenure denial means you never will. If you have published and were still denied, people assume you're an asshole. Nobody wants to give a job for life to an asshole. And they didn't have to in this economy. Outside of a miracle, after denial I would be lucky to scrounge up adjunct teaching at a community college somewhere cold, barren, and far from the ocean. A life of little health insurance, bill collector calls, and classrooms with metal detectors, all compliments of this college president, Mr. Bowtie. The least I could do was shit in his space for an hour.

We trudged. The building looked like an old church that had lost its faith, every step up the stairs a sacrilege. Garth huffed, but followed. I'd chosen an office in the back of the top floor to dissuade students, but my lectures had done a better job of this. My office was a narrow A-framed cathedral with a matching window. A shrine to the books that lined the walls and my own solitude.

"Bro, I'm not going to lie to you. I got a lot of books in here," I said, letting him in first.

"You do?" Garth asked me. Because I didn't.

It was empty. I should have been greeted with the hundreds of colored spines of literary loves, but there was nothing. My books were gone. My office had been cleared out. Everything was gone: my pictures, my lamp, my Persian rug, everything not school property or nailed down, gone. A chasm of vacant whitewashed bookshelves opened up before me.

I was breathless. Garth was out of breath, but for him, it was just all the stairs.

"They took my shit, man. They took my shit," I kept repeating. I walked over to the desk and pulled out all the drawers. There were some chewed yellow pencils left, and a few folded Post-its and bent paper clips, but that's not what I was looking for. I kept searching, desperate, sliding pencils and papers around, looking for more.

"Damn, dog. You didn't have no porn in there, did you?" Garth already had his Little Debbie out and was chewing on it like it was his reward for making it up three floors of nineteenth-century stairs.

"Just a picture," I told him.

"A picture of what?"

"Angela," I admitted.

"Worse," Garth said, head wagging.

I slammed the drawer shut, and it was loud. And I liked that sound, a moment of violence, but this time coming from me. So then I started banging on the empty shelves with my fists, and they vibrated. You could hear the echo in the room, then bouncing off into the empty building beyond us until Garth closed the door.

"That's wrong, man. Disrespectful. Forget them, job's over. That's life, what you going to do?"

I was going to show up at the president's house and kick his ass, it occurred to me. This act suddenly seemed like the only thing worth running away to Detroit for. I didn't tell Garth this, because he would have stopped me. He was big enough to fill up the door. He was even bigger since he'd been laid off. I remembered when this man was skinny, ran track. Ran it poorly, but still. It was depressing looking at every extra pound on him, each a reminder that we were both moving swiftly into decline with little else as accomplishment.

"Wait in the car, man. I just have to check my mail," I told him. Garth did it. I'm a bad liar, but he was tired and it was really cold outside, and brothers don't like the cold.* It was late spring, but it had been raining for a week and upstate New York was frigid in a way which was more gothic and empiric than the Philly chill we'd grown up with.

"You drunk. I'm tired as all hell. The sooner you get your ass out of here, the sooner you get to get your ass out of here," Garth offered, but he left. So then I walked over to the president's house to punch him and maybe kick him a few times too.

In my head, I was getting "gangsta," which I've always felt showed greater intent than getting "gangster" in that it expresses a willful unlawfulness even upon its own linguistic representation. I was going to show him how we do where I'm from, go straight Philly on him, and I knew all about that because, although I had never actually punched someone in the face before, as a child I myself had been on the receiving end of that act several times and was a quick study.

The president's house was at the other end of the campus, but it was a small liberal arts campus. An empty space, dorms and buildings deserted, solar streetlamps popping on and off for just me. While I was walking, stoking my anger, thinking of all the work I'd done and all that security I was now being denied, I came

* Matthew Henson excluded.

to the administration building, and I saw that there was a light on. Downstairs, in the back, in the president's office. No one just left interior lights on, the environmental footprint too massive, the cost too high, and with every attack the prices went even higher. So he was in there. The outside door opened, and I knew he was in there.

And then there was this overwhelming emotion. It was not rage or anger. It was something even more illicit, unwanted. It was hope. Here we were, two men alone. Society vacated, and now just two men and a problem, one that somehow in my stupor seemed workable. There was a guy down the hall, a Romanticist, who had been denied tenure ten years ago. Approved by the faculty committee, just as I was, only to be shot down by the same president in the same manner. And he had, in his grief, approached the all-powerful boss man, and he had repented all of his sins, real and imagined, and was granted a permanent teaching gig. It made sense too, for as Frederick Douglass's narrative tells us, it is more valuable to a master to have a morally broken slave than to have a confident one. That Romanticist's story had always seemed humiliating to me before this moment, but suddenly it became inspirational. At the president's door, I paused, prepared myself for what could be simply the final test before I overcame my troubles. I took a deep breath to prepare for a performance of dignified groveling. Then I heard the music coming from inside.

What I saw scared me. Took me out of my confidence, my momentum. What do you make of a Jew sitting in the dark listening to Wagner in this day and age? I could think of no more call to the end of the world than the one I was looking at. Random violence on the news had become background noise to me at that point, but this scene genuinely scared my ass. Still in his bow tie and tweed jacket at this time of night, it was disgusting. He hit his keyboard quickly, and suddenly the sound became Mahler, but I knew, I knew what I'd heard. As the sound cleansed the room, the bald man just looked at me, drink in hand. As drunk as I was, I could still smell the sweet singe of alcohol hanging in the air.

"My shit!" it came out. It lacked the eloquence of a planned rebuttal, but he understood.

"Packed by movers, delivered to your listed residence. A thank-you, really, for your service. Thank you." He said the last bit as if I should be saying this to him, but still it robbed me of a bit of my momentum. I had been surviving on righteous indignation and self-pity for weeks, I realized once the supply seemed threatened. But then I remembered I'd been canned and my fuel line kicked in once more.

"Is it because I refused to be on the Diversity Committee?" I demanded. I was loud, the halls were empty. The echo enhanced my argument.

"Well, that certainly would have . . . ," he began, but seeing that I was hearing every word, already planning my deposition for my discrimination lawsuit, he stopped himself. "Your file was examined as a whole. You were hired to teach African American literature. Not just American literature. You fought that. Simple."

"So you want the black guy to just teach black books to the white kids."

"We have a large literature faculty, they can handle the majority of literature. You were retained to purvey the minority perspective. I see nothing wrong with that." He shrugged, poured a second drink in a second glass and pushed it forward to me with the base of the bottle.

"You have academics going off the farm all the time. Yeats scholars who end up following their way to Proust. You have a film professor who was hired as a German linguist."

"A Guggenheim, a Fulbright, and a Rhodes scholar. Mr. Jaynes, you . . . you have accomplished no such honor or distinction. I do not mean that as an insult, just an unfortunate reality."

A big part of me hurt a lot hearing this said aloud, in a big way. I blushed, and as pale as I was I blushed possibly as no black man had done before me. Staring at him, I settled myself staring at his bastard tie. Look at it. That bow tie was hypnotizing. Usually men of power have useless fabric tied around their necks, but his was smaller, and tied at a different angle. No big phallic thing for this guy. No, it was even worse, it was "Look at me, I have an itty-bitty micro-phallic tie around my neck, and yet I still have all this power over you."

"Please, listen to me," I pleaded. "My work, it's about finding the answer to why we have failed to truly become a postracial society. It's about finding the cure! A thousand Baldwin and Ellison essays can't do this, you have to go to the source, that's why I started focusing on Poe. If we can identify how the pathology of Whiteness was constructed, then we can learn how to dismantle it. The work I am doing, it's just books, sure, but it's important, essential research. You're going to fire me for refusing to sit on the campus Diversity Committee?"

"You could have compensated for your lack of national presence by embracing our role locally, but alas," he told me and looked away. "Everyone has a role to play."

I put my hand out to him, and before he could meet my palm with his own I reached higher and grabbed the tie on his neck. It was a clip-on and came off easily, barely shook him when I yanked it off in my fist. I was right about it being his power source. He was totally quiet after it was taken from him. I didn't hear a peep behind me as I ran from the confrontation.

· · ·

When I got to the car, I told Garth that my academic career was probably over, but since I'd been saying the same thing for a couple days he just tuned me out as he tuned in the radio.

"Take me to this place, before we go. It was done at a park about two miles from your house. I already Googled it," he said, reaching across me to get into the glove compartment. Garth pulled out this print of a painting, all scrolled up, and dropped it in my lap. I unraveled it and saw a syrupy sweet landscape of the Catskills, the kind of vista painted on how-to shows in a half hour. The kind of painting Garth adored, done by that artist he idolized.

"It's called *Stock of the Woods*," he said. "It's a Thomas Karvel Hudson Valley School Edition. A tribute to the painters they used to have here. I have an original signed print. That's part of my nest egg, and you're there laughing at it. Look at it. Really look at it, you need to. Don't it make you all peaceful just looking into that world?"

"Looks like the view up a Care Bear's ass."

"I got stress!" Garth turned and started yelling at me, his tree air fresheners dancing over the dashboard from the wind. "I got no type of job. I got no savings. The whole world's hell. The world is pollution and terrorism and warming and whatever, I don't know, whatever gets dropped next. I drive a bus! Or I used to. I'm a thirty-eight-year-old man who drives a bus and I ain't even got that now. I got stress!" Garth pushed past me to get another Little Debbie snack cake from the box beneath my legs, and calmed down eating it.

"My man, you're like a home experiment in type 2 diabetes. Your picture, it's real nice, okay? And I'll take you wherever. But you need to calm the hell down," I told him, and he did. So we took to the road the last few miles to my home.

He was stressed. I understood. I understood even before we got to my house and saw all my books sitting there, on the front porch.

Not in boxes, just stacked there. Hundreds of them. My books, my treasure. Sitting in the rain, bloated with a week's worth of water and dirt and mold. Pages bursting open like they were screaming. Some lug nut from the physical plant had just left them there and driven off again. Tens of thousands of dollars, years of collecting. Destroyed. Irreplaceable. Gifts, inscriptions, ruined. I picked one up, threw it down, started screaming. Jumping. When I finished, Garth held out one of his Little Debbie cakes to me, cellophane already pulled back for convenience. Poking closer and closer to my face till I took it from him.

"Come on, take a bite of the white girl. It will make you feel good."

"I'm going back to campus. I'm going back to campus and I'm going to get that bastard."

"Damn dog. You already got his bow tie."

. . .

I went to the bar. Garth was tired from driving and so stayed back. On the way I made a call to my lawyer, and one hopefully to my antiquarian as well. The latter told me he had something special, something signed, first edition, and I caught myself almost smiling in response. Life would move on, I tried to remind myself. Presumably, it would take me with it.

There was one bar in town and there was a black guy sitting in it, and this I took as a divine miracle, maybe even another sign of my impending turn of fortune. It was a town of only 1,163, just eight miles north of the campus. Aside from a handful of students during term, there were no black people in the area. In the summer tourism months, on occasion you could spot a black woman with her white partner passing through, but often these visitors were particularly disinclined to coethnic bonding. This brother wasn't, though. When I walked in he looked up and smiled at me like he knew me and I gave him the nigga-nod and he hit me right back so I knew we were cool. I sat down next to him.

"Mosaic Johnson. Hip-Hop Theorist." Of course he was an academic. Of course I was. There was no other reason for two obviously educated black men to be there. And it was obvious, even of him, dressed as he was in his carefully selected baggy jeans, hat to the side, and other matching oversize pop culture juvenilia. But he was a professor of music, so allowances could be made for the styling.

"Chris Jaynes. Americanist." And our fists bumped in blackademic bliss. Mr. Johnson was a younger man than I, in both years and manner. Dressed like he was straight out of Compton, but clearly straight out of a postdoc instead. Just arrived in town to start teaching the following term, coming in the summer because his lease in Chicago was up and this was his future. Eager. Earnest. Through drunken eyes, I looked at Mosaic Johnson and I saw myself there. I saw myself showing up in this town, seeing it as foreign territory I was hopeful to invade. Twenty-one years of academic training culminating in permanent entrenchment on the business side of the classroom. Theory finally turned into practice, a practice of yapping about theory. Just like me. I wept for this bastard.

"Don't join the Diversity Committee," I told him when the third round hit. We'd been talking well, for a minute, mostly me bemoaning the history of Dutch slavery in the area, but he hung with me. A squat dude whose only thinness was his mustache, Mosaic seemed to roll a bit away from me when I said this, but I leaned closer because he needed to hear it.

"These historically white institutions, they get that one black professor, they put him or her on something they call the 'Diversity Committee.' Don't let them put you there. It's a slave hold.

They'll fight you: they'll really want you on the Diversity Committee because if there aren't any minorities on the committee, the committee isn't diverse."

"Man, in my work, I deal with the ghetto. The real shit, you know what I'm saying? Reality," he told me, motioning around the room with a silver-ringed hand as if our present setting was mere computer simulation. "I'm not trying to run from the folks. I want to be on that committee. I'm a fighter. I want to be on that committee, to bring the fight here." The hand in the air formed into a fist. I looked around the room, at the twenty or so white liberals taking him in on the sly. They loved it. They loved that fist. If I was still here tomorrow, they would come up to me and ask why I never raised the black power fist like the new guy. Undaunted, I continued.

"No, you don't, and I'll tell you why. The Diversity Committee has one primary purpose: so that the school can say it has a diversity committee. They need that for when students get upset about race issues or general ethnic stuff. It allows the faculty and administration to point to it and go, 'Everything's going to be okay, we have formed a committee.' People find that very relaxing. It's sort of like, if you had a fire, and instead of putting it out, you formed a fire committee. But none of the ideas that come out of all that committeeing will ever be implemented, see? Nothing the committee has suggested in thirty years has ever been funded. It's a gerbil wheel, meant to 'Keep this nigger boy running.' "

"Ellison." He smiled. I knew a black author reference would get to him. "Now that cat was straight hip-hop," he continued. I would have corrected the hip to be, but what's a difference of black American musical traditions among kin?

"Chris Jaynes. You know, I've read some of your early work, your Ellison theory. That had the beat. Why don't you bring it like that no more?" he asked me, and I glowed at this. Old musicians asked to play their classic songs, they must get this feeling. You're tired of it, sure, but at least somebody cares. I thanked him, told him how I've developed, how I've been drawn toward nineteenth-century fiction, Edgar Allan Poe.

As I'm getting up to hit the john, right as I'm turned away, Mosaic Johnson says, "Man, nobody cares about the Poe thing." And I laughed back at him and told him thanks for getting my pain and in moments I was off to pissing.

In the can, standing in front of the urinal, I was still for the moment. It felt like it was the first time I was truly still since this whole disaster had started. Even when I was pulled into a ball on the floor, I was rocking and reeling internally. But this bathroom, this empty bathroom, it was like a temple. Utterly serene. And within that silence, clarity came to me. I started thinking about my past, and my new friend. And I started to think about everything he had said, and all of his responses. And I was surprised to find a previously undetected negative tone there. Not in his words, but in the little performances in his demeanor. His last statement being the irrefutable proof of this.

"You're not in the music department are you?" I said to him on my return. I didn't even sit down. I was standing. I was shaking. My voice was cracking a little bit too, which was beyond my control.

"No, I am not. My instrument is the QWERTY keyboard," he admitted. Took the last swig from his Hennessy, and then swiveled to face me.

"You're here to replace me, aren't you? You're here to take my job. To take my office. That's why you're in this bar tonight, isn't it?"

"Man, just relax. Ain't nothing personal. Yes, I'm the new hire. Yes, it was your tenure line. I never said I was a music prof. I said I was a hip-hop theorist, okay? That's my school of literary criticism, right? I'm here to bring the beat to the text, that's it. It's all good. And hell yes I will represent myself as the strong black man I am on this campus."

"Right. You're here to be the Diversity Committee."

"Look, cuz, unlike you, clearly, I believe in trying to change things. Fighting against racism where I see it. I don't back down, and I don't apologize for that either. Hell yeah, I'm down for the damn committee. I'm down for the fight, know what I'm saying?" A Ph.D. can't manage a lot of menace, but we are good at reading between the lines. I knew exactly what he meant, no footnotes needed. Still, I stepped in closer.

"You know what I think? I think that when you fight the same battles, with the same tactics, you don't get any further. That unless you address the roots of the problem, it will continue to grow."

This was fairly eloquent for me. Given that it was off the cuff. No peer review or rewrites. And I was proud that I had thought it there and not later via *l'esprit de l'escalier.* It was the arrogance brought on by this success that made me pause two steps into my exit, turn, and continue.

"And the white folks here know that. And they like it that way. You're hired to be the angry black guy, get it? You're not fighting Whiteness, you're feeding its perversion. You're here so you can assuage their guilt without making them actually change a damn thing. They want you to be the Diversity Committee. Because every village needs a fool." Still, I felt I was sticking to my thesis closely, not diverting off into too much bullshit. If Mosaic Johnson had kept his mushy buttocks on the stool instead of getting in my face then, it would have made a decent closer.

"Oh I get it. I get it now, why you love Poe. You two share one big thing in common. Neither one of you is a damn bit relevant anymore."

"This college can really use you," I returned, preparing myself to hoof it. "Every good zoo needs a caged gorilla."

It was an inflammatory statement. I lit that shit on fire too, just to watch him burn. Even I was offended, to tell the truth, and that's why I chose that level of toxic phraseology to hit him. He hit me back, though. First in the gut and then, when I went down to the floor, in several other places.

Mosiac Johnson could definitely bring the beat. To me personally, he brought the beat down.*

"Poe. Doesn't. Matter," he said as he pummeled. I respected him for that, though. He guessed correctly his weak suburban mini-mall kung fu punches might not be enough to hurt me.

"Tekeli-li!" I laughed, as the crowd pulled Mosaic Johnson from my body.

"Tekeli-li!"

* Not to be confused with the "downbeat."

CHAPTER II

TEKELI-LI. Tekeli-li, Tekeli-li. I got that from *Pym*. I got that from Poe. *The Narrative of Arthur Gordon Pym of Nantucket* by Edgar Allan Poe, specifically. *Pym* that is maddening, *Pym* that is brilliance, *Pym* whose failures entice instead of repel. *Pym* that flows and ignites and *Pym* that becomes so entrenched it stagnates for hundreds of words at a time. A book that at points makes no sense, gets wrong both history and science, and yet stumbles into an emotional truth greater than both.

The Narrative of Arthur Gordon Pym was Edgar Allan Poe's only novel. It shows. A self-proclaimed "magazinist" who plied his trade mostly with Virginia's *Southern Literary Messenger*, Poe attempted the long form only because that's what the editors at Harper & Brothers were looking for. Poe was broke, his relationship with the *Messenger* soured, his intended entrée into New York literary society failed in drunken spectacle. Spiraling into the wreck he became known for, Edgar Allan Poe was barely writing anything new and couldn't find buyers for a collection of his short stories. The novel was a novelty, a lucrative one, so he cashed in. As for the idea of a book in "which a single connected story occupies the whole volume," Poe went along grudgingly, belligerent.

We start the story as Pym and his best friend, the ace sailor Augustus, joyride on a small boat at their home port in Nantucket, only to have Augustus pass out drunk not long after they set sail into the night. The two get rescued and, having escaped near dismemberment and drowning, decide the sea is the life for them. The novice Pym can't get passage on one of whalers headed out of town, so Augustus stows his boy away in a large crate in the hold, placing a mattress, a bit of water, and a few snacks inside with him. The plan is that Pym will spring out after a few days at sea and reveal himself to the crew when it's too late to turn back and dump him. Problem is, Augustus never comes back for him. We don't know why, and neither does our impish hero. As a result, Pym starts starving to death, dehydrating in the dark hull, where the oddly jumbled cargo threatens with each wave to fall over and crush him.

Then Pym is attacked by a lion (an African lion, in the darkness: begin trend here). Except it's not a lion, it is Tiger, Arthur Pym's exceptionally beloved canine companion, who just happens to be in the hold with him. "For the presence of Tiger I tried in vain to account," Pym tells us, and we agree, because for the thirty-odd pages that led up to this point, not one goddamn line was mentioned about any dog, a narrative error Poe tries to compensate for by telling us how much he really really really loved this pet. Eventually, after an extended period of time and pages during which even the reader becomes claustrophobic, we get word from Augustus about what has happened: the Negroes have uprisen.

Really, the mutineers are just the lower classes of the ship's staff, led by a massive black cook.* Among this group is a man described as a half-breed Indian (the other half is given no race, so European ancestry—nonracial norm that it is—is the implied assumption). His name is Dirk Peters. Odd, however, is the description of this Peters:

---

* Reference: Buck Nigger archetype. Meaning: Any large, physically imposing Negro whose very presence demands that others get the "buck" out of his way.

He was short in stature—not more than four feet eight inches high—but his limbs were of the most Herculean mould. His hands, especially, were so enormously thick and broad as hardly to retain a human shape. His arms, as well as legs, were *bowed* in the most singular manner, and appeared to possess no flexibility whatever. His head was equally deformed, being of immense size, with an indentation on the crown (like that on the head of most negroes). . . . The mouth extended nearly from ear to ear; the lips were thin, and seemed, like some other portions of his frame, to be devoid of natural pliancy, so that the ruling expression never varied under the influence of any emotion whatever.

Negro what? Brothers and sisters, pause to check the backs of your skulls. Notice the primitive dwarfish size, bowed legs, and mouth ever conspicuous. Then compare Peters's description to some of the other *darkies* haunting Poe's collected works:

He was three feet in height. . . . He had bow-legs and was corpulent. His mouth should not be called small, nor his ears short. His teeth, however, were like pearl, and his large full eyes were deliciously white.

—*Describing Pompey, in "A Predicament"*

They had never before seen or heard of a blackamoor, and it must therefore be confessed that their astonishment was not altogether causeless. Toby, moreover, was as ugly an old gentleman as ever spoke—having all the peculiar features of his race; the swollen lips, large white protruding eyes, flat nose, long ears, double head, pot-belly, and bow legs.

—*Describing Toby, in "The Journal of Julius Rodman"*

These big-mouth animalistic pygmies with pairs of legs shaped like fallen over *C*s, they are of the same nightmarish breed. Dirk Peters, we're told, is not a Negro but a half-breed Indian probably of the "Upsaroka," which we can assume is Poe's reference to the Absaroka people. Or as we commonly call them, the Crow (darkness!). Narratively, Dirk Peters needs to be half Indian despite his Negroid traits because there is no such thing as a half Negro, according to the American "one drop" social reality. Either you are a Negro, containing some African ancestry, or you are not; half whiteness is not allowed. Peters must be at least half white because it is his shred of white decency that leads him to abandon the mutineers and assist Augustus in taking back control of the ship. To save the day, Pym imitates a ghost by covering himself entirely in white powder, then jumping out and startling the black-hearted mutineers. True to metaphor, the superstitious Negro mind is no match for the Enlightenment European intellect, and the three heroes regain control of the ship.

Shortly after this, as luck would have it, the *Grampus* is destroyed by inclement weather. These things happen. For another near third of the book, the sole survivors—Pym, Augustus, Dirk, and a guy named Richard Parker—cling to the driftwood that the capsized ship has become, steadily starving and dying of dehydration. The first imagined hope for rescue comes in the form of blackness, with a black ship moving toward them across the horizon, a man with "very dark skin" on deck nodding and "smiling constantly so as to display a set of the most brilliantly white teeth." On arrival, it turns out to be just a decayed, blackened corpse, his smile the result of his lack of lips and his nodding the result of the fact that there is a seagull actively gorging on chunks of the dead man's head, the bird's "white plumage spattered all over with blood."

Before long, the boys are forced to soil their own whiteness with gore as well. To fight starvation they must partake of the ultimate act of savagery: cannibalism. Not surprisingly, Parker, the least fleshed out character and a former participant in the mutiny, is the one who recommends this culinary choice, only to go on to literally draw the short straw. The line, the definitive line that separates civilized man from the primitive, is crossed. This is the sin that kills off Augustus, who poetically dies on the first of August despite his feast of man-meat. With little fanfare, this once central character melts away from the novel as if he never existed.

Why not eat the dog first? you might ask. Well, the dog is missing, having gone AWOL immediately after the mutiny. We know this not because we're told but because we are not: no fate is given, Tiger's simply gone, vanished from Poe's mind without a mention despite his before stated importance. Not that this is simply an act of animal cruelty, because from the moment Augustus dies (a death we are at least informed of), Augustus too receives no mention for the rest of the book, which is only half completed by this point. Serial publication minded, Poe seems to have had little concern for the past or for continuity in this text. The work veers inconsistently from straight prose chapters to a dated journal finale. The only thing that appears to matter to him is the chapter at hand.

Before the doomed Parker can even be properly digested, rescue arrives in the form of the merchant ship the *Jane Guy*. By this time Pym and Peters, now the best of buddies it seems, discover that they have sunk far into the Southern Hemisphere. And they will be going farther, continuing down as the *Jane Guy* sails off to the South Seas for trading.

This is where things start to get interesting (really, they haven't been tremendously until now). Here's where things start to get surreal, where Poe starts to go off. This is where the darkies really start to bubble to the surface, where the Africanist presence jumps out and does its jig on the page.

I used to complain that the only things the white literary world would accept of Africa's literary descendants were reflections of the Europeans themselves: works that focused on the effects of white racism, or the ghettos white economic and social disfranchisement of blacks created. I still think that, I have just come to the understanding that I'm no better. I like Poe, I like Melville, I like Hemingway, but what I like the most about the great literature created by the Americans of European descent is the Africanist presence within it. I like looking for myself in the whitest of pages. I like finding evidence of myself there, after being told my footprints did not exist on that sand. I think the work of the great white writers is important, but I think it's most important when it's negotiating me and my people, because I am as arrogant and selfish a reader as any other.

• • •

The *Jane Guy* finds a polar bear living wild in these southern seas. That's right, a polar bear. It's not simply that this bear shouldn't be in the earth's Southern Hemisphere—Poe gets many of his science facts wrong, particularly egregious considering that he plagiarized contemporary firsthand travel reports. At least he could have copied the information down correctly. No, what's remarkable is the description of the bear itself:

> His wool was perfectly white, and very coarse, curling tightly.
> The eyes were of a blood red, and larger than those of the
> Arctic bear—the snout also more rounded . . .

Tight, curly hair and a round nose . . . on a polar bear? Right. Strange things to imagine, particularly together. Makes you (me) wonder, who else is known for tight curly hair and round noses, whose attributes might have inspired Poe, consciously or sub? This improbable bear is, of course, just a teaser in his symbolic offering. One of many, along with Pym's growing descriptions of the massive black albatrosses which haunt the *Jane Guy*, or the black *and* white penguins whose rookeries seem to offer a chance of order between this visual dichotomy. The real treasure comes at the arrival at the island of Tsalal, which despite being floating distance to the Antarctic continent, is a tropical land, well populated and idyllic in a way that harkens back to Diderot's Tahiti. Except this island is not populated by a previously unknown enclave of Polynesians, or an even less probable lost tribe of hot-weather Inuits. No, the inhabitants of Tsalal are Negroes.

> They were about the ordinary stature of Europeans, but of a more muscular and brawny frame. Their complexion a jet black, with thick and long woolly hair. They were clothed in skins of an unknown black animal, shaggy and silky, and made to fit the body with some degree of skill, the hair being inside, except where turned out about the neck, wrists, and ankles. Their arms consisted principally of clubs, of a dark, and apparently very heavy wood.

Not just skin of black, which is the classic European mythic negative, but woolly hair to match. These brothers are black. These brothers are so black they wear only the skins of animals that are black. The only wood they carry is darker than ebony. These brothers are so black, we eventually find out, that even their teeth are black.* In fact, the entire island of Tsalal is hued in shades of

---

* After noting that immigrant ethnic groups in the United States have traditionally used the word *nigger* to define themselves as white, the comedian Paul Mooney once said that he didn't brush his teeth. He simply woke up every morning and said "nigger, nig-

blackness. Poe leaves no detail unturned in his assertion of Tsalal as a fantastic place; even the water is poured into this metaphorical construct:

> It was *not* colourless, nor was it of any one uniform colour—presenting to the eye, as it flowed, every possible shade of purple. . . . Upon collecting a basinful, and allowing it to settle thoroughly, we perceived that the whole mass of liquid was made up of a number of distinct veins, each of a distinct hue; that these veins did not commingle; and that their cohesion was perfect in regard to their own particles among themselves, and imperfect in regard to neighbouring veins.

The water is purple, a product of the mixes of the shades of white and black. The water's veins hold up even when a knife cuts through it. So many shades yet they do not "commingle," they exist separate but equal. Connected but completely disconnected. Metaphorically, it is synonymous with the racial fantasy that Booker T. Washington would put forth so many decades later in his "Atlanta Compromise," that all Americans will be a fist of strength together, but in socializing we'll be as racially segregated as the fingers of a hand.

The island of Tsalal offers horror, clearly, immediately. These black people—and it is a stretch to call these people "people," with their animalistic primitivism and baby talk—are clearly horrors from the pit of the antebellum subconscious. And yet still for me, despite the filter, on my first reads through there was simply wonder at the thought of a lost tribe of Africans, even one distorted through the eye of the paranoid myopic vision of a white pro-

---

ger, nigger, nigger" until his smile was like so many pearls sparkling. Perhaps the Tsalalians' black teeth were the first sign that the island was effectively removed from the Diasporan dialogue, the word clearly never having been uttered among them.

slavery southerner. Tall, athletic—Yoruba, Igbo? Hair long and woolly—like dreadlocks? To me the Tsalalians were real but obscured and caricatured, hidden from our view in the erratic work of a drunken, pretentious madman. This is an American thing: to wish longingly for a romanticized ancestral home. This is a black American thing: to wish to be in the majority within a nation you could call your own, to wish for the complete power of that state behind you. It was the story of the maroons and black towns on the frontier, it was the dream of every Harlem Pan-Africanist. *Tsalal*—put it on your tongue and let it slither.

Immediately, the Tsalalians betray an aversion to all things white, manifested in their reaction to the skin of the *Jane Guy*'s passengers. Of course, the complexions of the mates of the *Jane Guy* (not including Dirk Peters of course) would probably be more of a pinkish beige. Yet the Tsalalians react to their *metaphorical* Whiteness. It's as if, as cut off as they appear, the Tsalalians already seem to know of the larger colonial struggle, understand that they should fear the infection of the Europeans' amoral commerce. Of Whiteness as an ideology. And of course, the *Jane Guy* brings that pathology with it, immediately setting about building a production plant to process Tsalal's natural resource of *bêche-de-mer*, or sea cucumber, for trade on the world market. True to form, not only do the colonial Europeans instantly commodify paradise on arrival but after they have begun the rape of Tsalal's natural resources, they get the Tsalalians themselves to contribute the hard manual labor.

The chief of the Tsalalians, Too-wit, goes along with this invasion, acquiescing, having his people offer not the slightest resistance. On the surface, it appears another case of Enlightenment man, armed with only the products of his rational brain, conquering the ignorant savages despite their superior numbers. Too-wit, however, lives up to his name and, after a month of shucking and jiving for the invaders, leads the men of the *Jane Guy* and their false sense of security into a narrow pass. Once the crew is vulnerable there, Too-wit has his warriors cause a landslide to kill the lot of them.*

Amazingly, two people survive this unforeseen attack. Less amazingly, those people are Arthur Gordon Pym and Dirk Peters. Stunning no matter how many times you read it: after the attack has happened and the rest of the crew have been killed, after Pym realizes he is stuck on an island overrun with super niggers, he looks at the man he referred to as both a "half-breed" and a "demon" just a few pages before and says:

We were the only living white men upon the island.

Fascinating. Whiteness, of course, has always been more of a strategy than an ethnic nomenclature, but Dirk Peters's caste shifting so quickly, so blatantly in reaction to the current dilemma is still something spectacular to behold.

When Pym and Peters return to the shore, they find the Tsalalians in a panic as these natives examine the corpse of that white polar bear thing, having pulled it from the now ransacked *Jane Guy*. And this, having taken the long route of entry, is where I first encountered the cry.

"Tekeli-li! Tekeli-li!" they scream.

Clearly this references something, something white and petrify-

* This was really the way to deal with first contact with the Europeans of this era. The Hawaiians, they wish they'd thought of this. So do the Arawak of Jamaica, and the Mayans too. And the Ashanti. And the Iroquois also. Smile in their faces, be the harmless darky they think you are. And then, when they are fat and confident with their gunpowder and their omnipotence, kill every last one of them. Kill them before they go back to their overcrowded countries and tell the rest of their people where to find your home and what to steal there.

ing because, after being taken prisoner, this Tsalalian shouts the same expletive in response to the white linen shirts Pym and Peters use to construct a sail for their getaway canoe. The Tsalalians, having blown up the *Jane Guy* because of their primitive incapability to negotiate technology (and in the process having killed a thousand of their own people), are soon far behind Poe's heroes, as the two men and one petrified Tsalalian hostage sail southward.

Oddly enough, the greatest allure of *The Narrative of Arthur Gordon Pym of Nantucket* comes from these final pages, from this ending. And it comes not from what Edgar Allan Poe does with the finale but from what he won't do.

After drifting uneventfully along in this canoe toward the Antarctic, the narrative breaks into dated, diary mode. As their black Tsalalian hostage fades further toward death the closer they get to the polar whiteness, we're left with this final paragraph, a complete daily entry in a novel that has suddenly reverted to journal form:

> The darkness had materially increased, relieved only by the glare of the water thrown back from the white curtain before us. Many gigantic and pallidly white birds flew continuously now from beyond the veil, and their scream was the eternal *Tekeli-li!* as they retreated from our vision. Hereupon Nu-Nu stirred in the bottom of the boat; but, upon touching him, we found his spirit departed. And now we rushed into the embraces of the cataract, where a chasm threw itself open to receive us. But there arose in our pathway a shrouded human figure, very far larger in its proportions than any dweller among men. And the hue of the skin of the figure was of the perfect whiteness of the snow.

And that's it. That's the ending. That's it, that's all, nothing more. That's the end of the book. No explanation of who the white figure is is given. No word on what happens next. No pseudo-scientific or mystical explanation for the chasm. No explanation of the human figure, or of how they make it back to America. Just over.

There is an afterword "Note" section to the novel, but it offers basically nothing, just more confusion than solution. For one, it tells us that Pym died, and died suddenly, having not completed the final three chapters of the book—but he somehow managed that earlier preface, supposedly written after the journey. What was this mortal accident? Doesn't say. In addition, the supposed ghostwriter, Edgar Allan Poe, who knows the final story, refuses to tell it as it is entirely unbelievable. And then we're told that Dirk Peters, who now resides in Illinois, is unavailable for comment on the matter.

Stunning. An ending that confounds more than it concludes. Within this we can see genius as well, as amazingly the reaction of the reader is not to throw the book across the room, as we are tempted to do with most literary disappointments, cop-outs, and blunders. Instead, our reaction is to grip it closer. To make our own connections and conclusions where there is no material provided. Our impetus is to find the satisfactory ending that has eluded us, to walk away with an answer.

You want to understand Whiteness, as a pathology and a mind-set, you have to look to the source of its assumptions. You want to understand our contemporary conception of the environment, commerce, our taxonomy of humanity, you have to understand the base assumptions that underlie the foundation of the modern imagination. To truly understand evolution, Darwin couldn't just stare at dead finches. No, he studied mammals in their embryonic form. How else would he have known that the inner ear owes its structure to what appears in larva stage as amphibious gills? That's why Poe's work mattered. It offered passage on a vessel bound for the primal American subconscious, the foundation on which all our visible systems and structures were built. That's why Poe mattered. And that's why my work mattered too, even if nobody wanted me to do it. That's what people like Mosaic Johnson couldn't understand. It wasn't that I was an apolitical coward, running away from the battle. I was running so hard toward it, I was around the world and coming back in the other direction.

· · ·

Garth failed to see the beauty in this rationale. The poetry in it. He was unamused when I showed up bloodied to wake him on the couch to retell my saga, and he didn't seem to give a damn more for it as I gave him more detail while we trudged out to the site in the park at sunset like he'd demanded. We'd spent the morning and afternoon taking visitors—my lawyer, the college's lawyer, my insurance claims agent, the college's team of them—to the mountain of mold on my front porch. The closest I would get to an apology came in the chagrin of the campus attorney reflected against the joy in my own lawyer's face as the word *settlement* was first said.

"We're late. We going to miss the golden hour. You talk about me being fat, you so damn out of shape, we're not going to make it till dawn," Garth huffed. Once he got going he could still move fast. Like a dump truck on the highway.

"It's right there, that's your painting, isn't it?" I managed, relieved that he shot on up the path in front of me and I could lean on my thighs and wheeze a bit in dignity. When I caught up to him, Garth was pacing the open field on top of the hill that overlooked the Hudson and the Catskill Mountains that began on the other side of the water. This was a good place to live. We were far enough north from the Point Pleasant nuclear reactor that if it was hit, we'd survive the radiation. Even a dirty bomb in Manhattan would be okay; the wind blew south from here. People moved here for that, and for the natural beauty. And that spot had a stunning view, locals hiked out all the time to see it. Garth was barely looking at it. Mostly he was looking at the ground, walking around a bit, pulling up his print of the painting to compare nature's majesty with Thomas Karvel's manufactured mess, then walking to another spot and trying it again.

"Well is this the right place or not?" My phone was ringing, but I was already impatient.

"Yeah. But I'm trying to find the really right place. Karvel spotting is a discipline." Like a dog looking for a place to piss, he kept circling. Small and smaller loops, and then he was still. I thought he was going to look for artifacts at his feet, try to find a paintbrush or something, but he just looked back up and finally took in the vista. Garth held out the painting before him one more time, and then sighed. It was windy, and he was not close anymore, but I could hear him.

"*Stock of the Woods!* He must have been standing right here. Right here, in this very spot. The Master of Light!" Garth yelled back to me, and more such ramblings. I nodded and forced a smile, and when he was done, I checked my voice mail, and was soon as high as Garth was pacified.

"There was an item listed today in a certain Hertfordshire house's catalog as a 'Negro Servant's Memoir, dated 1837,' I yelled after I heard the news. Garth was too chilled to even get my meaning. He didn't understand, but I knew. Just that winter a well-known Africanist intellectual had found a place for himself on several of the major news outlets merely because of his purchase of a previously unknown slave narrative.

"This is the stuff academic names are built on, man. Careers. Careers are made on this kind of thing." As we walked back to Garth's car, images of a rogue intellectual career flashed before me, and I pictured a new life for myself, one of glamour and packed lecture halls. All the recent damage repaired.

"I like seeing the original site of the art. It's like being able to climb in one," Garth told me. I felt the same way, but it took me a moment to realize he was talking about the print he'd tucked in his coat like it was a sacred scroll.

When we arrived back at my rented house, the Ichabod Crane frame of Oliver Benjamin, book pimp, was on the porch, poking through the rotted mound of my literary history.

"How could you do this?" he said by way of hello. He had a moldy reproduction of the only issue of *Fire!* in his hand, holding the soggy thing as gently as if it were an original. I gave him a synopsis of the calamity and his response was "But still. You don't know how to treat your things."

He kept going. Pacing the travesty, listing off titles and cursing. He wouldn't shut up. So he knew how to hurt me. I was so depressed at the end of his rant that I let him smoke in my living room, and even still Oliver spent the first minutes inside repeating a catalog of all that I had lost, specifically the volumes he'd found for me. Garth gave him coffee, and finally he relented. Oliver slurped and his Adam's apple bobbed, and then he pulled his leather portfolio onto his lap and said, "This is going to cost you." It wasn't clear if he meant a lot of money or that he might not sell it to me at all, seeing that I was such a disastrous guardian of literary antiquities.

"I told you. I'm suing the damn college. I'm getting paid back for all those books. For what they did. They're responsible."

"Oh hell no. Don't talk that lawsuit nonsense. I'm not waiting to get paid for some court to make a decision. This is going to cost you cash. Today."

I agreed, got the money for him. Even untenured professors at private colleges make a decent salary, and you add up 10 percent of that each year for several years and you get a decent chunk. It was money I needed, but I needed the pain to stop more. When I came back in the room, Oliver had the white gloves on, had the thing on the coffee table. A rumpled pile of brown papers, folded up and ripped. I could see from the rough edges of the pages that the stock was brittle and disintegrating. Besides the fact that it was dry, it looked like it belonged out on my porch with the rest of the antiquarian cadavers. Oliver saw the disappointment in my face and the cash in my hand at the same time and found that a powerful combination.

"Okay, not mint condition here. Clearly not mint. And yes, there are some other issues. First, let's get this out of the way: it's not technically a slave narrative. I read through a bit of it. What I could. Early nineteenth century, but it's not a slave narrative. The back is signed with the date and location. The guy's born in a northern free state in the nineteenth century, so this is not a slave we're dealing with here. Sorry. But regardless, it's fiction. It's got to be."

Fiction! My mood improved. An African American work of fiction predating the Civil War was an equally impressive find. Depending on the quality of the story, it was possibly even a greater find than a memoir. Eager, palpitating, I took the box that contained the withering sheets into my hands.

"Well see, that's the other thing. You might see different, that's why I'm going to give you a good deal, but the manuscript is kind of, let's say *elusive*. Nobody else today even wanted it. It was an estate sale, mostly art and furniture types bidding, but there's other reasons. It's more the notes for a book than a book itself. Parts of it are written like a journal, parts of it are just these disconnected scenes. There's a lot of random scribbles in it too, and maps. But you don't know; it could be useful. Look, we do this deal, I don't want you to think I screwed you on this. I'm being up-front. So sure, the whole thing is a bit of a mess. But it could be your mess. Something to build a new collection around, maybe."

Not letting my excitement completely abandon me and fully conscious that Mr. Benjamin was more of a literary hustler than a literary scholar, I lifted the brown and delicate linen cover. It was self-made and bound along its side in a messy hand stitch. On the page was the etching of a pale man, mulatto by feature and skin tone: his hair hinting at the slightest of kink, thin lips betrayed by a wide nose and the high West African cheekbones. The man was dressed in the frilled collar of the period. Drawn sitting at a desk. Beside him sat a periscope, a compass, and an open journal in which he was caught pleasantly getting his scribe on. The title read:

The True and Interesting Narrative of Dirk Peters.
Coloured Man. As Written by Himself.
Springfield, Illinois
1837

"See, that's what I'm talking about. It's a weird one," Oliver continued, pushing his glasses back up his sharp nose and giving a good sniff as if that would jam them there. "I mean, what kind of black guy is named Dirk anyway?"

• • •

I knew immediately that it was true. That this was truly the autobiographical work of a living man. That Pym's adventure must for the most part be true as well. Even before the days ahead when dates were researched, the censuses checked, the obscure biblical birth and property records investigated, I saw the text with its handwritten pages and loose script and knew that Dirk Peters had been a living man. I reeled, I careened, but I knew it was true, although the enormity of the revelation was almost beyond my ability to understand.

At the least, this was the greatest discovery in the brief history of American letters. That I was sure of. My boldest ambitions had instantly been met, and in the next instant surpassed beyond equal measure. Because if Dirk Peters existed, if this was a historic person who had walked this country just like me, what else did that mean in relation to Poe's *Narrative*?

It meant, I discovered at my desk that night as I turned the work's fragile pages, that there truly had been something living down in Antarctica. Something large and humanoid in nature. Maybe it was a lost strain of Neanderthal, or simply a variant of *Homo sapiens* that through location had managed to avoid modernity.* And more important to me, it meant that Tsalal, the great undiscovered African Diasporan homeland, might still be out there, uncorrupted by Whiteness. That there was a group of our people who did achieve victory over slavery in all its forms, escaping completely from the progression of Westernization and colonization to form a society outside of time and history. And that I might find them.

---

* While Poe's narrative makes note of a figure "very far larger in its proportions than any dweller among men," I have often wondered what Pym, presumably as short in stature as the majority of men of his period, would have made of an average National Basketball Association center.

CHAPTER III

THE dialogue that is African American literature really gets going with the slave narrative, the first book-length manuscript of which was published by Olaudah Equiano in 1789. Equiano's slave narrative, with its swashbuckling seafaring adventure scenes, moves the reader with the story of the narrator's own kidnapping, subjugation, and eventual escape from the slave system. Every word in Equiano's narrative, every sentence, every page, is dedicated to one thing: convincing its reader of the moral necessity of abolitionism. And that's the beginning of the primary conversation in African American literature, right there: the African descendant explaining to the European descendant about how white people's actions are affecting the lives of black people.*

In the two centuries to follow, thousands more personal stories would be recorded, but in the next sixty years in particular, the slave narrative became a genre in itself. It is into this context that we must place *The True and Interesting Narrative of Dirk Peters*. That said, in those first days of plowing through the text, the differences between *The True and Interesting Narrative of Dirk Peters* and the major slave narratives of the late eighteenth and early nineteenth centuries became fairly stark. For one, Dirk Peters was never a slave. Peters was instead the progeny of a free woman of European, African, and Native American heritage, and an Acadian

---

* (Negatively.)

trader.* The fact that Peters omits the African ingredient from his personal recipe, emphasizing the Native element instead, is altogether common and consistent with American Creoles of the period. Wishing not to be branded with the stigma and considerable social and legal limitations that accompanied a "black" classification, people of mixed heritage contended with the "one drop" rule of blackness by denying that one drop's existence completely. While Native Americans were also a lower caste, the existence of diluted Native blood in most portions of the growing nation carried significantly fewer societal implications. Often, Native heritage was falsely claimed by African/European mulattoes attempting to "pass," using indigenous ancestry as an excuse to explain away clearly non-European physical features. Similar claims have also been used by contemporary African Americans attempting to lessen the stigma of their personal "blackness."†

Structurally, *The True and Interesting Narrative of Dirk Peters* does not actually conform much to the novelistic prose form either. Like Poe's *Narrative of Arthur Gordon Pym*, Peters's narrative is episodic, disjointed. The book begins with twelve pages on Dirk Peters's isolated upbringing in rural Michigan. Similar to the *Narrative of the Life of Frederick Douglass*, Peters's tale focuses on his earliest memories of the woman who gave birth to him, the rumors about who his father probably was, as well as the agricultural, cultural, and socioeconomic breakdown of the area, and the narrator's first recorded encounters with a racist society. From the unnamed mother we get the sole yet pivotal advice, "You got straight hair, you got light skin: if they don't know you ain't colored, don't tell them!"

The next twenty-seven pages consist of Dirk Peters's maiden

---

* *Laissez les bons temps rouler!*
† Usually, these claims take the form of the sentence "You know, I got Indian in me."

voyage at sea. A fairly uneventful tale that spends the majority of its efforts describing in minute detail the duties of each member of the crew, and then more details of how each man failed to fully fulfill his responsibilities.* It is revealed that, because of his small stature, he was assigned to understudy the main lookout. Apparently, up on his crow's nest perch, Dirk Peters spent more time looking down than out at the sea around them, which seems plausible since the body of water was not an actual sea but Lake Michigan. In the following twenty-six-page section, Dirk Peters serves as a mate on a completely different boat, the *Precipice,* and he is somewhere in the Gulf of Mexico. How he managed to go from an inland freshwater ship in the North American Midwest to a merchant ship in Central America is completely unremarked upon.

Let me say here that it became evident to me that there were logical reasons why this text, *The True and Interesting Narrative of Dirk Peters,* while momentous in its historical significance, avoided publication and therefore its righteous place in history. I'll begin with the obvious: the handwriting is downright fecal. Given the time period, when blotting quills and poor paper stock commonly obscured the scripted word, the hand of Dirk Peters still managed to be spectacularly illegible. It took me six eighteen-hour days to push through a first reading of the text. And I was trying really, really hard. This atrocious penmanship was allied with an equally poor grasp of grammar. When deciphering a blurred word, it helps to know what it should be. But Dirk himself doesn't usually know what it should be. If it wasn't for the revelation in the clearly printed title, I would have given up after the first page.† On the

---

* The most repeated line in the manuscript was "_____ was a lazy sod."

† Having examined the hand and paper stock of that first cover page, I came to the conclusion that that page alone was not the work of Dirk Peters himself. Rather, I believe, it was the work of another, earlier owner of the manuscript. Apparently this owner attempted to translate the text into readable English, but after slogging through the opening title, author, et cetera, admitted defeat and went no further.

seventh day, I took a train into the city to check a ship's log for the *Precipice* held at the New-York Historical Society. Taking the subway from Penn Station, unable to get a seat, I stood up with the firmly packed crowd and attempted awkwardly to record a thought on Peters's saga as the local train swayed violently to and fro. The lights went out, and I kept writing. When the lights came back on a few seconds later, what I saw on the page stunned me. There I was eerily greeted with an exact duplication of Dirk Peters's own hand. *He was writing the manuscript at sea,* I realized. Beneath the rocking deck, in little if any candlelight.

Another probable factor in the Peters manuscript's obscurity was its timing. After a little old white lady published her lengthy melodrama about the evils of slavery in the American South in 1838, *Uncle Tom's Cabin* changed the dialogue of African American literature dramatically. Overnight, African American autobiographical storytelling became antiquated, and fiction, with its ability to directly manipulate the emotions of the white masses, proved a far more effective political tool. While the majority of Dirk Peters's manuscript was written before 1837, for a variety of reasons it was not quite ready for publication then, and truly never was.

While I have said that the narrative of Dirk Peters, much like Poe's *Narrative of Arthur Gordon Pym,* is episodic, let me further state that in the majority of other ways their structures are dissimilar. Poe's *Pym* is serialized, the product of a magazinist whose imagination constructed narratives in fifteen-page, stand-alone segments. Dirk Peters's chapters are crude and roughly structured. To be specific, Peters barely even has prose, just handwritten notes, brown and crisp from time, hand-sewn together haphazardly by thick thread (some of which appears to be fishing line). Each bound section is an individual tirade or description of events complete without reference to any larger context of the man's life.

One minute he's on one ship. The next he's on another boat yammering about a completely new set of mundane events. The next he's at shore complaining about the price of the produce and prostitutes. If it wasn't for the later entries, where Peters actively describes trying to sell his work, it would be logical to conclude that the collection was not intended for publication. What truly distinguishes *The True and Interesting Narrative of Dirk Peters* from the rest of the pantheon is that Dirk Peters was never a writer. This was a work constructed by a man without talent for structure. Or for character. Or poetry.

. . .

That first week of studying the manuscript, I felt drunk. When I wasn't researching, I actually got drunk, so I could sustain the sensation. Garth didn't fully understand what was going on, but he knew I was instantly overflowing with joy, and he was cool with that. We put off leaving for Detroit longer, and that meant he got to hike back to his painting site every sunset and pretend to climb into a better world, so we both were happy.

It took ten days to get verification on the age of the manuscript based on a sample of its ink and paper I sent to a grad school connection now working at the Smithsonian, and in that regard it was either an unlikely masterpiece of forgery or an actual product of the nineteenth century. This was all good, but what I really wanted to verify was whether or not it was true. Did this Dirk Peters really live and work among us? In the months ahead, I planned to continue my thorough and academic inquiry. In my more ambitious waves, I imagined an expedition to Antarctica. I had a cousin who might offer insight, someone I knew only from family rumors and newspaper clippings, who'd done oceanic salvage in the area, and for a romantic afternoon I hunted him down and left messages, trying to get him to contact me. The next day, Garth promised to drive me down to the National Archives in Washington, D.C., as long as we detoured on a Karvel spotting mission to find the site of a monstrosity titled *Cabana de la Chesapeake*.

It was going on two in the morning. I was spent physically and mentally. The limits of my official online database searching had for the day been exhausted, there was no historical library catalog left that I could think of to unravel the mystery of Dirk Peters. So I Googled him.

There are a multitude of Dirk Peterses in the world, it turned out, and most of them had nothing to do with books. When I tried adding the keyword "Pym" to the search, I was drowning in information on Poe's fictional account. Largely out of curiosity, I tried an image search for the name instead. The result: "Dirk Peters" was fairly common in the planet's paler regions, as many a white Dirk Peters smiled for the camera in various snapshots. I was pushing absently through pages of these images in the hope of seeing perhaps a lithograph of Peters's fictionalized portrait when a wholly inconsistent image struck me. Below that same Anglophonic name was the head shot of a woman, a black woman, probably in her sixties. It was a glamour shot, taken through the forced dreaminess of a Vaselined lens. Her chin rested on her hands, and one of those hands held a large red rose, like it was a singles ad. The entire photo was no bigger than my thumbnail, and even from that I could tell that flower was plastic. Clicking the link below took me to the obviously amateurish website of the woman in the picture, a self-proclaimed "Singer, Actor, Poet, Novelist, Dancer, Actress and Noted Psychic Person," who went by the name Mahalia Mathis. By this point I was just browsing for laughs. I stopped laughing when I came to a page titled "Genealogy." And there, at the top of a long and haggard willow of a family tree, was a patriarch who held the same name as the one I had been searching for, next to a tag that read "Crow Indian, Michigan."

It wasn't hard to reach Mahalia Mathis: her phone number was listed in twenty-four-point font on every electronic page. In fact, the next morning Mrs. Mathis proved to be one of those rare individuals who picks the phone up on the first ring. Before it even rang on my end, catching me off guard. Even though I gave her a vague line of questioning about her website, Mrs. Mathis answered my opening questions immediately in a raspy but bubbling voice, as if we had an interview appointment prearranged weeks in advance.

"I am of Greek, Hopi, Crow, Blackfoot, Chinese, and Danish descent," she interrupted me to declare immediately after I mentioned the genealogical page on her site. Hearing this, I poked my head back at the computer screen to look at the image of the Negro there looking back at me.

"Actually, I'm calling to inquire about one of your ancestors in particular. You listed a three times great-grandfather, by the name of Dirk Peters, is that correct?"

It was then that for the first time in this already five-minute call Mahalia Mathis actually paused from talking and came up for air. And what a great intake of air it was: a massive, dramatic gasp that seemed less appropriate to a question than to a mortal wound. The inevitable release of wind was no less a performance: the resultant sigh was labored and bass filled. I asked if there was something wrong.

"I will not be able to do this over the phone. You are a stranger, so I do not mind telling you: I am a very sick woman and I am not long for this world, honey. No, not long at all. If you expect me to discuss this . . . alleged Dirk Peters business with you, you will need . . . you will need to inquire in person. And considering my condition, you will have to do this immediately." I eagerly agreed, and despite the clear theatrics, she had me hooked. Even though it would mean getting patted down at the airport for an hour, and risking an airborne explosion flying to Chicago.

I didn't know that meeting Mrs. Mathis also meant I would be forced to travel from Chicago to the bleak urban landscape of Gary, Indiana; after thoroughly reading her website, I was under the impression that Mahalia Mathis was a resident of the Second City. I soon found that what I thought was a residential address in Chicago was in fact a post office box, and that her driving directions led me not only out of the city but out of the state of Illinois altogether. This information arrived at my cottage in an overnight package from Mrs. Mathis, along with an elaborate press package that included glossy head shots of the lady and several print clippings from her neighborhood newsletter, some more than a decade old, all attesting to her numerous creative abilities.

I found her residence an hour out of O'Hare without much trouble. It was harder to leave my rental car parked on her street, with its thugs hanging about the concrete like bats hang in caves.

"Niggers!" Mrs. Mathis yelled out at them as she let me into her town house, a response which only increased my concern that the car was done for, despite the fact that she insisted this would scare them away for a while.

The home of Mahalia Mathis was elegant on the inside, ornate. It was crowded too. There were many possessions on display in this house, and many, many cats to guard those possessions. Mrs. Mathis struck an impressive figure herself, wearing a muumuu of green paisley silk and a sparkled turban to match. She was a statuesque woman, both in height and in weight; aside from an occasional violent fit of coughing, she didn't look sick or weak to me as she went about her overcrowded house, with its many boxes and piles of antiques and random curiosities. She was a hoarder, and I was happy about this: if this woman had ever possessed anything of use to my quest, it was clear that she still had it.

It was in Mrs. Mathis's living room, seated at a large mahogany table covered in antique lace, that we began our discussion in earnest, tape recorder and notepad on my side of the table, a dusty box marked "pictures" on its lid in a handwritten scrawl between us.

"You must realize that the man you speak of—"

"Dirk Peters," I interrupted. I wanted no mistakes about this.

"Dirk Peters," she acknowledged with a hand to the side of her temple, as if even uttering those words made her anxious. "You have to understand, in my family, we weren't even allowed to say his name out loud. No one in my mother's generation talked about him, and that's because no one in her mother's generation did, or the one before that."

"But why?" I asked, largely because Mrs. Mathis took a couple of seconds off after her opening confession, dabbing her head with a handkerchief repeatedly even though it must have barely been more than sixty degrees Fahrenheit in the room. I was still wearing my coat.

"Because he is *the* Dirk Peters written about by that great author Mr. Edgar Allan Poe, all those years ago. The one who accompanied Arthur Gordon Pym on his southern adventure!" she shot back at me as if I was a fool. But I did not feel like a fool at that moment. To the contrary, I felt brilliant: I hadn't even mentioned Poe's novel before this point.

"Mrs. Mathis, do you realize that this is a major historic revelation?" I asked, struggling to constrain myself. "It's an important discovery for American literature and for America herself. Why did your family keep this a secret for so long?"

In response to my query, Mahalia Mathis made no attempt to

hide her disappointment in the poor display of intelligence on my part for even pursuing this line of questioning. After much eye rolling and elaborate head wagging had been completed, Mrs. Mathis finally saw fit to compensate for my lack of intuition.

"Well, he left that poor white man down there to die, didn't he? Not only did he go along with a mutiny, which would have brought shame enough to my family's name had it been widely known. But the fact that he left that poor white man to die on some iceberg, to freeze to death. The fact that Arthur Pym was a famous white man just made it worse. Time was, if white folks hear your kin killed one of them, they libel not to let the fact that it was a hundred years ago stop them from getting their rope."

"Oh, I get it, I see, right. Why didn't I think of this before? Of course there would have been larger, real-world repercussions to worry about, particularly as an African American man in—"

"A what?" Mrs. Mathis's hand shot down to collapse on my own.

"An African American man?" I repeated, assuming I had garbled the last of my words in the excitement of the moment. When I said "African" again, Mrs. Mathis squeezed my fingers so tight it left me with the impression of being gripped by a blood pressure machine.

"Honey, I got lots of Indian in me. I got Irish and I got a little French too. I got some German, or so I'm told. I even got a little Chinese in me, on my mother's side. Matter of fact, I'm sure I got more bloods in me than I knows. But I do knows this: I ain't got no kind of Africa in these bones," Mahalia Mathis delivered, poking her naps back under her turban as she snorted at me derisively.

After taking a moment to gather herself from my apparent slight, Mrs. Mathis proved to be as helpful as I'd hoped. From the cardboard box that sat beside her, she removed a folded piece of yellowed paper carefully wrapped in aged cotton cloth, and placed it on the table before me. Although clearly impressed with the white gloves I had brought with me for the purpose of revealing to her my own Dirk Peters manuscript, Mrs. Mathis still smacked my hand when I reached for her document. She chose instead to hold open her fragile paper for me to read. I was expecting to see Peters's chicken-scratch handwriting before me, and when I didn't I could feel my body deflate slightly in response. It was good that it did, because when I read the words written there I needed room for my mind to expand.

Mr. Dirk Peters.

I will kindly ask you to stop harassing me, as I have now addressed your fear of defamation in regards to this matter. I will write again that I had ended my tale of long fiction without showing our mutual friend coming to any sort of demise, by foul play or other. But, in light of your request and the energetic ones of your local legal counsel, I have considered the matter further. Instead of adding your requested disclaimer, however, I have written an epilogue in Mr. Pym's hand to serve as the final linking entry. Thus it will end the book, and I trust as well this correspondence.

Sincerely,

E.A.P.

After a lengthy recounting of her family history and the presentation of many a brown photo of many a brown face, Mrs. Mathis kindly agreed to make a deal with me. For her part, she would make me a color photocopy of her priceless letter, done on archival paper for historical purposes, and in return I happily agreed to escort Mrs. Mathis to some kind of local social gathering on the following day, when I was to return to pick up my treasure.

"It's good luck, you coming when you did. You're going to like this. It's right up your alley" was all she would tell me of what she had planned.

CHAPTER IV

IT turned out that Mahalia Mathis was not the only resident of Gary, Indiana, to claim Native American descent. Despite the fact that the satellite city of Chicago was 84 percent black, there were enough "Indians" to form a club, and it was to participate in its gathering that Mrs. Mathis had recruited me.

The Native American Ancestry Collective of Gary (NAACG) met on the first Thursday of every month at the Miller Beach Senior Center.* During our long and illuminating ride, I was simultaneously given a tour of the modern-day Gary, complete with a commentary on its most famous entertainment family, and told of the saga of Mahalia Mathis's own family, the Jacksons.† Mahalia's late husband, Charles, had passed a decade before. Charles, Mahalia acknowledged, had indeed been "colored." Mrs. Mathis went on to note that both her sons had married white women and that her grandchildren had been spared Charles's burden. It seemed that her sons had been spared the burden of their mother as well, because it was clear from her tone that she was estranged and isolated from all of her people.

"Your mother must have been so relieved when you came out," Mahalia Mathis turned in her passenger seat to say to me, reaching

---

* To my surprise the Miller Beach Senior Center was not actually in Miller Beach but in an adjacent community that merely aspired to appropriate the airs of its more reputable neighbor.
† No relation.

out to lightly touch the back of my neck, where my stringy hair met my fired alabaster skin. I giggled nervously, jerked my head, and eventually the older woman put her hand back at her side again.

Once the community center had been entered it was rather easy to locate the dozen or so NAACG members. This was not because the group looked like Native Americans; to my eyes, they looked like any gathering of black American folks, some tan and most brown. What distinguished this group was their attire. The first man I saw in the room had a full Native American headdress, a *Stegosaurus* spine of white feathers that reached all the way down to his moccasins. He was sitting on the edge of a metal foldout chair trying not to harm his plumage while he sipped his coffee from a Dunkin' Donuts cup. As I walked in with Mrs. Mathis on my arm, he turned toward us and the red war paint he had on his nose and cheeks spread as he smiled. Others in the room were more muted in their attire, but all seemed to have their flair. By the open box of donuts a woman wore a casual coat made of simulated Hopi cloth. Over by the blackboard a tall, slender brother chuckled and chatted on his cell phone, his raised hand a miniature museum of turquoise finger ornaments. Past him, a portly man with chemically relaxed hair tied into two greasy ponytails twirled one of those wet ropes with his finger as he waited for the meeting to begin. The only person besides myself who was not outfitted in some form of indigenous attire was a brown-skinned woman in a pink raincoat sitting in the farthest chair from the door as she read a magazine, but clearly she was the waiting escort of someone in the group.

Somehow it had been spread around the room that I was a reporter sent to cover their event.* The folks, pleasant and welcom-

---

* By "somehow," I mean that I don't know if Mahalia Mathis had emailed the other members or called them, or rather I have no proof of this. But as to the source of this information I, personally, have no doubt.

ing, made their introductions by telling me both their names and their Native connections. Tanisha Johnson—Cherokee. Antony Thomas—Chickasaw. Tyrone Jackson—Seminole.

"We're so glad you're here, so glad that you came to record this special day," Tyrone told me, and the others who began to take their seats as well agreed.

"Well, you know I couldn't just let this day go by, could I? This is historic," Mahalia Mathis boomed, her own hair hot-combed back into a Pocahontas bun for the occasion.

I whispered to her, "I'm sorry, what is today?"

"Today, we get our proof. That was my surprise. It will make an excellent essay for you; I know it. Today the truth is revealed, at long last. DNA testing isn't just for criminals trying to get out of jail free; it's for decent Indians trying to prove their heritage."

"It took us a year, and a lot of phone calls, but we found Dr. Hollins over at the University of Chicago to do our test for us, part of a program I read about in the *Telegraph*," bragged Antony, handing me a cruller on a napkin. "All expenses paid, all we had to do was scrape a Q-Tip in our mouths and they said they'd do the rest."

"I'm going to send my baby to college on this evidence, just you watch. We tried to join the Sioux Nation a few years back, and they had the nerve to turn us down. We'll see about that now," Tanisha humped, the tassels that lined her coat and pants rippling like the legs of a centipede.

The others were equally excited, and as they told their stories of ostracization by their respective Native nations, I empathized with their obvious pain. Although they didn't mention it, I imagined walking around Gary, Indiana, dressed in Native American attire had probably led to other incidents of alienation as well.*

---

* As a child growing up in the Germantown section of Philadelphia, I remember one such gentleman who regularly strutted through my predominantly black neighbor-

It was out of empathy that I removed a pad from my pocket and began taking notes, half convinced that I might just write an essay about this, that maybe I could play at being a pop psychologist. If this Negro in a Rick James jacket could call himself a war chief, then why not? Then the brother from the University of Chicago's lab finally arrived.

"Well, as many of you thought, your tests have proven that, as a group, you do have a percentage of Native American heritage. There is a margin of error, of course, but overall your tests proved to have between zero and thirty-two percent Native DNA, between eleven and sixty-four percent European DNA, and as for your African DNA—"

"On average then," Tyrone interrupted eagerly, "how much Native blood do we have?"

The professor stiffened visibly, put down the chart he was reading from, and leaned back on the desk behind him. "Well, the average . . . On average you have about six percent. Six percent Native blood among you, which is about the average for African Americans on the East Coast, for instance."

"Six percent? Six percent?" Tyrone stood, indignant. "That's all you could find, six percent? Well what the hell is the margin of error?"

"Six percent." The professor coughed into his hand and then immediately began shuffling his individual results, moving to hand them out just so he didn't have to stand in the center of the room anymore.

---

hood clad in a brown suede pantsuit and a matching strap tied around his forehead. You could hear him coming because he would sing "powwow" songs to the beat of the many beads that hung from him. We used to tauntingly say, "Howdy, Tonto," to him when he passed, to which he invariably smiled, raised his open palm, and replied, "How." For years I wondered just that: *how? How* the hell did that brother end up like that?

As the NAACG members inspected their individual test results, it became clear to me that the natives were getting restless. Antony, for instance, dropped his Boston creme right onto the floor and declared, "It's scalping time!" Mrs. Mathis, clearly trying to keep herself composed as the elder of this village, not even bothering to look at her own results, attempted to calm the room. "Professor, you did say that some of us have thirty-two percent Indian, right? You did say that."

"Well, one of you does. The rest . . . not so much," the professor, in motion, offered. Amazingly, his coat was already on when he said this, and most of his many papers had been speedily repacked into his briefcase.

"Me!" came a slight but jubilant voice from the far corner of the room. It was the woman in the pink raincoat, who now pumped her fist, staring at her report as if a great bounty had been won. Her round brown face did look like she belonged to a tribe, but more Igbo than Apache.

When I turned back to Mahalia Mathis, she seemed to have aged nearly ten years in as many seconds. Her mouth was agape, her top denture clacked loosely down for lack of support. *Mrs. Mathis thought the thirty-two percent Native was her,* I realized. That was the only thing that had let her keep her composure before now. Putting a trembling hand to the folder before her, Mrs. Mathis looked inside, and I peered discreetly over her shoulder. Two percent Native. Twenty-three percent European. Seventy-five percent African. This last bit I saw when I picked the findings off the linoleum after Mahalia Mathis collapsed, unconscious.

Discovering to my great relief that the older woman was neither dead nor in a coma, I carried Mrs. Mathis off the floor and out of the room, placing her barely conscious body in the backseat of my rental car. There she moaned and coughed as I returned her to her residence, invisible in my rearview mirror, her occasional sobs the only proof I had that she had recovered from her faint. At her curb, my steadying arm was all that managed to get her to her door. Not a word was said, not even "Good night." I was so freaked out by the entire incident, so in a rush to distance myself from the entire event, that I left her front stoop before I realized that I didn't get what I had come for: Poe's letter. It took all of my social strength to return right then to Mahalia Mathis's door and knock on it. "The letter," I bellowed to the wood, attempting to be both loud and empathetic, repeating this refrain until my throat was as sore as my rapping knuckles. It took me a while to accept that, even if the older woman heard me, she was beyond my reach now.

· · ·

By the time I got back to the Hudson Valley, I could laugh at some of it as I told Garth what had happened. Garth had his copy of *Chesapeake Cabin* rolled out on the coffee table, along with printed out driving directions to possible site locations. It wasn't till I'd finished my story and he looked up at me that I realized he was pissed.

"So that's it, everybody has to play their roles, right? Black people can't be Indians, don't matter what's in their blood or how they was raised or what the freedman did for red folk. You just got to be on Team Negro if you got any black in you. Even your octoroon ass." Garth took a bite of a Little Debbie fudge roll so big it seemed to end the conversation right there, as a matter of physics.

"Look, I didn't mean to offend, okay? I'm just saying it like it happened." Garth claimed a line of Seminole on his mother's side, I forgot about that. "I'm sorry. I'm not trying to judge."

"Oh, you judging. Don't back down now. You let me judge back first. You so scared someone's going to kick you off Team Negro that you think everybody's got to stick to some crazy one-drop rule. That's me judging now."

I wanted to ask him about his paintings then. I wanted to ask him if there were ever any black people in them, or did they look to him like a window to a Eurocentric fantasy world where black people couldn't even exist, like they did to me. If that was the attraction. But I took my lumps because he was my boy and I wanted to walk away from this.

"A guy called for you. Booker Jaynes." Garth's tone eased, which in its way was its own apology. "Left a New York number, said he's in the city next couple of days, recruiting a job for the place you called about. Said he wants to meet you. Yo, he ain't looking for drivers, is he?"

I smiled at my unbelievable luck. Finally.

"Oh, this is big. This is very big. We're going to Antarctica," I told Garth. Our conflict was forgotten, smothered by the decades of friendship.

"You on your own there, dog. Ain't nothing for black folks down there in the cold."

"White people don't own ice, Garth. I'm pretty sure they didn't even invent it.

CHAPTER V

DIRK Peters was not a stupid man. He knew. He knew he was bad. Peters didn't come to this conclusion on his own—he lacked even the talent for literary judgment—but from the written reactions of the few publishers he failed to entice with the manuscript, he could tell. Faced with this reality, Peters thought it of "considerable good fortune" that he knew of a man purported to be an exceptionally good writer, a friend of his former shipmate Arthur Pym. During their long and eventful tenure together on the wreck of the *Grampus* and those days on the *Jane Guy*, Pym had often reminisced about the fellow, a prankster he had come to know during a prospective visit along the Hudson to West Point. The two found an immediate intellectual kinship. They even looked the same. When they were walking the campus together, many assumed them to be reunited twins. To Peters, a resident of the sea and therefore a believer in fate, his own path was clear:

Way I figure, I figure he writes good. So I'm going to use him. I make a stop on the *Green Goose* in Baltimore City. Stop into a general store, what's known to sell reading things and what. Got subscriptions and such. And I ask for this Poe gentleman, ask they got something by him. Man tells me, they knows this man real well, then pulls out this thing, this magazine, turns to the page to show me, and that's it, that's the man's name. They won't let me buy just those pages, they want 20 cents for the whole thing. I says, them the only 13 pages I need, I'll pay you 3 cents and you just rip them out. They say no. I open it up and there Pim [*sic*] name right there. I know this my man, this Poe he can't wait to see me.*

It was Peters's great fortune to happen upon Issue 34 of the *Southern Literary Messenger,* in which Edgar Allan Poe's first telling of the beginning of Arthur Gordon Pym's story was delivered. It appeared that the influence of the friendship had gone both ways, and Poe was now exploring the life of his friend who at this point was thought to have disappeared, presumably lost at sea. Poe seemed to be creating an homage† to a cherished associate, which would weigh in Peters's favor when he attempted to retain Poe's services. Dirk Peters, of course, was the only one who could solve the mystery of what happened to the missing Nantucketer, a bit of information Peters had never considered of much worth before that moment.

Interestingly, what remains of the letter that Dirk Peters sent Edgar Allan Poe is a heavily corrected first draft in an unknown hand. In addition to numerous basic grammar corrections, the unknown party—presumably a member of the officer class on his merchant vessel—adds into the text more elegant lines such as "it is my desire to commune with you about that most able gentleman, Arthur Gordon Pym, with whom we are both so pleasantly acquainted." More linguistic embellishments followed, creating an altogether different impression of the letter's author than Peters's own literary voice was capable of. This was a particularly shrewd strategy considering Poe's attraction to the upper classes, which Peters may have deduced from his former shipmate's stories. Aside

---

* Dirk Peters, *The True and Interesting Narrative of Dirk Peters,* p. 277.
† Dirk Peters used the phrase "remembering thing," actually.

from his promise to share the information on the fate of the absent Mr. Pym, Dirk Peters made no further reference to the fate itself, deciding instead that it would be better to bait the storyteller. With this in mind, Dirk Peters included a segment from his manuscript along with the letter. It was a chapter he didn't seem to think was particularly special, one he wasn't worried about sending the sole copy through the post to a stranger who might not ever hand it back. It was "far from my good good work," Peters lamented in the margins, but he sent it with the letter anyway. His intent was to entice Poe into ghostwriting his autobiography.* The segment's sole strength in Peters's eyes was that it contained mention of his and Poe's mutual acquaintance. The selection began when the two met after the mutiny on the *Grampus,* and ended with the two of them sailing toward a chasm in Antarctica. All in all, from the opening sentence to the final letter, the piece measured three handwritten pages.

In basic substance, the tale that Dirk Peters told, in his throw-away little note, is the same as the one told in *The Narrative of Arthur Gordon Pym.* Of course, there are differences in style. For instance, from Peters's "we caught some big animal in the water, floating, not the best eating I will say," we get Poe's fascinating description of the misplaced polar bear. From "They got these fish down there what looks like that what comes out the buttocks," Poe springs forth with the culinary ravings on the *bêche-de-mer.* And most fascinating, from Peters's skewed, identity-denying perspective, comes the following:

Going further south, we came to an island full of niggers. Niggers just everywhere, black as night. More niggers than I could count. Coming up to the boat, making a big fuss. If I'd

---

* Peters's repeated phrase for this was "Help me make good on the thing."

wanted to be around this many niggers, I would have stayed in Michigan. Acting such the fool that the white men just relaxed like they was a bunch of black babies. Don't trust a nigger what's acting like a nigger, any damn fool tell you that. I know that. Didn't trust them one bit. One day, they started marching us up a mountain for no good reason. White folks just kept walking along like this made a damn bit of sense. I slowed down, just kept looking at these niggers, waiting for them to try something. Sure enough they did, let slide half a mountain on the white folks' head. Damn near killed me.*

It is at Tsalal that we get more of the richness that is a monument to Poe's greatness. Where Dirk Peters sees mere "smelly water all dirty and with slimy stuff in it," Edgar Allan Poe imagines liquid of a variety of shades of purple veins, each separate like the fingers on a hand yet similarly connected, inseparable. From "The guide that chief stuck us with was clearly a dimwit, his teeth rotting dark in his head,"† we get Poe's vision of a people so black that—breaking with the rest of humanity—their very smiles were denials of whiteness.

It is certain that Dirk Peters read the first and procured the second selection of Poe's early Pym narrative. It's clear that Peters enjoyed them both, and excitedly considered the man worthy of helping him convey his own ongoing saga. What is less clear is what Dirk Peters made of the rest of the *Southern Literary Messenger*. It was, as one would expect of its period and location, a somewhat pro-slavery publication.‡ If in fact Dirk Peters took this fact into his assessment of Poe, he made no note of it. What, however,

* Peters, *Narrative*, p. 184.
† Ibid., p. 185.
‡ That is to say, it advocated lifelong human bondage for those of African descent, as well as their children and grandchildren, great-grandchildren, et cetera, for eternity.

should be made note of here is one rather large and integral piece to the Peters puzzle: Dirk Peters was an Uncle Tom. This was a particularly impressive achievement, considering that *Uncle Tom's Cabin* had not yet been written. But Peters managed it anyway.

While Peters did think Poe to be an important enough writer to sculpt his own life story, he didn't bother to keep Poe's corresponding letter for posterity. In Peters's own record of the subsequent events, which like the Pym narrative alternates between first person and journal format, we are told that Poe was eager to hear more of his lost associate, giving thanks for the intriguing three pages included. Astutely, Peters also discerned that Poe might be even more interested in the chance at a paid commission. Poe was broke.

On April 17, 1837, Dirk Peters, now on the merchant ship the *Armitage,* landed in Philadelphia along the Delaware River. His meeting with Poe had been agreed upon months ago in their correspondence, only the exact date was uncertain. Peters found 1342 Pine Street a little more than a mile and a half from where his vessel was docking. When Peters reached the address and knocked, the door was answered by a man who declared himself landlord of the property. On mention of the name Edgar Allan Poe, the owner became immediately agitated and proceeded to lecture Peters on the lack of responsibility in the modern world and the interest that can accrue on a debt of eleven dollars and forty-three cents in a short time. From the grocer up on Spruce Street (owed $3.21 himself), Peters learned that Poe was rumored to be residing another two miles up the Delaware in a settlement known as Northern Liberties.

"How shall I know him?" Peters had the foresight to ask.

"Drunk as a bee in honey and a head like one of these melons," the grocer said, holding up a particular round one and making bags under where the eyes would be with his fingers.

"And he's got a mustache," the merchant cried after Peters had turned the corner.

Once Peters made his way into Northern Liberties, it didn't take long to locate his prey. The first public house he stopped at pointed him straight at the door in question, the bartender giving directions with the wearied confidence of a man who'd been forced on occasion to take some drunk home to that very address.

The door of 532 North Seventh Street was opened by a small, mousy young woman who seemed so frail that Peters's immediate inclination was to step in the foyer and close the door behind him lest she be swept away by the breeze. It was a brazen move that must have alarmed the lady, for she began nervously repeating, "My husband is not on the premises, sir, and I assure you there is nothing for you here."

Peters then did some assuring of his own, explaining he was not a creditor but a prospective business associate, but the poor Virginia kept stepping backward as if Peters was preparing to spring upon her.

"I have a shared associate with your husband. Arthur Pym?" Searching frantically for some way to authenticate Poe's presence, Peters glanced into the room beyond and looking at the small table spied pages with his own distinctive binding and handwriting. Charging into the room, Dirk Peters quickly explained himself to a shocked Virginia, "See, I sent your husband a business proposal, for him to do the telling on my own tale." To his surprise, grabbing the pile of papers and waving them at her did nothing to improve the situation.

"Edgar doesn't like Negroes," she blurted out. Dirk Peters was not put off by this, for aside from himself, he didn't care much for Negroes either. But then Virginia told Peters what bar she thought her husband might be in. Peters left with a bounce in his step, perceiving a victory in having proven his character to the woman. Wrongly.

> My feet were hurting, fierce, when I come to the public house that was suggested. I figure I will have a drink, regardless. At the bar I see him, him that was in daguerreotype at the house. At first I wondered, because he was wearing his coat inside out and showing the stitching, though he don't seem to know this. But still I am very happy to see Mr. Poe. He sits at the table deep in his cups, a fellow about the same build as I. I approach him with my widest grin, hands at my sides, explain myself and my business. What he says back to me is "Who is your master?" To this I tell him again who I am and that I have no master. Mr. Poe, who is Mr. Poe because I asked him and he told me so, he says, "Off with you, boy." I says again, I'm the friend of Mr. Pym, but he makes no motion, keeps drinking. Then I says it again, and removes from my pocket the pages I'd reacquired. Well then, he takes notice. His face, the color goes out of it, there being not much there to begin with. He starts to say something, but it not coming out, he grabs my papers and begins to balling them. Them being my property, I pulled them away and made haste away from him.*

If Dirk Peters perceived any possible racial implication to Mr. Poe's reaction, he took no note of it. Peters was accustomed to being on ships, and he was accustomed to others accepting his own racial explanation. But Poe, of course, was a southerner of the planting class. If not by birth, then by upbringing and inclination. His preoccupation with the gentility of Europe simply further solidified this classification. And an astute southerner, particularly one as

* Peters, *Narrative*, p. 278.

conscious of caste as Mr. Poe, could discern negritude in the palest
of those mixed in race. Even if Poe did not make a conscious discovery of Dirk Peters's race at the moment, and Peters's treatment
was simply the irrational act of an alcoholic stewed in his poisonous tastes, the evidence of Poe's reaction to the man can be found
in Poe's *Pym* itself, where, again, Peters's head is described as having an indentation "like that on the head of most negroes." The reality of Poe's insight seeps forth, held in check solely by the
demands of the narrative.

On my desk, those three balled and flung pages of Peters's narrative were still rumpled from Poe's coarse handling, permanent
planes giving depth to pages that were, nearly two centuries later,
as brittle as the leaves of November. They showed the orbiting
stains from whatever mug was once placed down repeatedly upon
them, revealing the reality of Peters's later description of the event
during which he repossessed them. Most important, it is within
the final paragraph of these pages that Dirk Peters, inadvertently,
hints at the greatness of his discovery, which he described again in
a second version:

> Just Arthur Pym and I weren't dead. The heathens blew up the
> *Jane Guy* the next day. So we got a canoe, got out of there. Took
> one of them niggers for rowing, but he ended up dead. Pym
> wanted to cook him up right then, but the tide had pulled us
> all the way down to the bottom of the world land by then and
> we come to the end of the ice. The current pulled us towards
> the ice shelf, but being as high as it was, there was nowhere to
> go to. Then a big piece just falls out, down into the water, and
> reveals a hole inside. Tekeleli I keep hearing, just like those
> island niggers used to yell when they saw white things. Then
> this really big pale guy in a white robe comes out.*

* Peters, *Narrative*, p. 185.

So ends the final crumpled page. This was to be all that Edgar Allan Poe would see of Peters's narrative, all that his imagination would have to draw from.

But in Peters's manuscript, there is more to the story. Sewn together with a thick purple ribbon reduced to pale lavender by time, there it is: the fourth page. An unrumpled, withered, yet clean sheet that clearly shows none of the harsh use of the other three. And on that fourth page, in Dirk Peters's signature liberally inked chicken scratch, is written the following:

> He points at us to land our boat and Pym got out first, and I went to follow and this big thing makes like I'm not welcome, pushes me back in the boat and gives it a kick. At this time, I don't even mind, because this white thing gives me the shivers. He ain't born right, I can see. I was far down there, about longitude 3.34 and latitude 34.3 by my calculations. And being as weak as I was, and as tired as I was, I assumed death was waiting at sea for me. But the same tide that pulled me down from the Tsalal Island in a few days pulled me back again. I came in at night, gathered up some of them dried sea turds fishes, and in a few days I sailed off again. Picked up by the crew of the *Blue Fortune* on what they said was November 17th.*

Longitude 3.34 and latitude 34.3. What we today know as Morter's Point on the Ross Ice Shelf. Longitude 3.34 and latitude 34.3; on the map it was a rather big place. It was the size of a small city, actually. But in the right place, at the right time, aimed in the right direction, what Dirk Peters's notes told me is that you could sail from there off this frozen continent to a hidden tropical utopia within a few days of floating. I knew this in my heart: that if I

---

* Peters, *Narrative*, p. 186.

found the right place at those coordinates and launched a vessel from it at the right time of the month, that regardless of global warming or centuries, the path to the isle of Tsalal would still be viable. That just as it did for Dirk Peters, the current would pull me to the island, and to discovery.

· · ·

I called my cousin Booker Jaynes at the number he left for me. Garth's handwriting wasn't much better than Dirk Peters's, but I got through anyway.

"Booker Jaynes?"

"*Captain* Booker Jaynes." The voice was abrupt, graveled. I apologized and started in with family small talk but only got a few seconds before he interrupted me.

"Mr. Chris Jaynes, I have three questions to ask you before we say anything else," he told me. I stuttered a bit, then went silent. After a few seconds of this, satisfied, he put them to me.

"One. You want to go to Antarctica, to the Ross Ice Shelf, take a group down there and do some research. Is that correct?"

It was. I'd told him in my original message. Clearly this was why he bothered to call me back. He sure didn't want to talk about Great-Uncle Oley.

"Two. Do you have the kind of money it would take to get down there, rent equipment, hire a professional crew, and make it through any weather delays necessary to get the intel you need?"

It looked like I did. The first settlement offer from the college was a little more than I had invested in the books themselves. Not as much as I knew the books' worth had probably appreciated to, but getting in the ballpark. Added with the year's severance I'd received for not suing them for firing their only black professor, I could do this.

"Three. Are you willing, are you willing to swear on your God, swear on your heart, swear on the very Jaynes bloodline, that you will not tell a soul about our meeting, or reveal any information therein—not one goddamn word—without my approval? Can you handle that?"

I could, did. I wrote the address of the bar he wanted to meet at the following night. Then I hung up and started calling some cousins on his side of the family to see if Booker Jaynes was actually as crazy as he sounded.

CHAPTER VI

MOST of the people on the Jaynes side of the family fell into two categories, brilliant or lunatic. My mother, who raised me alone, gave me both her surname and its problematic lineage. The Jaynes family was stricken with overactive intellectualism, which is why so many were clinically or functionally insane. But my other cousins insisted that Booker Jaynes was in the brilliant category. Mostly.

From calling around, the story I got was this: Booker Jaynes hadn't started out paranoid, he'd just worked his way there through life experience and due diligence. Booker Jaynes was probably the world's only civil rights activist turned deep-sea diver. The successes of the struggle in the South left him feeling distraught and betrayed—he was just getting started when those Negroes down there decided to call it quits—and he went as far away from it as he could. While his other disaffected radical brothers went underground, he went undersea, diving commercially mostly and wreck-diving when he could. The man had made his career before technology increased the range and duration of dives, back when you made it on oxygen and a prayer. It was a world where you owned no treasure unless you dragged it onto the boat yourself, where the rights to a fortune were often protected only by the sea that hid it, where claim jumping was called "fair game." Booker Jaynes was as much a product of this world as of the northern Bronx he grew up in. For Booker, going from diving to polar exploration was as natural as making the transition from H_2O in its liquid to its solid form. When he was a kid growing up with my great-uncle Frazel, Booker had his interest in polar exploration sparked by an article about the explorer Matthew Henson in the *Brooklyn Sun*. After saving Green Stamps from the local Shop N' Go for a year, Booker used the coupons to buy ice shoes and ski poles. By the time he could actually afford the things, it was June, so his pop arranged for Booker to have time climbing the discarded shavings from an ice-skating rink in Rosendale. The most important thing my calls to cousins and aunties told me, though, was that Booker was a man who made things happen. Or at least tried to.

Booker looked like a Jaynes, forehead like a block of caramel toffee, neck stolen from a giraffe, unfortunate attributes he'd tried to cover with a snake orgy of gray dreadlocks. As we'd planned the night before, we met at a bar in lower Manhattan, past City Hall by the docks. I didn't like going near Wall Street. More specifically, I didn't like going near high-risk bombing targets, it just wasn't my thing. He sat in the back of the room staring intently at the front door, Malcolm X style, which considering we were in an organic juice bar was a little heavy for the scene.

"I used to come here before. Used to serve you underage, if you worked the docks," he told me. "Wasn't all bright with these damn lights in here. It was called Hughson's. It was a place you could get stabbed with a knife. It changed on me," my cousin told me, in a way that sounded like he was adding it to a long list of things in this world that had betrayed him.

He asked about my motive for the expedition and I launched into the story of *Pym*. As his eyes drooped, I suddenly appreciated Garth for his ability to feign the slightest interest in literary history.

Next, he asked me about the family. It was clear he wasn't interested. He was just checking to see if I was really me. Once that was confirmed, Booker Jaynes cut short my family update.

"This bar holds a lot of memories for me. I was here, taking a break from working a dock in Brooklyn, the morning the truck bomb went off in the shipping entrance of the Twin Towers. I heard the bomb go off, went outside. Smelled the smoke and saw the soot-covered people, and it all kicked in. I knew exactly what I had to do. It was time to *march,*" he told me, hit the last word slow and hard so that I could feel the impact, then took a swig of his carrot juice. Immediately locating a Kinko's, my cousin had a flyer typed, printed out, and copied by the hundred before the smoke had even cleared. Setting the rally for four hours in the future, Booker Jaynes barked the news and handed out the flyers as he took his long walk north, from City Hall to Fourteenth Street. Hours later, flyers dispensed and throat parched from calling others to the cause, Booker Jaynes arrived at his rally point at Union Square, the historic site of American civil disobedience, and received the shock of his life.

"Not one goddamn person came to the Twin Towers Bombing Rally. Not one, not even the Negroes bothered. Not even one news crew either, and I called them all. What type of shit is that? Not a one; people just walking by. What the hell has this country come to, that people won't rally against injustice? What the hell is wrong with a society that won't even bother marching anymore?"

"But, you were going to march about what?" I asked my cousin, somewhat confused.

"What? What was I going to march about?" Captain Jaynes spun in my direction, shoulders, chest, and all. When Booker Jaynes looked at you, he really looked at you with his whole body: an errant billy club in Little Rock in '64 had resulted in a loss of rotation in his neck. "Negro, we were going to march! Don't ask me about marching; what kind of ignorant ass question is that? Let me tell you, I marched at Selma, I marched in Mississippi, I marched in Montgomery. I know how to march." The last sentence was delivered in a loud staccato, each word nearly a sentence in itself.

"I'm sorry, Captain, I'm a bit lost," I continued carefully, truly unsure as to whether I had missed some form of information. "March against whom? *Why?* I don't understand, how would that help anything to do with the bombing?" Maybe I did lack some insight, but my cousin didn't bother sharing his with me. Instead, he just stared me down, the gray snakes around his neck now still as if steadying themselves for a lunging attack. He paused to take me in. For a second, I thought he was going to stand up and walk out, leave me there sipping my wheatgrass. I could see he wanted to. But he didn't. Instead he leaned forward, and in little more than a whisper, he let me in.

"There are people out there, people who have made fortunes just following me around, finding out where I'm taking my boat next, so they can come right behind me and steal something. White folks who wake up every morning and say, 'Hmm, I'm getting kind of low, I wonder what Captain Jaynes is finding that I can take from him.' So this doesn't go beyond this table, do you understand me?" he demanded. I didn't really, but assured him I did. After making me swear a few more oaths, he continued.

"This is the deal. Drinking. Water bottling. In Antarctica. All above sea level. Go down, cut and drill blocks of glacial ice, then ship it on tankers back up Stateside. Big corporate thing, but I got an in. Government is giving huge tax breaks for using minority-owned businesses. We get some black people, front a bit of our own money, incorporate with a few others who can do the same, and it's a guaranteed fortune. Here's the number to get in on it. Can you do this?" Checking around the room first for prying eyes, Booker Jaynes pulled out a folder from his satchel, let me see the numbers. The number to get in and a much larger number, the number I would leave with after the money started flowing. I could pay it. It would be all of my money, but the projected earnings would set me up for five years. Enough time to construct a detailed analysis of Peters, even if we didn't find anything. And the plan made sense too. No one drank tap water since the Dayton Dirty Water Disaster; the clean stuff was worth as much as petroleum. The ice down there was centuries old, formed long before the modern world began collapsing.

"Looks good, but can we go to this location?" I said, pushing the coordinates across the table with equal paranoia, giving the room my own once-over.

"We can go and do whatever we want, that's the thing. Long as we get the water, put up the funds, we'll be on our own. We can drill for whatever's down there, the petroleum treaty is over, and what we find we can keep. Get it? Nothing but upside to this. Just need a skeleton crew. That's it. All black, so we qualify. And also because I don't trust white people."

"Who do you have in mind?" I asked, thinking of Garth. Thinking this could be employment for both of us.

"I start asking around for people, and it's out the bag. Any of my contacts could turn around and take the whole thing before we can seize this opportunity. But you, no one knows you. So you have to find the people. We'll need another general helper like yourself, two water treatment engineers, and two lawyers. Got to have the lawyers, I want protection. The laborers we'll ferry-boat in for week shifts from Tierra del Fuego. Find the crew, and I'll take you right down to your chasm and you can have the coldest damn book club on the planet."

· · ·

I'd reserved a hotel room in Queens for the night; it was cheaper and safer than Manhattan and I'd thought my family reunion would be longer and more social than it was. On the way there, I got off the train to stop in at a Thomas Karvel Emporium of Artistry on Fifty-second. The painter didn't just sell his work in galleries, he owned his own, and the store was awash in sunsets and saccharine. I was planning to see if the "Master of Light" had done any South American vistas, maybe even set in Argentina or Chile, that could be used to tempt Garth to come Karvel spotting below the equator. The closest I could find was a red sunset shining past the Jesus looming over Rio de Janeiro, a vision which had magically erased the actual city below in favor of green hills, sea, and sand. Waiting in line to purchase the overpriced print, I looked into the glass room at the back of the store. To get in there, you had to see one of the clerks, and then they walked in with you and hovered while you checked out the premium Karvelia on the walls. From the line I could see one of the paintings in the back. The top of the frame was yellow laced with orange and red and pink, and capturing the same end of day as the rest of the visions that crowded the place, but beneath the sky it was blue. I saw snow. I ditched the line and got closer. The guard was answering questions from a jewel-encrusted woman perusing some English cottages on the other wall, and in his moment of distraction, I took a shot of the snowy scene with my phone. Outside, my excitement barely let me control my thumbs. I texted it to Garth, along with its title. *Shackleton's Sorrow.*

I had an assignment from my cousin, to fill out a crew, but I knew absolutely nothing about aquatic engineering. An Internet search that night led me to several large companies that I was sure Booker Jaynes would hate if I notified, and not much else. The best I could find was two water treatment guys from Queens who ran what they called an "Afro-Adventure Blog" on the side. Sewage management wasn't exactly the same thing as aquatic engineering, but I figured if they could handle all the shit in Queens, they could handle anything.

Their website was a strange hybrid, half devoted to their sewage treatment services, half to video clips of their adventure exploits. I clicked on the first clip. One of the two men, Jeffree, was on-screen, the other, apparently, behind the shaky handheld camera. They were running west on the Brooklyn Bridge, fighting through the traffic of a terrified mob. The camera shifted away from Jeffree and to the Twin Towers in the distance, their tops flaming. The footage was bouncy and jumbled. But it was sincere. They were running against a panicked tide to get to the disaster. There is Jeffree, this dark-skinned man past forty with a shaved head and theatrical goatee, and he just wants, as he says again and again when he looks back at the camera, to "do something." It's black superhero shit. But then the fantasy ends. They reach the site of the World Trade Center and in moments it's in rubble. More chaos and running and horror. Tidal waves of dust and then sirens and rogue herds of insanely frightened office workers. But they can do nothing.

Jeffree and Carlton Damon Carter are just two guys who make dirty water clean again, guys who share the same little Lefferts Garden apartment, where they sleep in the same marriage bed. Poetically, the last image that the ever silent Carlton Damon Carter films of Jeffree on that day is of the water engineer handing water out on the street to those last survivors straggling from the World Trade Center.

"See, I'm the performer, right? I'm like, to these people watching, the hero they want to be. But my man Carlton Damon Carter, he's the one that filmed it and made it art. He's the one that designed the website, the one that brings all I've done to the world,"

Jeffree declared in another clip, one in a series of video journal entries. He had a hand firmly on Carlton Damon Carter's neck and was roughly pulling on him as the other, lighter man blushed in response. It would have been a very masculine gesture if Jeffree hadn't kissed Carlton Damon Carter lightly on the side of his forehead in the end.

"He's my muse," Carlton Damon Carter nearly whispered into the microphone. "I'm his lens."

It was clear from the number of comments beneath each clip that they had a huge national and international audience for their exploits. But as I kept watching, I started to wonder if the national and international attention for their little site may have distorted their original intentions. The duo's attempt to drive to Ohio during the Dayton Dirty Water Disaster was a disaster in itself, and the reams of tape basically just covered them stuck on I-95 in a U-Haul filled with barrels of New York tap sludge, only to be turned away by the National Guard. Here the same agonized futility on display in the 9/11 footage just comes off as plain stupidity. Clearly I was not the first person to perceive it this way; Jeffree admitted as much to me on the phone the next morning, calling me back a few hours after my fishing email.

"Something like this, that could really increase traffic. *Negroes on Ice.* That could be a whole documentary," he told me, his live voice filled with even more bravado than the video editing had captured. Already I found him a bit annoying, but I was looking to discover literary history not make buddies, so I pawned him off to Booker Jaynes anyway. I was already preoccupied with the next stage of the recruitment.

· · ·

I knew where she lived. I knew where she worked. I hadn't talked to her in seven years, but that was because I held on to the hope

that she would come back to me first. When I went into the city I
made a habit of passing through those blocks that housed her residence and her job, walking from one end to the other in the hope
I'd see her from a distance, but that was all I did. I didn't call her. I
clung to my hope instead, hope built on a shaky foundation of science.

With love, the scientific literature on the subject reveals that the
human brain works according to a series of dependable cycles,
ebbs and flows as natural as the current. We were seven months
into our first love phase, and Angela Bertram's endorphins ran out
before mine did. I clung, she pulled away. I clung harder, and she
walked out on my ass. I wasn't bitter, this was actually my preferred understanding of events. Another way to look at it is that
she grew up poor, and staying in a grad student's little stinking
hovel invoked a future life of pretty much the same. The fact that
she left me for a lawyer fits into this theory too well—evolution
had hardwired women to be attracted by ambitious, successful
providers, as it had predisposed men to physically fit women capable of bearing healthy young. So I gave her this. It was not Angela
Bertram's fault, it was evolutionary reality. She already had my
heart, I didn't have much choice. I didn't fight her abandonment,
because you can't fight science. Fighting science just makes you pathetic, like spitting in the wind or breathing underwater. The best
thing to do is let the wind abate, float to the top. And then breathe.

Science is a glorious thing. Angela divorced after seven years, a
number predicted by her endorphin cycle. Even though I heard for
years that the marriage was in trouble I stayed away because research shows that the vast majority of relationships that begin as
extramarital affairs end within a year after the partner has left her
or his spouse, and my love for her was undying. Angela Bertram
had been separated completely from the bastard for almost two
months. I'd heard something about infidelity, but made sure not to

torture myself with specifics. I'd stayed away because rebound relationships initiated in the first three months after the conclusion of a long-term relationship had a dismal success rate. I had been planning on contacting her in three weeks, on the exact date of the third month of her final separation, before fate had changed the calendar. If I was a religious man, I would have seen the hand of God. Instead, I saw the wonders of the scientific method and the fruits of self-discipline. There had been other women in my life, there was sex and sometimes romance and much flirtation. But no love. No one had gotten to my heart because my chest was hollow. Whatever was once there, Angela Bertram now possessed it.

She came out of the subway, and she blinked and looked around for a few seconds, orienting herself. Her sense of direction was poor, her eyesight worse. Angela refused to get glasses because she was a little vain and was afraid of falling into a downward spiral of myopia, that the lightest prescription would soon lead to lenses thicker than the Hubble Telescope. She found the street sign, found the direction, and walked toward the restaurant, where I sat by the window. The look when she reached me at the table, the hug that started with the arms and pushed in with the full body behind it, it was everything I'd been waiting for. Always let them be the last to contact you when you split, even when they dump you and say they don't love you anymore, so that you both know that you are the one who never called them back.

"You look great. You look the same. Like you haven't changed one bit," Angela told me, still holding my hand as she took her seat. Another victory on my part. Seven years without increasing your body mass index is a great accomplishment. Especially for a man soon to hit forty. It was the great age, when poor lifestyle choices and bad genes started to show dramatically on the human form. For her, I'd kept myself encased in amber, mind and body. From this position, though, up close, I could see all the ways Angela Bertram had changed over the years of name hyphenation. Her once braided hair was now untwined and ironed. The darkness of her skin banished the thought of wrinkles, though. It still shone like the skin of an orca. Accented now by diamonds that covered most of her earlobes.

"Don't you ever wish you could go back, make different decisions?" she asked after entrées, a sadness there I planned to rub away. "The divorce has taught me, I'm creative. Even if I'm not doing art anymore, I need to be a creative person. I needed a partner who's a creative, adventurous person. How did I think I could be content with someone whose idea of life was just raking in the cash from corporate acquisition contracts?"

I knew she'd never be happy in that life. I knew that when we were together. What I didn't know was how terrified she was of growing old in the same poverty she'd been raised in. This I figured out later. This I deciphered from "I love you, but I can't live like this. I'm going with David . . ." And then she probably finished the sentence—maybe she was going with David to the store or on a Caribbean cruise or to the chapel to be wed that very day—but I've long since deleted the rest from my memory banks.

"You always knew that. You always knew me." Angela laughed. And I laughed back because I did and I didn't hate her for it. She had fear. I had fear. Our demons had just been working at cross-purposes.

"I do know you. That's why when I heard about this, I knew I had to let you in," I said and pushed Booker Jaynes's folder across the table. I'd already sent her the scans, but I felt like the actual papers might serve as a talisman.

"Well, I'm at a crossroads. The marriage, the job even—I can't work with him anymore. Infidelity will do that," she said, and I gave a little shrug. Not enough to show my awareness of the irony in her statement. Bitterness was the enemy.

"Well, I'll have to look further, but I'm intrigued, that I can say now. I know I wouldn't have a problem getting a second lawyer to join as well." She smiled, took a sip of the white I'd picked for the occasion. A pinot—a refined version of the rotgut I used to lug for her up to my fourth-floor walk-up. It worked. We made it all the way to dessert, talking about the lost days we once had together. She listened to my *Pym* ravings. She was fascinated. We kept talking in front of the bistro as the lights went off inside the place.

"Look, Chris, I could use a capital investment like this right now. Hell, I need adventure too. But, I'll tell you, if I do this, if I do the crazy thing of coming all the way down to Antarctica, it won't be about me," Angela admitted to me, walking to her subway. "There's someone I know who this would be even more important to. Someone who this would be a dream come true for. A special guy who needs this. Someone very important to me."

I didn't go for the kiss. At the gate, I shook her hand and received another hug for my restraint. Excusing myself before I burst, I floated back home. Technically I took the train, but I felt like I could have glided on the tracks and made it there just the same. No present worry, not a thought that wasn't future or past. All my patience, my self-control, then victory. I promised myself I wouldn't contact her again until we were below the equator. I wasn't going to crowd her, scare her off. Give her any reason to second-guess the odyssey. I turned her over to Booker Jaynes, and I would just see her down there. See her on the ice. Wait for the opportunity to be cooped up with Angela Bertram on an utterly isolated Antarctic base. Let the inevitable take place.

"Niggas on Ice!" Garth yelled at me when I got the door open. It was late, he was early to sleep and rise, and I was surprised to see Garth even awake. But there he was, smiling, Antarctic images on his laptop and a doppelgänger of *Shackleton's Sorrow* on the page he waved, compliments of my own printer and a whole cartridge of my colored ink. "Get this, they say he's down there, dog. That's the rumor, this is where he lives. The ultimate in Karvel spotting," Garth ranted. I paid attention to him, but more to the large package I'd picked up at the door. "Mathis Estate" was listed at the top of the return address, in care of a law office in Hammond, Indiana.

I'd tried calling Mahalia Mathis, asking her to mail Poe's letter to me, of course, but no answer till now. This wasn't just a letter, though. It was as large as an icebox, and this made sense, because when I removed its outer paper, I saw that it was just that, a Styrofoam cooler. On top of the lid was a folder with not one copy of the Poe letter but five. All quality, professionally done. But the box, this huge box. Electric taped. Razoring the edges, I lifted slowly as Garth continued babbling about Thomas Karvel hidden away in Antarctica behind me. I was prepared for several things, a hat, tom-toms, maybe one of her performance gowns, but none of those were close to what I saw inside. A severed human head, sockets empty, staring back up at me.

The flesh was gone, all that was left was a brown skull resting on a puzzle of aged skeleton pieces. It was enough to make me jump. It was enough to end Garth's rant when he came up next to me. Beside this head was a note, handwritten in the elaborate cursive loops of the woman herself.

To Be Sent to Christopher Jaynes, on the Event of My Untimely and Unfortunate Passing:

My family has carried this burden, cast down from one generation to the next, since 1849, when they had to dig him up to hide his bones from Rufus Griswold. My plan for our last unfortunate meeting had been to ask that professor to test them next, but you saw how he made a fool of himself with his little Q-Tip nonsense. Please find me a good

Jewish doctor who can run that DNA test right. Redeem him,
Christopher Jaynes!!! You're my only hope!!!*

There was the skeleton of Dirk Peters. The man himself, in my
possession. It was almost as great an honor as the book. And I
made a vow to myself right then that I would redeem him. I would
redeem him, beyond the petty prejudices of his family, distanced
and departed as well though they were. Someday, I would find
Tsalal. And I would go to Tsalal with these remains. And there, on
the highest mountain, I would bury Dirk Peters in the ground, on
the island of blackness that he, a black man, had discovered and, by
leaving Pym behind, had preserved from the predations of white
supremacy, colonialism, slavery, genocide, and the whole ugly
story of our world. This was Dirk Peters's legacy. Even if he was
an Uncle Tom.

"Damn, dog. A box of bones, ain't that some shit? From here,
nothing can surprise you. You're not going to get a bigger shock
than that in this life."

• • •

Garth was wrong. Very wrong. A bigger shock came three months
later, when we met at the hotel in Ushuaia, Argentina, the day before the journey. To save money, Garth and I were sharing a hostel
room with four other considerably unwashed German backpack-
ers down the street, but I made sure that when I began my journey
with Angela Bertram I was ironed and fresh shaved.

She was standing in the lobby, the woman I used to call the

---

* Although represented as three, there were in truth at least a dozen exclamation points
at the end of the note's final sentence. And each of those had a frowning face drawn
carefully into its base dot, which I am both unable and unwilling to re-create here.

Ashanti Doll, her skin a wealth of rich melanin above the white vinyl of her snowsuit. And I saw myself with her, I saw a vision of us spooning on an iceberg, within an iceberg, the blue and white and the rest of the world impossibly hard and cold but the two of us warm in an embrace. And then I literally saw myself, right there, behind her. Me but chewed up me. Me but chewed up, digested, and shit out again. This guy. Like me but bloated and stupid and going bald where I was going gray.

Angela introduced her new husband. Nathaniel Latham told me how "fucking psyched" he was that "his babe" chose this as their "honeymoon journey." Garth put a hand on my shoulder to make sure I wouldn't do anything. Aside from murmuring "someone adventurous, creative," I didn't. I couldn't. My brain was flushing down my spinal column. My head was empty, my eyes blank.

"He's an entertainment lawyer," Angela Latham said and beamed back at me. "Being here, doing this, now I know the divorce came too late. Nathaniel reminds me so much of you too." The rock now on her finger matched her earrings. "You guys are going to get along great."

VOLUME

...II...

CHAPTER VII

IT was the last continent; man had overrun all the others. It hid on the bottom of the planet, below, white and silent and as still as it was cold. And it was very very cold. Our crew was black and loud, running and stuck, always freezing and yet sweating in our insulated clothes. It was boring. It was too bright. The sun never set, just went red at two in the morning and then back to yellow an hour later. And I was stuck in a double-wide aluminum box with Angela who was now Angela Latham, not even a hyphen this time that I could cling to.

The miners sailed down from Argentina to work in fourteen-hour shifts, Monday straight through till Friday, and slept on their own boat till their week was done. We oversaw them, provided direction, counted up the ice blocks they piled into their tanker's hull before taking them back north for bottling. During the week, the site boomed as the engines of the giant mining machines did their banging. At 3:00 P.M. on Friday, our world immediately became quiet once more. The last large sound was that of the latest tanker belching as it drifted, fully loaded, away from us. Heavy with clean water, it began its journey back up the planet again, first to Buenos Aires to drop off the workers and then all the way to exotic locations like Newark and Bayonne, its melting cargo becoming more valuable with every nautical mile.

When the drilling was going on, we bitched about the

sound.* The day after the workers sailed away from our Antarctic home, the silence was louder. The God-I-can't-hear-anything roar, building in your ears like a snowball on a cartoon hill. The constantly rustling wind didn't help. That was just the sound of silence moving.

Every Saturday after the workers had gone back to the warmer continent, Booker Jaynes sent Garth and me on out to drill in the surrounding tundra. Soil samples, ice samples, we even had a standing order to grab a penguin if we got the chance. Booker Jaynes had several "clandestine business opportunities,"† had promised things to a lot of people, it became clear. I wasn't sure how much of his intended take was outside our agreed upon communal take, but I didn't really care. It was a chance to get out of the box, away from her. Seeing her with this man, the ring, smelling the cigars he reeked of mingling with the scent of her, it was a lot to bear. I spent my time either working for my cousin or translating Dirk Peters into English from the blurred script he wrote in. I consoled myself with the self-evident truth: Their marriage would fail. He was clearly lazy. He had "taken time off" from the agency in L.A. she worked for, and on return, he would burn through their savings. Once he was stripped bare, she would see him as the fraud I knew he must be. Her fear of being broke would kick in and she would walk away from him as she had done to me years before. By this time, I would have published my edition of *The True and Interesting Narrative of Dirk Peters* to major fanfare. All would be restored. This was my fantasy. In the moments when I allowed myself to see past my despair, this is what I hoped for.

---

* Or rather, as the cliché goes, bitched and moaned, but you couldn't hear the bass of moaning over the machinery hum.
† These are sometimes also called "scams."

By week eight, Garth and I had fallen into a routine. Our little surveying trips were like vacations. Outside our windshield was no hint of humanity for miles and miles. Just ice and air, wind that shaped the snow on the ground into modernist curves and Victorian angles. Garth seemed almost comfortable out there. Cold climates look good on fat people. With all the layers, everybody else looks fat too. If you still managed to look skinny under all that cloth, you also looked miserable.

"They out there, dog. On the ice. Hiding."

"The shrouded white figures?" I asked. I was thinking the same thing. When you were looking out there, into the emptiness, it wasn't long before you could imagine anything you wanted there to be.

"No. Karvel and his people. Makes sense, don't it? You got all that money, you want to go where no bombs or nothing can get them. That's what I'd do," Garth told me, again. In bringing him down here, I had introduced Garth to his new favorite conspiracy theory.* I'd stopped countering with logic by this point, because doing this made me even more tired of him.

When Garth became excited he talked while he ate, his Little Debbie snack cakes inevitably smearing some sort of cream or multicolored glazing across his thin outline of a mustache. Garth knew his appetites and had come prepared to fill them. He'd brought cases of the cakes, as well as videogames (most of which involved him shooting imaginary loads into fantasy people) and porn (same). The actresses in the latter clips were older, matronly

---

* I should say here that, in America, every black man has a conspiracy theory. (That statement in itself reveals a conspiracy, omitting as it does the conspiracy theories of black women [copious though they may be].) Some theories are quite creative, fascinating. But most are quite mundane, because they're true. This obsession with conspiracies is most likely due to the fact that our ethnic group is the product of one.

looking women with large breasts and hips and guts who hugged the men assigned to act with them.* He'd also brought his entire collection of paintings of Thomas Karvel to be signed by the artist when he found him, certain that this ultimate feat as a Karvel spotter would be rewarded by the Master of Light, who would use his pen to magically ink Garth's investment into a fortune.

"*Shackleton's Sorrow* looks just like those mountain ridges out here. Tell me it don't. Now how could Karvel know that?" With a sweeping movement, a coconut creme roll clutched in his glove, Garth motioned to the space beyond our frozen windshield, his thick parka and snack cake cellophane rustling in unison to accent his gesture. It did look like the painting to me. So did all the other mountain ridges Garth had made the same claim of in the weeks before. This range was about ten miles away; its pale ridges were all that gave the landscape a sense of scale. Antarctica felt to me like nothing. Frozen nothing. Nihilism in physical form. If it was to be loved, it was to be loved for its lack of content, people, possessions.

The drill was mounted to an all-terrain vehicle (ATV) the size of a Volkswagen, and it took a good ten minutes just to get it unchained off the flatbed tow and then driven down to the ground. It was my turn, so Garth helped me set it up, then abandoned me for the warmth of the cab. It was an expensive piece of equipment. Every time we took it out, Booker Jaynes told us it was an expensive piece of equipment, but it looked mean and old. Once again it shook, it shuddered, and burrowed its way down the hole to its bottom, pumping and thrusting into the cold ground. Once it reached its target, the drill would remove an eight-inch tubular sample, and then we could drive on.

---

* This I found out after searching through Garth's laptop while he was in the shower (bored). Confronted, Garth responded, "I like to look at women who would actually sleep with my fat ass."

After I got the drill going, I walked back to the cab to refill my thermos. Garth was looking through his rumpled Karvel catalog. Nearly every page was worn from overuse, its corner intentionally turned. I tapped on the window, and he rolled it down, reached his thermos to mine, and poured.

"You hear that drill? Your mom wants one with rubber on the end," I told him. When the cup was filled, I took it into two thickly gloved hands, where it was not so much held as laid.

"Dog, you joke. But she had one. And your pop stole—"

Midsentence, Garth's expression turned from squinting speculation to wide-eyed revelation. Before I could react, one of his padded mitts reached out to grab my shoulder but slipped and took a firm sirloin grip on my neck instead. I reflexively jumped back, but not far because the big man had a grip on me, his face twisted with an emotion I had never read there before. I grabbed Garth's wrists just as he hit the accelerator on the truck—if I hadn't he might have run over me. With the engine roaring, we lurched forward, me holding on to Garth's arm with both mittened hands as fiercely as he was holding on to my neck. Under our mittens, we locked onto each other with a death grip. I looked up at Garth, his face ashy from the blistering cold, eyes facing the windshield, and saw that he was screaming. Between the roaring engine and the jackhammer of my adrenaline-pumped heart, I couldn't make out what he was saying. It might have been "Chris, I am about to ram into a snowdrift about twelve feet high, so you should brace yourself," but I didn't hear it. Just felt the jolt as the truck slammed into a powdered wall.

The truck bounced lightly back from the resistance; I came to rest less gracefully. Maybe it was the shock of the moment, or the shock of slamming into the drift, but I felt nothing on impact. Only confusion as I looked back at the truck.

Garth got out of the cab, his jacket unzipped in the polar wind, and didn't even glance at me, collapsed on the ground. He was looking back in the direction from where we came.

"Sweet baby Jesus." I could just make out his mumbling. "Ain't that something?"

In the space where we had just been standing, there was now nothing. Nothing: not the drill, not the ATV it was attached to, not the ground it sat on either. There was only air. A crater the size of a good-size Texas house. The abyss spread eighty yards from one crumbling side to the other. The twin tire lines of the truck led straight up to the lip of the hole and disappeared.

Garth was an expert on driving away from danger. On the day of the November Three Bombings, Garth Frierson was driving down Shankaw Boulevard as the third attack of that national bombing campaign went off, right there in Detroit. I'd heard the story only once before, right after it happened, but after we stood there silent, in shock, for near a minute, Garth, wired, started talking about it again as if I had just asked.

"Man, when they went off in Houston and D.C. that morning, I was driving my route thinking how safe I was, right there in Mo-town. Then *boom*. Passed the bomb site right on the left side, blew half my passenger area's windows straight out. Couldn't hear nothing in my ears for hours. Right then, I drove straight home, dog. I mean straight—didn't even let the people off the bus, didn't brake for red lights, didn't stop till I got to my apartment. Ran up-stairs, I don't know what those people in the bus did. I got to my house and kept going, headed straight to my bedroom. I look up and I got this painting over my bed, Thomas Karvel's *Mississippi Mist*, and I look at it, and I stop. First time since the explosion, ears ringing, I stop." Garth shook his massive head. "But that was it, that was that feeling again. Like the world's coming to an end. Now you know."

We stood close to the edge of the crater, and after a few minutes our minds shifted to the lost drill and other suddenly uncertain ground: financial stability, job security. We came as close to the edge as we dared, which was about fifteen feet away from it. The thing just went down. How far down it was difficult to say. The opening seemed to be smaller than the cavern inside of it.

"I hate ice," I admitted. "I don't even like ice in my soda." At the ends of my wrists, my hands were still shaking so bad you could see the movement through the gloves.

"Goddamn global warming." Garth leaned forward to get a better view. "Ain't our fault. It was all them Escalades in the ghetto."

Inching a little farther with one of the portable spotlights from my pack, I caught a reflection inside the crater of something red and metallic—the rifler was still visible. The only reason I could still see it was that the drill was lodged into a snowy ledge about two stories down. The hole went farther below that, but the depth swallowed my flashlight in its darkness.

"They going to stick this on us." Garth shook his head beside me. "They just going to say it's on us, dog. They're going to try and make us pay out our checks for this. You have any idea how much something like that drill costs?" I didn't, but it had to be a good chunk of what we were planning on earning. The money wasn't what bothered me. The look of disgust I knew I would see on Angela's face when we confessed our incompetence, that's what I was thinking about. And the sight of Nathaniel, right behind her, smirking.

"I'll go down there, bring it back," I told him.

"Negro what?" Garth politely asked me, turning to see if I was ridiculing him.

"I'll go down there, attach the rigging to it, and we'll drag it up. Hook it to the truck and just pull."

"You crazy, dog. Out of your goddamn mind." Garth paused, put his weight on his leg as he grabbed the spotlight and leaned forward, staring down below at the rifler on its precarious perch. He was silent for a few seconds before his reason took control of his desperation once again. "Hell no. You're bugging."

"It's my life," I insisted.

"It's my bank account. If you die, they going to make me pay for the whole thing."

"Or we could just take care of this and pay nothing at all."

Garth stared at me, then stared back into the hole for a while. Finally, he unzipped his jacket further and lifted off his hood to reveal his unpicked Afro. "Fine. But if you break your neck, I'm going to tell them it was all your fault to begin with," he said and started walking away. Pausing after a few feet to look back, Garth added, "I'll tell a better story, though. Something heroic, make you like the man." He walked another three strides before turning again and adding, "I'll tell them you died fighting a polar bear. Three of them."

There are no polar bears in Antarctica. There are certainly not three of them. This didn't matter to me because I had no intention of turning this into yet another polar epic of man succumbing to nature. I was not thinking about personal risk at all at the moment. I was thinking about attaching the harness properly to my chest, making sure the gear was securely fastened and could hold me. I was thinking about saving the money. Having the money. Using the money. I was thinking about how I might still be in shock or overrun with adrenaline, but that this manly act felt good, like something Nathaniel would never dream of doing. Even in death I would be redeemed, in life I would be a hero. Or was I just being a fool? Again. Too late. I refocused. I tried to find precisely the right angle to drift down, one that would land me right on top of my goal: a ledge that seemed composed of a solid enough lip of pale blue glacier ice on which both my own weight and eventually the hoisted rifler could be levered. And then, once I had successfully attached my line to the machine, I dropped below the edge of the surface, slowly letting go of my line through the clasp so that I hung out into the chasm. Dangling in the air, I distracted myself by thinking about white-shrouded humanoids.

I used to do the climbing wall at the gym and be embarrassed by the pretense that I was training for anything more than other climbing walls. Who knew it would pay off in a frozen chasm at the bottom of the world? My spotlight hung by my belt's loop, its power on and its beam circling erratically as I took care to ease into the slack and drop farther. The lamp created the feeling of movement below me, and that was all my imagination needed. Was it an illusion of dim light and shadow, or were there really tunnels and their openings just beyond me? Tunnels whose course had been interrupted by this recent avalanche? As I slowly dropped, my attention focused far below toward the crevices, hoping for something more, so I was surprised when I felt the hard and real metal of the rifler jam my toe.

"Don't land on it! You not supposed to land on it, man. You could set off a whole other cave-in," Garth boomed from above. He was leaning over the edge and his morbid obesity suddenly seemed like a mortal threat. I yelled him back.

I dangled in front of the drill. It looked to be in fairly good condition, considering the fall. A bit dented but functionally unharmed. Grappling hook in hand, I maneuvered myself to attach the line to the sturdiest section of the carriage it could hold. As I did this, giving it a good yank for security, the bulk of the rifler shifted from the vibration, sending a shower of loose snow farther below, into the darkness. As my eyes adjusted, I could make out more than I had before below me. Even at these depths, light managed to permeate the frozen crust, leaving the ice to illuminate the surroundings. The Antarctic gives the impression of being white, but really it's blue. Almost entirely constructed of that pale, powder blue that at times can darken to rich, cobalt haze, as it did now around me. Through this glow, I could see the bottom of the pit, not more than another two stories below me. I could also make out the rough pattern of the fallen snow at the bottom of the cavern. In some places the debris was thick soup, in others chunks of ice the size of coffins stood upright in the floor. It was already an impressive sight before one of the large spears of ice started to fall forward, giving movement to the static scene.

Except it wasn't falling forward, it was walking. Walking forward, arms swinging, along the crater floor. And then it was looking up to me.

Let me say this as I said it to the others, soon thereafter. I know what I saw. And what I saw was a figure. I saw a figure of massive proportions and the palest hue, standing below me. I saw a creature with two legs and two feet, with arms that shook off clouds of snow as they sprang out beside it. I saw that what I first took to be a slab of ice was in fact a shawled figure, one whose cloth now rippled with movement as the beast hustled forward.

And what did I do? I looked up, I looked to see if Garth also saw it, catching the quickest glimpse of my greatest revelation. But Brother Garth was gone. Above was just the taut rope that held me.

When I turned back to look down, *it* was gone. So that's when I did the only thing I could do, the only thing that came to my mind.

"Tekeli-li! Tekeli-li!" I yelled into that now empty crater, the words echoing lightly against the walls of the abyss. "Tekeli-li! Tekeli-li!" I kept screaming louder and louder, till Garth started pulling me up once more. I fell silent now, waiting for a response.

CHAPTER VIII

WHEN we got to the base camp we found the crew in the communal room at full attendance. The TV news channel was on, and on the screen was chaos.

It was the familiar trauma. There were the jumpy camera angles of smoke in the streets and people coughing into cloths ripped from their shirts. There were flashes of blood with no clear points of origin. There were people leaning quietly on other people who screamed loud enough for both of them. There was dust piling onto running crowds, as if they were being buried not just alive but in motion. There were legs that lay still in the streets, feet flopped out and hanging lifeless. But this time there wasn't just one place identified in the chyron, one nation, one landmark in flames. This time there was Tokyo, and Paris, and Berlin. And then there was London, and New York, and L.A., and Sydney, and Seoul, and at one point even Stuttgart, and then there was bouncy footage from locales that were defined by solemn commentators as being "_____ miles outside of" other places.

"The drill fell in a little crater. It's down about two stories, we're going to need help getting it up. Wasn't our fault." I saw the bad news on the TV, but the only good thing about really bad news is that it provided good timing for a less bad news dump.

"Man, it's blowing up, up there. Blow. Ing. Up," Jeffree responded, not listening. I'd accepted Jeffree's theatrical nature over the weeks, but that made it no less annoying. But he was right. On the set, the trusted news anchor relaying the latest events started choking up. The television blared but we were quiet. Nobody talked or moved much. Nobody had to because the television was relaying all the words and action a mind could comprehend. An image of smoke coming out of the subway entrance flashed by. I saw the green balls of the 4-5-6 train lines logo.

"Your condo," Nathaniel said, pulling Angela closer on the couch.

"My cousin Antoine works two blocks from Seventy-second Street Station," she returned, pushing into him. I remembered Antoine. I said, "Antoine's probably fine, just fine," but I don't think she noticed.

"We should be out there," Jeffree offered, no small bit of heroic longing in his voice. Carlton Damon Carter, Jeffree's lanky partner in engineering and love, was always silent, but at that moment, his silence felt profound. We in the room were all listening.

When the satellite suddenly lost its reception and went to static, we didn't even look away from the screen. Our satellite was always going down, and the signal was never very strong. I remember thinking that the white noise was a bit of a relief, a chance to brace ourselves before the next wave of chaos blinked into view.

"Turn it off. Turn it," Captain Jaynes said, pointing. His voice was deep and bellowing and full of enough drama that it demanded authority or confrontation if he could get it. "There's nothing you can do, nothing any of us can do down here. We're not just going to sit and watch all day going crazy. That don't make no kind of sense. Best thing to do: turn the news off for a bit, get our work done, get our minds off of what we can't change for the moment. When the satellite feed comes back through, we'll deal with it."

"Boss man, I likes the way you think," Jeffree agreed. "But it's

Saturday. The day off. The Shabbat, baby. We got nothing to do but wait for the TV to come back on, then watch it."

"No," Captain Jaynes disagreed, his voice rising so that the whole room could take in his declaration. "What we have is a very expensive piece of mining equipment that has to be retrieved from a hole in the ground."

• • •

The only white folks Captain Jaynes, Race Man, invited onto our crew's Antarctic mining mission was White Folks, his dog. And even that dog was a thickly spotted Dalmatian. My cousin loved calling his name in anger, and the poor mutt gleefully suffered it. I was nice to him, though,* and as we drove Captain Jaynes to the site White Folks leaned into my hands to be scratched.

"I saw something. I saw someone down there. A creature. Just walking by," I confessed to my cousin. Past him, Garth gave me the funky eye. Jaynes looked over like he knew there were two kinds of Jaynes minds too, and he was pretty sure how I should be categorized.

"This ain't going to be some great excuse for you to start going off about your book again, is it? People don't want to hear it, man; that shit on the TV just makes it more so. So promise me, no more stories about super ice honkies. Understood?" he asked.

I nodded. Because I did understand. I was obsessed, I knew it even though I couldn't stop being that way. I bored myself, truly. But I saw what I saw, and I said so.

"To think that a work of fiction, no matter how old or what you think you've discovered about it, has any reality. It ain't normal, son," Captain Jaynes offered. "I'll tell you something else, life is too

* I really, really liked that dog.

short to be reading more books by white people. Especially dead ones. We got our own books. We got our own culture. We don't got to borrow theirs."

Garth followed the tire tracks we'd made on our last visit, deeply concentrating on the road, lining up his wheels with their initial journey to save the trouble of replowing. The others behind us did the same. Nobody talked. Besides the last comment, the only sound in the cab was White Folks panting between his master's legs, his enormous pink tongue hanging out past his muzzle. Around the dog's neck was his uncomfortable looking collar: an old iron chain, weathered and with links nearly two inches long. I'd seen it before, but staring longer I realized what it was: old slave bonds.

"Are they real?" I motioned to White Folks's neck. I even repeated it as the captain stared mutely back at me.

"Real enough for White Folks," he told me. My cousin was a collector of black memorabilia, this was one of the things we had in common. Most of Captain Jaynes's acquisitions were of the remnants of slavery: chains like this one, bills of sale, sale adverts, runaway notices, cages, neck spikes, face masks, the like. Jaynes even had a vintage hogshead barrel that he'd filled with various cat-o'-nine-tails.* I would imagine that the links would pull at the Dalmatian's short hair or pinch his skin, but White Folks didn't seem to mind as he pushed back eagerly into his owner's hand.

"Why do you do it, then? Why exactly do you collect all the slavery stuff?" It was an obvious question, but we still had ten minutes to the accident site to kill. Captain Jaynes was quiet for a good two minutes before he answered, visibly turning the question over in his mind.

"I'm collecting evidence" was what my cousin told me, and the

---

* This he displayed in his office in a way that others took, rightly, as a veiled threat.

great trial that Booker Jaynes was preparing for unfolded before
me. In the captain's living quarters, office, and many storage lock-
ers, crowded with artifacts as they were, the case was perpetually
made, stuck in closing arguments with judgment ever forthcom-
ing.

My cousin was not the only one with an idiosyncratic collection
on base. Booker Jaynes understood people needed their passions
to keep sane on the ice. Everyone was provided a storage space.
Angela and her usurper had fitness equipment in their hold. At six
most mornings she dragged their machines into the cargo space,
where she moved her limbs until breathing heavily as the blubbery
Nathaniel sat on a foldout lawn chair, reading the *The Wall Street
Journal* on his tablet. Garth brought his sizable collection of Little
Debbie snack cakes by the case. When he worked the late shift,
Garth could be seen passing the sweating blur of Angela en route
to his stash of calories, and the difference in physicality between
the bus driver and the lawyer was like a display in the natural history museum. The remaining space of Garth's hold held his prized
Thomas Karvels. His own sleeping quarters had so little wall space
that, like the finest museums, he circulated his collection regularly.
In their hold, Jeffree and Carlton Damon Carter stored the extra
servers for their website, their video equipment, sets, and lighting.
At times, their small area became a miniature television studio,
recording clips that quickly found their way around the world via
their site. "If we wanted to do porn, we could be rich overnight,"
Jeffree joked, repeatedly. Painfully (personally). "Not sharing you"
was Carlton Damon Carter's constant response, his statement no
less adamant for the fact that it always came in a near whisper.

· · ·

The chasm didn't seem nearly as deep upon return to the site, or
nearly as wide. But then I started thinking about having to hang

102 · MAT JOHNSON

down on a cable into the abyss again and it seemed as scary as it always had. I was already sore from the first attempt, but that was
fine because Jeffree* eagerly volunteered for the task of trying to
rescue the drill this time.

"Ever since we got to Antarctica, the traffic to the blog has
started building again. We're getting more unique hits every day.
They love it. Polar adventure. I'm like a super-nigger on ice! The
people, they need someone to live through. Trust me, I used to be
in roller derby back in the day. People need a hero."

Even as Jeffree prepared to go down and secure the drill, he
managed to create a dramatic air about himself. It was in the beat
to his jaunt, the elaborate kufi that covered his bald head, the fact
that he let his parka crack open just low enough at the top that his
cowrie-shell necklace still affirmed his blackness into the frozen air
as his breath turned white before him. Carlton Damon Carter, as
always, hung behind. Like Garth, Carlton Damon Carter would
not even remove himself from his truck's driver's seat. I found
Carlton Damon Carter much more intriguing than his louder ac-
complice, because Carlton Damon Carter seemed to have no need
for attention at all. Sure, he kept himself looking dapper, his lightly
processed hair sculpted neatly with Dax pomade, but while Carlton Damon Carter clearly took pride in looking attractive, he
seemed to feel no need to attract attention from anyone but the
protagonist of his own life story, which of course was not Carlton
Damon Carter. Even there, staring across the distance through his
truck's frosted window, I could see that Carlton Damon Carter sat
preparing his camera equipment to focus on what really mattered
to him.

"Looks like you didn't fuck it up too bad" was Captain Booker
Jaynes's estimation on seeing the drill below. With that blunt as-

* Or Jeff-Free, as it said on the website, although I don't think that was the legal spelling.

sessment I felt better; the fact that it was Jeffree who was attaching the climbing harness through his legs and not me added to my mood. In that moment the earlier vision of the white shrouded figure, the stress of the initial accident, it all began to dissipate. Melt away, just like we hoped none of the snow that surrounded us ever would. My obsession was starting to scare me. It was leaping off the pages of the old manuscript and into my real world. That thing I saw was either real or a sign of just how advanced my mania had become. Back now, though, was the ever present mundane. We would get the drill, we would fix the damn thing, we would keep going. Back on TV and in reality, the world would not end, and just like all the other unrest, this spike would gain a vague name and be sectioned off into the land of anecdote. I would address my obsessions, and no longer let delusions of massive pale monsters get the better of me.

When Carlton Damon Carter finally arrived on the scene with his video camera and lights ready, Jeffree prepared to begin the rescue. He made a big deal about going down the hole too; despite the wind blowing as it did, ruffling the fabric in our hoods, further muffling our hearing, it was possible to hear his generous sighs and huffs. Even at the time of his complaints, I knew enough about Jeffree to know that he would be bragging about this later, replaying the clips of it on the computer for us even though we'd been here to see it happen. The man was physically built for this. Even through his parka the thickness of his arms was visible. I had never seen Jeffree lift weight one, and yet there the muscles were.*

"Rock and roll, baby. Time to get all action star out here." Jeffree was smiles before this jump. Captain Booker Jaynes, his hood and hat removed, his dreads so many silver snakes dancing in the wind,

---

* I'd heard grunting in the area of his and Carlton Damon Carter's storage unit but didn't pry.

tested the suspension line for him, giving it a tug for attention. "No cowboy bullshit. Go down slow, hook the pulley to the frame. Gentle, clean, easy."

"Don't worry, it's going to be easy," Jeffree responded, looking down at his target. Then to the camera.

"You hit the ledge with your full weight and you're going to knock the rifler off the shelf and send it in an avalanche another twenty feet down," I warned.

"I'm like a cat. Let me show you how a real man gets it done," Jeffree responded, pointing at me with the last sentence. Then with a smile and a salute, not even looking down or over into the crater, he quickly jumped up and flew down. Standing on the opposite lip beside Jaynes, I watched Jeffree slide in a quick, smooth, and effortless glide. Then I watched him hit the drill so damn hard when he landed that he set the whole thing in a secondary avalanche, falling another twenty feet down. Angela screamed.* Carlton Damon Carter kept the camera on and focused.

"I'm okay, didn't break anything," Jeffree yelled, but the weak cracking of his voice betrayed him. "Least I don't think," he retracted.

Captain Jaynes had two gloves over two calloused hands over his one face. He was breathing heavily; I could see the mist shoot clouds between his fingers. "Ig'nant ass fools," he said, which I felt was a bit rude, but Jeffree was so far down he wasn't hearing anything.

"Yo, Chris, you got some big-ass feet," Jeffree quickly followed. I could still see him from where I stood, brushing himself off, trying hurriedly to regain his jovial persona. I had small feet. I wasn't going to yell that down on account of the myth, but I didn't know

---

* Or perhaps it was Carlton Damon Carter, who was also a high alto when speaking above a whisper.

what the hell he was talking about. Before I could respond, Jeffree offered, "I thought you said you didn't come down here? You got your big-ass boot tracks all over the snow."

"I didn't go down there," I yelled immediately, looking to Captain Jaynes, largely to make sure he knew that Garth and I hadn't been just goofing off this time. But I hadn't gone down there. Leaning forward to peer over the edge for a moment, besides Jeffree's dark form, now covered in powder as he stood by the rifler, I saw footprints as well. They were like little craters, oblong, in a pattern that suggested the gait of a biped.

"Hey, this is wild. You got to come see this. You got to take a look at this, Chris Jaynes. Carlton, you got to get a shot of this." Jeffree was getting really excited now. You could tell, because for once he didn't sound as if he was reading lines off of a teleprompter.

I turned to Captain Jaynes, showing too much excitement before the first word, because he knew where I was going.

"Look," my older cousin interrupted me. "I don't want to hear none of that snow honky bullshit, you hear? We got reality to worry about. Real issues, real money. I don't want to hear any of your dead ofay book theories, conspiracies, or anything else." Captain Jaynes raised his head to address Carlton Damon Carter and the Lathams, who were only now deeming the event worth coming out of their own truck's heated cab. "And I don't want anyone else hearing your nonsense either. We're going to suspend down there, get our drill out of the snowball it's stuck in, and then we're done here. Not another word."

So I didn't offer one. Not as we attached our own harness gear around our waists and between our thighs. Not as we dangled slowly in the air into the hole and carefully controlled the slack as we drifted down. I didn't offer to say anything, not even after our feet touched firmly on packed ice, and I looked over at Jeffree, who was standing on top of the drill's snow-encased carcass where it rested against the wall, staring into the space around us. As I looked around, they did seem to be real footprints—an observation I made quickly and while Captain Jaynes was busy disengaging himself from his line. The spacing of the holes was a bit wide for footprints, but it was consistent.

"Help me get this goddamn drill out of here," Jaynes ordered, and I went over and pulled on it with the others. It had to be flipped, but the impact had packed the snow into its every groove, and the only reachable part was the bumper. If we tried to lift it up from that, chances were the bumper would just rip off it. Forcing myself to focus on the task at hand, I joined my muscle with Jeffree's, pulling as Jaynes offered direction from off to the side. There was the difficult first lifting, then the teetering, then it fell over with the slightest of bounces on the giving surface. I turned to Jeffree when it was done, but he wasn't even looking at the thing. Staring back from where the drill had just come, Jeffree was instead focused on the hole of maybe four feet that the machine's removal had revealed.

"You see that too, don't you?" he asked. I just saw a hole. Behind me, Captain Jaynes just saw something that was not worth his attention, and he was already fastening the harnesses to the rifler's frame.

Jeffree pushed past us, went to the little opening in the side of the hollow. I followed. The hole seemed to lead to another chasm. Or rather something more, its depth becoming more apparent as I got closer. It was a room that someone had recently entered; when I approached I saw those massive footprint-looking indentations, obscured as they were by the falling snow and the rifler's landing, heading directly toward this space.

"What is it, some kind of crevice?" In spite of my belief, or maybe because of it, I felt the first pangs of fear at what might be beyond. Jeffree shook his head at me. Or maybe not at me—his eyes were wide and distant, his thick jaw slackened in a rare moment of self-reflection. I could see Carlton Damon Carter adjusting his zoom to catch the expression as well.

With the sounds of Jaynes's diligent working still behind me, I crouched to look into the space. No, it was not simply an ordinary crevice. It was long, it was expansive, the footprints going far off into the distance and fading into the rest of the snow. It was tall too, this ceiling; the opening was just a space in the collapse. There are many natural ice caves under the surface of Antarctica. But it was hard to believe that this was one of them. The walls looked chipped away, the space too straight, and if there had been any debris it had been cleared away.

"It's a cave," Jeffree managed, beside himself at the sight of it. Even at this depth, the sun shone through the surface, offering illumination. Everywhere glowed a haunting blue that seemed electric from the throb.

"No, it's not a cave," said a voice that surprised me before I realized that Captain Booker Jaynes had stopped what he was doing and crept up behind us. Jaynes, to my surprise, now wore an expression much like Jeffree's, and I realized that I also wore the same foolish, overwhelmed look. Jaynes's eyes were focused on the things that I dared to think were the tracks of a creature that had walked upright through here only hours before.

"It's a tunnel," Captain Jaynes finally managed.

We kneeled silently in the cold, taking in the sight and its repercussions. Far above us, Carlton Damon Carter filmed, and unseen beyond him, Garth and the Lathams sat warm in the trucks that hummed and roared. Finally, as my knees began to numb and my excitement threatened to overpower me, I broke the meditation.

"Captain, what do you want us to do now?" I asked. Booker Jaynes was a man who lived life by either being in control or pretending he was long enough to gain control again. Here was a situation that no one besides myself had ever thought they'd face. Captain Jaynes met it with belligerent, folded arms, but then his attitude just fell away. My cousin turned to me, slapping me several times on the shoulders as if discharging any responsibility for this new discovery.

"Me? Hell, looks like we got a snow honky problem. You're the expert."

CHAPTER IX

OF course, I was *the* expert on the phenomena we seemed to be encountering. Unfortunately, my sole primary source was those few lonely paragraphs in *The True and Interesting Narrative of Dirk Peters. Coloured Man. As Written by Himself:*

> As we go south, the sky darks in a polar dusk and the fog gets thick. The birds, white gulls (or albatross or some such) were not stopping, gray ugly things that kept croaking "Tekeli-li" like we supposed to understand them. Infernal! The Tsalalian had been dying for days, then in a few minutes he dead. I says that we should dump the corpse immediately, for the sake of decency if not good health and stink, but Arthur Pym was looking by the body. Dripping more spit than I thought he still had in his self, he says, "That wouldn't be prudent." Alas, the flesh that had been Nu-Nu got saved for then as we were soon up on a strong current that shot us past the broken ice at fast speed. What can I say of what was seen next? Not nothing. So let me just say that we approached an ice shelf too long to be another iceberg, going into the distance of east and west. As we were move forward, a slice of this thing fell into the ocean before us, showing both a crack in the ice and a shrouded figure in white standing within it.*

---

* The last paragraph in *Peters, Narrative,* chapter XVII, the following paragraph being the lead paragraph in chapter XVIII (pp. 146–148).

Floating forward, we moved into a cave within the ice itself. There we come to a landing, and they surrounded us. Arthur Pym stepped out of the boat despite me yelling to stay put, so transfixed was he. The group surrounded him. And then I kicked off and made a quick exit out of there.

After that, Dirk mostly talks about how the current pulls him back, and how he's really fortunate that he listened to Arthur Pym and didn't get rid of the body of the late Mr. Nu-Nu, coasting as he did in the monthly return tide back to Tsalal. "You never know what you'll eat if you [sic] hungry enough. I cut up Nu-Nu's corpse into bite-size pieces, then I used them as bait for the Bich de Mere. Those things taste like horse shite," was the entirety of Dirk's recorded reflection on the experience.

So from my research I knew that we should avoid eating bêche-de-mer. Beyond that I had no idea what we were supposed to do next.

We lifted ourselves back up to the trucks. Now that I had their complete attention, I replayed in detail what I had seen the first time.

"Come on, Professor, what the hell is it?" Booker Jaynes demanded. "Some kind of monkey? Some kind of Neanderthal? Or just men, the CIA or something?"

"It's the twelfth tribe of Judah," Jeffree asserted as he stroked his goatee, nodding to Carlton Damon Carter, who stood behind him in our circle, reviewing his video footage. It was not clear that Jeffree actually believed this, but it was obvious that he liked the sound of it, its biblical and Diasporan overtones. We huddled in a makeshift tent, a tarp pulled between the roofs of two trucks and hung over the sides to keep the wind out.

"It's definitely government shit," Garth added, sounding like a weary big man preparing for a fall. "It's the feds that built that, dog. If not ours, then someone else's. Believe me, I know: I used to work for the government."

"You worked as a bus driver, Garth. As a bus driver for the city of Detroit. That hardly qualifies you as an expert witness on the government," Angela said with a roll of her almond eyes, and it was almost possible to see the air deflate out of the big man, sending him drifting into the corner. He gave me a look of sympathy from over there, but all I could do was marvel at her power.

"No," I boomed, trying to assert my own. "This is nothing like that. Whoever it was that I first saw, whoever it was that built that tunnel, it's not something modern, not something that's been seen recently. No mechanical equipment we know of built that tunnel. It looked almost natural. It looked *old*." I leaned on the last word, let it hang in the air for a minute. When I saw I had them, I dug in and declaimed.

"Look, folks, as you know, I am not here by complete accident. I am with you, on the crust of the Cape of Good Hope, because that is where I believe the events cited in *Pym* from two centuries past took place. Historical precedent. Whatever it is out there, it has been noted before. We are simply the first to experience this phenomenon since the chasm—"

"Excuse me." Jeffree, who had been whispering with Carlton Damon Carter, turned around to interrupt. "Before we get any further with this, this cave—since I was the one to discover it, I believe it should be referred to as, um, the Jeffree Tube. Yes. So if you could refer to it as the Jeffree Tube from this moment forward, I would appreciate that."

"So are you meaning to imply some form of ownership here?" Angela stopped him, pointing her finger in a way that threatened permanent ocular trauma to its target. "You must be, if you're already invoking naming rights. You don't even know what this thing is besides a big crack in an ice block and already you're claiming it as your own property?" There she was. This petite woman, small but centered. Her beauty alone would have made some men* cower, but along with the way she paced the tent, the way she shook her arms violently as she spoke, she erased any questions of stature. The woman at dinner had been less assured and a bit reeling, but already Angela had grown stronger. With Nathaniel. Like a beautiful blossom growing in horse manure.

"Hey, sister! Sister, please!" Jeffree jumped forward, his hand stretched out in suppressing motions, his face giving off his best impression of an individual hurt and affronted by false accusation. "I'm not saying I own it outright. You the one said our contract with _____ Cola says that the Creole collectively owns what we scrounge on our off days. I'm just saying, since I found it, I should be able to name it. That's all."

That's all. That's all you need to start a fight among a bunch of people sacrificing everything to get rich, to build a legacy. The largely deflated Garth Frierson still had enough air in him to float out the tarp as the conversation grew steadily more heated.† In the mix of things, amid the accusations and retractions, Captain Jaynes left the space. When he returned, my cousin had his full gear laid out before him: the steel spikes for his hiking boots, his face mask, pick, climbing rope, goggles, all in addition to his normal polar walkabout gear. As he prepared, the room became quieter. Even I, who had just been in the process of mounting a fierce defense of my more elaborate conclusions, joined the growing silence.

* Me.
† One of the unfortunate side effects of the imposed artifice that is "race" is that it forces its way into every categorization. For instance, as the crew of the Creole began to become increasingly argumentative and confrontational, instead of thinking A: "This group is plagued by overblown personalities and is socially dysfunctional" or B: "The issue at hand, with its extraordinary circumstances and implications, is one that

"Pardon, Booker, but what are you doing?" Nathaniel Latham asked Jaynes. Nathaniel seemed perplexed that the man appeared to be taking action when an argument was still being waged. Particularly when his wife was winning.

"Out," Captain Jaynes responded. Tying up his dreads behind his head in a bun, he looked up at us and saw that further explanation was demanded. "I'm going down that tunnel, going to see what's in there."

Nathaniel opened his mouth to respond, but Angela interrupted him before he started. "With all due respect, sir, you don't know what is down there. You don't know that it's safe." Her tone was definitive, the hand on her hip conclusive, but the captain kept tying and zipping, working to get his boots back on over his thicker layers of socks. Frustrated by his lack of response, Angela continued louder. "What about the naming rights, Jaynes? That's real intellectual property. If there is something down there, something huge, something with major social or scientific implications, whose ownership claim is that going to be?"

"Well hell, I guess it's going to belong to whoever else comes to explore the thing with me," Booker Jaynes declared and shrugged, pulling his bootlaces tight. Within moments, the others began preparing too.

---

sparks immediate difficulties," what one infected with the American racial mythologies might have come up with was, instead, C: "Why can't Negroes get their shit together long enough to get anything done?" This, of course, is a fallacious and offensive implied accusation. There are countless successful organizations in a variety of professional arenas founded and run by people of African descent to prove the implication wrong. At that moment, though, in this tent with these specific individuals tearing at each other before the event had even begun, I must confess that, when summarizing the scene in my own warped mind, I succumbed. In my mind, I had skipped over reactions A and B, even managing to degrade past response C to come another down, to D. This response consisted solely of the word N*ggers, which I confess I uttered, wagging my head in frustration.

. . .

There were seven of us standing before the chasm, ready to plunge below. Some of us felt like there was fortune waiting just beneath our feet, unseen. Garth came not because he believed that there was anything worth the effort but because he didn't want to be left alone in an empty truck. "Dog, that shit is creepy," he told me. As he struggled to be lowered into the chasm, the big man forced his eyes closed and clung to the two climbing cables supporting him. I took his box of Little Debbie Banana Twins cakes from the glove compartment and threw it to the bottom of the chasm so at least he had something to look forward to.

It was among the requirements of employment by the Creole Mining Company that all personnel should be skilled in rock surface climbing, with specific training in ice climbing. It was the captain's belief that anybody who lived on the ice should at least have it in his or her power to climb that ice. Unfortunately, like many job requirements, this one was fulfilled more in the letter than in spirit in our little squad. My own wilderness training, for instance, consisted of an intensive two-day course on the climbing wall at the Reebok Sports Club/NY at Sixty-sixth Street to refresh my indoor, plastic wall climbing skills. The polar qualification of the certification came from the fact that, even though I took this course indoors, it was in January. I felt a bit guilty about that until I found out that Garth believed he had fulfilled his requirements by walking to his bus station once the day after a seven-inch snowstorm. "Don't look at me that way. It was real slippery and shit," Garth, catching my glance as he signed his waiver, told me. Although they presented a much better face on the subject, Nathaniel's and Angela's training wasn't much better. While Nathaniel made a big fuss about their having gone glacial hiking in Seward, Alaska, in the early days of her separation, further anecdotes revealed that they'd flown to the flat glaciers in a prop plane and walked around for a few minutes before setting up a foldout table and having a picnic. Nathaniel had showed me pictures of the outing soon after we first met: the two sat in their matching snowsuits on metal chairs before a table covered in red checkered cloth. They toasted the camera with champagne flutes, their snow picks dangling loosely from their wrists as they smiled. "The pilot was a licensed masseuse too. It was sweet," Nathaniel recalled. I don't know what Angela had told him, but he seemed to have no concept of the fact that I despised him, or why.

This is not to say that no one of the Creole Mining Company had any training for the environment we found ourselves in. Jeffree and Carlton Damon Carter put us all to shame, and Jeffree clearly took great joy in this. It was their thing, the climbing, cross-country skiing, snowshoeing—whatever was the fringe sport of the moment. They were Afrocentrics who loved the adventure. It was an eccentricity that they (or rather Jeffree, as Carlton Damon Carter never bragged at all) were very proud of. Theirs was a type of pride peculiar to our ethnic group. It said, "Look, I'm black and I'm taking pleasure in something I'm not expected to." I don't know if it was the snow itself or the act of defiance they found more enjoyable.

After returning to our opening in the white wall, the entryway I did not then or will ever refer to as the Jeffree Tube, I was shocked to see the footprints still there, moving off into the expanse. Like dreams or haunts, in part I expected them to dissolve back into imagination and mythology. In fact, as we moved as a group, tentative and hushed by the cathedral-like quality of the tunnel, it became clear that the footprints had not only remained in our absence but multiplied.

"There's another set, look. There is one set walking off, and then there's a set that comes back, and then walks off," Jaynes told us. He pointed them out with his flashlight. Looking back toward the entrance, we saw that we weren't more than twenty yards into the journey.

"These weren't here before," I said, but it seemed the others had already deduced as much from Jaynes's tone. In response, Jeffree bent down on one knee, snapped a bit of the packed snow in the track with his fingers, and took it to his nose for a heavy snort before declaring, "It's fresh."

"What does stale ice smell like, Jeffree?" I asked, but if there was an answer I didn't hear it as the marching continued.

Nathaniel had brought a still camera too this time. When the whiteness of its flash hit, the explosion of light revealed nothing. The dimmer, persistent blue sunshine that made its way through so much ice was far more revealing. The ceiling of the expanse, cathedral-like in its arch, reached a good twenty yards above us. The group walked to the side of the tracks, careful not to crush them. As they did on their regular fitness walks, Jeffree and Carlton Damon Carter wore aluminum teardrop snowshoes, which let them float above the snow's crust nicely. Despite the heavy steps of the hiking boots that the rest of us wore, after a few minutes I noticed that my own steps did not go as deep as the footsteps we were tracking, my own feet packing the snow mere centimeters while the prints pushed down inches.

"What's the rush, y'all? You know there ain't nothing down there," Garth yelled ahead to me when I stopped to let him catch up, while the others moved on. Garth could move fast, but he couldn't move fast for long.

"Well, we'll find whatever soon," I assured him.

Garth paused when he reached me, leaning on my shoulder to do so. Pulling off his hood for a moment, he looked up, gazed around at the stillness.

"Nope. If there was something down here, this would be quick, because there would be something to find," he declared. "But searching for nothing: that takes all damn day."

Contrary to Garth Frierson's pessimism, there was something ahead. The path did have a direction. Aside from its straightforward line, it was also clearly heading down, the angle becoming more steep as we moved. It took Garth and me only a few minutes to catch up with the others despite Garth's slow pace, the road dipping at points significantly enough that until we were within thirty paces of the group we couldn't see them. Couldn't see them even when they were just black shadows within the snow, a clearly alien presence in this environment. Around us the walls were glistening and curved; I could even hear the echoes of water dripping in the distance.

"Which direction you think we should go?" Captain Jaynes asked me when I reached him. Our tunnel broke into three possible routes. Looking down at our two sets of tracks I saw it: *a third set,* and what could even be a fourth. There, beneath so many tons of ice and for the first time feeling its suffocating implications, I felt the vertigo hit me.

"'That don't mean there are more than one of . . . whoever this is . . . in here." My cousin exuded his usual confidence, but it wasn't working. The marks seemed all to be made by feet of roughly the same massive size. Regardless, retreat was never even discussed. When I look back now, I wonder about this. We were all down here for our own hustles, pursuing our own self-serving delusions, maybe, but now that we found ourselves on the trail of something genuinely new, something undiscovered, all that could wait. We had to see it through. It was decided then that we should break up into pairs and explore the three tunnels ahead, returning to this spot after five minutes.

Jeffree pushed off with Carlton Damon Carter before the rest of us had even adjusted our gear, so the captain moved to the left en-

trance with Garth in tow. I tried to follow them, but my cousin literally pushed me back to the last group. Nathaniel and Angela
Latham. Nathaniel smiled. Angela wouldn't even look at me, the
way she hadn't since we'd gotten here. Not like she was mad, or
even uncomfortable. Just like her eyes naturally went three feet
over and down in my presence.

"If we were to find something, Chris." Nathaniel left her to run
up beside me, the most energy I'd seen him exert since we got
down here. He tapped on my hood to get me to reveal an ear to
him. "Naming rights would be no small issue. Of course, it's really
intellectual property rights that are prominent here." The ceilings
continued to lower as we went. It was all downhill, taking Nathaniel, Angela, and I farther into the depths.

"Fortunes can be made in being an expert, I'm sure you know,"
he damn near purred. "There's documentaries, coffee table books,
reality shows. But even if you get to play the expert role, you'd
need management. Someone to deal with the finances, publicity."

"Slow down, Chris. Listen to him. He's the best." Angela followed me on my other side, tugging on my arm in a way I decided
to read as seductive. Nathaniel, watching, smiling, knew his wife
hypnotized me, but he also knew she was so far out of my reach
that my obsession posed no threat. "There's not much left to be
new in the world anymore, Chris," he told me, grabbing her
gloved hand right across me and squeezing it. I stopped, just to
look at them. This sent Nathaniel into a riff on international property rights and the Internet. I turned to Angela. She was looking at
me now, but just to impress upon me that I should be listening to
him. Her face modeled the seriousness with which she thought I
should be taking Nathaniel's pitch. I mimicked her without meaning to, until I caught myself.

"That's enough. For today. Let's go back." I turned to walk in
the other direction. I tried to split through the two of them, but

Angela held tight and they stepped out of my path before I could reach them.

. . .

"We're lost, aren't we?" Nathaniel asked when he caught up to me. It had been five minutes and we were heading back to the first cavern, and from the dread in his voice I knew that he too had noticed the mess of tracks that had formed behind us. Tunnel entrances I had ignored on the way down now seemed to tempt me as possible return routes. Had we really walked down in a straight line, or was that just an illusion? Was one of these side openings actually our way out?

"These are the freshest tracks right here." Angela, bent down on her knees, took a picture of the evidence with her cell phone for posterity. "The others are shallower; the wind's thinned them out. And they're crusted over." The two of us looked down at her, and when she got up, we followed behind. She walked faster leading, but it wasn't more than a minute later when the little woman halted abruptly. Flung a flat palm up in the air to motion for us to cease as well.

I followed Angela Latham's eyes, saw nothing.

"Listen," Angela mouthed, and this I tried as well. There was nothing to warrant the wide-eyed expression that had seized her face.

"Breathing," Angela mouthed, and I knew that I was breathing very hard, not quite used to the level of physical exertion currently being demanded. Then, logic clicking into my brain, I stopped my breathing, or at least paused it for a little while.

But the breathing kept going.

Harder than my own this time, although fainter from the distance. Just beyond the next corner, the next bend, something was alive. Something was alive and breathing like a thing wounded, its gasps heavy and deliberate, broken up by occasional forced sighs. *It sounds almost like a horse,* I thought. That is what it reminded me of.

I stood there waiting for Angela to continue walking toward the sound, which she did not. It seemed that Angela had changed her mind about being the first to discover our big-footed prey. Nor did she appear to want to let Nathaniel engage with the unseen beast either. Me, she was willing to sacrifice, and she reached out and pulled my sleeve, giving a slight push in the small of my back in the direction of my destiny.

Never had my own footsteps seemed so loud. Fortunately, the closer I came to the source, the louder its inhuman breath seemed to boom. Turning the corner, I saw the beginning of the beast, a massive black form in the shadow. As I inched closer, I could see that whatever it was was sprawled out, legs before it as it sat leaning against an ice wall. Heading forward in my slowest gait, I could see its chest heaving in the shadow, shuddering from the effort. Then as I came even closer, I saw the creature push a massive hand into its side and remove a small, high-fructose-corn-syrup laden Little Debbie snack cake and shove half the thing into its mouth.

"Damn Negro, you about scared me half to death. Why you creeping like that?" Garth managed. I say "managed" because he had a good amount of pastry in his jowls at the time. Hearing his voice, Angela and Nathaniel came up behind me. Angela used her adrenaline-fueled energy wisely: by giving Garth a good unwarranted kick in his leg before turning around and stomping back in the direction of our starting point. Nathaniel offered a smile and a shrug before he followed her.

Leaning an arm over me for support, the huffing Garth let some of his girth onto my shoulders, and as I walked us out I was soon breathing as hard as he was.

"You're weak," Garth huffed.

"You're fat," I pointed out.

"Yeah, but I'm strong, see? I carry all this fat around every day like it's nothing."

Angela and Nathaniel were far beyond us. By the time I'd pulled Garth up and started moving, they'd made a significant distance. Even in the halls that didn't turn for hundreds of yards, I couldn't see the end of them. Despite the rustling, despite the considerably heavy wheezing of my boy, the massive silence of this cavern started to hang over me. It occurred to me, more so than before, that if the ice above us gave in to its own weight, we would be completely lost. Enveloped in the cold, the labyrinth returned to nothing more than the packed solid mass it was supposed to be. Just when I was really starting to feel the strain, Garth removed his arm and attempted to walk again unaided.

"Listen," he said as he trudged along. "You laughed at me before, but let me tell you something: Thomas Karvel is down here, you know, in Antarctica. He's down here, waiting all the bad shit in the world out. Just chilling, hibernating almost. This could be his hideout."

"What the hell does that have to do with anything? Look: I'm sure the rich have taken off to faraway places to escape the poisoned reservoirs, the bombs, wars," I acknowledged. "But it's to places like Aruba. White sand, not white snow."

"Naw, dog. Karvel, he's too smart for that. This is a man that went from a nobody to a billionaire selling pictures. *Pictures.* No, Karvel's down here, away from everything. Nuclear, chemical, suicide bombs, everything."

I got pissed. At him, at his fantasy. Here I was, on the cusp of my own great dream, my own impossible truth, and this gluttonous man was crowding it with his improbable vision. There wasn't enough magic in the universe for both of us. Worse, Garth's mad theory put mine in an altogether new light. Was I as crazy as his fat ass? You saw something, the footprints, I told myself, but as soon as I did, my rational mind began asserting dominance once again. The corporations were everywhere. It was a fact that a major corporation had hired the Creole itself—wasn't it possible that our efforts were being surveyed, or that we were hired as a front for a greater subterranean effort? It was all viable, and the viable always outweighed the improbable.

Looking at the ground beneath my feet, I saw the footprints, numerous now and going in a variety of directions. Mundane, lost, mindlessly treading. I could hear with some relief that the others were shuffling along in front of us, their crunching steps and muffled voices audible.

"There are no billionaire painters down here, Garth. And let me admit this, there are no albino monsters or Neanderthals either. Nothing other than the mundane abounds, as usual."

I said this last bit, this stubborn pessimism, just as I turned in to door—a narrow crevice in the ice between corridors. What I saw on the other side was a crew standing around, talking to each other. I say "a crew" because they were not *my* crew, not the members of the Creole. Nor were they a crew of humans. At least not in any understanding I had of my species.

Garth came behind me, continuing his mumbles about a rumor some Karvel dealer in Buenos Aires had told him, then bumped into my back, looking up at his surroundings just as these other figures were doing, and he was no less startled.

There were six of them, standing there, mountainous creatures. Their white robes hung loosely around them, and while they stood frozen by the sight of us, those robes continued to sway. There was a moment when I questioned those first seconds of physical movement, being tempted to believe instead that the monsters were merely statues carved from the snow around us, garbed for effect. But then one turned his eyes from Garth to me, and held his massive, pale hand out before him. I knew by some instinct that this was the one, this was the one that I had seen earlier in the day. Even before I spoke, I understood the scene we had walked in on: the creature had been explaining to the others what he'd seen and what it meant, much as I had done earlier to my people.

His hand continued to move in the air before him, whether reaching to me or pointing at me I couldn't tell. I could, however, testify to what the creature said. In a slow, deliberate imitation of my own nervous chatter, the creature spread his colorless lips, revealing an alabaster tongue as devoid of blood as his skin was, his slick gums as pale and shiny as porcelain.

"Tekeli-li" is what he told me.

CHAPTER X

THE others came running quickly down the snow-packed path. This was because I was shrieking. It seems that Garth, the white creatures, and I were not far from that opening hall through which we had first descended, and that the rest of Creole's crew were waiting just beyond the bend. Considering this fact, it was probable that these other beings, standing so close and so still, were very conscious of our group's presence. That they'd been monitoring our presence. Assured that our group was contained and about to head back up to the surface, the beings had swooped in for further observation. Not counting on two slower members to get lost, not counting on us swooping in on them instead. Regardless of the alien nature of these figures, their expressions of shock were clear. The cringing, the cautious backstepping. They were enormous, and even their frightened movements of retreat were terrifying. If it had not been for the arrival of the rest of my co-workers at the opposite entryway, they would have quickly escaped me, returning into fantasy and rumor, the story ending on this very page.

We looked on the six of them as they looked at us, but we were the more awed of the two camps. Their size alone, their towering presence, would have been enough to provide a spectacle. Given my own height of six four, I would have to say that their median height was at least seven four or higher. Their bodies were mountainous and hidden, covered in hooded capes that hung broadly from the shoulders and concealed their bulk in folds. What we could see of their very thick legs and feet were bound as well, but by how much material it was impossible to tell. All the cloth was off-white, composed of what appeared to be the rawhide of skinned animals. In the dim light it was difficult to make out depth and distance. The only things that were clearly visible were their heads, and those were what froze us. What I at first glance had assumed to be horrific masks proved instead to be *their actual faces.* The color, or lack of it, was striking. Albino, it seemed clear, but their eyes contradicted that. Looking into them as they stared intently back at my own, I realized that I had never truly seen pale blue eyes before. I had seen blue but never in this shade, the lightest possible variant, which had more in common with the snow around us than with any accepted form of ocular pigment. These darting, acute, haunting orbs bobbed over noses that were so long and pointy I assume they served some sort of evolutionary purpose that was at the moment unclear. The nostrils were cavernous stretches of ovals, from which gusts of steam—the sole visual evidence that these were actually hot-blooded creatures—pulsed. Also from the holes in their noses came hair, straight and brittle, that fed into their beards, thick corn silk completely devoid of coloring, pouring out of their ponchos. The only pigment attached to them was a yellowing around the mouths and noses, presumably from feeding or bodily fluids.

"Chris? Say something. Do something," Angela, poking me from behind, put to me, as I was standing the farthest forward. I don't know if attempting communication was the consensus plan of the others, but to me it seemed profane to break the silence of this moment. And for a second I couldn't be sure the creatures before us wouldn't kill us for the sacrilege.

"Your hands," I whispered to the others. It was thought said aloud. "Drop whatever's in your hands, and hold them out to show that they're empty." Simple deduction. That's what waving and shaking hands are all about: showing we have no weapons to attack with. Since they were tool users, it made sense that the beasts would get this logic, and they did, looking at each other before cautiously holding their own hands out as well.* The only one not making a gesture was poor Garth, whose hands wagged as loosely by his sides as his chin did on his neck. From behind him, Angela gave the big man a forceful jab to his hefty underside. Perhaps a bit more nervous than most, Garth awoke from his frozen stupor, saw what the rest of us were trying to communicate, and flung his hands forward in a sudden motion. It was a spastic display that sent a forgotten snack cake once in his glove out into the snow between our two parties. When it landed in its crinkly covering, the monstrous beings seemed to view it as a gauntlet, nervously reaching back for their weapons once more, causing our side, en masse, to take a few stutter steps back in response.

"We come in peace," Jeffree managed to get out. He had one hand on Jaynes's old shoulder and the other on Carlton Damon Carter's, seemingly prepared to push the former into harm's way as he pulled the latter away from it. As Booker Jaynes yanked himself free, one of the creatures, the shortest of the bunch, shot down to grab Garth's pastry off the ground, causing another wave of backstepping by us. He huddled off to the side of his group with the Little Debbie, seeming truly agitated by his find, holding it at arm's length for quite a while before bringing the open packaging closer.

"Yum yum," I told him. I think it was something I'd seen in a Bob Hope movie once, where the sophisticated American tries to communicate with a bestial savage. *Our animalism connects us,* I

---

* I thought of smiling at them too but held off on this with the distant memory that chimpanzees take grinning as a hostile bearing of fangs.

struggled to remind myself. "Mmmm, mmmm," I said, making feeding motions with my hands. His eyes were firmly affixed on me. He raised the now crushed cake to his lengthy nose for a series of quick snorts, then pulled a loose piece into one of his massive, hairy hands. With a slow, dramatically deliberate underhand swing, he threw a piece of pastry lightly across the expanse at me. His companions stared dumbly at this interaction. I caught the missile and—before I could think of what unknown contaminant these creatures might share, what hidden virus they might be infected with—I swallowed the cake down, humming "mmmm" all the way and rubbing my belly. It was cake with the texture of a sponge soaked in oil since 1952. Pausing for a few seconds after my last swallow, seeing I didn't fall to the ground and meet a quick death, the creature ate what was left of the portable sweetness.

"AAAAAAAAAAAAHHHHHHHHHHHHHHHHHHHH"

The sounds it made, the groans, were loud, vulgar. They were appreciative too, and the now excited snowman gathered over his buddies. The international sugarcane trade that fueled the colonial world—these beings had obviously missed that. I watched, struggling to be culturally relative and hide my revulsion, as they moved the crumbs around in their mouths, their alabaster tongues glistening.

"They like the food," I turned to tell the others. They were all nodding, uniform looks of frozen shock on their faces.

"Them shits is good," Garth mumbled, eyes glued to the display of ecstasy before him. "Let me see if I got more," he said and began patting himself down, pulling through all the pockets. The others soon joined in, frantically groping him like those sweets were the only things holding off a rabid dog. Garth looked like a sculpture they were putting together.

"Uh, guys? They're leaving," I interrupted. It was true. A quick word from the main yeti had sent the others, one by one, back out into the tunnel beyond. Except one. He was moving toward us. Moving toward me.

I didn't appreciate how massive he was until I was swallowed in his shadow. The smell, the horrible fishy smell, like the penguin cage at the zoo. The hand, a mitt of calloused, pale, dead skin, raised slowly up to me. Up toward my chest, open, flat. Still. Like he wanted me to take it.

"You going to leave him hanging?" Jeffree asked, incredulous, to which the others agreed in a united chorus of "Don't leave him hanging."

I grabbed the hand. I was touching it. Not as cold as ice, but as cold and hard as leather laid on it. The massive fingers slowly circled mine, and the creature gave me a gentle pull, motioning with his head beyond.

"He wants me to go with him," I translated. "Shit" slipped out next.

"I'll go." Jeffree stepped beside me, hand forward. "Carlton Damon Carter and me. Will film it. We'll bring the footage back."

The creature, seemingly sensing the meaning of the discussion, let me loose. He looked at me with those eyes. I met them, barely. Long enough to motion over to Mister Adventure Man.

"But let's get this straight now: it's called Jeffree's Tube."

"Fine," Captain Jaynes offered. He was already backing up out of there, the others following.

"And we'll call them Carlton's Carrions. That has a real ring to it." Carlton Damon Carter looked up from his lens at this, smiling.

"They're not birds, Jeffree. And you can't name everything," I told him.

"Look, if we go down, we take the risk, then we make the decisions. That's supposed to be how this deal works, right? Finders keepers. That's the deal. Whoever goes down there owns this.

Movie rights, book rights, TV rights. Action figures. Because I don't see anybody else stepping up."

And with that, everybody stopped stepping away. And slowly, one by one, stepped forward.

We all went. Everybody but Garth, who was out of breath and exhausted from the task of carrying his own weight, but he was my boy, so I argued successfully that he should stay above to serve as our lifeline in case we disappeared below. As for the rest of us, down we trudged behind the snowmen, deeper into the subterranean blue, not knowing what awaited us. Down into the ground at the end of the world.*

·   ·   ·

The beings were fast, the lengths of their gaits alone put us at a disadvantage. Jogging lightly for a bit as the labyrinth of tunnels moved farther down, we struggled for purchase when the surface became steeper. As the angle increased, so did the time these creatures kept their feet to the ground, using the rough ice of the floor to add a skating motion to their stride. The farther down we went, the wetter the ice that surrounded us seemed, glistening in a slow but undeniable melt. This, of course, was the opposite of what I'd expected; it should have been colder the deeper we went away from the sun. But the caves that widened to cathedral heights dripped above us. We were silent, focused on not busting our tails, until we arrived maybe a half hour later at an opening that brought our path to an end, dumping us out into a hollow so fast it took a moment to realize that the blue sky we now saw far above us in the cavernous space was a distant frozen ceiling.

---

* The events that follow are fantastical and challenged the imaginations even of those of us who experienced them firsthand. I will therefore attempt to relay them to you in the most straightforward manner I can manage, taking on the same level of distance I did on that day, simply to avoid being completely overwhelmed.

Americans use the description "as big as a football field" as if that is a legitimate form of measurement. But really, what other single unit of measurement is there that's comparable? The space here seemed to be at least the size of one large sports arena, possibly two, seats and concession stands included. And there were enough creatures present to fill that field's audience as well. Thousands, tens of thousands, of the humanoids could be seen moving about below us as we stood at the tunnel's mouth. In an instant, creatures that seemed the greatest rarity in the universe now outnumbered our own group by a legion.

"We are going to be *very* famous," Jeffree said, looking around. The sweat on his brow steamed. Carlton Damon Carter, his eyes nearly as wide as his lens, nodded in agreement as his camcorder took in the wonder.

"We are going to be very famous. We are going to be very famous, and very, very rich," Nathaniel declared as he pulled Angela by her gloved hand over to him. She looked at me, though.

"You said it was true," she said, dumbfounded. I was struck by the privilege of witnessing this spectacle and the dizzying possibility that my strange obsession might come to fruition. But the way Angela looked at me was the greatest treasure and maybe the whole point.

All around us, the creatures climbed along the walls, drifting upward in lines to the ceiling in hivelike precision. In fact, the hollow itself was just like the inside of a beehive: I could see rows of identical portals covering the walls around us for hundreds of yards in the air, each the entrance to one of many hundreds of rooms, and each room delineated by pockmarked indentations in the ice that served as ladders. The creatures secured a hand or foothold, effortlessly gliding their oversize bodies both down and up the cave's high walls. Above us, the distant ceiling dripped across the expanse, giving the appearance of soft rain. And as more of the beasts saw us, more of them climbed out of their high-rise caves and slid down the walls to crowd around us.

"This is not good. This is not good at all," Captain Jaynes said as we were surrounded. It was already too late for complaints, whatever was going to happen had already started. So many faces, so many pale eyes, now staring at us. So much familiarity within the alien. They pointed just like we did. They whispered. I had no idea how genetically connected we all were, but I felt some link must be there—if not as fellow humans, then as fellow primates, or at least as mammals.

As I was guessing at their taxonomy, a male stepped forward, a shriveled specimen in comparison to the stoutness of the rest. This was clearly an elder, his silver beard was fuller, longer than those of the other males.* He came directly forward, past the imaginary boundary around us that his tribe had respected, and stopped in front of me. This was odd: the gesture seemed intended to initiate a meeting of leaders, and Captain Jaynes was obviously the elder of our group.

"Tekeli-li," their chief said to me. The pronunciation was so different from what I had imagined, containing warbles hidden within the word that no tongue groomed on Romance languages could duplicate.

"Tekeli-li," I responded back to him. This was greeted by a polite nod—I doubt he imagined that I was trying to respond to his greeting—and then a motion to one of the other creatures who stood behind him. The second humanoid looked similar to the one who had taken a bite of Garth's cake upstairs.† Big and pale, pale and big. But this one was clearly a leader—his paunch of

---

* And the rest of the females too, because really they all seemed to have some kind of beard.

† I'll confess that due to my lack of knowledge they all pretty much looked the same to me. Same skin color, same hair color, same hair texture. All the same.

overindulgence poking out like a massive phallus beneath his robe, his face bloated in comparison to those that peeked from behind him. And the nose. In comparison to those of the other monsters who came to gawk at us, this guy's nose was freakishly massive; gray, long, and lumpy, like poorly packed boudin. The sausage-nosed beast spun off at the old beast's orders, and then the elder tried to continue.

"Ergg Eyy Ossen Aublatt?" is what the odd old thing said to me. This is as near as I can manage to catch how it sounded to my ears, and the only thing I understood was that it came in the form of a question. I looked over at my captain for guidance. He looked back at me and slowly shook his head. He'd had enough.

"I don't know who these folks are, I don't even know *what* the hell these folks are, but I do know that now we got to get the hell out of this place. We seen enough. Jeffree can stay if he wants," he barked. I could hear in his voice that it was clearly too much for the old man.

"Agreed," offered Nathaniel. "We've established first contact, and established our respective stakes in intellectual property and other rights of exploitation. Let's go while we still got the good health that makes money worthwhile."

"We come in peace," Jeffree, stepping forward and past me, declared suddenly, Carlton Damon Carter zooming his lens in on the intensity in his partner's eyes. The elder paid Jeffree no mind, quickly sidestepping him while keeping his glare on me. He looked at me expectantly, as if I was about to give an answer to his burbled question. I felt obliged to comply. Pointing to myself, I said, "Chris Jaynes." The long beard simply stared at me with an expression of confusion.

"EEEEErrrrrggggggggggg—" was what the elder was winding into when another call came from behind the crowd and beyond the cluster of igloo-type buildings in the distance, from a large cave opening much like the one our own crew and guides had descended through minutes before. Hearing the sound, the speaker cut short his wailing with visible relief and joined with the rest of the crowd in looking back toward the newcomers. Jaynes nodded his head to the side, as if we should just turn and run for it right then. But there was nowhere to go. We couldn't possibly hope to climb back up those caverns, or even to navigate the route back to the surface, fast enough to distance ourselves from these creatures so clearly bred for the environment.

Besides, I was caught up. Hypnotized. For now, coming to our gathering, Sausage Nose and another of the larger creatures seemed to be carrying a child, each with one hand holding a shoulder. A diminished, dangerously thin boy, with a slight pinkish color that contrasted with the bluish tones of the other creatures. He appeared to be unconscious, flopping like a stringless marionette. The three figures came through as the crowd opened a path for them. When they dumped the smaller creature between the elder and myself, I saw that it wasn't a child at all but the body of a man.

It was undeniable. It was the single most bloodless corpse I had ever seen in history, but it was definitely a human one. A white man, with dark hair on his head and a dark mustache. I carefully stepped toward the body and stuck a hand on its shoulder. Aside from fabric tied around his neck in a makeshift scarf, the Caucasian was dressed very much like the creatures who had produced him, swaddled in cloth.

"He's dead, isn't he? Is this like an initiation or something? Do you think they want us to eat him?" Jeffree asked as he hunched next to me, not at all kidding. I was in the process of dismissing his interpretation when, to my surprise, the corpse opened his eyes and looked directly at the two of us, startling us even more than we already were. Equally surprised, the guy scrambled backward across the ice to get his distance. Eyes wide, trying to lose himself in a crowd of creatures that scrambled away from him as soon as he arrived there, the white dude kept pointing and muttering, "You're not there, you're not there, you're not there."

"Yes, we are," I told him. The comment seemed to have the desired effect. The man ceased his panic and turned to look at us directly.

"Did you actually say something?" he asked, crouched and cowering. He spoke with an odd accent, a hint of the American South but a bit of the Brit too.

"I did say something," I told him, and then the obvious questions were lobbed over my head by my yelling co-workers: *What is this place? What are these people? Who are you?* It was only the last question he seemed willing to discuss, the rest he just looked away at and shook his head at nervously. But his identity, that he seemed clear on. Adjusting the material on his collar, standing straight and short, and looking directly up at me, the man said:

"Well of course my name is Arthur Pym, of the Nantucket Pyms, sir."

I wasn't stunned. I wasn't shocked. I wasn't even impressed, because he was clearly a lunatic and I didn't believe him. Because unless we'd stepped into a time warp, that would make him over two hundred years old. He looked bad, but still.

I nodded my head, smiled, and said my name back to him. Politely, the madman nodded as if to pretend my own name held some weight with him. Then this Pym looked quickly at Jaynes, then at Jeffree, then at Nathaniel, lingered over Angela, and then turned back to me.

"So tell me then, Mr. Jaynes," he began, his voice hoarse from disuse and possibly misuse, "have you brought these slaves for trading?"

CHAPTER XI

A point of plot and order: I am a mulatto. I am a mulatto in a long line of mulattoes, so visibly lacking in African heritage that I often appear to some uneducated eyes as a random, garden-variety white guy. But I'm not. My father was white, yes. But it doesn't work that way. My mother was a woman, but that doesn't make me a woman either. Mandatory ethnic signifiers in summary: my hair is fairly straight, the curl loose and lazy; my skin lacks melanin—there are some Italians out there darker than me.* My lips are full and my nose is broad, but it's really just the complexion and hair that count. *Octoroon* would have been the antebellum word for me. Let me be more clear, since some people can't get their heads around it even when I stand before them: I am a black man who looks white.

I grew up in a working-class neighborhood in the "Black Is Beautiful" era and suffered in school from my poor timing. Fifty years before, being the only European-looking brother on a black campus might have made me class president in the Adam Clayton Powell mold, but during my era it made me the symbol of Whiteness and all the negative connotations it held. This is probably assigning too much political acumen to my fellow middle-schoolers. A less ambitious assessment might be just that I stood out, and the wolves attack the weak separated from the herd. Because of the

---

* To the horror of both of us, I'm sure.

color of my skin, I was targeted for abuse as much as the kid who wore his Boy Scout uniform every day.

In sixth grade a little effete frog named James Baldwin whupped my ass. He was a foot shorter than me, but he hung with hulking eighth-grade girls, who towered over both of us the entire time, taunting. It was by the bushes in the asphalt driveway of my apartment building and it was because I'd gotten lazy. I had a whole plan for getting home unmolested, it involved shortcuts along the train tracks and alternating building entrances, but it'd been two weeks since the last attack and I let my guard down. I bought a Reggie bar at the drugstore before heading toward my building: they must have monitored the corner, followed me. I didn't fight back, because if I did the ladies would have really hurt me, and the only thing more humiliating than getting my ass kicked by this little shit would have been getting my ass kicked by a gaggle of girls, even ones as prematurely huge as these postpubescent vultures. I had never even met James Baldwin, but it didn't matter, he attacked me anyway. I was different. He was puny, weak, but I was weaker. Kids have to feel like they're more powerful than someone.

The worst part of all this was when my mother forced me to report to the school where James Baldwin kicked my ass. Mrs. Alexander, the librarian, was not much darker than me but was armed with a mouth full of ghetto to make up for it. She couldn't get enough of my story. She asked me to repeat it again and again, "James Baldwin beat me up." "Who you say?" "James Baldwin," and the librarian, as round and yellow as the sun, shuddered with laughter. I asked her what was so funny and Mrs. Alexander told me, "Young bru, you gots to gets your little yellow butt down to my library. You gots to learn who you is." Mrs. Alexander was no great fan of books; everyone knew she had been placed in her position after suspension for beating her second-grade students with a ruler. She had a bachelor's degree in education but talked like her college was located in the back of a deli. Still, even for her the broken grammar she used to tell me this message was exaggerated, and I heard another meaning within it. That I, like her, would have to overcompensate for my pale skin to be accepted. I would have to learn to talk blacker, walk blacker, than even my peers. Or be rejected as other forever.

Going to the library was excellent advice, it turned out. The library was open for another hour after school, the byproduct of an academic initiative long since forgotten. Hiding in the library immediately after dismissal allowed the tsunami of juvenile violence that occurred at the end of each day to ripple on beyond me, clearing the area for a safer retreat to my apartment once it was gone. So I went every afternoon from that day forward. The only one not pleased with my new routine was Mrs. Alexander herself, who'd grown accustomed to leaving in time to watch her stories. But after a week or so of missing *General Hospital* for my sake, Mrs. Alexander showed me how to turn out the lights and lock the door behind me, and then we were both happy.

Alone there, wasting the hour, I couldn't bring myself to read the real James Baldwin. I wouldn't read the man until college, another thing I blame on my abuser. But the cover of another book on the African American literature shelf spoke to me. A picture of a weak-looking boy, one who was still proud, one who wanted the world to see him as the person he knew he could be. He was wearing an ascot—I didn't know the word for this accessory at the time, but I knew that if he wore that at my school he would also get his ass whupped. The book itself revealed that I was right. The entire story was a chronicle of who had robbed him, who had beaten him, who had ripped him off. Sure, there was slavery as well, but Olaudah Equiano's narrative was about more than that for me. It was the diary of the first black nerd. And the language, it sung and pleaded and was as graceful as I wished I would become. Reading it I knew that if I was to acquire the language of blackness, if my own survival and sanity depended on it, then this was the voice that spoke to me. What blacker form could there be than African America's first literary son? It is a great moment in every freak's life when he or she finds out that at least they are not the only one. Diving in to the pantheon of slave narratives, through Mary Prince and Harriet Jacobs and Solomon Northup and the others, I found my people. I was by myself in this era, but across time I was joined by a great and powerful tribe. But even that solitude didn't last. I would not be alone for long.

When I heard the sounds from the back of the library, I knew they had come for me. Mrs. Alexander had driven away at 3:15 P.M. after the principal's car was gone, like always. It was them. The violent horde had noticed my absence and would now be correcting the order of things. I heard the sound and knew that I had always expected this moment to come, that the ignorant's natural fear of books could only keep them at bay for so long. Emboldened by my literary peers, though, I stepped forward into the darkness of the art history stacks. If a beating was inevitable, I would at least retain my pride by facing it directly. There were books strewn across the floor, oversize, colorful painting books and for a moment I thought they'd just fallen down. That this is what I'd heard. Then I saw him. Standing there, naked, at the end of the aisle. Naked except for a red scarf around his neck and a copy of Norman Rockwell's *World of Scouting* held to hide his genitals.

"Why doth thee have no garments?" I asked the boy.

"They took my badges. They took all my badges, and my clothes. And they took my French horn too," he told me. Saying who "they" were wasn't necessary. They were the beasts at the door. They were the unthinking. They were the elementals of destruction we both knew intimately. We looked at each other, relaxed. He knew who I was, and I knew who he was too. He was the

Boy Scout guy. He was Garth Frierson. Garth sat down Indian style on the floor, continued slowly turning through the pages in his book as if he was looking for someplace to escape to. I sat down, joining him, and did the same with my own book. We locked the library up together from that afternoon until high school.

· · ·

Even in comparison to my own, sometimes ambiguous, identity, the claim of this found Caucasian to be Arthur Pym seemed like bullshit. The cracker was crazy, I assumed. While possibly an obscure little story in the whole of the English-speaking world, *The Narrative of Arthur Gordon Pym* held a vaunted position in the literature of the Antarctic, being as it was the first great text of this continent's imagination. And when dealing with a place of such desolate reality, the imagination can be as important as the place itself. So as noms de plume went, "Arthur Pym" made sense. Soon after his introduction was made, "Pym" suggested we move to more private quarters for further discussions. I turned to Booker Jaynes upon hearing this, and my cousin nodded, clearly eager to get away from the monsters, so our group made to follow Pym. Noticing that the rest of my party would be coming with me as well gave this Pym a pause.

"Are you sure you might not rather deposit the chattel elsewhere as we conduct our business?" he asked me. There was a fermented smell to his breath that I hadn't noticed until we came close to each other. I didn't see how wobbly he was on his feet either till he was walking next to me.

"You're not actually serious, are you?" was Nathaniel's response. He had a polite, indulgent smile on his face as he said this, whether because he was amused by this character's display of racism or in disbelief. I told Pym that we were all of the same crew, and when he heard this *c* word, the guy relented.

The hut we entered was a construction entirely of ice, as was the rest of this primitive subterranean village. It was a good thing to be in a small space for the moment, because the majesty of the larger hollow was just too damn much.* While the space was still considerably colder than what we would ever think of as comfortable, I noticed that it was significantly warmer. The skins of some unknown animal, probably some form of walrus or seal, had been placed along the bulk of the floor, paler side up, enabling us to take seats without literally freezing our asses. This Pym, for his part, seemed to come further into consciousness the longer he was awake, and the more awake he got the more excited he was about our presence. Mine in particular. The white man began to rant on about how long it had been, and how bored he'd been, how eager he was to finally hear stories of the North he had left behind. Here, I was forced to interrupt him.

"Mister? Mister, listen. Who are these people? Where are we?"

I spoke to him loudly enough that he paused from his verbal riff on "the calming effect of staring directly into the ice walls." A look of utter perplexity came over this would-be Pym's face when he realized the depth of my confusion. He solemnly took my arm and spoke in comparatively sober, measured words.

"My good man, do you not realize? These creatures around you, they are perfection incarnate. They are the end of being, for after them there is nowhere to go. You, sir, are in the presence of the *Gods*," he said calmly. Hearing this statement, I looked to my co-workers where they sat behind me, and they looked back at me. In that moment, silently, we agreed that we were indeed in the

---

* Imagine the farthest cloud, on the brightest day, in the bluest sky. Imagine that just past the very top of that cloud was a hard, constructed ceiling. Then imagine how small you would feel under it.

presence of an exceptionally delusional white man—which is of course one of the most dangerous things in the world.

"And what exactly is this place here? Tekeli-li?" I followed with.

"Well, is it not obvious? Where else would the Gods reside? Tekeli-li is *Heaven,* of course," he finished, his mustache hairs twitching at the ends much like the whiskers of a mouse.

• • •

"Well they're obviously not gods, so we can begin from there," Nathaniel offered after the uneven crunching rhythm that was this Pym's gait had sufficiently receded into the distance. "But what in God's name are they?"

"As spectacular as it sounds, I think it's pretty clear we're dealing with some sort of lost Neanderthals here. Or possibly another line of hominid, a spur of *Homo erectus,*" I offered. They were already looking at me funny, as if what I had to say could somehow be more fantastic than what was just beyond our frozen walls. I didn't care.

"Their size: there was a humanoid that walked the earth relatively recently that we call 'Colossus,' nearly the same size as these beings. It's said that the race died off because they couldn't radiate enough heat for their size, but down here that wouldn't be a problem." Booker Jaynes just kept staring at me, a suspicion of madness reflected back. "Hey, I said I've done the research," I tried, but their looks continued unchanged.

"They're just crackers," Captain Jaynes returned. He stared down at his boots' spikes as he continued, the weight of it all clearly on him. "Trust me, I know white folks, I can smell them a click away. These are just plain old, backward-ass white people. Big ugly ones, but still." He spoke with an air of unassailable finality.

"All due respect, are you for real?" Jeffree said. "I know white folks too, and these guys don't look nothing like any white folks I ever seen in my whole life. Did you see how pale they are? Everything about them—they got nails like ivory, you catch that shit? And you could hammer a nail with those foreheads."

"Just some ugly, big-headed honky albinos," continued Booker Jaynes, undaunted. "I don't know, maybe some Vikings got lost down here a long time ago, something like that, inbred for a few centuries. Who the hell knows? But these things are white folks, I'd bet White Folks on that. Maybe the whitest folks you ever met, but white folks just the same. They sure as hell ain't some sci-fi monkey creatures out of your imagination. They even got that smell too, that white folks smell they get in the rain."

"We just have to ask Mr. Arthur Gordon Pym," Nathaniel calmly interrupted. Nathaniel smiled when he was nervous, he smiled when he was calm, he smiled when he was attempting charm as well. Individually, all these uses of the expression were appropriate, but together their uniformity was disgusting. "Stop and think about this another way for a moment. Think about it from a business standpoint. Let's say for a second he actually is your Arthur Pym, alive after what? Two centuries on? That would be an even bigger discovery than a village of albino monkey people. It would mean *the fountain of youth*—the most sought after resource in human history. It would mean an infusion of wealth like nothing ever seen before."

"Nathaniel's got something." Jeffree's breath billowed before him in excitement. "Maybe being on the ice slows down the aging process—like people who survive drowning because of hypothermia."

"Right. See, I don't know, but you don't either. And either way, marketing wise . . ." Nathaniel drifted off on the last syllable as he waited for us all to fill in the rest of his thought. Apparently the others did, or at least Angela did, because she started nodding excitedly behind him.

"Honey, we could bottle that whole concept up and sell it with the quickness. Run tours down here, set up one of those ice hotels like in Finland," she absolutely bubbled.

"Think of the documentaries—you remember all that stuff on the Yanomamö tribe we watched on the Discovery Channel?" Jeffree said to Carlton Damon Carter, who nodded eagerly back to him. "This could be even bigger. A reality show, an ongoing serics—"

"Whatever they eat could be the next great diet," Angela interrupted. "Do you know how much those synergistic diet corporations pull in a year?"

"Just honkies. Just really cold, really big honkies, nothing more," the captain chimed in, not amused by the direction the room was taking.

"I love the way you think, baby. Right here could be a bar-nightclub. We could serve vodka shots in ice cups for twice the cost of the bottle. Honey. Honey. The *money*." Nathaniel, lost in his own vision, kept going.

• • •

When my darker cousin, being the true leader of our group, tried to engage Pym in a dialogue on his return to this small ice house, you could almost see the well-glazed eyes in the pale man's head take on an additional layer. Instead of responding, Pym would simply look over toward me nervously, as one might toward the owner of an unruly and possibly dangerous pit bull. It was clear by Pym's mannerisms that he would listen only to me—his fellow white man. That isn't to say he did this task particularly well. On his return, it took the good part of an hour to convey to this Pym that I

was not in fact a slave trader but rather a member of a crew populated by the descendants of slaves. He kept nodding, but then he
just nodded off. At one point I really felt he was listening to what I
had to say, but then out of nowhere, distracted, he started reaching
for Carlton Damon Carter's mouth.

"What are you doing?" I asked. Carlton Damon Carter simply
jumped back, muttered to himself, and got a new seat behind
Jaynes.

"Checking the gums. Is that not the best way to discover the
beast's health?" When he heard the word *beast,* Jeffree leaped up to
slap Pym upside his head, but to his credit he didn't struggle too
hard when Nathaniel held him back. Pym continued on as this was
happening, without embarrassment. His eyes, already fairly wide
to begin with, grew momentarily larger. "They are a feisty bunch"
was all he had to say. And despite my efforts, the idea that we
wanted Pym to accompany us off of this frozen continent so that
we could reintroduce him to the modern world was clearly incom-
prehensible to the man.

"Why would I want to leave Heaven?" he started repeating absently, which indicated he understood at least part of what I was
saying.

"Well, Arthur, don't you want to go home? You said you were
bored. Don't you want to see your family? Where are you from?"*
Nathaniel stepped in to ask all this, and when Pym ignored him, I
repeated the questions.

"I'm a Nantucketer," he replied.

"Well, are your family landowners?" At this the supposed Nantucketer shook his head with enthusiasm and then annoyance that
I would even question that fact.

* Americans love that last question, "Where are you from?" They see it as an excuse to
go on about their peculiar local identity and tell you everything about themselves as
people without really offering anything personal at all.

"Well, you've been gone awhile, things have gone up in value," Nathaniel followed, and this time Pym deigned to hear him directly. "Land in Nantucket sells for about two million, two hundred thousand *an acre* on today's market. You probably have quite an estate to attend to." Already growing a bit more alert, at the sound of the figure Pym's eyes seemed to gain a greater level of consciousness. The ghost of a man leaned in toward me.

"Is this true?" he muttered.

"Yes, it is," I told him, relieved that we finally seemed to be getting closer to an actual conversation.

"In a world where people would pay so much for sand," Pym started, clearly awed by the thought of this, "how much did these niggers cost you?"

I flinched and looked over at my cousin when the derogative was said, waiting for a reaction. Despite being confronted with someone who was, in his racial outlook at least, a throwback to the white American nineteenth century, Captain Booker Jaynes did not lose his composure or for that matter seem in any way surprised or offended by Arthur Pym's word choice. In my cousin's head, this was how all white people were. Of this Jaynes had no doubt: they were all racist, they looked at all of us as niggers and were blind to us in every human way.* Even after Obama; a black president in Booker Jaynes's mind was just the nigger white folks voted to be their servant.

Calling these strange beings back in to see us, Pym soon proved to serve better as a translator of information than as a conversationalist. The older creature of before again took a position of leadership, and Pym spoke directly to the snaggletoothed elder in what sounded like a series of attempts at dog barking. The chief

* My cousin felt that a white liberal was a Caucasian who said to himself or herself every day, "Don't hate niggers. Don't hate niggers." And that the rest of white America's racial perspective was "Don't let the niggers hear you say 'nigger' out loud."

moved as the old do, with the knowledge that things broken might never heal.

"Please tell him we would like you to accompany us far away from here, back to our native land" was what I said to our translator. This was a fairly direct sentence, meant to put our primary position on the table. While I couldn't understand the harsh sounds Pym was making, I could not believe that it could possibly take so long to relate this relatively simple proposal. The old creature, sitting on a rumpled pile of skins and leaning against his own upright knee as if it was the most stable thing in the world, listened and listened to Pym's monologue. I saw what seemed to be an increasing hemorrhaging of patience the more Pym's verbosity continued, which was confirmed when the old creature, in a surprisingly swift movement that left no room for misinterpretation, put his long, vein-traversed palm directly over Pym's mouth,* clamping it shut instantly. Once assured that Pym had received this in no way subtle message, the elder removed his hand and barked one fiercely declarative sentence directly at the man.

Hearing the dismissive nature of that sound, I felt for sure we were denied. Worse, I feared we'd caused offense as well. When I asked for the translation, Pym turned back in my direction and said, "Khun Knee says, 'Go.'" There was no question, from Pym's deflated manner, who this directive was intended for. Him.

"Make sure to tell them you want a pair of the creatures to come with us. A male and a female," Nathaniel approached my other ear to coax. Among the crew we had already decided that two would be a good number, since one might be misconstrued as a hoax or a genetic anomaly. Apparently, Nathaniel's current manner seemed too forceful, because Arthur Pym leaned in with his own whisper to me soon after.

* Still talking.

"Would you like the guards to discipline them? The Tekelians can be quite . . . *vigorous* when motivated," he said, rubbing an unseen knot in the corner of his balding head that I assume proved this point.

"No thanks," I said and turned my attention back to Khun Knee.

"Also, we would like to take two of your . . ." I stumbled here, because the word *people* didn't seem to be quite right, "community to accompany us in our employ."

"Do you intend to purchase slaves from amongst them? Is that what you are implying?" Pym looked at me aghast, casting a rare glance to the others and shuddering at the unthinkable vision: of his gods in the same position he imagined the Creole crew to be in.

"No, no. Never as slaves, not at all," I continued, carefully. "More like, ambassadors really, to be put in our legal care for the duration of the tour. We'll pay well." This rephrased job description seemed to be a bit more palatable to both Pym and eventually the elder Khun Knee, who nodded sagely as if he knew just what we wanted, and just who should do the job.

• • •

When the dozen or so potential ambassadors were paraded before us within the hour, we were at a disadvantage in choosing who among them to take as samples of this species, having just that day been introduced to their existence. That said, while we didn't know much about their alien physiology or beauty standards, it was pretty clear that the gathered specimens were not the most exquisite examples of this remarkable life-form.

"These guys are clearly morons, right? They look retarded," Jeffree said to me, adding a second note directly to Carlton Damon Carter's video lens, "I mean that in a literal sense, y'all. Jeffree got no prejudice against the handi-able."

"They all look like monsters," Angela whispered, as if they could understand any of this. "How can you tell the difference?"

"They're a bit irregular in comparison with the others we've seen, honey, I'll agree with Jeffree on that," Nathaniel said. "But irregular isn't necessarily a bad thing. It heightens the difference between them and us. It's dramatic."

"Inspect their teeth with your fingers, poke a finger into the backs of their mouths to see if they're missing any," Captain Jaynes declared, his tone implying that he was both well read and practiced in the art of ice monkey commerce. "Check their hair, make sure it's not falling out. If they're sweating, taste it to make sure they're not salty and sickly. That's how these things are done."

Using these traditional methods more and less (luckily none of the creatures were sweating in this ice block), we picked two: a male and, going on the assumption that swollen pectorals were a sign of gender, a female.

Pym, who had spent the proceedings nodding off as he leaned against a far wall, was roused once more when Khun Knee returned. Seeing our selection, the elder gave a polite nod in my direction like a waiter pretending to be pleased with his customer's order.

"In return, the Tekelians have decided on a price for the services of Krakeer and Hunka." Pym paused, and for a moment I imagined that they must want a blood offering. "They would like one dozen hogsheads, that is twelve individual hogsheads of the normal size, filled to the brim with your special sweetmeats, delivered on Krakeer's and Hunka's return."

"A 'hogshead'? Why would you want to shove sugared meat into the head of a pig?" Jeffree interrupted. "That is so not kosher. That is some sick shit, right there."

"He means a barrel filled with the pastries. And it's probably the equivalent of about three or four cases of those Little Debbie snack cakes," I told Nathaniel. "Garth has that."

"How much would that cost? They're only like a dollar a box." In my memory, a calculator appeared over Angela's head as she tried to figure it out. "About two fifty? Three hundred dollars? That's it? That's nothing," she answered herself.

"Each!" Arthur Pym adjusted hearing this, clearly pleased at his own negotiating skills. "If that is too much, I'm sure you could exchange your chattel for payment."

"They're not my 'chattel,' Pym: I'm black too," I snapped, my patience having evaporated after the third time I made this revelation to him only to have it ignored. "And you know what, I must inform you that you are really fucking with the wrong octoroon." At this final word, Pym recoiled in horror, staring at me and then at his own hands, seemingly terrified of what he may have touched unknowingly.

Nathaniel squinted at me in disgust, then stepped between me and the cringing white man. "Two dozen 'hogsheads,' final," he declared, recovering the negotiations. "Our word is our bond."

And then Khun Knee hugged me, and up close he smelled of dead fish left too long in the freezer, and his old body felt more solid than any biped had a right to. And I knew immediately that with his gesture the deal was done and there was no turning back from it.

• • •

"My stash? All they want to trade for is my Little Debbie stash? Why not your stash? Why not all your books and shit?" Garth asked as we were driving away.

"They don't need books on *Pym*, Garth. They have the real thing."

"I'm saying, I'm the only dude that wasn't down there, and then you come back and tell me how you traded all *my* stash, all my comfort foods—and man I need comfort—and nobody else's? You don't think that sounds a bit suspicious?" Garth demanded.

"Why do Negroes always have to have conspiracy theories?" I asked directly.

"Why are motherfuckers always conspiring?" Garth turned to face me, taking his eyes off the frozen road without slowing down a mile.

"They don't just want those goddamn boxes of junk food: that's just what they want first." Booker Jaynes interrupted our standoff. He was downcast, resigned. "Garth's food: that's just what they knew we had. They'll want more later, trust me. They're white folks. Eventually they'll try to take everything." Behind us, White Folks the dog seemed equally hungry, barking without pause as he stared out the back window at the Tekelian monsters, who followed our moving truck.

I turned to look at the sight too. Outside the truck's misty back window the white shrouded figures jogged, trailing us. Bouncing up and down like the wooden horses of a carousel, going nearly as fast on foot as we were in the vehicle. They had insisted on joining us as we returned to our base and had turned down our offers to accompany us in the bellies of our metal beasts. Even Khun Knee was among them, although I couldn't see the elder at the moment. All I could really see was their outlines through our truck's crystalline wake, the figures dancing on the horizon like the northern lights.

When we returned, Garth and I checked the hulking satellite dish placed on top of our cramped, one-story encampment. Although the dish had a heater, it still sometimes failed from the cold, so to avoid a loss of reception we covered the entire thing in electric tape and sprayed the receiver with nonstick cooking aerosol. At the moment, the dish did appear to be in complete working order, a fact I intentionally made note of so that I wouldn't be sent out in the cold to check the thing if the reception wasn't working. For a moment or even half of one, I believed I hallucinated the image of a white shrouded figure up on the roof, ducking behind the disk as we approached, but this sensation passed rather quickly.* A green light on the base of the satellite receiver indicated that a strong connection was engaged, and that was my primary concern at that moment.

When I came inside they were all there, in the common room. By all of them I mean not just our crew but the contingent of creatures too, with Pym in tow. Literally in tow: one of the group of large, militaristic-looking warrior beasts had carried Pym in like a shawl over its monstrous shoulders and was only just letting him down. And it was freezing. Whether the heat was even on in this portion of the building I don't remember, but I did see one of the guards holding open the front doors in a successful effort to make the climate more to their liking. Past my sober-looking cousin, our television projected a black, blank screen onto the unpainted white drywall. This, in my experience, simply didn't happen: when there was no signal from the satellite, the TV said, "No Signal," the words slowly bouncing around the screen in an almost taunting manner. If there was a problem with the connection on our end, a blue screen was usually the symptom. But the screen projected was simply black, sucking the light from the space it landed on.

"Why is it doing that? Is the cable loose? Is there a cable loose outside or something?" I asked.

"It's not the cables, inside or out. That's what comes in on every station. It ain't a problem on our end. It's something up there,"

---

* Let me assure all who inquire that I did spend time considering this image later. At the moment it didn't seem possible. None of it did.

Captain Jaynes said with a nod out to the beyond, and I couldn't determine if by "up there" he meant the satellite orbiting in the heavens or the rest of the world north of the pole. "Chris, I want you to do something for me, okay?" The others, my crewmates, were staring at me as though I had a grenade in my hand.

"You and Garth, go over to the computers, check your email."

"What are those boxes of light and text?" Pym said, pointing at the computers as if they were aberrations only he noticed. I don't know what he found more fantastic, that there were such fantastic inventions in the world or that black people had mastered them.

"The modem's working. Look, it's green, you can see the signal light from here," Garth informed our captain.

"We know, we already checked our accounts. Now just look up your email clients, see if any mail came for you since we went away."

There were several terminals around the room, each of which had been staked out by us individually. With the connection as unreliable as it was, it was good to have a computer up and attempting to retrieve your mail all day, so that even if a viable signal was present for only a ten-second interval, your letters from the outside world might get through. When I checked, there was one email message waiting for me, although even before I opened it, it appeared odd. First, I have fairly sophisticated junk mail protection, barring emails from all but the most recognized sources, known associates, et cetera. This email, however, was from no one. There was no name listed, only a blank space in the sender's name category. Even more ominous was the subject line: AR-MAGEDDON. That was it, ARMAGEDDON, in all caps, which seemed a bit dramatic and just the type of email you never open lest your computer spontaneously implode. The message itself was blank, whether because the toxic text had been filtered out or because the sender felt the subject heading said it all, I had no idea.

" 'Armageddon'? You get this thing, 'Armageddon' in your box too?" Garth looked over my shoulder for his answer before I could give it to him.

"Well I'll be. We all got it," Captain Jaynes confirmed. "In all of our email accounts. Personal mailboxes, business mailboxes, addresses that in no way should be linked. We all got this one email and nothing more, all day. 'Armageddon.' "

We were all silent for about five seconds, our pale guests unaware that anything was amiss, and then Jeffree began crying. Actually no, crying implies one subtle tear down a somber cheek. *Wailing* is more apt. Wailing and praying at the same time. The sobs made the individual words difficult to decipher, but when he cried out "It's the end of the world!" into Carlton Damon Carter's shoulder, it was impossible not to hear him.

It was only then, as my cousin turned from the embarrassment of the engineer, that he seemed to remember our guests were even there.

"It appears we have a problem," Booker Jaynes told Arthur Pym, who was before this moment marveling over an electric reading lamp in the corner by the couch, turning it off and on. Catching his attention, our captain continued. "We had planned on bringing our collection of snow monkeys and you back to civilization."

"Yes, I am here. As are Hunka and Krakeer," Pym said as the other two, apparently recognizing their names, revealed themselves, coming from behind the more average-heighted of their species. "We are here, and we are in your employ. We are ready to go."

"Well see, that's the thing," I intervened. "There doesn't seem to be anywhere to go to, at the moment. We're trying to reach the rest of the world, and it doesn't appear to be, you know, answering. We're not going anywhere, at least not at the moment."

There was a bit of commotion on their side at this revelation, and our crew watched the cloaked figures having an animated discussion with their disconcerting vocalizations. They were making such a violent fuss that once again the size of them was really impressed upon me: they were so damn big. It was after a lengthy discussion directly with the aged Khun Knee that Arthur Gordon Pym said to me, "The debt, it has begun with our employ. If you are not to take us, then Khun Knee says our price must be paid immediately."

"Well, we don't have the bounty now, do we? Would he take something else in its place? Some matches, perhaps? Blankets?" More snow beast discussion followed. I noticed that the more the old beast Khun Knee talked, the more the room smelled of herring.

"He says the debt must be repaid," Pym translated. "If you lack the bounty, you can work it off."

"Work? Well shit, how long will that take?" the captain shot back at him. His voice had risen an octave. There was something about a white man saying you had to work for him that I knew repulsed Booker Jaynes to his core.

"A few hundred cycles."

"What's a cycle?"

"The time from darkness to light," Pym responded, and although his voice still seemed a bit distant, numb, I detected a bit of nervousness on his part as he kept glancing at the beings around him as if to avoid ownership of those words.

"A hundred days? You're trying to tell us we owe you *a hundred days' labor* for a deal that didn't even go through?" The captain was getting exceedingly agitated at this point. The strain of the past hours, of this improbable discovery and the fate of all that we had left behind had finally overtaken him.

On orders from Khun Knee, the warriors under his control suddenly stood at attention. In response to the elder's barked command, the soldiers bore arms. Literally bore arms, rolling up their sleeves to reveal horrifically muscled and veined biceps and triceps that seemed as hard and heavy and white as marble.

"Not days." Angela stared at the approaching soldiers, her voice shaking slightly with each of their steps. "The nights here last all winter, right? And the days the entire summer too. He's not saying we owe a hundred days of work. He's saying we owe *a hundred years*." The uncertainty in her lovely voice had nothing to do with her lack of faith in her own interpretation of this contract. It came from a deeper anxiety, one that in that moment fluttered through every black heart in that room.

And thus our slavery began.

VOLUME

...III...

CHAPTER XII

I am bored with the topic of Atlantic slavery. I have come to be bored because so many boring people have talked about it. So many artists and writers and thinkers, mediocre and genius, have used it because it's a big, easy target. They appropriate it, adding no new insight or profound understanding, instead degrading it with their nothingness. They take the stink of the slave hold and make it a pungent cliché, take the blood-soaked chains of bondage and pervert them into Afrocentric bling. Parroting a vague "400 Year" slogan that underestimates for the sake of religious formality. What's even more infuriating is that, despite this stupidity, this repetitious sophistry, the topic of chattel slavery is still unavoidable for its American descendants. It is the great story, the big one, the connector that gives the reason for our nation's prosperity and for our very existence within it. But still, aren't there any other stories to tell? So many have come to the topic of slavery because they think the subject matter will give them gravitas, or prizes, or because they find comfort in its familiarity. To be fair, something so big (nearly 20 million slaves kidnapped), for so long (from A.D. 1441 until the end of the nineteenth century) is nearly impossible to dance gracefully with. But still. That is the source of my love for the slave narratives: they are by their nature *original,* even when they draw on the forms of earlier literary sources. They are never duplicitous, because they all have one motivation: to document the atrocity of chattel slavery and thereby assist in ending it. Their artistry is surprising, considerable, devoid of pretension and with passion in its place.

Turns out though that my thorough and exhaustive scholarship into the slave narratives of the African Diaspora in no way prepared me to actually become a fucking slave. In fact, it did quite the opposite. The amount of real manual labor these prehistoric snow honkies expected me to do was insane.* The day after it was revealed that we had no connection to the outside world, and worse still of course that the outside world might not exist anymore, the Tekelians came for us. We had spent the night discussing our situation as Jeffree and Carlton Damon Carter kept trying to contact the mainland, trying to get someone on the radio, thinking as much of our own situation as of that of the rest of humanity. Nothing. They found nothing—no email, no text, no call. No signal, no satellite. At first it seemed like it was just a delay. After a while, the dread grew. There was nothing out there. And then, after hours of desperation, came the banging on the outer door. Slow but hard. Steady. Unavoidable.

Gathering our warmest garments, we were forced to leave behind all but what we could carry, as the hulking Tekelians insisted that we follow them on foot. Even my most prized possession, Dirk Peters's antique skeleton, which I kept in an oily green canvas sack, had to be left behind in my room for now. Given minutes to reduce our belongings, unsure of how long our stay was to be, excess baggage and clothing were thrown across our break room floor.

"Don't let fear take hold of you. We go into the unknown but

* I realize *honkies* is a racial slur and the Tekelians might not even technically count as human, but this was the word that Booker Jaynes kept using and as such was stuck in my subconscious as well. In addition, the noises that the creatures made to communicate did have some literal honking sounds, which made the slur that much more difficult for me to shed.

not the unconquerable," Booker Jaynes addressed the now down-turned heads of his crew. I tried to take my cousin's advice, but I wasn't sure if I could carry the load with his flinty determination. Each of us had been withdrawn all night, whispering our private concerns and suspicions, I with my cousin, Angela with Nathaniel, the engineers in their coupling. Gone was Garth Frierson, who after the situation of our being forced into servitude by our credi-tors was revealed, quietly removed himself from the ensuing dis-cussion. I saw Garth whispering for a few moments with Pym, but thought little of it at the time, or truly of Garth in general for the rest of the stressful night. At half past three in the morning, giving up on the hope of intercepting a radio signal from the world to the north, I passed Garth's door on the way to my own. Stopping in the hall, I was struck at that moment not by what I heard from his room but by what I didn't: no snoring. Garth suffered from the worst sleep apnea I had ever heard, his bass snores started loud and then built toward industrial levels before waking him for a few sec-onds of lip-smacking incoherence before repeating the chorus. But there was no such solo; instead I heard movement, and the crin-kling of more wrappers than I was willing to imagine. Despite my suspicions, morning revealed that the sound was not the product of an epic preslavery pig-out, but was the sound of strategy. As the rest of us did the last of our zipping and the massive Tekelian war-riors crouched in our low-ceilinged break room as they waited to take us away, Garth appeared before us comparatively unclothed. Dressed in just his bathrobe and long johns, the big man held be-fore him a large box, a box I immediately recognized as one of the bulk containers of Little Debbies from his storage unit. Not look-ing at us, and particularly not looking at me, Garth lumbered over to the closest and the largest of the shrouded guards and handed the freight to him. The guard, for his part, took the gift without bark, concealing it within his robes as if it had never been there.

Garth Frierson sheepishly turned around and was quickly walking off toward the hall when I grabbed him by the fatback of his shoulder.

"What the hell was that?" I demanded.

"Um. A couple things. Some Cosmic brownies, some Swiss cake rolls, a few Devil Squares, and some Banana Twins. Actually, mostly it was Banana Twins: I ordered those by accident" was all Garth said back to me, trying unsuccessfully to build up enough momentum to break my grip. Accepting the futility of this action, he continued. "Look, dog. I'm sorry. I paid off my portion of our debt with a box of snack cakes, okay? What can I say? I'm so sorry."

Nathaniel Latham, having also witnessed the transaction, interrupted excitedly. "Sorry? Don't be sorry. If they're willing to barter for the remaining debt, you can pay it off for all of us! You must have two dozen boxes of that candy crap in there, I saw them the day you loaded them. That's enough to pay off everyone. Hell, that's probably enough to get ourselves a few servants."

"I'm sorry 'cause I ate the rest" was Garth's reply, and it made me sad to hear the big man's voice crack like that. Nathaniel tried to strangle him, and it took both Jeffree and me to pull the lawyer off of the big man.

• • •

Garth had bought his freedom, but I figured the rest of us would be in servitude together. I found out soon that this was not to be the case. When we reached Tekeli-li's cavern once more, the Creole crew was dispersed. Before much discussion on our part could begin, we were being divided, urged through pale hand motions and the Tekelian guttural barking to follow others among the small crowd of the creatures that awaited us at Tekeli-li's cavernous center. Angela protested when she realized that she and Husband II would not be taken together, but even those complaints were relatively muted considering the amount of anxiety present in those moments. They were less pulled apart than physically urged into opposite directions, massive, freezing hands put firmly on shoulders and arms until resisting would be a noticeable act of violence. For the most part, we didn't fight the monsters. We didn't complain or try to assert our own agenda because we didn't truly understand what was going on or have a clue as to the penalties for noncompliance.

At least I recognized the creature in whose care I was now placed: none other than Krakeer, one of the two Tekelians we had claimed ownership of only a day before, the specimens we had intended to present to our world. The entirety of my debt, Pym explained, was owned by him. Despite my lack of familiarity with the species, Krakeer was easy to spot in a crowd. He was exceptional. Most of the Tekelians had long, nearly luminescent teeth that were so narrow they looked as if the creatures might ritually pull them down from their gums as some sort of beautification exercise. But Augustus—as I chose to rename him in honor of Pym's fallen shipmate and my own morbid passive aggression—had teeth that seemed to go down at odd, unrelated angles, each bit of fang with its own dental agenda. The only two of his teeth that seemed to coordinate were a pair that turned in as if they were talking to each other. Augustus's hair, or at least his lack of it, was distinctive as well. He wore the same shroud as the rest of his group, but he lowered his hood for a stretch to itch his scalp as we walked back in silence through the long frozen corridors. The hair there appeared in barren patches, the skin it failed to cover was the gray of dog bellies. And those chewed fingernails, devoured to the point that even the flesh around the nails had been eaten. Augustus's wretched fingernails were utterly unique to him among his breed; all of the others I saw had long talons that they clearly took pride in. It was also clear that Augustus took little pride in anything. My only consolation in this whole affair was that, by the time we reached his dwelling, a half hour later, the creature was breathing so heavily from the effort of the journey that I knew, if the situation warranted it, Augustus was also probably the only Tekelian I could whup. Even the small, ghoulish children of this race that taunted both of us as we marched seemed more of a threat, wiry little things as feral and gray as squirrels. One, no higher than four feet in his little shroud, threw a snowball directly at Augustus's head and offered only wheezing giggles when my captor turned to feebly bark a complaint before slinking away.

Augustus's lair was what I expected for a large hominoid, similar in my mind to the descriptions of the much speculated upon North American Sasquatch (who I suspect might be a relative of this southern breed). The room was a dark cave with almost womblike overtones, the floor scattered with debris that had become embedded in the ice in sedimentary layers where the floor was bare and in clumps in the furs that provided partial cover. Despite the low temperature, the space had an overpowering musk and an unmistakable odor of flatulence, which I took to be the stank of Tekeli-li. Later, however, I came to understand that this hygiene issue was particular to Augustus, and that most of the other Tekelians lived under the ice hygienically.

Soon after we arrived, after catching his breath and informing me with hasty hand gestures of a task I was to do, Augustus went to the far side of the room, lay down in his robes, and went to sleep. I started to theorize that the Tekelian metabolism must necessitate extended multiple rest periods throughout the day to conserve body heat, but the nap thing also turned out to be another quirk unique to Augustus.*

---

* There are two types of lazy bosses. One is so lazy that they make you do not only your own work but theirs too. Worse, they lie to you about it, unloading all responsi-

The task which Augustus had signaled for me to do was simple, and with nothing else to distract me, I gave it my full focus. The Tekelian's pantomimed instructions were easily understandable. There was a frozen tub of loose fat, presumably taken from seals above. My job was simply to smash it with a pestle. The tool was the height of a small man and made from what I assume was whale bone. Although the actual manipulating of this fat cauldron was different, it reminded me instantly of the preparations of fufu I'd seen during my vacation travels through Ghana.* Similarly *krakt,* which is the closest I can come to capturing the Tekelian name for it, served as a staple diet. While fufu is a firm, doughy paste served along with stew, krakt was more like porridge in consistency, or a mushy rice pudding, composed entirely of squashed animal fat. Prepared properly (and this I never actually managed to do, not that Augustus seemed to mind), smashed utterly and chilled by the natural climate, the paste achieved a taste similar to that of unsweetened ice cream, or a mayonnaise without the vinegar. The fatty, unsweetened custard was packed with energy, fitting a normal human's daily protein requirement in only a few swallows. Krakt was a meal that satisfied your hunger, or at least extinguished it: every time I ate that paste I never wanted to eat again.

My first night in the compound, while Augustus snored, I explored my surroundings. The dwelling was in a tunnel like the ones we had been in when we first came down here, only a hole

---

bility for their actions. The other is so lazy that not only do they not do their own work but they can't even be bothered to provide you work to do. These bosses lie as well, but only to themselves, passively. The first is the hardest boss to work for, the second the easiest. In Augustus I sensed immediately which one I had.

* Fufu is a starchy paste made of boiled yams or cassava that comprises the staple of the Akan peoples. It is also used as glue for minor automobile repairs by tro-tro drivers in parts of Accra, Tema, and Kumasi.

had been burrowed into the side and beyond that a room carved. Along the way, we had passed several other residential holes, giving the hallway the appearance of the interior of a flute, and in these I saw others of these creatures going about their lives. Despite my novelty here, I was ignored by all but the children, who would stop what they were doing in order to taunt me. Surrounded by the little monsters, I was struck mostly by how utterly alone I was in this world. No sooner had this thought appeared in my mind than I saw a flash of brown, similarly engulfed by a gaggle of toddlers.* It was her. Angela. Despite the distance we'd traveled, fate had placed us on adjacent properties, and when she saw me approach her, the look on her face said that she seemed to rejoice at this.

"Have you seen Nathaniel? Is he with you?" was the first thing Angela said when she saw me. The last time I saw her second husband, he was being pushed into the exact opposite direction. Whether Nathaniel reached his destination shortly after or had kept moving far off into the reaches of the outer tunnels I had no idea, and I didn't care. It seemed to me that we were on the extreme outskirts of this village. If we weren't in the rural area, then certainly we had landed in the Tekelian suburbs. Or maybe, off in this well-worn frozen backwater, inconveniently remote from the main area, we had landed in its ghetto.

"Chris, this is crazy. These things expect me to clean up after them. They're disgusting. I tried kicking loose what I could, putting it into a pile, and this bitch in there—I mean I think it's a female, it looks like it has tits—just keeps pointing at the frozen-in bits going 'Ung!' Pointing at stuff stuck to the ice for god knows

---

* Unlike the young of most mammals, the Tekelian children managed to be diminutive and large eyed and yet still utterly unendearing by my human standards. Their little white piranha teeth helped.

how many years, how many inches down. I'd need an ice pick to get it out."

"Wait." I calmed my excitement over the fact I could do some-thing to the benefit of her. Retreating to Augustus's quarters, I reached through my backpack for one of the only possessions I had deemed worthy of taking with me. Pressed in my reading edition of *The Narrative of Arthur Gordon Pym,* stuck right by the page where Richard Parker was being served up for dinner, was a nine-teenth-century bronze letter opener that had served as my favorite page holder since I had bought it off Benjamin. Without a statement about its history, either sentimental or antiquarian, I made a gift of it to the lady. The gift Angela Latham gave in return, a re-lieved smile, was greater.

"You're always there for me, Chris. I always knew that, always loved that about you." Angela poked the Tekelian air with her lit-tle saber as she winked at me. "Look at this thing. I bet Nathaniel could stab a couple of these bastards with this in his hand."

• • •

I didn't expect to stay the whole night in this Augustus's hole, hud-dled for warmth inches away from the site of my labor. I expected Garth to appear in a matter of hours, declare that our communications with the world had resumed, and that we were all shortly going to be getting out of here. I didn't know how Garth would get this information to me, but I was certain our situation was just temporary. Unfortunately, it didn't go down like that. The first night was one of suffering. The diet of krakt, as rich as it was, proved quite a shock to my system, the result of which was that I discovered the Tekelian form of plumbing: a visual nightmare that consisted of a hole in the ice (one can only guess how it was exca-vated) and a Lovecraftian horror within it. It was the following morning, after retreating from this communal commode, which in a bit of olfactory fortune was far down the hall from where Augustus had us staying, that I saw Angela being led by her family of Tekelians.

"Come with me," she urged, grabbing my hand. Her own temporarily gloveless palm was a skinny thing, I could feel her bones through skin as light as oiled papyrus, yet nearly as cold now as the ice that surrounded us. She was too good for this—I would have felt more guilt in inviting her down here if I wasn't so relieved to have her near me. With Augustus napping for the second time this morning (Was it morning? I don't know. There certainly had been a slight ebbing and receding of the glow), I chose to join Mrs. Latham as she walked down the tunnel toward town with her captors. Her hosts apparently accepted the addition of my presence to their party, because after a few hundred yards the monsters were poking and prodding me in their desired direction, just as they were doing to Angela.

At the market, strutting amid the stares of so many of these robed creatures, we quickly noticed the presence of both Jeffree and Carlton Damon Carter in the distance. They had been fortunate, it appeared: they were the only two who had been selected for labor together, their bond so visible that perhaps even these alien creatures could recognize it instantly. Despite this, the men's demeanor did not indicate that their hosts had given them much consideration at all.

"We got to get the fuck out of here" is what Jeffree said to me when we approached him. Jeffree was one of the darkest-skinned among the Creole crew, but his melanin count did nothing to hide the bruise that had welted along the side of his face, punishment for what offense I couldn't imagine.

"I'll admit it, I thought we could just hang here for a few days, wait for the next shift of workers to sail in from Argentina, get some footage for the site, some anecdotes for the talk-show circuit.

But this is bullshit, man. We got to break out. If they think, they think Brother Jeffree is going to put up with this treatment for another night, then they got another thing coming."

"Have you seen Nathaniel? Or Captain Jaynes? Has anyone heard anything from the mainland?" Angela tried to press him, but whatever affront Jeffree was reacting to was still spinning behind his glazed brown eyes.

"Man, we ain't seen nobody, I ain't heard nothing, and we ain't about to hear nothing down here either. They even took my man's camera. Tell them what they did to your camera, Carlton."

"They *took* my camera," Carlton Damon Carter explained.

"Can you believe that? What's the point of being here if we don't get it on tape? Forget news of the outside world, we got to make our own news, sister. And the news is freedom. Fuck this!" Jeffree declared, nearly yelling.

"Word!" Carlton Damon Carter echoed behind him, and it was this one loud declaration from the quiet man that made all three of us turn to note the anomaly.

"It doesn't have to be that bad," I tried to calm them. "Garth's still at camp, at the radios: when he hears something, when the satellite malfunction or whatever is resolved, I'm sure he'll come get us. Think about the story here, think about the experience you're having, this priceless material falling into your lap, Jeffree. When the world comes back, and it's got to, think of how many hits you're going to get on the blog. You'll have to increase your bandwidth. Think of the *movie rights*." This last bit was for Angela, and it seemed to work, because she paused from darting her head around in search of a sign of Nathaniel to look at me. "Right, you're right." She nodded the affirmative before her attention drifted off again.

"Yeah, okay. Okay, man. You right. I guess, I guess I can—" It was just in that first moment of Jeffree's pacification that his host, a creature whose draped figure I'd previously assumed to be a curtained wall, turned around. What fierce, dead-eyed monsters these were, I thought, staring at it. This one was the most horrific beast I'd seen among them, a full head taller than the rest of his colossal kin and that damn sausage nose, like it had been chewed by a bear before being judged inedible and abandoned. While the overgrown homunculus I called Augustus seemed soft and harmless, like a rotting marshmallow, looking at Jeffree's sausage-nosed specimen, I was reminded of the ferocity of these barbarians. Without warning and without letting Jeffree finish his sentence, the creature shot out a hand toward Jeffree's bald head, the impact causing the cowrie-shell necklace that Jeffree always sported to clack like a rim shot.

"Motherfucking kielbasa-nosed prick!" Jeffree responded, and immediately I knew where his welts were from. Jeffree pulled his hand back as if to use it for punching but, taking in the size of his target and the hopelessness of his task, dropped it again in frustration. For his part, Mr. Sausage Nose paid him no mind, merely walking farther along the village path as he had just urged Jeffree to. Carlton Damon Carter, giving his partner a tortured glance, smartly started following the beast, but this had no effect on Jeffree, who after wagging his head several times, turned to me instead.

"You stay here. You put up with this, I'm going. I'm going back to join that fat bus-riding bastard, and I'm going to get somebody up on that radio, and then we are all getting the hell out of here."

"Don't you think—" I started, but having made his decision, Jeffree began walking off. Back toward the tunnel we had first come through on discovering this place, in the opposite direction of his personal monster.

"RKARKKARKIV," Sausage Nose roared with such a violent collection of consonants that my own body froze up. First the sound hit, then the air that made the sound. Angela's petite hand flew to her equally diminutive nose to shield her from what came out of the screaming creature: the breath of a lifetime diet of lard processed through the body of an ape. Jeffree may have smelled the aroma too, but by now he'd walked pretty far away and made no motion to stop. Clearly infuriated, the beast repeated his roar, leaving poor Carlton Damon Carter to curl his arms over his ears and head in response. It was then I noticed that the other Tekelian breed, those that had been casually walking past us and stopping only to give us curious stares through their albino eyes, now had come to a complete and expectant halt as they waited to see how this situation was resolved. It was Jeffree himself who gave them an answer, although I doubt that the creatures had any under-standing of what the raised middle finger signified, or of Jeffree's verbal instruction to "sit on it and rotate." What the crowd did un-derstand, what it was impossible to misunderstand, was the mean-ing of Jeffree's creature's response. When Mr. Sausage Nose shot his hand out from his robe, I assumed it to be another violent hand gesture in response, but it was violence itself. The dagger, which is the only word I can think to describe it, was clearly made of bone that had been sharpened on one end. Thrown from fifty feet away in a blur barely visible, that point went directly into the socket that held Jeffree's left eye. When Jeffree collapsed on the ice, red pool-ing into the ground around him in an unexpected burst of color, the crowd decided it had seen enough and moved on.

Close up, the wound was even more grizzly, even more so for Jeffree, still being unmercifully alive. It was only the angle that saved him from death—the dagger exiting at his temple instead of depositing in his brain. Judging from the blow, he should have been dead, but we knew he was alive because of how loud he was screaming.

After a few minutes, Angela and I had to pull Carlton Damon

Carter off his lover, because Sausage Nose still demanded his attention. It took all of us to get Jeffree off the ground: he was stuck to it. In just minutes his own blood had frozen his soaking clothes to the floor.

"My eye," Jeffree kept saying as he staggered to standing. "We're sorry," we kept saying back to him. And then in a sudden movement Carlton Damon Carter grabbed the knife poking out of Jeffree's head as if the weapon might fly away, just as quickly yanking it free. I thought Jeffree would pass out from this, but he didn't. To his credit, he stayed conscious and was still screaming a good ten minutes later, stopping only when his captor returned. That's when Sausage Nose shoved some fabric in Jeffree's mouth, then threw him over his massive shoulder like Jeffree was a bag of brown rice. Carlton Damon Carter trailed them as the monster stomped off again.

• • •

I found my captain, my cousin, not an hour later, having pantomimed his beard to a horrific assortment of beasts until enough pointing fingers added up to his location. Booker Jaynes was crushing a collection of glacial ice by stomping in a basin of ice shards.* Just past him, noting his progress, was a Tekelian form at rest, reclined on a slope carved into the wall behind. Leaning as it was, with its robes hanging back across its body, I realized that this beast was the one they called Hunka, the first creature I'd noticed to be clearly female: the collapsed gown held the shape of what appeared to be engorged breasts.† After seeing me, Captain Jaynes

---

* This process I would soon be acquainted with as a method of preparing drinking water.

† The way she was sitting, leg up and leaning on her arm, disgusted me. Later I realized it was a mockery of the Farah Fawcett poster many of my white friends had when I was a child.

paused in his march, but when he heard his host's guttural exclamation from behind, Jaynes resumed his motion, crushing the ice
cubes beneath him with his boots as if he was stomping on grapes
south of Napoli.

"That is the way of it. That is the way of our bondage. He's
lucky he just lost an eye" was his reaction to the news of Jeffree's
maiming, and this came after a long pause that seemed to offer
even less than that paltry response.

"Booker, what if the ships never come back for us? What will we
do if it takes a week for telecommunications to be restored? What
if it takes a month? What if we can't reach the world for years?"

"Then we will do what our people have always done: we will
wait for our chance. And we will endure," Booker Jaynes shot
back, the words filled with disdain and disbelief that I would need
this answer found. Returning to his crushing, he seemed more at
peace in it than I had seen him in any of his Creole desk duties.
Crunch, crunch, crunch. Stomp, stomp, stomp. That was his only
answer. There was another overtone to his statement as well, one
that I digested in the long, cold walk back to my own tunnel, my
own servitude. There was relief in his voice. As if the man's worst
fears in life had been realized and justified all in the same moment.

CHAPTER XIII

NATHANIEL Latham was a Morehouse Man, and to me this said everything about him. This is a distinctive breed, one possible to identify without the sight of a college ring or knowledge of its academic history. There is the entrepreneurial optimism, visible in his buoyant steps, there is the near-religious belief in the self and a refusal to acknowledge that any obstacle could thwart him. The Morehouse Man is a uniquely American creation and shares the young nation's traditional certainty that the days ahead will be greater than the days behind. His clothes are crisp, conservative but energetic, ever waiting for that magazine cover that will one day reflect on his success. The Morehouse Man, at his finest, is America at its finest. Once, while sitting at a dusty café in Accra, I looked past my dog-eared copy of *The Garies and Their Friends* to see the red polo shirt, perfectly trimmed dreads, and platinum watch of a Morehouse Man sitting at the table next to me. What struck me about the scene was not seeing such a familiar sight thousands of miles away at a little burger stand in West Africa. No, what I found most impressive was that even so far out of context I could recognize the Morehouse Man, which a conversation with this brother soon confirmed.

Unfortunately, while Morehouse had trained Nathaniel Latham for many things, none of those things had to do with physical survival in Antarctica. His college had forged Nathaniel's will, filled him with enough optimism to convince him that his will was suffi-

cient to overcome even the most absurd situations, but as for practical polar matters, such as choosing proper metal studs for ice
spelunking, it was woefully inadequate. I say this because after
only a week of walking back and forth between his captors' lodg-
ing and his wife's, Nathaniel's top-of-the-line, custom-order boots'
lack of proper studding had resulted in a sprained ankle. Sure,
Nathaniel's soft feet were kept warm, but on the iced-over floors
on the path that separated our two neighborhoods he would have
been better off with spiked golf shoes. I heard Nathaniel moving
outside my door five nights after Jeffree lost his eye, calling my
name, calling out a bunch of cusses as well, although those
weren't directed at me.

"Yo, Chris. You watch out for Angela, okay? That's your job,"
Nathaniel told me, not even bothering to look at me directly. I felt
a shameful rush at this request, like he was acknowledging that
had always been my job, no matter what role he served for her at
the moment. As Nathaniel talked to me, he limped forward a bit,
and his injury became apparent. "This ankle is killing me; it's
puffed up like a . . . Forget it. But I'm not going to be able to walk
back here for a couple of days. Maybe a week. I should really take
the week because I need to recuperate. I'm going to start getting
migraines, at this rate."

"Did you tighten your shoestrings at the tops? That will brace
the ankle," I generously offered.

"Yeah, I tightened the goddamn shoestrings, Chris. Jesus Christ.
What do you think is keeping me upright? I'm barely going to
make it back to those bastards where I am tonight, and you would
not believe what they're capable of. So your job is to watch out for
Angela. I don't like what's mine fucked with, and I don't want
them fucking with her."

She wasn't his, but I did watch out for Angela Latham. Minutes
after the usurper limped off, I found my way down the hall, using

for illumination one of the fatty candles that were ubiquitous down there, made from a substance that seemed to be stale krakt or, if not, something almost identical in composition.* The neighboring residence, the one of Angela's enslavers, was only a hundred yards away, and yet I had never visited, waiting instead in my off moments in the halls for Angela to pass through so that I might stalk her without seeming to. Now that I was actually taking time to investigate her residence for the first time, I immediately felt a moment of disorientation. Expecting to find another small hovel, I instead discovered something much grander. What I had taken before to be the front entrance to a simple hollowed-out cave like Augustus's (not a home but home to a few smelly sealskin rugs) was merely the back end, the alley exit, of a palatial fortress. Instead of rough markings made into the ice, these walls were perfectly smooth, except where moldings and primitive candelabra had been expertly carved into the surface. And there was furniture as well, not just heaps of animal carcasses but elegant pieces carved out of the very ice into chairs and tables and even baskets for storage. I saw this and was amazed, and also shamed: if you have to suffer the indignity of being a possession, it's an even worse insult to be the possession of a pauper. Angela certainly seemed to have landed a prince, or some other branch of royalty, although to look at him you couldn't tell. Or at least I took the beast I now saw to be her principal captor, but that was just because I found the thing standing behind her, staring intently at the woman as she worked. Angela was in what appeared to be the dining hall, a cavernous room immaculate aside for the smell that hung in it. There was a soft-shell crab place in South Philadelphia on Passyunk I used to go to, open for decades nearly twenty-four hours a day: this cave smelled like that joint's sidewalk. But the

* Blubber.

place was spotless, clearly owing to the labors of the brown woman making it so. Still, there was a haughtiness to the creature sitting behind her on a raised surface, as if he himself was responsible for the efficiency of her work. He was no more responsible for his clean home than I was for Augustus's messy one (I wasn't touching that place, it was disgusting), yet there the creature was, as arrogant as a Shar-Pei.

At the moment, Angela was down on her knees, digging at the debris in the pale floor with a bone tool, pouring wet slush over the crater to smooth the surface in her wake. Despite the thick Gore-Tex and fleece which padded the majority of her body and limited her movement, Angela had the task down to industrial-level efficiency. She was so consumed by her efforts that she didn't notice me for a long moment and, when she did see my boot, barely looked up.

"Is he still there?" Angela asked finally, not pausing from her digging. The debris she threw onto a skin which lay beside her, one that kept freezing to the floor, so that as she progressed she kept giving it firm tugs. I looked over at the creature directly and, thinking of Jeffree's now missing eye, smiled the best I could at him, bowed my shoulders a bit, and tried to look stupid and harmless.

"Still there. Is he giving you trouble? Do you want me to do something about it?" It felt manly at first to offer the help, but the moment after I said it, fear quickly performed its castration. What we both knew: there wasn't a damn thing I was going to do. This monster was huge, and even if he was made of more krakt than muscle, like Augustus was, the whole of their society was too much for me. This was their frozen territory, I could barely keep the turns correct in my mind to make it through the tunnels to town. As to how to make it back to the Creole base, I knew the direction was up but not how to get there without getting lost and freezing to death first.

Angela flashed her eyes to mine just long enough to make contact, and even then the creature made a bellowing sound, removing his hand from within his shroud and making me wonder uncomfortably about where his paw had been resting moments before. "You have to get me out of here, Chris. I'm not going to make it. I'm not made for this life, you know that. I went to *Spelman*, Christopher. I am a soror of *Delta Sigma Theta*," Angela emphasized, her whispers otherwise barely audible over her snow-cone scraping.

"You're even more than that. I love you, and I don't want to see you like this," I told her. She didn't even flinch at the L-word. She just got a little tear in her eye, which she wiped on her glove, where it froze. It had been almost a decade since I had told her that I loved her, and last time she didn't cry at all. I did. "And I will get you out of here. I promise," I told her. And we both believed me.

Back in Augustus's hovel, I lay on the pungent skins by the hearth, staring into the blue gloom of it all. Augustus's sty was increasingly cluttered. I began to realize that when I had first entered the hole it had been at its cleanest; maybe he'd straightened up in anticipation of the trip that never happened. Now it was horrendous, with pieces of everything that had frozen to both our shoes cluttered around us. Augustus, true to form, was eating, and I could hear the krakt swooshing around his jowls. I actually considered cleaning the place up a bit. Most of the mess was not mine, of course, but for the moment I did live here. After witnessing Angela suffering, however, I couldn't motivate myself to do any work. Augustus for his part chomped away, staring back at me with curiosity.

The more the image of the other Tekelians became normalized for me, the odder Augustus appeared in my eyes. My captor's peculiarities extended beyond his wretched smile: his back was bent forward, stuck in a perpetual bow; his shoulders collapsed on either side of him so that his head was the only thing that kept his shroud from sliding down to the floor. I also noticed that while the rest of the Tekelians seemed to travel in groups, or at least congregate in groups in the city center, Augustus seemed to be perpetually alone. In my entire time with the creature, I never once saw him socializing with another of his species. Staring across at him, watching his pale, watery eyes looking at me, I actually felt a moment of pity. Perhaps in response to this empathy, Augustus did the most human of things: he rolled his marble eyes at me. Shaking his hands free from the krakt (and thereby making even more of a mess of himself) he reached into his cloak with a sigh. In my mind, the casual amusement of the situation immediately dissipated and thoughts of Jeffree's maiming emerged once more. As pathetic as he was, Augustus was still one of them, and so I had reason to be on guard. The next dagger could come for me. Immediately, I got on the floor picking things up, frantically attempting to bring order to the place, smiling all the way. That is, until Augustus put his cold and pudgy claw on my shoulder. It was a bracing grip, belying a strength that was not immediately apparent, and I almost expected a blow to follow. Instead, I heard crinkling.

"Aaaggaakkaarraagagh," he said. Looking at Augustus's greedy paw, I saw something startling: the empty wrapper of a Little Debbie snack. No, not just one but several, balled into his palm and now falling to the floor, each with the last traces of their caloric goodness sticking to the cellophane. Augustus had eaten every one, clearly, and just as clearly, his appetite was in no way satiated. In his primitive, albino snow monkey way, Augustus had just discovered what every food-stamp foodie had before: the more you ate of the things, the greater your desire to eat more. Poor Augustus was already addicted. And there was only one man left on the continent who could offer him more.

• • •

While the Tekelians were by far the most notable of our discover-
ies, there were less sensational revelations to be had in Tekeli-li,
ones no less substantial. Chief among these were the white bee-
tles that infested the frozen city and were in particular abundance
in the cramped hovel of the insulin-fueled ice monkey I called
Augustus. Going for a more scientific angle, I named this insect
Scarabaeidae colonialis, although admittedly this appellation soon
degenerated in my mind to *colons* for short. At first I mistook these
pale bugs for pieces of snow, as which evolution had camouflaged
them, but after I felt the evil little things climbing on me, I soon
discovered their true nature. It was an age of discovery, even when
you didn't want it to be, even when you just wanted to sleep for a
few hours and hope that the world hadn't been destroyed. But in
my waking hours, with nothing else to amuse me (upon reflection
I found that, as a modern man, I had spent most of my day amus-
ing myself), I had taken to watching the creatures go about their
day.

All these bugs seemed to do was eat, their meals being the scat-
terings of krakt and whatever pieces of dried leather they got near;
they even ate bits of rubber off the bases of my shoes. They didn't
seem to be too particular about what they ate, they just consumed
and consumed, and when they got food they almost instantly
seemed to breed so that they could eat it faster. A few would arrive
on a previously "undiscovered" property, and after immediately
claiming it for their own they would eat and multiply, and only
hours later they would be swarming in disgusting multitude and
their object devoured. It seemed like such a short-term survival
strategy, one based on the premise of abundance. When, however,
they were placed within a finite space (such as four blocks of ice
around them high enough so that the bastards couldn't get out),

they mindlessly continued with the same strategy of overconsumption and overbreeding. After a few hours of my experiment, the last of them had turned as cold and hard as the little snowballs they resembled. In the back of my mind, with my last sliver of optimism, I was hoping that I might write some sort of academic paper on the subject, something I would dedicate to the memory of Jeffree's left eyeball.

Before I managed to wipe out the most recent wave of the colon bugs in Augustus's hovel, the little bastards were able to enact a bit of revenge in the form of the holes that now perforated my nylon snowsuit. These holes caused a draft that, after a few miles of trekking through the tunnels with Augustus as my lead dog, threatened to freeze my sweat right onto my long johns. The only thing to do was to keep walking, which I did, and try to avoid slowing down enough that I lost the crucial body heat that was the key to my survival.

I had no fear that I would lose sight of Augustus as he walked on in front of me, because as he stomped forward he sucked the last remnants of Little Debbie goodness from his collection of wrappers, leaving a trail behind him when he discarded each bit of cellophane. Augustus, I now noticed, had a bit of a limp, whether from an accident or from abuse it was impossible to say, but based on how the others of his tribe derided him as we passed them in the halls, I guessed the latter. It wasn't just a limp but a sway, an oscillating motion I found almost soulful.* The trip was much longer than I remembered it, much more vertical, and I was petrified that after we finally got to the surface there would still be the miles of trudging in the open air before we arrived at the Creole's base camp. With time the ice around us became brighter, more solid as the

* For a good portion of our walk, I passed the time imagining that Augustus was moving to the rhythm of Stevie Wonder's "Superstition."

mild signs of perplexing melting that plagued Tekeli-li moved farther behind us and my eyes adjusted from the subterranean dim.
The wind that whistled through the frozen channel became
stronger, more direct, and soon there was literally the light at the
end of the tunnel. To my surprise, when I stood aboveground, I
discovered that the tunnel, all but the final opening of which
looked as if it had been carved centuries before, came out not a
hundred yards from our Creole Mining Company camp. Ours
were not the first footprints here either: the Tekelians had possessed a direct underground route to our front door all along.
Putting a hand on Augustus's hulking shoulder, I tried to ask him
about this, motioning to the cave opening and then to the Creole
barracks, where I could already see Garth had the lights on. Augustus looked back at me with his ghostly eyes to see what I was ges-
turing about, then held me in a stare for a moment before nodding
slowly and deliberately, as frustrated by our language barrier as I
was at that moment.

In the living room of my former Antarctic home, I hoped to find
the signs of a living society. I hoped to find the TV on, CNN blar-
ing, maybe Garth eating a serving of spaghetti in a salad bowl,
waiting excitedly for me so he could share the good news of the return of satellite communication with the rest of the planet and our
impending freedom, wealth, and world renown. What I found was
that while the TV was on, it showed nothing but static, a gray and
blue electric blizzard on the screen. The computers were on as
well, but each gave a "Failure to Connect" error message that
flashed on, then off again. With the feeling that my organs were
plummeting to my bowels in an attempt to escape my fate, I remained focused and kept walking past these screens to the lounge
area. There I saw an even more bizarre sight: the communal room
was covered with paintings. They sat across the couches and
chairs, they lined the walls like tiles so that only glimpses of the

surface behind were visible. Everywhere, in watercolors and oils and the reproductions of both, the worlds of Thomas Karvel competed against each other. The sun was setting. Oh, God, was the sun setting, but in parts of the room it was rising as well, and it was hidden by clouds, and it was at midday also. In some places, remarkably, it was actually dark, which was particularly impressive given the solar display that was going on around here. It was the entirety of Garth's art collection, and within it, in the middle of the floor, collapsed in the remaining stacks of his master's work, was my man Garth Frierson, snuggled next to White Folks, who barked a few times at Augustus after yawning a hello to me. Garth himself woke up but after an immediate head spinning didn't actually seem that excited to see me.

"I'm sorry, dog," he offered meekly as he rose. It had been only a week, but it was clear that the man had lost weight in that time. Maybe it was just water weight, but it was a whole fish tank's worth. "Can't eat, dog. Feeling all guilty and shit. You know you're thinking it: if I'd just had more Little Debbies, I could have bought your freedom too."

I assured him that I wasn't thinking about that, and once he saw that I had not returned to enact some sort of revenge fantasy, the big man's demeanor improved immediately. I was happy to see my boy, a human connection to the past and reality. I was also happy to hear that there was half a pound of powdered sugar in the cupboard over the stove, because this would take care of Augustus's "sugar fang." After I had guided his pale and now sweating paw into the bag, Augustus held up his powder-covered fingers to marvel at the warmth of this snowlike substance. The pupils of his gray eyes bulged in ecstasy when his tongue touched the smallest bit of pure cane sugar on his marble nail. I left my new roommate sitting down on the kitchen floor, his stained shroud balled on the linoleum, plunging his face into the bag like a dog.

Garth was as unhappy to hear about the fate of Jeffree's left eye as I was to hear that the rest of humanity was still missing. For the moment, there was nothing we seemed to be able to do about either one of those things, and in our conversational pause to digest that fact, the room's odd decoration seemed a safer topic.

"What's with all the paintings? You airing them out or something?"

"Just makes me feel at home."

I grew up with Garth, in the same neighborhood for ten years. This stuff didn't look like our home. There were no black people in any of Karvel's paintings, not one in all the ones that engulfed the room. Actually, that is not a fair assessment, there are no blacks in the paintings of Vermeer either, but I didn't get the same feeling from his work—and Vermeer was Dutch, the old, scary Dutch West Indian kind of Dutch too, not the modern, happy-go-liberal version. It wasn't just that there were no black people present, it was also that Karvel's world seemed a place where black people couldn't even exist, so thorough was its European romanticization. With its overwhelming quaintness, its thatched roofs and oversaturated flowerings, this was a world that had more to do with the fevered Caucasian dreams of Tolkien and Disney than with any European reality. During my African sojourn, I remember having seen my Afrocentric countrymen land at the airport in Accra and wander around a city that wasn't there. They were so firmly entrenched in their ideologies, so tightly wrapped in their kente cloth, helmeted from truth by leather kufis, that they failed to see the real Africa before them. They wanted only the Africa where everyone was either a king, a queen, or a descendant of both. Where a Wakandian fantasy civilization hid just beyond the palms.*

* Wakanda is the African utopia of the Black Panther comic books. Although initially I struggle with the fact that it is an Afrocentric romanticization funneled through the

Where black diasporans would be greeted at the airport as long-lost offspring, like the Hawaiians do with the leis. Determined, they walked on the continent seeing only what they wanted and blamed all they didn't like or understand on the white man. All the while ignoring that at the same moment the locals called them "white man" to their backs and faces. But on the other end of the spectrum, how much better than real Europe was this fantasy of Whiteness which Garth took for granted? The romance of castles and armor removed from the context of constant war, serfdom, and feudal lunacy. Conan barbarianism, Dungeons & Dragons alternates to plague-ridden reality. That delusion was everywhere, but it was a dreamworld that was no less absurd for its ubiquity.

"It's not art," I blurted out. It was a cruel thing to do, but at the moment I wasn't responding to Garth Frierson's taste in art, just fighting for intellectual space in this oversaturated room.

"Dog, you silly. Course it's art. It's the best art. Thomas Karvel, he's the bestselling painter in America, probably in the world. See this one right here, this one?" Garth grabbed a sunset over a sandy beach with seagulls flying by. "This is *Dawn at Surfside*. When Thomas Karvel was creating this, they did a limited release of like twelve hundred hand-painted, signed copies. I ordered mine three months in advance, and by the next day, it was sold out. By the time the FedEx man dropped it at my door, it was already worth damn near double what I paid for it. The majority of people love it. It's art."

"But what if now the majority of people are dead out there, Garth? Then what good would it be?" I asked, motioning to the paintings around us.

---

imagination of its white creators, the first issues produced by Stan Lee and Jack Kirby are the sole memorabilia that Captain Booker Jaynes and I share in our respective collections.

"Shit. If that was true, what good would anything be?" It was a question we both responded to with silence, just sitting there.

I was hoping that Augustus would want to spend the night at the Creole base camp, and that maybe I could even convince him this would be a much better living arrangement for both of us—given the state of his hovel, I had high hopes for this plan. Unfortunately, I wasn't back in my room for more than fifteen minutes before I heard an explosion of liquid violence coming from the kitchen area. There, sprawled out on the linoleum, was Augustus, heaving and clammy. A long stream of white vomit strung from his pale lips to the hard floor around him. I would have thought this reaction was due to his caloric overindulgence had we not experienced a fairly significant breakthrough at that moment.

"*Cold,*" Augustus said.

The creature had spoken! Making sure that Augustus hadn't simply caught something in his overused throat, I repeated the word I thought I had heard, and he, in progressively fainter tones, said it back to me. *Cold,* he kept saying. It made sense that he would have knowledge of the word's existence, having heard me use it repeatedly as I chattered my teeth. His comprehension of the word was obviously limited, though, because it was specifically not cold inside the Creole base. In fact, for the first time in days the frozen ache I'd felt all over my body had left me and I was even working up a light sweat, dressed as I was. Augustus was clearly not cold either because he was dripping with sweat as if he had a great fever and his pale pores were trying to flush it away.

"Goddamn. I think that boy is melting," Garth offered as he leaned over me. While not literally losing his solid form, Augustus did look like a Popsicle in a microwave. "Cold," he'd said, but "hot" was what he meant. Still, even this small breakthrough in comprehension was staggering. So was Augustus's weight: they say that muscle weighs more than fat, but I can't imagine any of the Tekelian warriors possibly weighing as much as the doughy creature Garth and I lifted up off the floor and out onto the tundra so that it could recover itself.

While Augustus moaned back into good health, I managed to shovel down a quick can of a premade pasta, filling my gut with just enough calories to see me back to Tekeli-li, the constant threat of falling and polar air staving off the 'itis. Garth's last words to me, *Just wait, when I know anything I'll come get you,* haunted my every step, but I distracted myself by teaching the words *hot, walk, ice, good,* and *bad* to the eager Augustus, who aped them back to me as we trudged along. While it was impossible to say whether he got the full concepts behind the sounds, listening to his effort was worth more effort, if for nothing more than the comedy of it all.

By the time we arrived back at Augustus's cave, I was hungrier than I had been in my life, but more tired than ever before also. Augustus predictably went straight back to his stash of krakt, but I didn't have the fortitude to stomach it at the moment. Neither, apparently, did he, because it was mere minutes before I heard the labored breathing of his sleeping, his sticky paw still in his glazed mouth. It was very late at night, I'd forgotten. But my body remembered.

"Sleep," I said to Augustus.

"I can't," Angela Latham said from behind me, her voice skipping lightly off the white walls and kissing on my spine.

She stood at the doorway, and she was lovely. Akan cheekbones that hinted at a smile even when her eyes had been crying, lips so full they seemed perpetually puckered for a kiss: she was as lovely as she had ever been, even in my dreams. And there was this pause, when she just looked at me, actually looked at my eyes for a moment for the first time in so long. And there was a second of veiled recognition when we both acknowledged that it was late, too late for her to be showing up at my door even if the impetus was insomnia.

"Nathaniel has been out to see me just once in three days. Three days, can you believe that shit?" she asked me. Of course I could believe that, the man could barely walk. How the hell was he supposed to get all the way over to this side of the city? Crawl?

"That's not right, Angela," I told her. "A man should be there for those who depend on him." When she sighed and nodded, relieved that someone could mirror her anxiety, my moral fiber was mushed into so much krakt. "That's what makes a man a man," I added, and with that, she was next to me.

I pulled her close, or rather I pulled her thickly insulated Gore-Tex Arc'teryx coat close. Angela laid her head on my heart, and through a good two inches of insulation and laminate I imagined she could hear my pulse accelerating.

"When this is over, I'm going to buy a mansion in Oak Bluffs, with a maid for every floor," Angela managed to say to me before drifting off finally. The absurdity, I thought, but knew that Garth and I were no better. Our goals, what had brought us down here, were out there on the ice like shining oases, luminescent to us individually. Now, frozen, trapped, I couldn't help thinking that maybe they didn't matter. That what really mattered is what our ambitions had led us to. That we were in this moment because of the futures we imagined for ourselves. That even without the snow beasts, we were enslaved. By our greed, our lusts, our dreams.

On my pile of tattered furs and leathers, we lay spooned. Intimate and clothed and with our boots on. No words were said, and for the first hour I could hear that Angela Latham was awake and swiftly breathing. And then, after that hour, her breathing slowed to nearly match that of the nearby Augustus. I, on the other hand, grew more awake and energized with every heave of her chest, pushing as it did into my own back. It was such a beautiful sound, this exhalation sweetly gusting, that I could almost convince myself that I really was the man she was pining for. I could push away the thought that ever since we'd come down to Antarctica, we'd all of us—I, Garth, and now Angela—fallen short somehow, revealed how enslaved we were to our own comforts, lusts, and delusions, even without the snow beasts.

Lying with her, I thought of Tsalal. I didn't think of finding anyone there, of excavating evidence of whoever had once inhabited it, or academic fame that might come from its discovery. I just thought of us, like this, alone on its beach. I thought of escape, but escape to an Eden. The two of us, spooned together, the heat of the sun above and the warm sand beneath us. Lying there, drunk on purple water.

CHAPTER XIV

THE issue of starvation in American slavery was a central one, for the slaves. For the slavers, not so much. But for the slaves starvation was *extremely* important. In modern America, most of us have never had to endure the constant hunger that was once commonplace among our people, but the legacy of centuries of starvation is still present in our culture. Before the stereotype of the black man running down the street with a TV under his arm existed, the same racist archetype was carrying a stolen chicken, or a watermelon. Similarly, the stereotypical embodiment of black masculine superiority, with his rippling muscles and flat abs, owes much to a slave history of endless toil fueled by little food, lifestyles no modern diet and exercise plan could compete with. All this is to say of the crew of the Creole that, after three weeks under the ice, at least we looked good. In the modern era, Americans starve with full bellies, starve on high-fructose corn syrup and hydrogenated oils, carbohydrates too complex for our bodies to bother deciphering. We starve and yet are fat as shit at the same time, morbidly obese and vitamin deficient, hands shaking if we take too much time in between pies. That was a much more desirable form of starvation than our current situation, if you had to pick, but an anemic existence nonetheless. Ironically, both forms of starvation can cause diarrhea, which shows you how limited the human body is in its range of defenses. There are those who say that it is important to "listen to your body," that "your body knows what it needs." If your body knew what it needed, it would listen to the brain, the only part of it worth a damn when it comes to thinking. Diarrhea is the worst possible reaction to not having enough food to digest. It's mutiny. It's everything inside you trying to get out while it still can.

I wasn't sure why I was afflicted with this symptom, whether it was from barely eating the krakt or from eating any of it. Either way, I wanted to eat more. I wanted more of the vile stuff because I wanted desperately to eat, and I no longer cared what the cost of that desire was. Yet ironically, there was food equally desperate to get out of me, forcing me to undress and bundle back up in a torturous cycle. But there was not enough food coming in, not enough to sustain me. When I finally managed to gather the energy to rise, Augustus sat across from me, staring at me like a retriever eager to be walked.

"Smell," he offered, pointing a cold, pale digit in my direction. "You. Smell," he followed with, conjoining the words awkwardly and, in my opinion, just showing off. Overwhelmed and undernourished, I lay back down again and drifted into unconsciousness to the sound of Augustus's wet, snorting giggles.*

When I next opened my eyes I saw that Augustus had drifted off, presumably in search of food, and I spent the day alone lying there, increasingly delirious, feeling the acid bubble inside my gut attack my stomach's walls. It was a few hours into this pain when I saw it scurry through the room, just out of the corner of my eye, just beyond visual recognition. *Scurry,* though, is wrong: that implies a sense of urgency this creature didn't convey. *Skip* would be the best way to describe the action of the thing, a casual hopping

---

* This sound was yet another trait I had seen exhibited only by Augustus and not by his race in general. The others either didn't laugh or did so in a way that seemed less like they were clearing their sinuses of a decade of congealed mucus.

motion that bounced buoyantly across the far end of the room. At first I took this to be one of the Tekelian pickaninnies, maybe lost or just being devilish by invading the local eccentric's eyesore flat. But as it continued to dart around, I began to realize that this creature in the room with me was something entirely different. First, there was the sharp percussion sound of its walking, crisp and metallic on the ice as if it was wearing tap shoes. And there was a whistling sound as well. I thought it was the wind, but it was more solid, stronger. It was a happy sound, although I confess in my state I wasn't paying attention to the tune of it. At that moment, I was too focused on the little head I saw poking out from some of the cluttered debris of animal refuse Augustus had accumulated. It was a human head. It was a child's head. A white girl, no older than four years by my estimate, whistling and skipping with curly chestnut hair billowing out of her blue summer bonnet. All that protected her from the freezing air was a blue and white, checkered sundress, but she seemed fine. There were no signs of hypothermia at all, in fact her cheeks were quite rosy (and not from frostbite). She just whistled along, pausing only to take a bite out of the Swiss roll snack treat in her lovely little hand, the pastry's delicate chocolate covering falling like ebony snow to the ground.

"Little Debbie," I called to her, but my delusion just giggled and kept skipping around. Skipping and chewing, swallowing then whistling. This was a girl whose feet didn't touch the ground. Literally, they didn't touch the ground, floating a good two inches above it yet still managing to make those lovely tapping sounds. Little Debbie's shoes may have missed the floor, but her crumbs didn't, and the more she skipped around, the more her crumbs fell where I could come eat them later. Skip, Little Debbie. Dance! If it would help, I would be her beige Bojangles. For that pastry good stuff, I would bug out my eyes and hop up and down the stairs with her in blackface just like Louis Armstrong had done for Shirley

Temple.* I didn't care about principles, and I didn't even care that this was surely all a hallucination. I wanted some of that sweet stuff too. Bite off her head and scoop the cream filling out of her neck with my hands.

· · ·

I made it down to the market area because I didn't want to die of starvation alone. It was not so much the "die" part, rather the "alone" aspect that most scared me. Before leaving, I managed a quick check for Angela, hoping to find both comfort and food, but she was gone. I saw a lot of Angela by this time, usually at night, and in my bed. Fully clothed and no kissing, but there she was. In fact, aside from those evenings when her captors didn't allow it, Angela was there with me every night she could be. I never attempted to push it further. It was enough that there she was in my heavily bundled arms, and there she would stay until the next waking. I hadn't yet transitioned past the role of placeholder, I understood this. But what a place to be.

While our growing interaction was unknown to Angela's second husband, it was keenly noticed by Angela's captors, who shooed me away from their kitchen vigorously on every occasion I made to go find her. Now that I was starved to the point of losing my mind, looking for whatever scraps she may have been able to give me, she was nowhere. Instead of the sustenance I needed, I received a blow when one of the more matronly examples of the beasts hurled a block of ice the size of a softball at my nose. I man-

---

* Shirley Temple was America's biggest star during the twentieth century's Depression, but she was a national obsession that from a distance of time now seems quite disturbing. Just a little girl, Temple was the ultimate symbol of purity: the sacred virgin, worshiped by all. There is an innocence to the virgin icon, but at its center it is still a sexual role. Little Debbie, I must say, was beyond such considerations, her purity unassailable. You don't talk about Little Debbie.

aged to avoid the brunt of the assault but took enough of it to leave my jaw swollen and my head throbbing with even more pain than my starvation had already inflicted. In this haze of nauseated famine, I made it into the village, guided by will alone. It was my guess that Augustus had relocated himself to the center of town, because often when he disappeared from our flat, he came home reeking of the grog I had seen him drink there. It was a good guess, because it was the only choice I had. It was possible that Augustus was coiled up in the smelly hovel of some other hermit, but the idea that he might have a friend besides me seemed improbable.

I was on my way toward that area of the village in which the bar had been carved when I came upon a crowd of fifty or so of the Tekelians standing around in a circle, muttering their harsh consonants as they stared into their grouping's epicenter. It is in man's nature to be drawn by the crowd, if only to see what everybody else is up to. Even when that crowd was composed entirely of albino snow monkeys, I wasn't any better (perhaps there was more krakt!). Weakly, I began to insert myself into the middle of the assembly, but thinking better of it, I decided to gain a more remote access point from which to watch the spectacle. Kicking a notch in the ice of a nearby building, I hoisted myself just high enough to see past all of those cloaked hoods that were getting in my way. What I saw at first I took to be an icon: appropriately, they were worshiping a block of ice.* It was about ten feet tall, roughly hewn, powdered white by snow on its sides, upright and phallic in

---

* I had wondered about these creatures' religious inclinations, whether they believed in a soul or felt they had one, and what I saw I took to be a sign of their primitive faith. Of course they worshiped an ice cube. Without natural predators—which were often the favorite subjects of worship of primitives—what would they bow down to? In the absence of bears or big cats to run from, the ice itself seemed a natural (though abstract) choice.

presentation. This was not the only phallic presentation in this spectacle. In response to some fierce barking call, the assembled crowd returned a roar of its own and from within their cloaks removed long, pointed bones, what appeared to me at first to be the tusks of a mammoth but were more likely the ribs of a small whale. To my great and growing horror, I saw that the ends of these were sharpened to fierce points like calcium swords, with grooves cut into their bases for handles.

"KARARUM!" one of the beasts yelled from his perch by their frozen idol, and above the tall crowd the bone sabers rattled, banging horribly off each other in deliberate percussion.

"They're going to war," I muttered in disbelief.

"No shit. You really are a genius." The sarcastic words came with a hand on my startled ankle, and when I looked down from my perch I saw that they belonged to Nathaniel. It was unnerving to see him in the state he was, in some ways more so than to see the monsters get more monstrous. The Morehouse Man was now unshaven, and a scraggly beard had gotten the best of him, clinging to the sides of his face like a mold. Strong cheekbones that had once protruded now seemed to just poke out, the cheeks below nothing more than sunken caverns. Stains of krakt were apparent on the front of his coat and gloves. The Morehouse Man is a well-groomed man. I didn't know who this Nathaniel was. This is not to say that at the moment I cut a stunning figure myself, but even in the real world I was known to let myself go for the sake of a good book with more than three hundred pages.

"You okay?" I asked, climbing back down. It was a rhetorical question, but the man Nathaniel had become was in no mood for rhetoric.

"Am I okay? Nigger, do I *look* okay? I can barely walk. It's going on three weeks and my ankle still looks like a cantaloupe. And once they saw I still couldn't walk, my snowmen kicked me out.

196 · MAT JOHNSON

Carried me down here and left me. Can you believe that shit?" he asked. I could. Behind us the creatures yelled the mindless syllables of nationalism followed by more waving of swords in the wind.

" 'The Melt.' That's what they're saying. That's what they say they're going to fight."

The Melt? How the hell do you know they're saying 'The Melt'?"

"The melt, or the heat, or something like that. It's the word they use to describe when things start dripping around here. And the next word is the one they use right before they hit you." With this, Nathaniel said the sound, doing a decent job of reproducing the barbaric Tekelian tongue. Although Augustus had never even attempted to strike me, I still recognized the word instantly.

"That's what the beast that keeps Jeffree said right before it poked his eye out for trying to escape." When I said this out loud, I realized how I had rationalized Jeffree's maiming: I had decided to believe that he had been disfigured because he was obnoxious. Because he was prone to clichés, garish behavior, and meaningless grand gestures. Not because he had tried to run for his freedom but because he could be a dick. But trying to break free had not been simply a grand gesture, or even a heroic one, although it was both of those things. It had also been a rational response. They were going to kill us one by one, I became certain. That had been their plan all along. That was what the rally was for: our genocide.

"They're not trying to kill us. Look at them, they look like an army." Nathaniel gestured with the ski pole he was using as a cane. "Do you really think they'd need an army to kill us off?"

"I think they're going to kill me next, Nathaniel. They're starving me," I explained. Suddenly, my hunger made complete sense: they were experimenting, trying out different ways to kill each of us. Just for sport. By the time they came for Garth they'd be ready to attempt burning him on the stove like a luau pig.

"Don't you get it?" Nathaniel was shaking me now. His pole fell to the floor, but with a firm grip on each of my shoulders he was at no risk of tumbling. "They're not trying to kill us, because we are commodities. I'm a businessman, Christopher. I know what I am seeing here. They don't hate us, or at least they didn't when this started. They just want us to do their work for them, to get a return on their investment. That's why they didn't just kill Jeffree; they didn't want the capital loss. They're not starving you, they're just keeping their expenditures low. My captors didn't hate me, they just declared me a loss and had me liquidated. It's not personal."

"It's personal to me: I'm starving. I take that very personally."

"And my ankle feels like an elephant's standing on it. But if you asked them, they'd probably tell you that my ankle's hurting them more than it's hurting me. And if they had a balance sheet, they could prove it. That's why I'm learning the language, get it? Life is all about improving your assets," Nathaniel told me, then added a series of growling syllables I took to be a Tekelian translation of the same sentiment.

Regardless of his plans for the future, it seemed that, in addition to suffering his sprain, Nathaniel was not doing much better on food than I was. I had little hope that I would be able to remedy the situation, but out of pity I asked him to travel with me on my quest to find something to eat. When I pulled Nathaniel's arm around my neck, through the frigid air I received a good whiff of him. His musk was pretty bad, but it couldn't have been much worse than mine, it having been weeks since either of us had had the supreme pleasure of a hot shower. As he limped and I dragged, we made our way through the midday village traffic, past pale stares, their hostility obvious regardless of their alien, simian nature.

Fortunately, the location I had in mind was not far along the

path. This was good because I don't believe that I could have carried Nathaniel much farther, and it was only the guilt of sleeping
with his wife (albeit only literally) that let me heave his burden as
far as I did. The spot was an ice cave like most in the main center,
carved into a wall away from the village's primary action. What set
this one ice cave apart was that a long window had been cut out of
the wall separating the room from the outside, and the open rec-
tangle was a bar for those Tekelians inclined to consume its liquids,
served in thick goblets of opaque ice whose blue tint turned dark
yellow when filled up. I didn't see Augustus with the crowd of pa-
trons. (Tekelians, I believe, were genetically predisposed to the
drink, and seemed to make its consumption a part of their daily rit-
uals.) Who I did see, however, surrounded as he was by his frozen
cups, was the only other human in this subterranean community.
The one whose ancestors came not from the Tekelian caves but
from the caves so far away in the Caucacus Mountains.

"Arthur Gordon Pym," I said to him. At the moment, the white
man was pulled into the far corner of the bar's wall, surrounded
by cast-off cups of past customers. Bent over, walking among
them, Pym was gathering up the mugs that lay discarded, picking
up a fresh one as a particularly tall Tekelian lobbed one in Pym's
basic direction. From his custodial actions, it appeared that I had
interrupted Pym at his job, that he was perhaps the pub's owner,
or at least one of its stewards. However, I then saw Pym find a cup
with a little drink still frozen solid to its inside. He immediately
dropped all the other cups again and began scraping out the prized
remainders of the one with his pink hand, shoving the garbage
into his mouth.

Nathaniel, seeing this process, let go of me, limping heavily
until he reached the pile Pym had dropped, and scooped his own
brown fingers in search of leftovers as well.

"This tastes like fermented whale piss" was his critique of the now frozen beverage, as he scooped a bit from an ice glass with his pinkie.

"Close" was Pym's response, and as soon as he had licked the last remnants of the stuff off his fingers, Pym dropped the glass in hand straight to the floor, turning to look for another one. I don't know if Nathaniel didn't hear Pym's confirmation of the drink's ingredients or if Nathaniel's own hunger was simply too great for him to object, but he kept eating from the discarded receptacle regardless. I too was tempted: if this was all there was left of the world, what else would there be for me to dine on?

"I say to you that good liquor is not light on the tongue," Pym continued, lips smacking. "And this is the drink of the Gods. It is the elixir of life, keeping me alive longer than I'm sure I have a right to live." Swallowing down another bite of his frozen spirit, the clearly inebriated man took a good look at me.

"This is how you survived two hundred years, huh?" Nathaniel perked up. It was clear that he didn't believe the Caucasian but just as clear that he knew he didn't need to believe him in order to sell this dreck by the barrel back on the mainland. The optimism intrinsic in this speculation, that there might still be a mainland to return to, put a little pep in Nathaniel's limp as he searched through the pile for other samples.

As Pym chewed, his mustache bounced up and down over his top lip like a caterpillar in a circus. He was taking me in now, really looking at me for the first time since he'd realized I was not a fellow white man. "You look awful. Or like offal. One or the other; I care not," he told me.

"Of course I look awful, these creatures have me living like a fucking slave. What the hell am I supposed to look like?" To this, Pym raised his eyebrows in disapproval before continuing with his binge. His manner seemed to imply that he found my reply not only boorish but pathetic.

"That is not what I have heard. Your master Krakeer was just over there—"

"Who, Augustus?" I asked in disbelief. The idea that Augustus, even with his considerable strength, could ever be the master of me was ridiculous.

"Do not interrupt me. As I was saying, I heard from the very source that in fact you were being put up for sale. I suspect in mere weeks your indolent character has revealed itself."

"He's not feeding me, Pym, he doesn't have any food. I'm starving. I'm not working around the house because I'm so starved I can barely move."

"Well, you managed to walk all the way into town, didn't you?" Pym replied smugly, very impressed with his own impish wit. "I suspect your master will have food enough shortly, for that is him addressing the great warrior Barro. In fact, I imagine your price is being paid as we speak. You know, when the Gods found you, they believed your people would make fine additions to their lives. Tis sad; you are shaming their generosity."

I followed Pym's pointing hand in the direction of the interior of the public house, and there, in the shadows, was Augustus, talking to another, taller figure I couldn't see from where I was standing.

"He wouldn't do that. He wouldn't sell me," I told Pym or myself. For the most part I thought all the Tekelians were the same, but I realized then that I had grown soft on my Augustus, as damaged as he clearly was. And in comparison, he was good to me. When he noticed my presence, Augustus pointed me out to the other man, and I could tell he was speaking of me in high regard from his expression and his hand motions. This began to make me nervous until, to my relief, Augustus's conversation came to a seemingly uneventful end, and soon my Tekelian roommate was joining me. In Augustus's hands were two great frozen cups of the pub's fermented liquid. One of those he held out to me. I drank that mess down too.

"Katow Knee Cracto Khee!" Augustus declared joyously.

"He says he sold you to Barro for two full glasses of khrud. Says it will be better for you—Barro has a fur-padded bed and can feed you," Pym instantly translated for me, not even giving me a chance to take my drink from my lips.

"You eat!" a grinning Augustus offered, tapping his frozen mug against my own, clearly proud of himself.

"Who the hell is Barro?" I got out after my first swallow. Khrud did taste like fermented whale piss, along with less pleasant fluids of the whale as well. Or Ballantine malt liquor. Either one. "Barro." Augustus shrugged sheepishly, acknowledging the minor drawback of his victory. Before more words could answer me, actions did, and behind Augustus his trading partner emerged from the bar. They all looked the same, but this one looked a lot like the one that had poked Jeffree's eye out. I was now in the possession of Mr. Sausage Nose, I shuddered to realize. When he passed me and smacked me upside my head without breaking his stride, I was sure my identification was correct.

"He said, 'Come to me tonight.'" Pym translated. "If I were you, octoroon, I would heed that beckon."

· · ·

The thought of having my own eyes poked out of my head in a Tekelian game of William Tell gave me enough energy to make a break for the surface. That and the odd Tekelian liquor I had swilled, which took the bite off my pain for the majority of my journey. Even slightly drunk, I knew better than to try to make it all the way back to the Creole base and risk being seen by Barro or his associates. Instead, I was attempting to get up to the trucks, which were still parked directly above us at the site of our original contact. And, as the alcohol quickly wore off, I decided not only that I would make it there but that if I could not get one of the vehicles to start, or find one of the extra sets of keys I knew to be hidden on them, I would instead die there. That I would simply lie down to sleep in a front-seat cab and not have to wake up again. This was actually a comfort in the final stretches of my journey, when I could no longer imagine ever gathering the energy to walk back again. Even for Angela.

After finding the crater we'd entered on our first descent, using the last of my energy and will to climb the rope that still hung down as we had left it, I located the vehicles. My eyes adjusting to the amount of unfiltered sunlight that shone from above, I saw something else: that the wheels of all three trucks had been slashed. Long, deliberate cuts that were identical on each wheel and machine, sinking all of them a good two feet closer to the ground than they ever should have been. And I saw that their gas tanks had been opened, that petrol had spilled and dispersed into the ground around them. Except on the last massive truck, which despite its equally flattened tires, had its engines running.

The windows were fogged, and I saw movement inside. I thought: Little Debbie, you have come to have a final feast with me, and imagined a cornucopia overflowing with every snack cake there ever was, every snack cake currently on the market and every snack cake yet to exist. Instead, after I opened the door, I found a black man, chomping on protein bars.

"I know where it is, dog!" Garth said to me, completely unsurprised by my arrival. "Thomas Karvel's base camp. I figured it out, found the mountain peak in the painting, found it in one of the photo books Jaynes has. It's right there!" he gushed, holding his snapshot of the painting up to the horizon and the mountains of ice that stood there. The resemblance between the two images was nonexistent to me.

"No, man. Look at the ridges, look at the outline. The top's basically the same, right? Just flipped. That's why it looked so familiar but I couldn't place it. This image was painted *from the other side.* That's where Karvel's base is, man. Over that ridge. Has to be. It takes him weeks to create a masterpiece; he would need somewhere to stay."

Looking at the outer shape of the formation, wanting to believe it so much because I had no other vision to invest in, I began to think that for a moment I'd seen what Garth was talking about. There were similarities. I ignored the fact that all the mountains basically looked the same to me.

"So, you down? You want to run away to the promised land?" Still staring at the photo and then back at the horizon, still wanting to see what Garth saw that gave him this level of conviction, I nodded my cold head in the affirmative. However mad the big man's suggestion, it was the closest thing to a logical course of action available.

CHAPTER XV

GARTH explained to me that the cutting of the truck's tires didn't matter to us, that our journey wouldn't require them. The ice ahead was uncharted, and any seemingly harmless stretch of untouched snow might conceal a deadly chasm, or paper-thin surfaces unable to carry the weight of the vehicles. It was better to take the snowmobiles and hope that even they weren't too heavy. Garth had managed to bring one bike by himself to the site and used it to drag another. There were two more waiting back at the Creole's base camp; the captain could get one and Angela could double up on another. Now that he knew I was game, Garth would make a quick trip back for supplies and meet me here again. That was our escape plan.

After this course of action was agreed on and I had blissfully filled my belly on forgotten glove compartment energy bars, my first order of business was to find my cousin and put Booker Jaynes back in charge, because now more than ever we needed his leadership. Captain Jaynes was a member of the baby boomers, the last generation of African Americans to fight the race war directly—I can admit without embarrassment that I have always been impressed by that. Leaving Garth on the surface so that I could bring the good news to Angela and the others, I headed immediately for the hold Jaynes served in, which fortunately for me was on the way to town in the tunnel I was traveling. When I got there I found Angela as well. Seeing her at the door of Jaynes's cave, leaning against the wall, I was almost immediately hit with a wave of euphoria that seemed to imply that everything was going to be okay. What a divine coincidence. That there was, contrary to my suspicions, an order to the universe, and that it was a benevolent one. The beauty of this woman only contributed to this feeling: even now, after she'd spent weeks in the same dirty clothes, her grip over me was not lessened. The scarf that wrapped up Angela's unwashed hair only increased her hold on me, made my mind think back to our grad school days, before any misstep had been taken. Hugging her, I told Angela how lucky it was that I'd found her here at this moment.

"No, it's not lucky. I've been waiting here in front of your cousin's door for half an hour. My thighs are frozen, my feet are almost numb, but here I still am waiting, all this time waiting just to ask the old man a question. This is so not covered in my job description."

"Babe. What do you need to know that could be so important?" I pulled out one of Garth's protein bars as I talked, taking the time to remove my gloves and unwrap it for her. To my surprise, Angela didn't grab the offering from me, instead with her gloved hands she cupped my bare ones, guiding them to her mouth. There was no risk of the chocolate melting on her gloves, as cold as it was. Looking at her, her lips drained to gray, I found it hard to believe there would be enough warmth in her gut to melt the food either. Seeing her lips part and then collapse as they chewed, I was overwhelmed by the desire to touch them. To touch any of her, and not just acrylic thermal padding.

"I want to know if he'll switch jobs with me."

"You want him to come all the way across Tekeli-li to scrub down that kitchen floor?" I asked.

"No, I want to trade households with him. Even if it's only for a day or two. You've seen Booker: he's the only one of us who looks

well fed and not beaten down." I had noticed this in my quick passing in Tekeli-li's main square. I put it down to the legendary Jaynes
endurance in the face of opposition, but a generous employer was
the more likely factor. "He's your cousin, Christopher," Angela
continued, squeezing my hand, which she still cupped in hers.
"You talk to him. I need this. I called his name into the cave a few
times; I heard something in there, the moans those Neanderthals
make sometimes. But I don't feel safe going in uninvited."

"You don't have to worry about that anymore. I have an escape
plan for us," I told her. There was intimacy in the way I said "us,"
and no small amount of expectation on my part. I admit I wanted
desperately in that moment to play the hero, for Angela to see me
in that light. This might be the final break she would need to mentally annul her second marriage. Not reacting to any of this, Angela instead became excited about the main point of my statement
and jumped to the conclusion that the modern world had reap-
peared in the form of radio contact or the workers' ship arriving,
and that we would be soon traveling back to it. This assumption
contrasted painfully with the reality that I was really discussing
Garth's belief that if we marched out onto the uncharted ice we
might find the hidden lair of his artistic crush.

"Chris, that's just insane. That's not even stupid, it's past stupid
and straight into suicidal madness," Angela nearly whispered,
pulling away from me and tugging absently on her snowsuit's zipper as if a half inch of flesh had been exposed.

"Staying here is suicidal madness," I rebutted, trying not to
sound hurt.

"Maybe. But at least it requires a hell of a lot less effort. And
anyway, Nathaniel isn't going to make it on the ice: he can barely
limp out of the village square." Angela paused for a moment, drag-
ging the image of her ailing second husband into both our minds.

"Even if I wanted to go, if I wanted to risk it all for freedom and just run: how can I just leave him?" she asked. For a moment I entertained the hope that it was a question of logistics. "Go. If you find a way to rescue us, come back for me," she said.

After arranging for me to make the request to my cousin on her behalf, Angela departed, leaving me alone in the corridor just as she had been. Immediately I missed her, but I comforted myself with the thought that Captain Jaynes most certainly would join the escape, and that, with his vote secured, Angela (and Nathaniel too, of course) could be convinced to join us. Given the urgency of the situation, I was much less timid about finding Captain Jaynes than Angela was, so instead of passively sitting it out in the hall, I crept into the opening of his captor's dwelling.

As I moved slowly through the entrance, past the curves of the first walls that hid the interior, I heard that moaning sound that Angela had mentioned. There was no question something was home, and in deference to the Tekelian inhabitant (and the breed's considerable strength), I attempted to move with all the stealth I could manage. Staring down at my boots, trying to limit their crunch, I became aware that there wasn't simply one voice moaning: this was a duet. And one of them was not the canine roar of the Tekelian, but instead the intermittent wailing of a human. Forgetting care and caution, I ran forward, turning the corner to enter the great room.

What I saw there I have no words for. Except these: Captain Jaynes lay prone on an elevated slab of ice with his Tekelian mistress, Hunka, on top of him. Together they were performing an act that I did not find entertaining. That's all that I'm prepared to offer on the subject, because to this day I haven't fully recovered from the trauma the vision inflicted. And to be real, it was a blur, the flash of an image rather than a clear one, because the moment my presence was known, the snow monkey was gone, having run off in embarrassment to more secluded quarters. So fast was Hunka that one second I was seeing a blur of white and the next moment, in the very same spot, a solitary brown member stood its ground, saluting me.

"What were you thinking? Don't you knock?" Captain Jaynes demanded of me as he struggled to cover himself and stand. There was, of course, no place to knock, as the melting ice tended to swallow the vibration of most percussion. As to what I was thinking, it would take me much longer than the time provided to decipher that. Once my cousin had repackaged himself, pulling up his snow pants and zipping up his zipper, he began to act as if I had seen nothing at all. In appreciation of this mercy, I went along with the act, telling him the details of our impending flight to freedom, and this time I made a real effort to sell the feasibility of the quest. I was so successful in arguing my case that as the words came out of my mouth my own ambivalence about Garth's plan slowly cemented into certainty. By the time I was summing up my pitch, there was no doubt in me. Our journey would be successful. Our destination was a real one.

From the look on my cousin's face as he leaned against the far wall, hugging himself with one arm and stroking his beard with the other hand, I could see he was taking it all in. Better yet, from the seriousness with which he was studying the situation, the moments of silence that followed, there could be no doubt that Captain Jaynes actually believed me enough that he felt the merits of the whole crazy plan should be weighed like gold. This was the man I had worked for, the one I was proud to call my family. This was the representative of that generation of leader caste that would take us to tomorrow.

"No, we shouldn't leave this place," Booker Jaynes interrupted my rush to euphoria. "Nope. No."

"What? What the hell do you mean 'no'? You believe me, don't you? This place is out there. It could be complete luxury."

"Could be, could be. There's probably something out there, I trust you on that. That's not what I'm saying at all. Sure, that all may be out there. But the problem, our problem with these people, is right here. They don't respect us. They treat us like animals. What we need to do is stay here and fight that."

"What are you talking about? You're the one always talking about getting away from normal white folks. Why the hell aren't you down to run away from these monster ones?" I demanded.

"Separatism; look where it got me. I come all the way across the damn ocean to the South Pole, and they still here. I was wrong. You can't run from Whiteness. You have to stand and engage it. They got courts: we can litigate our freedom. They like ice sculpture: we can learn the medium and then outshine them with our own artistry. We will teach them to respect us. We will show them how beautiful we are. And then, then they will be forced to love us, and that is our only salvation."

In movies, when someone is talking crazy, you are allowed to smack him.* Unfortunately, I lacked the speed to pop the lunatic in question, and the thickness of my snowsuit would have cushioned the blow anyway.

"Booker. They're enslaving us. They're not even humans. And they're assholes! You've changed, man. You've sold out. This is because you're screwing that ice ape, isn't it? You got Stockholm syndrome or something."

"Don't talk about Hunka like that," Captain Jaynes snapped back at me, his corded dreadlocks bouncing around behind his

* In African American vernacular, it's called "going upside the head," and because of that I have always imagined an open-hand assault in a literal upswing, gliding past the ear and making contact with most of the temple.

wagging head to add punctuation. "Shut your mouth. That is a special creature there. Don't add insult by pretending like you don't think she's fine."

Already, Booker Jaynes was brushing himself off, preparing to pretend that this discussion and my visit had never happened and the new road he was choosing was a sane one. He had lost it, it was clear. His Jaynes eccentricities had misguided him, and his Jaynes stubbornness now ensured he would go all the way. "No point in running anymore, can't you see that. We stay, and we struggle. Because the struggle is who we are," he told me with finality.

· · ·

Burdened by a profound sense of disappointment, I climbed once more from the bowels of the underground whiteness to meet the yellow sun above. I had intended to return from my trip with my three comrades, each high with the hope of freedom. What I returned with instead was a week's supply of krakt, a gift from Captain Jaynes which I held on my shoulder in an oily sealskin sack. "She makes it from her own recipe. Take it or I'll eat it all myself," my cousin said proudly as he gave me the parting offering, along with a promise to get Hunka to buy Angela from her captors.

Beyond those emotions related to my failure, I began to realize that there were other feelings boiling up within me as well. With every step out of Tekeli-li, I began to wonder if this would be my last moment in this improbable community, an idea I considered with absolutely no sense of nostalgia. So regret-free were my actions that when I came closer to the surface I began to experience a wave of paranoia as well: surely it could not be this easy. Surely, if I had realized that I was leaving, others must have realized it as well, noticed my absence already, and were at the moment making preparations to stop me. Not Augustus, of course, but others more invested in my servitude. Maybe even Sausage Nose himself.

In the light of this fear, I stopped several times along that final stretch of the path just to listen for footsteps behind me, ones I was sure I almost heard before I acknowledged that it was probably nothing more than an echo.

I found Garth in the truck's cab, asleep and prone, feet up on the steering wheel, his socks reeking like deep-fried corn chips. Instead of taking a seat and warming myself by the truck's running heater, I chose instead to leave the stash of krakt on the floor in front of Garth, then inspect the snowmobiles that would provide our escape. I wanted to be gone from Tekeli-li now. I wanted to have this place farther behind me with every second, lost in a cloud of snow and memory. I didn't know much about mechanics, but I did know enough to understand that the internal wires and tubes of the vehicles should not be strewn loosely around the snow, packed into the ice by an orgy of footprints. I knew enough to know the vehicles shouldn't have their front visors smashed, or be lying on their sides, hoods open and guts ripped out, metal corpses even more still because of their ruin. I brushed the snow from the snowbikes as if I could comfort them, tears starting to build in my freezing eyes. It was during the process of doing this that I saw him, caught a glance of him in a cracked rearview mirror sneaking up behind me to observe my mourning.

"Arthur. Arthur Gordon Pym!" I yelled to my tormentor. The culprit still held a piece of bone in his hand, preparing to do more damage. If it really was him, if he really was that old, I suddenly felt as if it would be my duty to nature itself to kill him. In that moment, eyes blurry, it was clear to me. If Pym was the destroyer of my dreams, then I would be the destroyer of the dreamer.

"*You did this,*" I yelled at him, with as much venom as those three words could carry. Pym paused just out of lunging distance, kept his arms open at his sides in case he needed to spring into some form of action.

"You would speak to me about what I have done, you dark character? I know what it is that *you* are doing," the Caucasian said to me, and when he did the full fear of our discovery and possible punishment hit me, and I felt a cold chill well beyond the one in the air.

"What the hell are you talking about?" I yelled back at Pym. Looking at all the tubes and wires at my feet, I thought nothing appeared so damaged by his human hands as not to be salvageable. If I knew how to stick them back into the machines properly, which I didn't.

"You have a secret treasure trove of the prized sweetmeats, I have no doubt. But you, sir, have been discovered!" Food. That was what he thought this was about in its entirety. There was a tone to his voice that was as self-righteous as it was wrong, and it warbled and bounced just like his finger did as it pointed at me.

"Why would I be hiding the snack cakes if I knew they could buy my freedom, Pym? That's not even logical."

"So you say, so you say, but logic is exactly what it is that I apply to your chaos. For if that is not what you are doing, why else did I see your mate attempting to harness your carriages, except to . . ." There was a pause here, a moment when the two of us were just standing out there in the snow, and I could almost see the cold synapses fire in his brain as Arthur Gordon Pym came to the realization of what Garth's and my true intentions were. "You scoundrel! You foolish beast! Do you really mean to steal your person from your rightful owner? Not only have you been a lazy slave but now you indulge in this madness as well? Are you such a fool that you intend to run away from Heaven itself? Has the taint of your blood made you so black and stupid that you can't—" Pym stopped abruptly, taking the time to recover from the blow that Garth landed on the back of his neck. Garth's big hands were like leather gloves filled with pudding, and the sound of the impact reverberated well beyond the site of impact. Spinning around to look at his assailant, Pym jumped forward so that now he was trapped between Garth and me. As he took in the massive figure of the bus driver, augmented even further by the layers of thermal padding to keep Garth's flesh warm, Arthur Pym suddenly remembered that he should be afraid of us.

"On further consideration and reflection, I must say I am sorry for the insults. You and your brethren make excellent slaves. You are truly born for it. Much more so than those poor specimens from Tsalal, I assure you."

It was that 'excellent slaves' part that made Garth walk toward Pym, landing another slap to the back of his nearly perfectly round skull, his balding raven mop bouncing in response. It was the line about Tsalal that startled me, though. I held a hand up to Garth, beckoning him to pause his thrashing. *Tsalal*. Oh, the sound of it. Even from Pym's dismissive lips it struck a fire in part of my soul that I worried had gone frozen. *Tsalal*. The dream was out there. And it was with Pym's pronunciation of the word, with all its slithering and disdain, that I knew it was within reach. That the greatest revelation was still in front of us.

"Tsalal? What do you know about Tsalal?" Even if there was no world left above us anymore, did that make this goal of discovering Eden any less lofty? Maybe now it was even more so. Tsalal was the world my crewmates and I were destined for.

"I have known of the island, for I discovered it, and the Tekelians did so before me. They sought to use its natives as a source of labor. But the human crop, it was useless. Unfit for proper bondage. Now they grow wild, I presume."

Trying to calm myself, to avoid betraying how much I wanted this information and letting Pym know he could extort it from me, I continued. "And what else do you know about these Tsalalians?"

214 · MAT JOHNSON

"They are black," Pym said as if this said it all, pausing after each of these three words so that I could perceive the weight of them.*

"Do you know how to get there?" was the most important question I had to ask. Garth paused behind, and his threat definitely affected the speed of Pym's answer, but I hoped not the content.

"Yes, of course. It's a simple matter of tides. I could show you. Although, I must tell you: there is no point trying to set up trade with those niggers."

Spurred by the last word of his statement, Garth gave the white man another smack, this time with the full force of annoyance. The blow left Pym on the ground, very, very unconscious.

"What the hell are you doing, man? He was going to tell us how to get to Tsalal!"

"I don't like that word." Garth shrugged. "And I ain't the kind of nigga that's gonna let some cracker say that to my face and get away with it."

Garth showed some bit of regret by grabbing Pym by the collar and smacking him further, more lightly this time, in an attempt to wake him up. But it was clear that Pym would not be regaining consciousness for a while, and the longer we waited the more our immediate plans were at risk.

"Did you bring Dirk Peters's bones from the base camp like I specifically asked you? I don't want to lose them."

"You're a weird dude, Chris. Really, you're not right sometimes. Yeah, I got it."

---

* Pym said "black" the way really white people do: not like they are simply naming the pigment, which those people do in one quick syllable, but in the way that made the word specific to Negroes. This black had at least two syllables, bě-'lAk, and there was always enough emphasis on the second syllable to convey all of the anxiety the speaker had about my ethnic group as a whole. Ba-laaaaaaaak.

"Good. We're taking Pym with us too. That's the only solution. We're taking him with us, we can't . . . I can't let this chance slip away."

"Man, do you not see what that fool did to the other two snow-mobiles? We not carrying nobody. Besides, why do we need Tsalal? We already got somewhere to run to. We already got a plan, and I think it's a pretty good one."

"I'll carry him. He'll be my burden."

• • •

With that, I rolled Pym's limp body over and tied him up. Then I took the rest of the rope we could find in the truck's cab and laid it out on the snow in the form of a Philadelphia soft pretzel. Once it was arranged, I poured water onto the line from the bottle that Garth kept in his coat, despite his complaining. And in seconds, when the water had frozen the rope and the snow around it into a hard shape and the makeshift sled was ready, I placed the knocked-out Pym on it and put our food supplies and my bag of bones beside him, securing all of them tightly so that they wouldn't fall off during the quest ahead of us.

CHAPTER XVI

I have always loved quitting jobs. Whether because the job itself was repugnant or the people working at it with me, I have always held my right to quit my job as one of my most sacred privileges. An entire ritual surrounds this shedding of employment. First, there is the glorious moment when, after the unpleasantness of my position and my general unhappiness become overwhelmingly apparent to me, I say to myself (and I quote), "Fuck this. I don't have to take this shit anymore. They think they can make me do what they want, but I'm out of here." Ah, there it is, the almost orgasmic release I feel when I first make the profane declaration to myself, the feeling of reclaimed power coursing invisibly through me. But not just that: this singular moment, this coveted private knowledge is formed into a golden kernel and popped into existence again in my mind as a reaction to every unfortunate work-related moment I'm forced to endure before I make my destined departure. It's such a glorious thing, the harboring of this secret knowledge, that in itself it has kept me at many a job even longer than I had originally intended, because just knowing that I would soon be free was the most effective of panaceas. So much so that there were times when even though it was impossible for me to quit I would say the same words to myself and mercifully delude my conscious mind that I could get the hell out of there if I wanted to.

As I marched through the snow with nothing but more snow in

front and behind for hours, I began to wonder if all of my quitting dramatics might have some larger meaning. That they might in fact be evidence of some form of race memory from my genetic past. How many of my slave ancestors used such gimmicks to preserve their own sanity? Spending years obsessing over the intended escape that only they knew of. The intricate planning that they shared with no one. I have thought of their escapes before, and was usually impressed by the bravery and fear that must have accompanied those breakouts. But I forgot to think about the glory of all the acts of flight that never happened. And how powerful their inaction probably was to the slaves who did not perform them.

But me, I quit. I have quit very good jobs, and horrible ones. I have co-workers that I still miss, and co-workers that I regret never assaulting on the way out the door. And overall, I have enjoyed my resignations, enjoyed that last moment of walking away from each of the places that housed my misery, knowing that I would never have to return. I have walked down the street each time and bounced away, literally bounced in a skipping motion, knowing once more the effervescence of freedom.

And always, immediately after my departure, then comes the next feeling, the next sentence, which is just as inevitable as the first. It goes, "What the hell are you going to do now?" And thus begins my terror. The hell I was doing now was slogging forward through the wind, rope over my shoulder as I pulled, trying to ignore the pain in my right hand as I kept my grip on my makeshift sled. What I was going to do was ignore the sounds of the screaming Arthur Gordon Pym, who was surprisingly awake and still tied to the luggage pile behind me. What I was going to do was keep following Garth Frierson, staring at the back of his head like so many of his bus passengers must have, and trust as they did that the man knew where he was going.

• • •

"What is this shit?" Garth asked, staring at the sealskin container. It was Pym who responded.

"That, heathen, is *krakt*. It is the chosen meal of the Gods, the most perfect economy of taste and sustenance." There was a snort that ended this description. I had untied Pym for the moment and replaced his many folded robes with one of the spare snowsuits just so that I could keep a better eye on what his limbs were up to. We sat out on the compacted snow taking a break, our footprints lost in the trail behind us, the mountain in front of us still infuriatingly distant. There was nowhere for Pym to run to, and this knowledge calmed him a bit. The fact that he seemed to be sobering up as our trip progressed contributed to his change in demeanor too.

"But does it taste good?" Garth retorted.

"No," I said over my shoulder, and then continued relieving myself into a growing yellow hole a dozen yards past them.

"It is a staple of the very heavens," Pym shot back, offended. "Everyone eats it there. Everyone eats it there for every meal, and for every occasion. It is the food of love. Everyone who consumes it has love for it."

"Everyone?" Garth asked, and emboldened, he took a sample, dipping a bare finger into the gook and putting it on his tongue. "Dog, this is delicious" was Garth's judgment.

"Great. Eat as much as you want, my man," I told him. "You sure you know where you're going, right?" I asked, but Garth was too engrossed in his culinary discovery to answer.

• • •

"Where the hell are we going, Garth?"

I didn't want to seem like the child on a long trip calling out *Are we there yet?* but yet and still, were we? We were stopped for yet another "bathroom" break, as it was clear that the krakt was proving too rich for the mortal stomach of Garth Frierson, who at least did me the honor of going downwind to shit himself this time.

I'd given up tying Arthur Pym's hands an hour before, since there was no point to it. For the most part, as I trudged along behind the tracks that Garth laid down just before me, Pym was the least of my fears. Mostly, I worried about Garth. I watched through the small cloud of snow in his wake as he stomped along, the fat of his hips swiveling to get him there. I watched as he Karvel-spotted, removing the picture of the mountain peak from his jacket and raising it to whatever new vista we approached. And I waited. Impatiently. Trying to calculate the point at which our bodies would be sufficiently depleted so that even the life of servitude behind me was literally beyond my reach. And only after that horror became too much to contemplate did I think of Pym instead. And I thought of something. I turned my body and mind to Pym, who was trying to scrape the last of the krakt out of the empty seal bladder onto his fingers.

"Arthur Pym, why'd you say 'the Gods found you'?" The Caucasian turned up from his feeding to look at me inquisitively but said nothing. Although centuries old, he didn't look more than thirty-eight. A drunkard's watery thirty-eight but a lot better than most two-hundred-year-olds nonetheless. Down here, white didn't crack either.

"You know," I continued, "when we were talking back at that pub before, why did you say 'the Gods found you' about the Tekelians, when I found them? I discovered the Tekelian at the base of the chasm. That was me."

"You are not half so clever as you imagine, Christopher Jaynes. Did you really believe yourself to be so lucky as to trip upon their perfection? Did you really think it was you that had the element of surprise?"

The tunnels that led to our base camp—immediately I made the connection. My mind lurched forward, fueled by explosive possibilities. *The Tekelians had been watching us all along.* They had planned for all of it to go down.

In a rush of euphoria, I began to believe that the entirety of humanity was probably still alive and carrying on in the rest of the world without bother. But then I remembered the emails and the missing workers' boat, and my mind came crashing down once more. There was no way the ice monsters could have made their own computers from bones and snow, or made phones to cancel work orders.

· · ·

"Do you intend to starve me? For if murder was your dark intent, it would have been better to kill me back in Tekeli-li rather than drag me this far." It was two hours later, and Pym had a good point on that one; even though it had been only a few hours, I was hungry too.

"Garth, two protein bars, please. No, maybe you should make that four." It was a hard thing to ask for; I'd eaten so many before we left that the mere thought of those faux chocolate fiber bricks threatened my gut. Still, it was better than the pangs of hunger which I was already starting to feel again.

"Ain't no more, dog," Garth said, not even bothering to put his binoculars down and face me.

"What? Of course there are more. There was a whole unopened box; just take one out of that pile."

"Ate 'em," the big man said while looking back through the binocular lenses. He kept scouring the horizon as if his magical mountain would just jump up and reveal itself if he stared at the distant ridges long enough.

" '*Ate 'em*'? That is a sentence fragment, Garth, among other things. What you're missing primarily is a defining noun. Your subject. If you are going to eat all of the food, you could at least say 'I ate them.' If only because now you're going to have to watch us starve."

Garth didn't respond. As he walked on toward the ridge, he just kept looking around.

• • •

By our next stop, the tip of my nose had gone numb: there was barely any of it showing past my hood. Mine was a wide, Negroid nose, and yet and still its tip had gone numb. For a good half hour, I lost Garth in front of me, his massive figure growing smaller on the horizon until the dot that he had become simply vanished. Pym trudged not far behind me, just one wrist now bound and attached by rope to the sled. The white man complained bitterly the entire way, but luckily the wind blew loudly enough that the specifics of his discontent were lost. It started to seem like maybe Garth had gone on to die alone and without accusations, because the idea that we were actually moving forward toward something seemed absurd. Not even looking up anymore, I just stared at the ground. Following the tracks of Garth's boots print for print, at some point I just stopped thinking, became hypnotized by watching the powder as I trudged by. Given my state, if it wasn't for Garth's screaming, I would have slammed into him when I eventually found him standing there.

Garth Frierson was yelling, but as I took his presence in, pulling back my hood to better hear him, I saw that he was doing something else even more spectacular: Garth was jumping. Jumping up and down, pumping his plump, gloved fist as he did so. Despite my exhaustion, it was a moving sight: given the general rotund shape of his outline, his actions gave Garth the appearance of a blubbery ball, bouncing up and down at improbable intervals.

"We're here!" he finally managed to communicate to me.

"The camp? You see the camp? Where is it?" I called back to him.

"The mountain ridge! That's it, dog. That's the one we're looking for, over there."

Following Garth's pointed finger, I did see the mountain ridge. It was true, it was the same one that I saw in the painting. Then, looking past and around that landmark, I saw something else. I saw that there was nothing out here. No sign of an eco-habitat, no sign of life, nothing. If not for the printed image that Garth had of this very spot, I would have assumed there had never been any form of human contact with this place at all. But I was sure it was this spot, just as Garth was as he held up the image and compared it to the landmarks around us.

"This is it!" he kept declaring.

"Yeah, this is it. Fine. But what are we going to do now, Garth?" I asked, searching around for salvation and seeing nothing but snowdrifts.

"So is this to be the site of our grave?" asked Pym, sitting on the sled as he massaged the blood back into his feet.

．．．

We pitched a tent. As we did, the wind picked up and carried a storm cloud directly over our heads, then kept it there, dumping its snow down on us as if we had asked for more. By the time I began to drag my gear inside the thin nylon walls, the top of our shelter was already lined with an inch of powder. I thought, Good, that will keep some of the wind out, because I had decided to lie to myself for a while until there was some truth worth hearing.

We dragged whatever we had inside the tent before it was lost in the storm. With the last of my strength, I took the gloves off my nearly numb hands and zipped down the front tent flaps as if this act would magically turned the fabric into the sturdiest of doors. Hunched over, turning around, I saw Pym at my canvas bag, my treasure. He'd opened the strap at its mouth. In an act completely lacking in respect, he'd pulled out a blackened and aged femur and was holding it as if it was a drumstick he might want to take a bite of.

"Enough!" I managed the energy to snatch it back from him, replacing the contents and hugging my collection as if the remains were still living.

"Why do you have a dead man among your luggage?" Arthur Gordon Pym asked me, the judgment and disdain as palpable as the wind that blew against our refuge's walls. "What is this, one of your victims?"

"No," I replied, pointing. "It's one of yours. It's Dirk Peters."

Pym dropped what was in his hands, pulled away from it for a second before looking into the rest of the sack. And then he looked back at me, smiled broadly, and gave a laugh of madness. Picking up the skull, he held it out to me.

"Alas, poor Dirk! I knew him, Christopher: a fellow of infinite jest, of most excellent fancy: he hath borne me on his back a thousand times; and now, how abhorred in my imagination it is!" The sight of this white guy holding the sacred remains of my black brother pissed me off more than any of the events before. I grabbed the skull back out of Pym's hands with the one-word curse, "Blasphemy!"

"Well, if this is who you say, which I believe not, then who are you to throw such a stone?"

"The weirdo's right, dog. What you're doing with it?" the former bus driver asked me.

"I'm taking it to Tsalal. For a proper burial," I said, holding the bag to me.

"I'm saying, if you ever do find Tsalal, this big black island, why the hell would you bury his bones there? Isn't that, like, the last thing this dude and this Mathis lady would have wanted?"

"It's not about what they would have wanted. It's about what's right," I told him. Consumed by cold and overwhelming hunger, I barely bothered to offer that explanation. Why struggle to fight such silliness?

• • •

We sat in silence for hours awaiting death, the three of us. Then, after a while, Arthur Pym said:

"Do either of you count straw or twigs among your many wondrous possessions? For I believe that to find sustenance we may have to look amongst our own circle." Despite myself I looked and saw a pool of spittle spill out the side of the Caucasian's mouth in anticipation. Although Garth was the one currently being stared at, the big man paid Pym no mind. Instead, as Arthur Pym argued to no one the merits of his culinary suggestions, Garth put back on his gloves, goggles, and hat, and left the tent.

"I am just going outside and may be some time" was his sole remark, and like Lawrence Oates before him he was gone. I was too far gone to try to stop his sacrifice.

"So, are you going to try to eat me now," I asked Pym, but he shrugged this off.

"Let us acknowledge this: yours is a rather odorous breed, and you, sir, are a particular pungent example of this. I fear even my starving appetite could not overcome that truth."

"My people don't stink. And I wouldn't stink if those Tekelians you love so much had let me take a bath." At the mention of criticism of his beloved snow monkeys, Pym's head shook side to side as if he'd bitten something nasty.

"This end is a judgment, I fear. For your theft of yourself," Pym returned, looking toward the tent door Garth had just walked out of, perhaps considering if he should go and chase after his meal.

"What are you talking about? Steal myself? You basically admitted that they scammed us into that deal, that they were watching us all along."

Again, the head shake. Pym wouldn't hear anything negative about the race from the caves. That is it, that's the trick, I realized as my brain began to go numb. Drifting off, staring across at the two-hundred-year-old man just to make sure that the needs of his stomach didn't overpower the needs of his nose, I saw it all become clear to me. That is how they stay so white: by refusing to accept blemish or history. Whiteness isn't about being something, it is about being no thing, nothing, an erasure. Covering over the truth with layers of blank reality just as the snowstorm was now covering our tent, whipping away all traces of our existence from this pristine landscape.

VOLUME

...IV...

CHAPTER XVII

And now we rushed into the embraces of the cataract, where a
chasm threw itself open to receive us. But there arose in our pathway
a shrouded human figure, very far larger in its proportions than any
dweller among men. And the hue of the skin of the figure was of the
perfect whiteness of the snow.

—*The Narrative of Arthur Gordon Pym of Nantucket*

IT can be argued then that the greatness of *The Narrative of Arthur
Gordon Pym of Nantucket* lies more in the ongoing reaction to its
cliffhanger ending, this flaunting and confounding literary challenge, than to the work itself. The backflips of those who seek to
prove that the book is actually a finished work in itself are matched
perfectly by the somersaults of others who say the work is an unfinished equation to be answered. Jules Verne, eager to solve the
riddle laid out by his American hero, wrote a sequel called *An
Antarctic Mystery*, or *The Sphinx of the Ice Fields.** Verne sought to
place Pym firmly within the world of the rational, regardless of
Poe's own lack of concern for this regard. The mystery referenced
in Verne's title is solved when his protagonist's exhaustive research
into *Pym*'s final scene comes up with an answer to explain everything: magnets. Ever fond of science (or even pseudoscience) over

* *Le Sphinx des Glaces*, in the original French.

mysticism, Verne came up with this rational explanation, that the white figure was a big Sphinx-shaped magnet that had pulled Pym to his death. H. P. Lovecraft took up the challenge in *At the Mountains of Madness.* In Lovecraft's version, Poe's white figure was revealed to be a penguin. A massive, albino penguin, of a breed that was left there by the alien Old Ones, who had also left behind an incomprehensibly hideous tentacled monster. This creature was slimy and, true to Poe's symbology if not to the setting, completely black.

Pym's literary critics, the ones stuck with working over the existing text rather than imagining their way out of it, have struggled valiantly, but with disappointing results. As examples of the many schools of thought on that infamous final paragraph, I offer the following:

A. The ending of *Pym* is simply a taunt for a possible sequel, a crass attempt to turn this novel into one of several, thereby solving Poe's considerable financial burdens during this period. This technique also harkens to Daniel Defoe's *Robinson Crusoe,* from which Poe borrowed liberally throughout. People forget that, after Crusoe escaped from the island, he and Friday went on to further adventure for another chapter in the wild hills of Italy, chased by ferocious wolves and the like. People forget that part because they want to—it's anticlimactic, pointless, and silly. Arguing against this theory is the fact that Poe says in the afterword to *Pym* that there are only two or three chapters missing. Why merely three if an additional volume was the aim?

B. If it is separated from the expectations that a novel has an arc, a direction, and that even the picaresque variety must undergo some final statement, then the ending of *Pym* fits quite well within the rest of the work. It starts with action, explores the scene, and then ends unresolved, with the reader wanting only to read on. The final chapter feels like every other chapter in the book, and Poe himself once declared that he was first a "magazinist," an assertion that fits his refusal, or inability, to end this story. Instead of an apposite and structurally determined ending, his finale seems merely to mark the moment when he surrendered to exhaustion and wrote no more. While this may be an attractive explanation, it should be remembered that Poe was a master storyteller, albeit of short-form fiction. Surely, though, a master of the micro could not blunder so largely on the macro level as to have a novel that simply doesn't end. Right?

C. The ending, the moving into the white chasm with the inhuman, shrouded figure, is an allegory for death. The ending is merely the poeticized destruction of both Pym and Dirk Peters. While it is attractive in its simplicity and for the way it compliments *Pym*'s author, I object to this rather common read because it's just plain stupid. First, why, in a book that has taken pleasure in so many gory details, would Poe escape into metaphor for the clincher? Also, how could Arthur Pym then write the preface, *which he does,* telling us that he is back on the East Coast? No, this is just a stupid interpretation. I usually refrain from name-calling, but it's true.

D. Just as Poe's vision of the blackness of Tsalal is perfectly horrific, his vision of this complete whiteness of his Antarctica is perfection itself. How then, as a writer of stories based on conflict (as all tales are), can Poe go forward with the narra-

tive? "And then we got there and everything was just absolutely without flaw in every way" does not make for a grip-
ping story. Or even a feasible story. So, this theory states, the
narrative reaches a dead end. It can go nowhere. Conflict, the
basis of all storytelling, itself has been negated by an overwhelming worship of whiteness.

CHAPTER XVIII

I woke up dead. I woke up naked, lying on a bed of soft green moss, my body warmed from the golden glow above me. There were voices. Men mostly, some women. Not a conversation, not listening, just talking, over each other and united only by their passionate tone. Angry voices, words and meaning lost in their muddle. I was in Hell. As my eyes adjusted, I found hope for Heaven instead. Looking around, I could see that it had to be one or the other, because Purgatory could not be this decisive, this stunning. Gone was the snow with its frozen white death, and now in its place were fauna and lavender and color. Bushes of every hue, more vivid than I could have imagined, stretched out around and past me, along the small hill to a waterfall that fed the Pierian spring that babbled a few feet beyond, large orange carp swimming visibly beneath the surface. Gone was the vast frozen whiteness that was the taker of life, because now I was lying on the green bank of a river, naked, smelling lavender in the air and hearing the faint sound of harps present under the chatter.

Yes, there was the noise of the voices, but it was so beautiful. The more I looked, the clearer that was. As a matter of fact, with the white doves flying by and the clouds which hung above perfectly billowing their fluff, it was so overwhelming that it was almost too much for my mind to negotiate. No, not almost, definitely, it was definitely too beautiful, too perfect, for my mind to wrap around, my ears all that grounded me. In fact, the air was so sweet it was saccharine. Really, it was like pouring perfume under your nose. I started to feel sick in my stomach at it, but there was something so familiar about this place and the voices in my head. That's when I noticed that, despite their appearance of flowing, the clouds above weren't actually moving. Tracing their path off into the horizon, I saw that right before the farthest clouds disappeared past a blooming cherry tree, *there were black letters written right onto the blue sky.* It was a signature, the autograph of this land's creator.

In my terror I realized that this was not my heaven, this was Garth's. This was my hell. I was trapped inside a Thomas Karvel painting.

"Dog, you up?"

I rolled over onto my side and saw my friend. Garth stood buck naked. Eating a bag of Cheetos.

"Where the hell are we?" I managed, taking him in. Orange cheese dust powdered Garth's various bodily hairs from his goatee down, his overhanging belly covering his genitalia, fortunately.

"We're here, dog. I found it—don't sleep on the big man. I told you I knew what I was doing. I found it and came back and got you."

"Where the hell is here?" I asked, raising myself up as well, a hand covering my groin in an act of modesty.

"This is Eden, dog. As in 'the garden of.' You standing in the *Dome of Light.*"

Dome was an apt description. And not just in the sense of the shape of the structure I now found myself in but also in the "sports arena" usage of the word. This was no modest little science station. The interior really was the length of a football field, and the waterfall that coursed on the far end of the room poured down from at least three stories high. As I looked at the falling water, I could see that there was actually a fenced deck just above the falls with a table and chairs, past that the reflection of windows. Above, the clouds were painted right onto the ceiling.

Garth leaned down and whispered firmly into my ear, "I told him we're Republicans. Black. Republicans. Got it?"

"What? What are you talking about? Why are we naked?" I had many questions, but this seemed the most pertinent.

"Contamination, dog," was Garth's answer.

"Contamination from *what*?" I must have yelled on that last word, because just then out of the turquoise bush beside me hopped an Easter bunny, clearly startled. Albino and obese, it darted its nervous red eyes in confusion at the scene.

"I was hoping you could tell *me* 'what,' " a male voice answered. And there, on an outgrowth of granite rock, stood a Caucasian with a thin black mustache, his arms outstretched like the Rio de Janeiro Jesus, white terry-cloth robes in each hand.

"You fellows hungry for some Welsh rabbit?" asked the Master of Light himself, whom I recognized immediately from Garth's catalogs. In response to Thomas Karvel's query, the Easter bunny to my side scampered back into the bushes, presumably for cover.

• • •

When I heard "Welsh Rabbit," I expected cheese on toast. So it was with surprise that I received my plate.* Instead of being populated by a metaphorical rabbit, it was instead occupied by a real one,

---

* The culinary term "Welsh rabbit," is of course a joke. A very old one as jokes go, dating back to the early eighteenth century. The joke, English in origin, was that the Welsh were either too poor or too stupid or too generally pathetic to have actual meat on their plates, so cheese grilled on toast was their delusional equivalent. The other version of this title, "Welsh rarebit," is in fact a degradation of the original, a mishearing that was later adopted as a less offensive alternative. To little avail. In fact, the English so derided their neighbors to the west of the isle that in their language the very word *Welsh* became synonymous with substandard or imitation goods.

dead and skinned and glazed. A cherry tomato stuck into its little bunny mouth.

"Is this one of those?" I motioned with my fork at the scattered white bunnies it was possible to see jumping around below. From the deck atop the waterfall, one could see the entire length of the life-size terrarium we were inside of.

"Those cute little white ones? Oh no, I would never do that. Those are for the missus. I shot most of these back in Ohio," Karvel assured me. I could barely hear him, though, over the sounds of all the voices, pumped through speakers attached to the wall.

"Nothing's come through the satellite in weeks, but luckily I had hours taped. I got Rush over here by the kitchen, because he's the granddaddy. I got Beck going in the southwest corner. Northwest is O'Reilly, southeast is Hannity, I think. Honey, is southeast Hannity?"

"How the hell would I know?" came from the kitchen.

"She's sick of it. Keeps me grounded, though. Makes this hallowed ground, the way I see it. Makes it America. America without taxes, and big government, and terrorist bullshit. I knew this was coming, end of the world, been saying it since the sixties. I got out because I love it too much, really. But I'll never leave the U.S. of A. God bless America." Karvel lifted his glass, and we toasted with him.

"Where's Pym?" I asked Garth when Karvel went to lower the volume of the speaker over our table. Given the current circumstance, the idea of a kidnapped Caucasian seemed like it might prove problematic.

"I don't know. Frozen on the ice? Maybe all the way back at our departure site? Last time I saw him, he was running off away from me, following the tracks back in that direction." I could tell by the way Garth said "departure site" that he had avoided telling our hosts of our Tekelian adventure.

"Don't worry about him, dog. He sure wasn't worried about you. You know that fool tried to eat you last night?" I told him that, yes, I did remember the cannibal conversation. "Conversation? Dog, when I got back, I had to pull that lunatic off you. Look at your leg." I did. There was the perfect oval of human teeth marks traced in red on my pale calf.

"Yeah, I saw that when I was stripping you down; I put a little peroxide on it. That'll heal," Karvel told me, returning. "It's a shame about your crew member. Some people, they can't handle being alone down here. All that PC nonsense, it made men soft. Hell, the lesbos are stronger than most of the men nowadays. Me, I love it down here. You make your own reality in this place. The ultimate luxury. But I always lived in my own world, least that's what my wife says."

"I do say that," Mrs. Karvel called from the kitchen. "Because it's the damn truth, even before you dragged me down here."

"So . . . what was with the strip-us-naked thing?" I used this opportunity to ask my host. I felt a big foot kick my knee at the end of this sentence and looked across the table to see Garth was staring me down. We were both currently clad solely in Karvel's bathrobes. It didn't seem like an inappropriate question.

"Hey, don't worry, I ain't one of those," he said, laughing. "Just didn't want to throw your clothes in the incinerator with you in them. Who knows what they're contaminated with? We don't know what happened out there in the world, do we? I was hoping you all would know, but it's pretty clear not one of us does. One minute I'm sitting here watching *Fox & Friends*, then they start talking about some riot. I go get some nachos, next thing you know I come back and it's all dark. It's dark everywhere: TV, phone, Internet. Nothing." Shaking his head, taking a swig of his beer, Karvel drops his voice both in volume and in pitch before continuing. "First thought: nukes. Iran, North Korea, Pakistan, they've been begging for it for years. But a nuclear attack couldn't have taken out everything at once, not even a big one. So I'm thinking, something biological. Then you got a bigger list: add in Syria, Afghanistan, Saudi Arabia, Venezuela, Cuba, Somalia, Chechnya, China, and I sure as hell don't trust Russia. Probably engineered or something, sitting dormant in everybody's system while it spreads across the world. Silently spreading all across the world, see? The smart people, they been talking about this for years. Then on a set time, on a set date, boom, it goes off. Just like that, everyone's dead. Blood in the street, blood pouring from eyes, babies screaming, dogs dying. Everything. We been talking about stuff like that for years, but still, when it happens . . ."

I looked at the painter for a moment, petrified. As he talked, Karvel became increasingly morose, his voice dropping with his shoulders, joining in with the chorus above. It was almost as if you could see the fear radiating off of him, that if you reached out your hand you could feel it blowing out his pores.

"Well, let's hope that's also highly unlikely, right? Could just be a satellite problem, or an international computer virus."

"Yeah, that's what I thought at first. Then the repair and supply plane stopped showing up. We were supposed to get that boiler fixed, damn thing probably won't go over seventy-two degrees without exploding like the Fourth of July—it's a menace. Course, they use computers for everything now, so who knows? Right? Let's just hope it wasn't the Rapture, 'cause if my wife finds out that Jesus came and didn't take us with the righteous, she's going to make my life a hell," he said. "I'm kidding," he followed with. I didn't know about which part.

. . .

After the meal of brown bunnies with Kraft mac and cheese, "Jiffy" mix muffins, and heaping portions of Betty Crocker roasted garlic and cheddar mashed potatoes, Mrs. Karvel cleared our plates and even complimented us on our appetites. Mrs. Karvel was a plain woman who was also plainly a bit intrigued by Garth and me: her smile was a little too wide, her laugh a little too quick, her retreat to the kitchen a little too nervous. I thought this might be a reaction to our race, but that was probably more about me than about her.* I did know that the food was a welcome change from our moment of starvation and weeks of krakt, and after I was done I felt more like a man again. Garth, though, seemed like less of one, having regressed in the presence of his hero. For one thing, he couldn't stop staring at the painter, darting his eyes in Karvel's direction every time the man looked away. When not staring, Garth just rotated his head, slack jawed at this life-size terrarium Karvel had created.

. . .

"It's a state-of-the-art 3.2 Ultra BioDome," Karvel told us as he gave his tour. We had each been given a pair of his pajamas at supper's conclusion. Unfortunately, like many men of big accomplish-

---

* I often forget that to some I actually look "black," not just ethnically but along the "one drop" line. I become comfortable in one category in the world's eyes and then am surprised by the next person's interpretation when it's altogether different. The difficulty lies not in the categories of looking "white" or "black" but in the inability to simply choose one self-image to rest in, never knowing how the next person will view or interact with me. In that sense, Mrs. Karvel's discomfort with my presence as a Negro was more comforting to me than the trepidation I often feel not knowing how I will be perceived.

ment, Karvel was a short guy. Only the pants fit us, and even those just made it as far as our shins before retreating. Above the waist we were naked, but thanks to Garth's bloated physique, I didn't mind this as much as I might have. In contrast to his C-cup breasts and overhanging gut, my own academic torso appeared almost sculpted.

"The 3.2 Ultra, that's top of the line; you don't get something like that at Sam's Club. Hermetically sealed, fully self-contained. Got solar panels all over the roof, even. NASA contracted for these things to colonize Mars someday. The fauna, the exchange of CO_2 and oxygen: it's all set up so we can get our own ecosystem fully self-contained. You can't even find it with infrared satellite imagery: the exhaust system shoots the hot air right down into the ice tunnels, which makes the heat signatures invisible. Not even the government could find us. This is the safest place on the earth, right here."

When one was standing in the middle of the construction, it really was awe inspiring. I'd seen other faux habitats before, but never walked around freely within such a big one.* Even more stunning was the amount of detail that went into the realism of the place. The sky, although stuck in perpetual sunset, was no mere clunky mural painting, it was clearly an actual photograph of a Karvel original, blown up to span the hundreds of yards that constituted the entire ceiling. The sides of the structure were equally meticulous in their attempt to continue the illusion: the room did not appear to end. Rather, the foliage around us became too dense to see through. Besides the apartment that floated above the waterfall, there was no sign that we were not really outside. And yet, despite these nods to realism, the overall look of the room was utterly unreal. The grass we walked on was green, but it was too

* Mostly at the zoo. And the mall.

green. The water that ran through the rambling stream that went diagonally through the space was actually *blue*. The azaleas and roses and tulips that appeared across the space were all, simultaneously, in the most vivid bloom. It was as if we were walking through a world that had been colorized with markers by an enthusiastic eight-year-old.

"God created nature. I just improved on it."

"NASA's biodome looks like this?" I asked, hard-pressed to imagine this landscape populated by bookish men in white overcoats. Garth flashed me a look, darting his eyes back to his hero in fear of finding him offended, but Karvel was indulgent, even jovial.

"Oh no, no, no. This is all custom," he said, walking to the water's edge. Bending down on his knees, he took a cup into his hands, sipped some water, and motioned for us to do the same. "For years, I kept painting all of those pictures, trying to create a perfect world. One day, I'm standing there with a brush in my hand, and I realize: I don't just want to look at this world, I want to *live* in it."

"See, that's what I been talking about. That's brilliance." Garth took to his knees too, gathering some of the stream's water in his hands. Thomas Karvel's palms went to Garth's shoulders, blessing.

"A man who lives a life worth living, he's a hunter. He hunts for something, he hunts for his dream. And his dream is always the same thing: to create a world he can truly live in, without Big Brother enslaving him to mediocrity. So I created this free land. First within my art, and now in life," Karvel said, motioning grandly around him, the king of all we could survey. "Had to come down here to do it too. As blank as the morning snow. A clean canvas. A place with no violence and no disease, no poverty and no crime. No taxes or building codes. This is a place without history. A place without stain. No yesterday, only tomorrow. Only beauty. Only the world the way it's supposed to be."

"This river tastes like grape Kool-Aid!" Garth exclaimed, staring at the bit left in his cupped fingers in disbelief.

"Yeah, but with Splenda instead of the real stuff. I tried to use corn syrup, but it killed all the damn koi."

The cottage we were to stay in was the adjective *quaint* made manifest. At least from the outside. With a real thatched roof and stone façade, it seemed as if it had been sitting there for centuries. Even from a distance, I could see that the windows bore the distorted surfaces of handblown glass, the candlelight flickering behind each one running beautifully along their imperfect surfaces.

"That's *Lamplight Brook*." Garth turned to me, as if this was supposed to mean something.

"That's right. This was the original model I used to paint it. Bought it with the money from that painting. I had it removed stone by stone from Bourton-on-the-Water, in England. Took them thirteen months, four jet trips to fly it down. No expense was spared."

This last part was not entirely true. While the outside of this house indicated that we might find a plush and comfortable household just beyond its threshold, what I found instead when I entered was just an empty shed. The floor itself seemed to be original, the wood beams were wide and old and well worn, but there was not much else in this space besides them. Gas-fueled "candles" hid just below the windows, as did some sort of piped device that hummed so loudly I could feel the vibrations through my bare feet, but no furniture. Our interior tour revealed that this house had no back. After only ten or twelve feet, the building ended abruptly at the metal wall of the BioDome, giving the impression that God was cutting the building in half with his knife. Worse still, that knife seemed to have cut off the part of the Lamplight Brook that contained the bathroom.

"You can stay here. I've got some packing material you can use for mattresses. It ain't much, but you'll fix it up."

"Don't worry about us, we'll be fine, Mr. Karvel, sir. We are taken care of, don't you worry," Garth gushed, ensuring I could make no statement to the contrary, not even "Where do I take a crap?"

"Good, good. Well, the tools are in the back. You might as well take that patch of land past the cottage; I can't see that from my place. Need anything, you just holler, 'kay boys?"

"What tools?" I asked as soon as Karvel had fully departed. I saw him walk down the path toward his quarters, pausing to snap an orchid off a low hanging branch on the way. What was that made of? I wondered. Mars bars?

"Well, they have a food budget, don't they? So when I first got here I promised we'd do some vegetable gardening. You know, to cover what we're going to eat, in addition to just helping out around the place."

"What else did you tell him? Did you tell him about the others?"

"Told him we were working for a corporation harvesting water. He liked that. I left out the snow monkey part. You want him to know that, you tell him."

"Good. I really don't think this guy's prepared for a Negro invasion," I said. Garth's head cocked to the side as if yanked.

"You can't help yourself, can you? The man takes us in. Feeds us. Almost clothes us. And there you go with the racism talk."

"Just because someone's not scared of minorities, doesn't mean they want to be one."

Outside our window, Karvel paused on his walk to pull another pink orchid from the low-hanging branch of a cypress tree. Then he put the flower in his mouth and chewed.

· · ·

It took most of the next three days to clear out the patch of vege-
tation to the far side of Lamplight Brook cottage. It was difficult to
define a "day," really, because the sun was always setting* in
Karvel's world. It did get a bit dimmer at "night," though, and this
helped our well-earned hours of sleep. It was hard, muscle-aching
work. I needed all the rest I could steal.

It wasn't that the roots of the plants were particularly deep, or
that the soil was particularly hard, it was just that there was a lot of
it. The spot we cleared was nearly half the size of a basketball
court, and the removed flora was strewn as high as the three-fifths
of a house we were living in. Still, we took great care to keep the
roots of our transplants intact, and the majority of the greenery
was still living. I was in shock those first days, I even knew at the
time, reeling from the trauma of the past weeks and the oddity of
the present. But it felt good to work, to focus on my hands instead
of my mind. To not be a freeloader on someone else's land. I even
started to tune the ever-present voices out. This habitat was so
much a creation of our host that, in a Lockean sense, it was a relief
to establish some form of ownership through our labor.

By the afternoon of the fourth day, Garth and I were finally prepared to stop the reaping of the aesthetic but useless flowers and
begin sowing the vegetables and fruits we could live on. When
Mrs. Karvel came by with our daily rations (Stove Top stuffing
mix, Sylvia's canned collard greens, and Spam) Garth made a point
to show her our progress before she scuttled away as usual, making the request for the seeds we would need for the next stage in
our victory garden. Mrs. Karvel seemed perpetually stressed,
rarely out of motion any time I saw her. Standing still for a moment, without food or an emptied plate or a feather duster in
hand, seemed almost a painful act for her.

* Or possibly rising, I was never quite sure.

"You gonna have to make that patch bigger, ain't you?" she said, looking out at the rows of rich, dark earth we had uncovered. This comment came to me as a surprise, because I thought if anything we'd perhaps been overzealous.

"You want it bigger?" I muttered aloud, more out of shock than as an actual question.

"Honey, we ain't got enough food to feed you. A few months, tops, but it ain't like the cans in storage are breeding new ones," she told us, leaning forward and dropping her voice as if her husband might hear us, as far away as he was. "This is the deal. Either you guys got to figure out a way to grow us all some new food or you tell me how the hell we can get out of this goddamn fishbowl."

CHAPTER XIX

IN the two weeks it took to clear and sow a patch of land big enough for a suitable amount of vegetables to be grown, my head was in my job. My heart, though, was still in the frozen hell along with Angela. It hurt, and when it didn't that was only because it had frozen numb. I thought of her, and of them, often. But not too often. I couldn't call, I couldn't write, and I had no real power to change this situation. So I made myself busy in work instead. And as I labored, I learned the truth behind the mysteries of this new world where I found myself. I discovered the smell of lavender was not coming from the flowers of the same name: it was pumped out from the air ducts that lined the far walls and appeared in the bushes, through vents disguised in concrete made to look like igneous rock formations. After a while, I didn't take notice of it, except during those times every few hours when the smell cycled, and all of a sudden there was a new odor in the air, spearmint or rose, or lemon scent. My favorite was the wave of jasmine that hit at exactly 12:30 P.M. every day, because this meant it was time to take our lunch break.

The vivid floral bushes that surrounded everything in this landscape were similarly assisted in their otherworldly blooms. Part of the reason that it took us so long to clear the space we needed for our vegetable garden was that there were so many different water lines leading out to the fauna beyond. These messily woven hoses would have been hard to untangle in themselves, but what made it even more difficult was that each hose contained water with a different color ink. There was pink water to make the pink bushes pinkish, purple water to make the purple flowers more purplectic, red water to make the red flowers appear to bleed the new blood of the vegetative world. And to even call it water is not truly accurate, because there was not only an ample amount of paint in these concoctions, but also a good amount of steroids, to keep the plants in perpetual bloom. These colored lines shot around the room in miles of tubing, crossing over each other to deliver their gifts in seemingly random order.*

The animals too, while appearing carefree (though really not wild), lived a carefully maintained existence. The white rabbits, for instance, were managed as closely as any rosebush. The afternoon following my discovery of a litter of fresh young rabbits hopping around close to the stream trying to taste what it had to offer, the bunnies were gone. Clearly they were picked up and moved out of the main arena, although what fate they headed to I didn't want to think about. Mrs. Karvel served a stew that very evening, but maybe the painter was right and this was just coincidence. Likewise managed were the white birds who populated the upper regions of the terrarium, the ones that liked to sit on our cottage's nonfunctioning roof and coo loudly. Each evening after supper these birds were gathered up by hand and placed behind the inner dome in cages, only to be released the following morning. Why anyone would make the effort to transport a dozen pigeons down to Antarctica I couldn't understand; just because they were white didn't seem enough reason. The birds' feces were white too, but they weren't cherished. All the animals were white: I heard some

---

* Unfortunately, the greener than green grass that surrounded our little three-fifths house, so mossy and moist beneath our feet, took its brilliance from a different source: it was fed by the runoff of the BioDome's septic system.

scurrying in the walls while sleeping on my mat and half expected to see a white lab mouse run by.

The person who did all of this work, the person who did all the work in the dome except for Garth and me, was Mrs. Karvel. I woke up every morning to the sound of her setting up her ladder to dust the wide leaves of the trees with her rainbow-colored feather duster. By the time I was dressed and down at the river for a drink, she was usually finishing combing it of any unsightly floating objects with a pool net, having cleaned the filter already. It was Mrs. Karvel who removed the dead monarch butterflies, placing them gently into Ziploc bags.* It was Mrs. Karvel who lit the very sun in the sky: we could see her shadow behind the ceiling's façade as she changed the lightbulbs accordingly. All of this was done in addition to her preparation of meals, laundry, and more mundane duties. If she slept, I'm sure she did so fully dressed, with a ladle in one hand and a Swiffer in the other.

"That's why she wants to leave here. She just needs more help," Garth dismissed: he wanted a petty reason for the rejection of his utopia. Sounded like a good enough reason to me, though.

In contrast to his wife, the great painter himself went to bed early and with regularity in timing. This I knew because the second he went down, the world went dark, the sunset simply blowing out, being replaced by the faintest of stars, stuck to the roof in the form of glow-in-the-dark decals. In the last stage of our garden installation, this was our cue to begin work, we having switched our work hours from the daytime to the night by that point. This was done by the request of Mrs. Karvel, and while no explanation was given, it seemed clear the reason was that, although Mr. Karvel wanted us to do this work, he wasn't interested in seeing it.

Working nights, I began to be able to tell when it was that

---

* Scrapbooking, her husband told me.

Thomas Karvel not only went to bed but fell fast asleep as well. It wasn't that he snored or, if he did, that his apartment was close enough that I could hear. What I would hear instead was the sound of his waterfall, whose roar accompanied the radio voices every moment of our day, spontaneously ceasing its voluminous Kool-Aid spew. The water went off, and the loudspeakered pundits with it. It was an abrupt silence, as if someone had simply turned off a faucet, and this of course is exactly what Mrs. Karvel did. Sound removed, the artifice of this environment was even more obvious, because without this roar a second, more mechanical one was revealed from the boiler room. This was clearly the waterfall's primary purpose: to mask the bass intrusion of the engines that kept this South Pole oasis a nearly tropical seventy-two degrees Fahrenheit. The waterfall was only off for maybe an hour, long after midnight. After Mrs. Karvel had entered the little door below the lightly dripping fall and attended to whatever hot and agitated machinery the room held, she emerged, climbed the earthen stairs to their apartment, and turned the waterfall's supply back on, its contents pouring down again and thus hiding the little door below it in both sight and sound. Karvel himself restarted the taped verbal spew hours later.

Once, after two weeks on our plantation, I was returning the dishes from our dinner to the kitchen to save Mrs. Karvel the bother. The painter himself was out on his deck, standing over his waterfall, staring at a canvas in the same way he had been off and on for a few days now. This canvas rested on an easel, and Karvel would look at it, get up as close as he could, and then step back and look at the room, repeating the action every minute or so, pausing at both places of inspection before switching again. As I walked closer, I tried to figure out what the hell he was focusing on but couldn't—his eyes definitely looked at different parts of his expansive view. Maybe his subject moved, I figured, maybe it was a bird or something and he was trying to find it again (although as far as I was concerned one albino pigeon looked pretty much the same as any other). I climbed the stairs, prepared to head for the kitchen, and as my head peaked onto the landing I got a good glimpse of Thomas Karvel close up, without him seeing me. That's when I noticed the weird thing. He had no brush. No brush, no paint. Nothing but the painting itself, which he walked up to so close that the oil almost touched his nose.

"You planning a new work?" I asked. It was none of my business, and in general I just tried to stay out of the man's way, not wear out my welcome. But I had to know. Not only did I have to know but I had to repeat myself, louder. The guy was gone, mentally. Stuck walking back and forth before his creation. When Thomas Karvel finally looked up at me, he was a man possessed, lost in a vision that had nothing to do with his retinas. There was a good two seconds before the realization of who and where he was seemed to hit him, and then a smile erupted across his pale face.

"You want to see it?" he asked me. Garth would be jealous. Garth would be blind with envy, I thought, and already planned to amuse myself teasing him about his missed opportunity. Hours of fun to be had, I was sure. I placed the dishes at the top of the stairs and went over to my host. The painting, it looked just like every other Thomas Karvel painting, and besides the one that brought us here, each one of them looked basically the same to me.

"It's nice. It's really nice," I told him, smiling down at the canvas. It was a compliment on autopilot, without thought, only purpose. Looking a moment more, just to be polite, I finally got it. It was his view of the entire dome. There was our little partial house at the far wall, his white animals, his sucralose stream. Our vegetable garden and the impact it made on the environment was obscured just as he insisted it be from his view.

"Are you done painting it?"

"Painting it? What? The painting was done years ago. Years. No, what I'm still creating is the land itself."

I looked around at his land, this hall, this cave. It seemed nothing if not complete. It was a world without chaos, or really even the hint of it. Every detail was man-made, controlled. And specifically controlled by this man, its master planner. A utopia in a bottle. Not my paradise, but certainly his. Unless he was planning to float expanses of cotton candy from the rafters, I couldn't see what was left to do.

"You want to change things around? Redecorate? Go for a different look?"

"No. There is only one look. There is only one vision. Perfection isn't about change, diversity. It's about getting closer to that one vision. And there's still so much, so much to do. Like the palms. Look at those damn palms, in the back there; they keep trying to grow any way they want. Look at them, then look at the painting."

I looked. There were palms, in the back of the dome's inner space, spreading out their umbrella foliage just beyond the rest of the tree line. They were a bit out of place, a tropical presence in this reproduction of European fantasy, but it wasn't like that was the oddest thing going on in this space.

"So you're going to have them cut down and taken out?" I asked.

"Do you know how much money it costs to ship fully grown palm trees to Antarctica? No, they're part of the vision. But look at the painting, then look at them again," Karvel insisted, clearly annoyed by the fact that I couldn't even notice what seemed to be bugging him so much.

"Coconuts," Mrs. Karvel said. I hadn't heard her arrive, hadn't heard her pick up the tray of dirty dishes or come up behind me.

"Coconuts!" her husband screamed, staring at the painting,

pointing at the little oil dots he'd made at the top of his palms' trunks. "Ever-loving coconuts!" I looked back out at the actual trees, and he was right, no coconuts.

"Because I told you, when you were ordering those things," his wife began with the weariness of an explanation often started, "that type of palm you wanted doesn't grow coconuts, but you said—"

"The other kind was too skinny. It needed to have a thicker trunk."

"It ain't natural is all."

"Nature was created to serve man. And now this man wants some coconuts up there." Karvel paused to get his message out, stopping where he could to control his temper. It wasn't menace there, a threat of violence. Just frustration. Just an utter conviction of what was right and what must happen.

"This man wants coconuts up there," his wife said back to him, the repetition of his point careful and deliberate as if she were dealing with the single-minded obsession of an overly indulged child.

"Thank you, honey," he said to her, appeased, and since he was already leaning in at the canvas looking for the next flaw, he didn't see her roll her eyes. But I did. Her bloodshot eyes. They rolled around like her corneas were going on a world tour. There was no sigh, no word of complaint, but there was expression. Following Thomas Karvel's lead, I looked away from this moment of intimacy as well and pretended I didn't see any of it.

I don't know if, somehow, she already had coconuts in storage. I don't know if she made the coconuts out of clay or papier-mâché: it was impossible to see if they were real because they were so high up. At least three stories. And I really don't know how she got them up there. I can't imagine a ladder that high, or her scaling the trunks in mountain-climbing gear. All I know is that she did it.

Less than a week later, they were there, out of nowhere. Some-
time in the night, quietly enough that neither Garth nor I heard
her. Brown balls in the air. Resting under the treetops as if God had
made them grow there.

· · ·

We were winding down in our little agricultural project. The seeds
were planted, I had no idea if they would grow. But to celebrate,
Mrs. Karvel invited us across the dome. The brisket smell started
twelve hours before mealtime, beckoning from the barbecue. We
sat on the terrace before a table set with sauce and napkins. Karvel
even turned the voices off the speakers, substituting hymnals. It
was Sunday supper, and Mrs. Karvel was in the kitchen getting the
next course ready, singing along.

"This whole thing, it must have taken a lot to create?" I asked
our host, looking out at it all.

"To get this ready, it took years. And most of my money—but
still cheaper than taxes. It's modular, made the pieces up north,
shipped it down, helicoptered it from there, then they put it up.
Took a lot. Plus, when you're talking custom-made, you're talking
extra labor. See that ceiling up there? That was special made. I
don't just mean the painting either. On the original plans, the
whole roof was supposed to be glass. They tried to tell me I had to
keep it that way. But the sky, that's my big thing, my signature. The
scene wouldn't be complete without the real Thomas Karvel heavens glowing above."

"It was supposed to be a greenhouse, then? To take energy from
the sun. Heat, food for the plants, everything?" I said, my mind
spinning. Seeing the direction I was revolving off in, Karvel
quickly interrupted.

"Yes, but I took care of that: I had them put solar panels all over
the new roof, then put in ultraviolet lights behind the gauze the

sky's painted on. Cost was no option; I do something, I do it right. Matter of fact, speaking of the panels, you boys want to do us a really big service?"

Garth, eager fanboy that he was, said yes before the proposition was spilled. Considering that our farming project was at a close, we needed some other purpose to serve to justify our citizenship, our pull on the resources. It wasn't that this was the world I would have imagined for myself, or even chosen. It was just that there were no other practical options. Because it was very, very cold out there. And despite our second-class citizenship, it was still pretty comfortable in here.

"Now I know, it's risky going outside. That air, who knows what's in it. It's a danger going out, but you did survive it before, an hour more can't hurt too much. And we got those solar panels up there, and every few minutes or so you hear—" Karvel stopped, reached for the audio remote. A rare moment of silence in the chamber followed. Then came a sound, one I'd heard but never paid attention to before. Metal scraping. Darting his head up to stare at the ceiling and its perpetual sunset clouds, Karvel grimaced. "There it goes. You hear that? You're not supposed to hear that. That's not how it's supposed to be, that racket," he said and turned back on all the voices talking.

An hour later, we were headed for the roof. Fortunately, Mrs. Karvel had been less than exact in her following of her husband's orders on our arrival, and instead of burning our snowsuits, she'd just washed them instead. We dressed and made our way back to the terrarium's exit hatch, located behind a discreet and wholly cosmetic cave formation, itself hidden by an abundant cluster of hydrangea shrubs that distracted attention in a pink trademarked by Mattel.

Past the door, what was revealed was the hard, cold, industrial shell that kept our controlled world from the real one's chaos.

Here, the sound of the all-powerful boiler echoed violently and you could feel it in the air like humidity. A narrow corridor of metal and concrete rose up several stories to the ceiling, lined with storage containers and what appeared to be freezers. There was even a sailboat back here, wrapped in a tarp. It wasn't a yacht, but it was still three times the size of a canoe, just small enough to ride the fifty yards down the Kool-Aid stream if you were so inclined. Past that, we saw the red "exit" signs pointed to an open garage door, where his and her snowmobiles with racing stripes sat waiting. On a metal balcony far above, I saw the image of Mrs. Karvel, so out of place in this industrial environment, waving at us. Braving one of the grated ladders that were embedded into the outer shell, Garth and I huffed our way up to her, climbing two stories of metal catwalks to do so. When we arrived on the right level, however, Mrs. Karvel had disappeared. It was only after we walked out to the exact place we had seen her that I noticed there was an actual room hidden up here, off to the side. And that's when the smell hit me, followed by the image of Mrs. Karvel sitting on a large cardboard box, smoking, a heavy pink parka draped over her wiry frame. The rolled joint smoking in her hand.

"I grow it over to the side of the waterfall, near the boiler. Gets good heat," she said with a shrug, by way of explanation. "Usually come out here, light up first, then do the washing, manage the machinery, organize the meals. By the time I'm done, you can't really smell it on me quite so much. Not with all that perfume he's got going in there. He knows, but, y'know . . ." She trailed off, the smoke from her narrow spliff dancing optimistically in front of her.

It was then that I noticed something even more shocking: a cold breeze that I could feel even in all of my padding. The window just past Mrs. Karvel was open. I must have let out a bit of a gasp at the sight of this, because my sound made her shoot her head back up, and her mind back into the present. It was Garth, though, who said what I was thinking.

"Hey," a wounded sound, less a word than an emotion. "I thought this place was supposed to be hermetically sealed and self-contained and all that?"

"Yeah, well, you gut a couple hundred feet of high-yielding plant life from the plans and replace that with lawn sod and rhododendrons, and you kind of have to throw that whole 'self-contained' thing out the window." And then, coming to the end of her smoke, Mrs. Karvel did just that, flicking her roach out the open window in such a practiced, casual motion that I imagined there must be a huge pile of similar butts forming a frozen mountain in the snow below.

"There's the door over there, that'll get you up on the roof, boys. I'll just wait here till you're done." Lighting a cigarette from a produced pack, Mrs. Karvel motioned to the metal door with her elbow. The little room was clearly a storage room, filled with tobacco cartons and identical yellow boxes with illustrated dead vermin stuck on the sides. "Tommy likes bunnies, but he sure don't like rats," his wife offered by way of explanation. Mrs. Karvel had stacked some of the poison boxes in the shapes of chairs and a table, a group of eight with an old blanket on top formed a makeshift bed against the far wall, rumpled women's magazines lined in a neat pile just beside it. It looked poisonous but comfortable.

"Mrs. Karvel, you don't have to wait. This could take a long time, trying to find out which of the solar panels is making the noise, out of a whole roof of them," I told her.

"Nope, that won't take you long. There's only one out there, and they're all together on one hinge." Mrs. Karvel took a long puff on her cigarette after that. "The original redesign, it had solar panels all over the roof, but then Tommy changed that so he could add satellite dishes aiming in six different angles. Y'know, so that damn satellite radio never goes on the fritz or nothing, God forbid. The solar panels there, they're just so our accountant could get us a tax break. Mostly, this whole place runs on gas. Tommy likes to forget that."

"Well then, what will you do when your gas runs out?" I asked in disbelief.

Mrs. Karvel thought about it for a moment, sucked on her menthol, then blew a cloud out. " 'Spect that solar panel is going to get mighty useful."

. . .

The entire roof surface, we saw, standing outside, was painted in the colors of the American flag. Red and white stripes ran in front of us, and there was a patch of blue with white stars all the way at the other end, in the corner. If he was trying to hide his heaven, he wasn't trying very hard. The dome was covered in snowdrifts along its sides, part of the reason we hadn't seen it at first when we originally arrived here. It was a flat roof at the very top, curved on the sides; it wasn't as much a dome as it was a giant jelly mold. But it was all-American. Whether Karvel wanted to make sure the helicopters had the right place or he thought Old Glory was some kind of talisman, I never discovered. Even the communications satellite dishes had been painted, each according to the stripe it sat on.

We sat too, Garth and I, on the flat roof of Thomas Karvel's BioDome for a long time. Appraising this scene. Sitting in our snowsuits with our asses cold and numb, but not as numb as the rest of me was becoming. The solar panel was right beside us, positioned perfectly to take the place of one of the flag's white stars.

It was the size of a Ping-Pong table. On a good day, a day of sun and light, it might have offered enough power to operate the coffee machine back inside. This was good news, because when this place ran out of power, we were going to freeze to death, and I imagined a good cup of coffee might bring comfort as we died.

"It's about to get dark down here. Not nighttime dark, but winter dark. There won't be any sunlight for months. These panels don't work without sunlight. And there's just one. What's he going to do then?" Garth said, his voice cracking.

"What's Karvel going to do? Man, are you crazy? Forget him. What the hell are *we* going to do?" I asked. Garth said nothing. For a long time, he kept saying it. I started talking again when I felt like he was going to start crying.

"First we have to get them to turn down the heat in there, turn down the lights more, anything we can. Then we have to go get some oil. There's a tanker back at our base camp. We could get our old solar panels too; even the Creole camp had more than this."

"And the rifler. Maybe we can drill for some damn oil."

"We don't know anything about refining crude oil."

"Dog," Garth told me, "I'll burn that shit in a cup to stay warm if I have to." Thinking of this image, he drifted off.

"And now we bring the others. Angela, my cousin, the other guys. This is our leverage, Karvel can't say no now."

"The snow monkeys," Garth whispered so low I could barely hear him over the wind. His eyes widened as he said it, and his jaw dropped when he was done and I could see the horror that was engulfing him.

"Yeah, but Karvel's got some guns. We'll do what we have to do to defend ourselves."

"No, the snow monkeys," Garth said, pointing. I followed his gloved digit out onto the snow-covered plain. And there, past a ridge not far from the direction I recognized we too had come from only weeks before, I saw them as well. An army of a hundred or more pale, shrouded figures, camped out. Rough igloos constructed in a circular formation. I didn't know how long they had been there, but I did know why they were there. They had come for us.

"But then why so many, dog? If they're just hunting us down, why bring an army when one could kick our collective black ass?"

CHAPTER XX

WE wasted a lot of time just getting Karvel to believe what we were saying: that they existed, that they were out there, that they had come. It was only because we were so relentless, and because the painter started to respond to our fear with ample fear of his own, that Karvel finally relented and agreed to at least see what had made us so excited.

"Nobody's busting in my dome, I'll tell you that right now. That's where I draw the line. I didn't come all the way down here to get bushwhacked by some mythological creatures."

To protect himself from being exposed to even a room that had been tainted by the outside air, Karvel insisted on wearing protective gear before entering the work area behind his grand illusion. I think he would have preferred a space suit, something airtight with its own supply of oxygen. In lieu of that, however, Karvel settled for a beekeeper's suit because it covered his body completely, particularly his head. It seemed the BioDome was originally intended to house a hive population as well, for the purposes of pollination and honey production.

"I like honey, hell, I love it. But I don't like bugs. I like butterflies, we got lots of them. And ladybugs." Karvel nervously chattered as he dressed. It was clear during our ascent to Mrs. Karvel's little room that Thomas Karvel rarely ventured behind the set of his own masterpiece. If ever. Garth and I, the recent visitors, the newly arrived guests, had to direct him through the scaffolding to navigate the place. His whole time back there Karvel wore a look of mild disgust, as if he was being forced to peer into the putrid bowels of his beloved. When we finally found our way back to Mrs. Karvel's poisonous little storage room up high, a wave of floral air freshener greeted us. Its spray was so recent and heavy that the smell of ozone hung nearly as heavily as the ones of weed and nicotine beneath it. Nobody bothered to mention these aromas, of course, because now there was something far more disturbing in the room than rat bait. A cache of rifles was leaning against the far wall. Mrs. Karvel was vigorously polishing the largest of them.

"Honey," the painter asked. "Did you see anything funny out—"

"I'm not looking out there, Tommy. You're looking out there. You look out there, and you deal with it," Karvel's wife interrupted him, rubbing the oil cloth down the shaft as if she thought a genie might come out. There was a scope on the camouflage hunting rifle in her hand, and for the moment she had no problem looking through that, her bloodshot eye engorged and magnified on the other side. Satisfied with its cleanliness, Mrs. Karvel handed it to me firmly. I took it to the window, looked down the gun's sight to the place of interest below.

"There," I said, looking up from the weapon, calling Karvel over to take my place. "There" were the igloos. "There" were the tracks in the snow. Even through his beekeeping helmet, Karvel could make that out, or at least something out.

"Oh boy. Yup. I see something."

"Shoot 'em!" his wife yelled. Though she wasn't getting any closer to the window, Mrs. Karvel threw me another hunting rifle from where she was standing. I handed it to Garth, so she threw me another one.

"Look, I take care of in here. I always have taken care of in here, in our home. And you're supposed to take care of what's out there. That's the way it's always been. That's the pact. So get out-side and shoot them." Karvel lurched up from the gun's scope in response, face hidden behind the mesh of his helmet. There was a moment when I expected protests about air quality and biological warfare to emerge from behind the metal mask, but after a few seconds the only words that managed to make themselves heard were "yes" and "dear."

. . .

Thomas Karvel looked even smaller outside, in the open world, the one he didn't create. The painter was clearly not someone who was used to being out of his element, and even as we walked those few feet, I noticed a change in his demeanor. I could see the Teke-lian base camp from where we stood; the rifle's scope helped, but it wasn't needed. I could see them moving around individually as well, even make out their robes flapping lightly in the polar wind. Squatting down, I lifted the heavy Browning to my head, undid the safety with my thumb, and aimed the barrel up and over in the direction opposite the camp, and pulled the trigger. Everyone jumped: both men beside me and all of those creatures down there.

"What the hell are you up to?" Karvel demanded, the mist of his exhalation rising up through his mesh face mask.

"I'm scaring them off," I told him, and I said it like I knew what I was doing.

"But how you know them things even know what a gun is?" asked Garth, and I nodded back that this was an excellent observa-tion, then proceeded to take another shot directly at the Tekelian stronghold. This bullet made a definite impression, taking a block off one of the structures they had created, spraying a cloud of sharded ice. The impact sent robes running, robes hiding for cover.

Who is God now? I thought, but then tried to calm my heart and temper.

"I still can't hardly see anything. Are they leaving?" Karvel asked me. When I looked over at him, he wasn't even facing the right direction. He was already staring back to the roof door of his precious dome as if he was embarrassed by my action, or just bored.

"Down over there, they're coming toward us," Garth shouted, and I looked to the far side and saw a line of five or six of the pale beasts trying to come wide around a snowbank and make it closer to the dome. Aiming again, I took another shot just in front of them, somewhat relieved when the bullet missed and only more clouds of snow were created on impact. To my surprise, though, the invaders kept coming. This platoon of Tekelians didn't run for cover, try to protect themselves behind a snowdrift or simply haul ass in one direction or the other. Crouched down in their garments, slowly stepping, they kept coming toward us. I reloaded, clicked the barrel back together loud enough for them to hear at a distance, but they didn't pause, just continued. It was then that I realized they weren't worrying about being seen. It was absurd, but from the way they were moving, it appeared they were worried I would *hear* them coming. They were so convinced that their supposed whiteness camouflaged them against the snow, they seemed to think they were invisible.

"See who?" Karvel asked when I said this aloud. "I don't see anybody. Are you sure somebody's out there?" the painter asked, annoyed. In frustration I whipped off his beekeeper's mask, took his head in my hands to aim it at the scene below as these monsters of the past came at us.

"There, right there, in front of your face. Those gray things," I told him, not even aware of my tone until Garth put a firm hand on my arm to calm me down.

"What? What? I don't see nothing. Is this your idea of a joke?" Karvel repeated without a hint of awareness, looking right at where the Tekelians crept.

It was then, looking past the painter and his biggest fan to the other end of the roof behind us, that I saw what we should have been worried about the whole time. First, at the far lip of the roof plateau we stood on, a small dot of albino head popped into view. Then, several more heads alongside it. Before I could even utter my warning, I saw the band of creatures those heads were attached to. They were pulling themselves up the side of the BioDome, over by the forty-nine stars and the one solar panel. A second line of attack. Garth turned in time to see the first creature hoist itself completely onto the roof to get us. The creature stood at almost the opposite end of the 3.2 Ultra BioDome's roof, its colossal frame nearly reaching the sun. Silhouetted as it was against the blue sky, Thomas Karvel finally saw what he was up against.

"Cheese and crackers. What the hell is that?" he asked, pulling on my sleeve as if I could truly answer him. "Man, he's huge. Look at the size of him. What's he doing? I think that thing's making a snowball. Well, if they're just going to throw snowballs then—" Karvel said, stopping abruptly when the first frozen projectile hit the side of his head, knocking him to the roof and into a mild concussion. More iced balls drilled into our backs as we struggled to pull the unconscious master back to the exit door.

• • •

The BioDome door was metal, meant to keep out Martians and snow-loving Islamic militants, so for the moment it held attacking hordes at bay. This was good, because the Tekelians were really trying to get in, and we really didn't want them to. Cowering as we were, we listened to the thunder of the door shaking under the brutal onslaught. Piling every heavy rat-emblazoned box we could in front of it just in case, we also locked the door to the corridor as we left the room. Dragged unconscious out into the hall, Thomas Karvel lay on his back before us, unaware as the three of us discussed our options, trying our best to yell over and otherwise ignore the sounds of angry fists that seemed to come from all over the outer hull.

"Well that plan didn't work, did it?"

"No, ma'am, it did not," we agreed.

"Then you boys need to call for help," Mrs. Karvel told us with so much calm and acceptance of our improbable situation that I began to realize she was probably heavily medicated as a rule. Trying to match her subdued tones, I made the point that unfortunately there was no one whom it was possible to call: no police, no national guard, no anything.

"Get your friends, the co-workers you said they captured. Whatever you have to do, you do it. We got guns, we just need the people to hold them off, kill them if they try to come in here. And get me some ice for Tommy's head too, he's going to have quite the lump on him."

In the excitement of the moment, motivated largely by a desire to simply run away, I seized on the request to get help as if it was my destiny. Not a thought did I give to the actual logistics of how we would manage to escape the 3.2 Ultra BioDome unprotected, or make it back through the frozen wasteland and repeat the journey that had almost killed me, or how we would do all this in time to make it back here for whatever siege this white woman had in mind. These questions must have also occurred to Mrs. Karvel, because as she stared down at her husband's slack face, her plans became more specific.

"We got two snowmobiles: Tommy got him a real good blue one, and got me a pink one to match. But you can't take 'em, can you? Because the garage door is right down there, facing their camp. As soon as you open it, they gonna be all on us. All on us," she repeated, standing up and grabbing me by the shoulder as if I intended to disagree with her. I wasn't. "You boys, you take the exhaust tunnel. Exit's in the mechanical room. Don't go near the boiler, that thing's an accident waiting to happen, just head for the back door. That'll get you far; that tunnel comes up out past where you say they are. You take that, you get out past them, and you get us some goddamn help. You hear me?"

• • •

I heard very well. Packing my old snow gear with Slim Jims and PowerBar gel this time, I was ready to get the hell out of there. The exhaust tunnel, it seemed, was perfect for our escape, a better solution we could not have asked for. In his fear that his precious dome would somehow be located by rogue nations with heat-seeking satellites, Thomas Karvel had also provided himself with the perfect escape hatch. Walking past it, I could easily see that this boiler system was a truly monumental construction, something I would have paused to be awed by had the moment allowed for it. After cranking off the water of the waterfall, Garth and I walked under its last sweet drops to get to the mechanical room's door and make our way out of Karvel's utopia. Without the waterfall, it was loud. In the room, though, it was absolute cacophony. The roar was the first thing that attacked my senses as we began our trudge. Clogs, pistons, lubes reverberating like a junkyard orgy. Before the vibrations could overwhelm me, I was hit by another assault. The heat. We walked through what felt to me like a nearly solid wall of heat. The main interior of the 3.2 Ultra BioDome was kept at a perfect seventy-two degrees Fahrenheit. Within the boiler room, though, it felt like twice that.

"This is unbearable," I complained, wiping the sweat that had instantly appeared upon my brow.

"Enjoy it while it lasts, dog. You going to be cold soon enough," Garth responded.

Still, in that moment, as sweat coated my body in a vain attempt to cool me down, it seemed that the walk back to the exhaust fan exit was endless. I had assumed that the boiler room was just little, merely covering the space under the waterfall and deck above, but this mechanical area went beyond the confines of the Karvels' living quarters and spread back all the way to the dome's edge. The supposed "room" was larger than a house, with pipes interlooping between the metal constructs in a way that only hinted at order.

The exhaust fan itself rose not to the height of my waist but twenty feet beyond, to the height of the ceiling itself. As the blades swung before us too fast to see, there was only the slightest of breezes to be felt and that came from behind us as the boiling air rushed to exit out of the dome to the great chill beyond. Through the blur of the blades, I could see there was nothing beyond the dome but darkness. Outside, the exhaust tunnel that led into the subterranean ice caves was large enough to park a bus in, and dark enough to hide it there. Although the blue of the ice could be seen beyond, it was far from a welcoming vision. As I looked into the dim abyss, the thought of walking out into it and all the way back to Tekeli-li to enlist our co-workers to do battle seemed the suicide mission that it was.

"Brother, listen to me," I yelled to Garth over the din. "This plan is crazy. We're never going to beat those monsters here, even with all of us." I put a hand on his beefy arm as he reached to open the exit door. Trying to give him a squeeze he could feel even through his padded coat, I leaned in closer. "We should go back. Go back, get that sailboat, drag it with us. Then when we get the others, we all make a break for Tsalal. *Tsalal.* It's out there, man, Pym knows where it is. We find him, we find a real way out of here. Black and warm and away from all this beyond the pale bullshit."

"Dog, I ain't doing the Karvels like that. Why don't you just shut *your* pale ass up and keep an eye out for those snow monkeys? Okay?"

Garth aimed a look of annoyance over his shoulder at me while he pushed the bar on the exit door. For this reason, he didn't see how prescient his advice had been. Looking beyond Garth out the door, I saw not the expanse of the tunnel but the expanse of a robe draped off of Tekelian shoulders. In that moment, my doom seemed immediate. In horror I looked, because what massive shoulders these were. Though it had been only a few loose weeks since my last close encounter with the breed, I'd already forgotten the improbable size of them. In my mind, I had pushed out their horror. This was the back of a creature that could kill us simply by falling. This was a monster capable of crushing our bones and the meat they held with such speed that we would feel it before we saw it coming. And one was guarding the exit door, ready to perform such an operation. It was only the roar of the engines that distracted the homunculus from immediately spinning around.

Close the door! I mouthed in the most deliberate and precise manner I could, staring straight into Garth's brown eyes as he faced me, oblivious to our fate.

"Close the . . . ? Man, when are you going to give up? There ain't no Tsalal, get it? And if you don't stop with that, I'm going to leave you and your bag of bones out on the—" was as far as he got before that wall of shroud that stood behind him started spinning around. This time it was my opportunity to save Garth from unseen danger, and I jumped to close the metal door. Unable to get past him in time, I was left with only the option of pushing back the big man himself, letting Garth's startled girth fall into the door to close it. Even still, it wasn't soon enough. The creature managed to fling his arm into the space between door and jamb, and the pale limb now kept the two from meeting. It wasn't until Garth saw those gray fingers struggling to reach him that he stopped swinging on me and joined my efforts to reseal the entrance. The only things that kept the monster from knocking it open and flinging both of our bodies with it were a bit of leverage and surprise. For our part, we seemed to be trying the impossible, to slam the door shut and amputate the creature's appendage at the elbow in doing so; neither one of us was trying to push the arm back out.

"Get the gun off me and shoot it!" Garth motioned with his eyes to his shoulder. There was no way Garth could lift his arms so the strap could be removed, so it was up to me to unhook the rifle with my shaking hands as it bounced around before me.

"Just break the damn strap. Yank it, dog!" was Garth's advice, but this didn't keep him from cursing at me when my first desperate tugs did little more than yank his neck. But the clip gave out before Garth's strength did, and I was able to get his Winchester, cock the bullet into the chamber. The protruding, pale hand, almost as if it knew that it was to be my target, flailed wildly as the beast it was attached to howled in pain at another of Garth's full-body thrusts. I couldn't get a good shot with it moving like that, especially since I was too scared to step much closer.

"Shoot it! Shoot it!" Garth said. And I did. And missed. Only for Garth to yell, "Aim it this time," as if that had not occurred to me. Garth leaned in with all his might and fat behind him, trapping the arm completely if only momentarily. Taking my time, breathing out and preparing to pull the trigger with my inhalation, I focused, staring over my scope at the thing. It was the perfect shot, the hand stretched out all of its fingers in a moment of pain, forming a clear target. So clear was my sight that, for the first time, I noticed those well-chewed nails on the ends of fingers that could only be considered pudgy in relation to the average of his race.

"Augustus!" I yelled, and after a confused look by Garth, I repeated my call, louder, loud enough to be heard over the twenty-foot-tall fan and all the machinery behind it.

"Chris!" came back to me. Not in the voice of my runt of a Tekelian. No, this voice was human. This voice was female. The woman I loved. And her voice brought a chorus of others behind it.

Hearing the responses, Garth eased up on the door, and the arm revealed itself to be that of my brief roommate and supposed captor. Augustus stood there, nursing his wrist, smiling at me.

"Friends," he managed, and I thought he was talking about us till he stepped to the side and I saw Jeffree and Carlton Damon Carter, Angela Latham and my cousin Captain Booker Jaynes standing behind him. Right on CP Time, they had joined me.

CHAPTER XXI

SPEAK no ill of the successful black male sellout, for he has achieved the goal of the community that has produced him: he has "made it," used his skills to attain the status that would be denied him, earned entry at the door of the big house of prosperity. His only flaw is that he agreed to leave that community, its hopes, customs, aspirations, on the porch behind him. It is a matter of expedience as much as morality. I say this to forestall any judgment on Nathaniel Latham, who given the state of the world, just might have been the last sellout in history. And it was not completely fair to say that, in the end, Nathaniel Latham sold out his community for the Tekelians, for what he did, he did not only for himself but also for his wife. Unfortunately for Nathaniel, this was not how his wife viewed his hiring out of himself as an interpreter to the Tekelian army. Unfortunate for Nathaniel, but very good for me.

"You know, historically, many of our people have joined up in the armies of our oppressors as a means of solidifying our place in society," I offered, refilling Angela's tea as the group of us sat on the porch of our three-fifths of a home in Karvel's paradise. I was comfort, solace, all things good and understanding. I could be. Nathaniel had proven unworthy and I the opposite. I could take my time now, and needed to. All of them, not just Angela, looked to be in mild shock in the plush, manicured surroundings after spending so long in the monotonous white hell that was Tekeli-li. Poor Augustus was nearly delirious now that he was removed from his natural habitat. And it was clearly not just a psychologi-cally traumatic reaction the creature was experiencing. The heat of the room, while a perfect sventy-two degrees and unnoticeable to me, seemed to have the effect of wilting him. Before he could faint, we relocated him to the walk-in freezer, a place Augustus was happy to go when he saw the culinary treasures there. The only one who looked worse than the savage was my cousin Cap-tain Booker Jaynes, who'd grown older in the last weeks at a rate accelerated beyond the limits of space and time. I couldn't tell if this aging had occurred back at his frozen love nest in the weeks since my absence, or simply by walking in the imposing threshold of Thomas Karvel's sanctuary. My grizzled cousin stared up at the colossal painted ceiling nearly the entire time, muttering what I as-sumed was the first prayer to make it past his full lips in years.

"No. No, my son-of-a-bitch husband has really gone and done it. He joined up. He's trying to be one of them, trying to get in good. I know it. I've seen him act that way with potential corporate clients, that same groveling act. It's disgusting. He's limping around the tunnels wearing one of their robes now, tripping over the damn thing because it's too long. He won't even look at me. And if he was getting any extra food, I wasn't seeing it." Angela sighed, rubbed her skin, which must have itched after being numb with cold for so long. "I thought you were as good as dead, and then come to find out you guys have been living high on the hog this whole time? Unbelievable. I should have left with you when you asked me."

"You should have," I told her. But I held her closer when I said it so it didn't come off as a dig.

Immediately, the thought of Angela Latham inserted into this utopia made the whole BioDome thing more appealing. More sus-tainable. Mentally I reshot the last few weeks with Angela by my side instead of just Garth Frierson, and this faux past seemed like one worth building a future on. This came in the briefest of flashes, because soon returned the noise of the Tekelian hordes banging away at the structure of the 3.2 Ultra BioDome like it was an aluminum piñata, just waiting for their target to implode and reveal its treasures. From the sound of it, they were all over the roof, and there were at least a hundred of them up there. Maybe it was just acoustics, but it started to sound as if all that beating might actually be working, and in moments the sky might literally come falling down upon us.

This monstrous reality wasn't the only thing that told me the idea of Angela and me staying in this artificial environment could never work. The other great clue was the look of Mr. Thomas Karvel, who sat a good fifteen feet away, staring at six of his seven new guests with unhidden trepidation. I recognized the look. It wasn't hatred, or racism, at least in any substantial sense. It was just that, clearly, the six of us were more startling to him presently than the one unfortunate Tekelian who was no doubt that moment ravaging Karvel's stores of frozen pastry products.

"How did you find us?" Mrs. Karvel asked, and her tone immediately challenged my observation: no hint of animosity in it, aggression.

"I'm a tracker. I'm a tracker; I can track things." Jeffree started talking, pausing between the first sentence and the second to give Carlton Damon Carter time to remove the lens cap from his camera and capture the discussion at hand. The fact that Jeffree had only one eye now, that his empty socket was covered in a white leather patch, did give him more gravitas. "You see, you got to get a feel, you know, in your heart, for your destination. You got to imagine it, see, in your mind, and then the ancestral spirits—"

"We took the tunnels straight here," Angela interrupted, unaware of the reckless eyeball attack being thrown by Carlton Damon Carter in response. "Augustus got us to the tunnel, and then we just came straight here. It's easy to pick the right path when you get closer: the walls along this route are melting. They're covered in wet ice. That exhaust fan you have there is blowing heat straight into Tekeli-li," she told us.

"Listen!" Mrs. Karvel said, and I thought she was going into some sort of rebuttal, but in fact she meant just that: *listen*. Slowly the hammering above us was decreasing. Together we stood, each looking up at his or her own bit of ceiling above. The unseen assault trickled from a hurricane to a drizzle and then dried completely up until Karvel's radio voices and Kool-Aid waterfall were, once again, the arena's loudest sounds.

"Shhhh!" Jeffree added totally unnecessarily. "It's stopped!" He used hand gestures, his arms fully out to his sides as he crouched slightly, patting down the remaining sound in a pantomime of the obvious.

"But why?" I asked, looking at the silent ceiling above us. We knew so little about them, about their intelligence, culture, or history of military engagement. We had no way of anticipating their next move. They could've stopped for tea for all we knew. But that didn't mean we didn't want to gut those motherfuckers.

"It could be a bomb. It could be a bomb that they planted and now they're running away while a bomb explodes, that could totally be it."

"Jeffree, that is the stupidest thing I've ever heard in my—"

"They must have a way in. They have no reason to bang on the walls anymore," Mr. Karvel said slowly, in a near whisper, his eyes growing up into slits and darting to the side as if at any moment the monsters might appear from behind a magenta rhododendron bush.

The knocking wasn't completely gone. Once we were back in the mechanical walkway, above the clanging of the machines

doing as they do, you could hear it. The last rapping. The sole percussion that now stood out. I do not know if it was less threaten-
ing because it was only a lone request or because there was
something to the rhythm itself that almost soothed us with every
quick hit. It was coming from upstairs. It was coming from the
room that the beast had last seen us escape into.

It was harder climbing the ladder to get to the top tier this time
since we were holding the rifles as well. Jeffree, for no practical reason I could see, held the strap of his rifle in his teeth as he pulled
himself forward, grunting loudly enough for Carlton Damon
Carter's camcorder to capture each guttural utterance. Mrs. Karvel and Angela stayed in the terrarium along with Captain Jaynes,
who seemed to be adjusting to the dome no better than Augustus
and clearly needed no additional shocks at the moment.

There wasn't a peephole in the metal roof door that separated
us from the unknown, and at the moment this seemed to be a
great failure of design. Couldn't an architect who had the understanding that such a door was needed to keep the metaphorical
wolves at bay have also understood that one might need a safe way
to see if there were wolves at all? Leaning against the door with all
our strength, Jeffree, Carlton Damon Carter, and I each attempted
to hold it secure as we cracked it open to peer out at whatever was
calling. There, standing with the same demeanor as any other
door-side solicitor I'd encountered, was *the* Nathaniel Latham,
shivering in the cold. His face was drained to a mortal gray by the
elements and the stress that was clearly weighing upon the
brother.

Angela was right. This was the face of a traitor, a man who for-
goes his own just to better himself. But maybe that's too harsh,
maybe I was biased. If the Confederates had won the American
Civil War, wouldn't descendants of the blacks freed by fighting

with the gray army have seen their ancestors as heroes? Maybe then it was simply a question of who would win this battle, this war.

"We need to talk." Nathaniel stood before me, urging. "Listen to me, Chris, this is not a joke. They're going to destroy everything unless we do what they say." In the word *everything* I heard not this building, structure, but all the people in it. Possibly all of humanity, if we were its last representatives. "This is not a debate. This is not a negotiation. You know what these things can do. Don't play games with our lives here."

"If there is a game at all in play, it's of cats and mice. And you, sir, are in the role of the vermin," said Arthur Gordon Pym, Nantucketer, pushing past his lesser envoy so that we could take in the power of his threat. Pym stood alone, but behind him we could see the albino hominids forming a martial line at an even fifty yards away along the side of the roof, their pale robes rustling as the Antarctic wind gusted. This may have been an attempt to seem nonthreatening, but if it was, it was a failed, miserable attempt.

"What do you want?" I said this more to the gathered army than the two men who had been sent to represent them. As if they could understand me.

"There is no need to yell. In betraying the Gods, you have already garnered their attention." Pym seemed more sober than usual; either they had cut him off before he reached his limit, or he was taking his job seriously.

"I'm about to betray your natural-born cracker ass if you don't get the hell out of here," Jeffree offered by way of bluster. This however went unfilmed, as even Carlton Damon Carter was more engrossed in recording the legion of warriors that stood just beyond.

"Control your man," Pym said to me, his spittle nearly covering every inch of the dozen feet between him and our door. I could see that no one wanted this conflict to end quicker than the man that stood before me, although for entirely different reasons than mine. Somewhere back in Tekeli-li there was a cool glass of fermented khrud waiting for him, its contents still and forlorn, and Pym missed it no less than any man had yearned for his true love. "We are here to discuss this civilly and calmly. Let us end the distractions and attend to the matter at hand."

"Which is what, cracker?" Jeffree snapped back. It was easy to be brave on the other side of that door, particularly standing as he did behind me, his momentary human shield. Our attempts at seizing the argument were pointless, though, because I noticed for the first time that Pym was not even looking at me or Jeffree. Instead, he was addressing the lady of the house, whom Pym perceived had the most authority of those present. Mrs. Karvel for her part responded to the Nantucketer's attention by moving farther away from the door, leaving me up front as her clear surrogate.

"I speak of the ceasing of your great fire, and the fans to blow their heat into the corridors of Heaven," Pym hissed back at us. It was clear he assumed that we were well aware of his grievance. That this was not simply a part of our knowledge but the key part of our intent that he was exposing.

"The exhaust fan," Nathaniel interjected. "You've got to turn off that exhaust fan; it's blowing hot air right into the village. That's what's melting everything. Just take care of that and everybody will be fine. Nobody gets hurt. Everything can go back to normal." His voice cracked, and the last word was perhaps an unconscious notification that there simply was no more normal to retreat to.

"The heat of your device is destroying the great city, vanishing paradise itself. We know not how you do it, nor do we care, but the assault must cease and for the solid foundation of our world to continue," Pym explained.

"That's all they want, Chris. Just go take care of this . . . whatever you have to shut off, and let's end this thing."

"And of course we will also need the return of the human chattel which owes its labor to the citizens of Tekeli-li, such as you yourself are surely aware. But nothing more, I assure you, honorable lady," Pym said past me again to Mrs. Karvel. "This theft cannot be tolerated." This last statement was directed at all of us, even Nathaniel standing beside him. When Mrs. Karvel, who I wasn't sure even understood that she was being addressed directly, made no response to him, the aged Caucasoid followed up his statement. "The latter might be negotiated if the former is abided by."

"Then you would be willing to talk this out, then?" Mrs. Karvel unexpectedly stepped forward, burning the side of my hand with her cigarette as she pushed past. "To handle this thing like decent, civil Americans?" Mrs. Karvel asked him. I don't know what she made of the odd man in his cultlike white robes making demands of us, out here in the epicenter of nowhere, but Mrs. Karvel was clearly a smart woman, and a smart woman made the best of whatever situation she was presented with. "Y'all will be my guests then, mine and my husband's. We'll do this nice and friendly like. You tell your people, or whatever them things are out there, you tell them we'll serve it up right here, bring tables right out onto the roof. Good home cooking and all that. Talk things out real civil. Invite as many as you want. How you like that?"

Pym looked over his shoulder, back behind him at the creatures he represented. How did he like that? There was a nervousness to Pym, a nervousness that he bore every moment I encountered him. His love of the Gods was based on his fear of them, and it was clear which of the two emotions was most overwhelming.

"What kind of food might you have?" Pym asked, preparing as he was to make the offer as attractive as possible to his masters.

"A feast?" I asked aloud as we closed the door behind us. It seemed a brilliant idea to me, truly inspired. The breaking of bread, the universal action of communal friendship. What more agreeable act could we offer? I was surprised at the rationalism displayed by Mrs. Karvel.

"A supper," Mrs. Karvel said in response to me, lighting another cigarette and nodding. "We'll give them a good, strong supper, and that will take care of all our troubles." She went to the back of her little storage room and started unpacking the boxes, lifting them out of their furniture shapes and lining them up on the floor before us.

"Well, I don't know if that'll take care of all our troubles, but at least that'll begin to—" I stopped when I realized what she was doing. Inside the boxes labeled with the images of rats were more little boxes with more little rats imprinted upon them. And as I watched Mrs. Karvel, I saw that inside those little boxes were little poisonous blue pellets, the kind you would feed to rats if you wanted them to cease being nuisances and start being dead.

"All our troubles. You said they have a village under the ice, right? A place big enough for a homestead, if we need to?" Mrs. Karvel asked, holding a box of poison and shaking it like a maraca before us. "Now help me look. I know there's some packets of Kool-Aid back here."

. . .

"You can't just poison them, dog," Garth kept complaining, simultaneously dipping his fingers into untainted cooking bowls to scoop up leftover food. Garth addressed me, but he was loud, offering criticism for the entire room. And, apart from my cousin, the room ignored him. Garth was different from us: we might have shared an ancient slave past, but we did not share our immediate one. Garth hadn't been caught with us below. Garth hadn't had his own brief taste of bondage to give him something invisible and bitter to suck on. No, Garth was an outsider in this regard, and we ignored him.

"I mean, what you guys are talking about is like some germ warfare shit, you know what I'm saying? It's like some anti–Geneva conventions shit. It ain't right."

"Right. It ain't tactical." Captain Jaynes took over the discussion. "See, when you fight against your oppressors, it's got to be tactical. There's no point in poisoning them, there's too many for that. And if you do that, you can't never win the argument. You can't never see that look on their faces when they know that you were right and they are so wrong." We ignored Captain Jaynes for entirely different reasons. For one, he was clearly in shock, shivering there in his blanket despite the heat, and he was now so pale from his discomfort that he had gone from brown to gray. But really, the captain never sounded much more sane than this, so there was no confusing his current physical condition with his mental one. No, the real reason we didn't listen to my cousin would've hurt the man if it'd been said aloud: even though I was the only one who had witnessed the actual intimacy between him and his personal captor, the truth was suspected by all. So we ignored him and kept quietly at our diabolic work. Garth filled the new silence.

"But dogs, you can't just kill people. It's not right, it's not how you're supposed to do things. I mean, these creatures freaked me out just as much as they freak you out, but there are some things that are right and some things that are wrong and poisoning a bunch of folks is just wrong. That's like torturing them to death."

"Young man," Thomas Karvel began, and his voice alone was enough to quiet his biggest fan. The painter was still hoarse since rising back to consciousness, and he held the site of the painful blow on his head as if he was keeping his brain from falling out of a hole there. "Young man," he repeated, emphasizing the words in such a way that through his southern accent "man" sounded belittling. "This isn't some uniformed army, this is something totally different. There are no rules here."

"But sir, it doesn't have to be this way," Garth asserted, jutting his gut forward in the center of the assembly, as if to use his girth to stop the momentum of the room. "Why not—I don't know—just listen to what the snow monkeys are saying. I mean, they have actual demands here, right? I'm saying, can't we just turn down the heat? That's what they're asking, right? We can just turn down the heat and figure out some other way to keep warm. We could save energy, you know? I bet if you turned off that waterfall for one, that alone would make the boiler chill a little. Dim the lights. I don't know. And then we could just turn the heat down to fifty degrees or something—"

"Fifty degrees! You're talking to me about fifty degrees? You lost your mind? If I wasn't worried the boiler wouldn't blow to high hell, I'd have it running at eighty. Fifty?! Forget fifty, why not thirty-two degrees? You drop it to fifty, then they're going to want it below that. You show them weakness now, and where does it stop? Where?" Karvel's face was flushed with indignation. Motioning with his arms to provide an invisible canvas, Karvel painted this horrific vision for the room. "Hell, we could even have snow in here." He spun around on his heels after that declaration, joining his wife in her culinary preparations.

"Well, all right then. That sounds settled to me." Angela was the first to break the silence. It was no small thing that her legal husband was out there, serving the savages of the cold as we spoke. If she could move forward, if she could move on, what could the rest of us say?

Although Garth's complaints were ignored almost as quickly as they were registered, it should be said that the final decision to poison the Tekelian Army wasn't made quickly. There were logistics to consider. For one, we had no real knowledge of their physiognomy: would this even work? What if it offered the beasts no more than a case of heartburn or just left them groggy?

"We'll feed them up on the roof. We got some foldout chairs, some pullout tables. It's too hot in here anyway. And if they get a little drunk, hopefully it will be enough to just push them off the side."

" 'The side'?" Angela asked, confused.

"Yeah. The side of the roof. That ought to take care of them." Mr. Karvel took up the direction. "Sure thing it'll work. When times get tough, you got to go back to the simple things to get them done. You do what you have to. And we have to survive. Even if we lose the dome, we have to survive."

It was simplistic and brute, and nobody argued with it because nobody had a better idea. Each of us on our own mumbled about the improbability of it all, but the simple fact was that there were no other legitimate options. Even my Plan B of getting that little boat and sailing to the Tsalalian refuge of blackness depended on us getting out of this dome alive, and that seemed impossible now. The Tekelians knew of the exhaust tunnel, and they had seen Jeffree here as well, so it was safe to assume that that exit would soon be obstructed.

In our absence, Augustus managed fairly well in the freezer. I went to visit him as Carlton Damon Carter and Angela helped Mrs. Karvel prepare her feast, to at least alert him of the invasion and take some of the prepoisoned Betty Crocker golden food cake out to where the creature lay in his robe on a sack of frozen burritos as if it was furniture. There was a moment there as I watched him that I empathized not only with this individual, who had been so kind to me, but with the race that he was connected to. These were living creatures, regardless of how abhorrent I found their social values to be. It was so easy to let that xenophobic element within me, that part inclined to dehumanize those different from myself, have its way. But it was my duty to fight this mentality. Watching my creature gorge upon his yellow cake, shoving his head into the plate much like a spaniel does, crumbs erupting around his jowls, I reminded myself that, though his mannerisms were bestial, he was still a living, caring being.

The food that covered the dining room table ready to be transported upstairs, it looked like it could kill you, but kill you by clogging your arteries or sending the kind of fat that sits in your gut and waits to stop your heart when you're not looking. Now the poison, it did have a smell. But that smell was as sweet and inviting as the marshmallows that melted over the tops of those salad bowls of candied yams. All the food that was in the white porcelain and Tupperware containers had enough rat poison in it to kill the kind of vermin that stalked the streets of Tokyo, knocking over buildings in black-and-white movies. All the food in the Fiestaware serving bowls was good enough to eat—good enough to eat and still live to the next day to talk about what a great meal was. We were betting that the monsters didn't know what poison smells like. We were betting that none of them collected Fiestaware either.

Once the food was properly prepared, Mrs. Karvel, triumphant, came forth upon the roof plateau to announce its impending arrival. All seemed as civil as the circumstance could allow for. Arthur Gordon Pym even volunteered to help us bring the serving trays out onto the landing, and for a while I saw him sitting in Mrs. Karvel's storage room, holding the exit door open. Presumably Pym was there to oversee any foul play, but the gift of a bottle of Kentucky bourbon quickly stilled his own apprehensions, a distraction we'd counted on. What we weren't counting on was that our party would be such a success. After we brought all the food upstairs, all the little paper plates and plastic silverware, after we located the foldout tables and chairs and removed them from their storage, passing them up along a bucket line to the roof exit, after it was all ready and we knew there was no turning back, again we opened the roof exit door. It was windy outside, and we hadn't even started when a whole pile of napkins blew past us and off the edge, but the napkins were white, and when they hit the snow you couldn't see the litter.

And there they were. All of the warriors, which we expected, but more. Beyond them, all of the women of Tekeli-li. And then among the females, I saw them. All the little Tekelian children had been brought as well. Screaming gleefully at the feast they were about to indulge in. Little, hairy albino kids of no more than six and seven, four and five, one, two, and three. Mrs. Karvel looked up at the spectacle of youth as she carried in her deadly Sara Lee easy cook and bake rolls, and I believe I saw her almost collapse for a second. It might have been the wind whipping across there or the slippery, slight curve of the plateau, but I know her shoulders did buckle for a moment and I thought she might fall down at the sight of them. They were hideous, but they were young in the way that's familiar across species: clumsy, endearing, trusting, inno- cent. But Mrs. Karvel recovered. Without anyone other than me noticing. And she kept walking to the serving table, looking down at her wares without breaking her smile.

"Oh, you brought quite a crowd. I hope y'all also brought your appetites!"

CHAPTER XXII

THE Tekelians sat on folding chairs on the roof, their asses stretching the fabric halfway to the ground, their minds conscious only of their own fingers and the food that they grasped and that stuck to every crevice and nail. The creatures ate without utensils, ate in the most natural way, but also in a style that was completely alien to me. There was a time when I lived in West Africa that I had to train myself to eat solely with my right hand.* Despite this simple task, I couldn't do it. Food fell from my fingers and back into the communal bowl, and I longed for the ease and dignity of a simple fork. But there is grace in hand-to-mouth eating for those who are used to it. These creatures were experts at their task. They were so focused on their meals that not a crumb was spilled, leaving only the smallest of visible evidence of their feast on the plates. They ate it up. And what they ate was poison. And they didn't seem to mind that either.

In fact, they didn't seem to mind the poison at all. Didn't seem to have the slightest bellyache from their specially prepared destruction. Not even the children; I have to confess it was painful for me to see the little ones devour this tainted bait, their little mouths eager to experience the novelty of it all. I was witnessing an act of genocide, I was sure. I have no delusions about myself in this: I was

* The left hand being used for toilet duties, unlike in the West, where we are willing to get both hands dirty to get the job done.

no less morally responsible than those that sat by while European traders sold infected blankets to Indians, or the first guns were traded for slaves on the West African coast. I was relieved to see that, much like with children everywhere, the novelty of a new food was outweighed by the inevitable repulsion to novelty itself. Leaning in toward their fathers' and mothers' food-laden fingertips, all of the children I could see took only the smallest of bites before shaking their heads in the familiar refrain of the picky toddler. I confess, I didn't see all of the children, and I don't offer this report as an excuse. I was participating in something horrible, and my only defense is that I was motivated by my own fear, which of course is no defense at all.

At that moment, though, I was engulfed more in practical matters than in ethical quandaries. The food had to be served; although we had planned for fifty Tekelian monsters, there were at least a hundred in attendance, and we weren't prepared to get the plates to each of the unfolded tables while they were still warm. This, however, turned out to be to our benefit: the beasts really liked the food cold. In fact, even when we managed to bring it to their tables quickly, the creatures let the warm plates sit there for a few minutes in the wind, refusing to touch them before the dinner became nearly as frigid as the air. We decided to play a zone defense with our serving duties to make up for the fact that there weren't enough of us to fully meet the challenge. This strategy soon met a snag when it was discovered that Jeffree's monster had been placed in my quadrant. Old Sausage Nose sat closest to the exit door with a table all to himself, an arrangement clearly referencing his importance. As soon as we got on the roof, I could see Jeffree staring at him with his one working eye. The beast saw him too. He saw what he thought was his and he demanded it. As the rest of the troops dug into their food, this monster just stared across at his injured chattel, one arm extended, pointing his long alabaster digit directly at Jeffree's moving body. There could be no confusing the gesture, so I was left to ignore it. I had no intention of bringing Jeffree near Sausage Nose's table; I could tell by the way Jeffree was looking that he was already imagining the finale in his personal movie, already imagining his climactic conquering of the big boss. As I struggled to figure out how to avoid the impending conflict, Carlton Damon Carter pushed by me with such force that I expected him to attempt to maul the molester of his man. Instead, Carlton Damon Carter immediately went to serve the food that sat before the creature, picking up a piece of the poisonous Hamburger Helper stroganoff delight in his bare brown hands and holding it out to the beast's mouth with all the tenderness of a man feeding a baby goat in a petting zoo.

"Eat up, big boy. You eat as much as you deserve, honey," he cooed, his free hand still holding the camera, which he'd somehow recovered before fleeing, to record the revenge for posterity.

And it was not just the Tekelians who were taken with the Karvels' supper. Since being awarded a bottle of the painter's private stock, Arthur Pym had made himself scarce and was nowhere near the tainted food in question. Nathaniel, for his part, was all over it. I watched as Nathaniel kept staring at the food while it was served to his masters, his eyes watering as much as his mouth when Angela paused from her serving duties to slap the dinner from his thieving hands. The Tekelians, thinking the servile wench was affirming Tekelian dominance by not allowing the human to eat, just laughed at this display, a congested snorting sound I was sure would make Nathaniel lose his appetite further.

Mr. Sausage Nose, for his part, showed no sign he would ever be satiated. He barely bothered to use his hands, vacuuming the food on his plate nearly as fast as I managed to replenish it. Regardless of his enormous intake, and the amount of food I saw the rest of the creatures seated on the roof consume as well, none of the beasts showed any sign of succumbing to the trap we'd set for them. Admittedly, I knew hardly anything about poisons and their effects, or the creatures' alien physiognomy, but after forty-five minutes of gluttony, there was nary a burp to be heard. Not even a cough. The creatures, besides an occasional shout and slap to the head of one of my human compatriots for perceived sloth, showed no negative signs at all. They were joyous. And they were horrid. The laughing and the fangs and those horrible white gums holding the yellow teeth in their mouths. But never a healthier bunch have I seen. Even the children, the poor children, the ones who had eaten our offering, showed no signs of slowing, and it was to these canaries that I looked for the first symptoms to develop. We had fed them nearly every bit of poison we could, I knew. Any more and the food would have turned blue from its active ingredient.

"It's just time for dessert, then. Get the pudding, Christopher. But this time, extra sprinkles," Mrs. Karvel said, sidling up next to me.

"But they've already eaten a ton of poison and it doesn't seem to be working," I said, forcing a smile and talking openly in front of the snagglenosed monster because he had no comprehension of my words' meanings.

"*Extra sprinkles*," Mrs. Karvel gleefully insisted. "All the sprinkles we've got left."

I would have preferred to take this journey on my own, of course, but it seemed Mr. Sausage Nose must have remembered that I, too, was his property and followed me with his eyes when he saw me walking toward the exit door. Ignoring Jeffree's attempt at a menacing gaze,* the beast jumped up from his seat. It was like watching a willow tree walking, the hulk's robes blowing in the wind, revealing the outline of monstrous proportions. That beast

---

* This was no longer that powerful, given he had only one eye to do it with.

wanted into the BioDome, which he made clear by refusing to let me close the door behind me. He wanted to see everything, and clearly felt ownership of everything he could see. Worse, when one of the pale children noticed our interaction, the child wormed its way into the entrance as well, and Mr. Sausage Nose just let it, patting the boyish mini-monster on the head as it passed him.

Regardless of the fact that I barely knew the species, I could see the awe in which the monster held the room we entered off the roof. Considering that he had never seen a building not made of ice, I have no idea what he made of the metals and plastics. Exotic bones, he probably thought. This wonderment only grew when we entered the outer hallway of the dome, where the ceiling soars to a cathedral majesty and Karvel stored several of his many treasures. Even still, none of this could in any way prepare the two creatures for the vision of Karvel's utopia itself. Looking at the beasts' faces in those moments of our arrival, I was struck by the difference between witnessing the improbable and witnessing the impossible. I don't believe these creatures had ever seen the color green before. There was no natural occurrence of it on their section of the continent, there was no reason they should have. And yet it was such a fundamental thing, this color of life. And I would not have believed it was so alien to them if I hadn't seen their reaction with my own eyes. They stood still, in utter wonderment. They stood and looked out into the vast arena not just because of its improbable size but also because they had never seen anything like this. Assuming they had the same access to the color spectrum as we did, and that evolution hadn't left them unable to see beyond whiteness, they must have been overwhelmed by the sudden engagement of a dormant part of their brains. And what can be said of that ceiling? Even though they surely knew the sky it represented, still they had to be awed by this human interpretation of the heavens. It was visible how much the scene moved them, and not just in their faces and eyes but in their very spines. I could see their shivers, even under their robes. As I watched them take in the vastness of it all, I began to see the shivers increasing, nearly to the point of convulsion. It was the heat. It was exactly the same reaction Augustus had had on entry to the BioDome earlier. Understanding what was affecting him, that there was no way he could handle this temperature for too long, the horrible beast looked at me and made motions to his mouth, chomping his disgusting jowls in a pantomime that left no hideous detail to the imagination.

"AAAAAAAAAAAARRRGH!" he finished with, throwing his head back and showing his fangs impatiently.

Aargh indeed. The child, perhaps sensing that the stream held cooling liquid, ran toward its banks with the universal glee of youth and laid its head straight down. Leaning in to lap up the Kool-Aid contents timidly, like a fawn. Moving away from the child and toward Karvel's deck, Sausage Nose kept a heavy hand on my shoulder, leaning down on it either to brace himself as he adjusted to walking on grass or to keep me from getting too far away from him. The creature didn't release me until I led him directly to the many cooking pans that still lay forlorn across the dinner table. Before I could even offer these remains, he was all over them, forgoing hands and lifting the pans directly to his mouth to scrape them with his dry alabaster tongue.

"More food," I said, pointing off toward the freezer. There lay the trays of pudding, each one having been boiled with the remainder of the rat bait for a definitive conclusion, in case the main course dosage failed to do its job. "I'm going to get more poison, to kill you," I added, offering the most servile of smiles before slowly moving away. Despite my physical caution, I still almost had a glass baking pan thrown at my head by the monster and probably would have if at the last minute the brute had not noticed the morsels of Betty Crocker's classic bread turkey stuffing stuck to the sides of it.

Augustus. It was not until just then, when I looked directly at the freezer door, that I realized my favorite Tekelian was still locked inside. Not wanting his presence to be revealed, not wanting our most recent guests to have an emotional reaction to this probable traitor, I barely opened the door before going through. And Augustus was still there, lying facedown in the back amid a few half-eaten Pillsbury crescent rolls. I was first struck by the smell. You would think that the frozen air would delete some of this stench, but no. The little storage room was putrid with Augustus's stank, which was so much more rank than usual. Soon I could see why: fecal liquid emerging from the midsection of his robes poured into a puddle around his limp body. It was even whiter than his hair; if it wasn't for the stank odor, I would've thought it was yogurt.

"Augustus? You've shit yourself," I called to him, first in a whisper and then repeated with increasing volume with each unanswered entreaty. Getting as close as my nose would allow, I reached out for his shoulder. What I held in my hand was hard, and it was not that muscle had miraculously appeared since the last time I had touched my ally. I wanted to convince myself otherwise, but I knew what I would find even before I turned Augustus over and saw his face and those pale eyes staring open and lifeless toward the empty pudding pans he'd managed to consume. Augustus, my friend, was gone. That damn pudding. Augustus was my responsibility, and I'd failed him. But at the moment there was no time for self-flagellation. Only revenge and survival. And sadly, there was this one horrible positive that emerged in the back of my mind: the poison did work on them. It was only a matter of time or dosage.

I would have stayed hidden in that freezer if I could have. Just waited it out till the poison did its job and freed me from the Teke-lian oppression. But an easy exit was not to be. The greedy monster outside beckoned, and within minutes he was throwing pots and pans at the freezer door as a sort of remote control, summoning me out again. Out of respect to our friendship, I closed Augustus's eyes with my fingers and kept them shut by placing a bag of frozen peas over them. Careful not to step in his disgusting bodily fluids, I wrapped the shroud around his rigor-mortis-stricken corpse before gathering up as many pudding pans as I could carry at once and walked out to meet my impatient guest once again.

"You're going to love this. It's guaranteed to kill you," I said and smiled on my arrival. The trays went down with a thunk before Sausage Nose, and despite the fact that he already looked ill, the shaking hands and sweating pale face evident, there was a clear expression of joy that he was going to indulge further in his unintentional suicide. Maybe it was my anger at the death of my friend or the simple bravado that comes from exhaustion, but before he could even dig into the first serving tray, I did something reckless. Slapping his marble hands playfully, I said, "No, no, no. It's not quite done yet." Reaching for the last box of Black Flag industrial-strength rat and vermin poison, I took a handful of those blue pellets into my palm and then, as if I truly was dropping rainbow sprinkles onto chocolate ice cream, I let them fall over the upper surface of the pudding in question. And they looked beautiful there. The monster gazed up at me, gazed at the box of poison that I had in my hand, saw the illustration of the rat there, and smiled. And then he started gorging.

· · ·

The monster was so engrossed in his final meal that he didn't notice much else, thinking little of anything but himself and his dessert. I was more considerate. Standing before the creature where he had come to lean against a stool, I thought of the Teke-lian child. Looking to the stream that flowed not more than thirty yards beyond, I could see the kid remained on its belly, head at the syrupy stream still. The child, who must have been very thirsty, was so close to the water that at times its head disappeared below the surface, the food-coloring blue covering the back of its gray hair. It was an odd, overindulgent way of sucking in the blue sugar water, and it was this strange technique that led me to walk slowly off the porch toward the back. I was not more than ten yards closer when I realized the youth's head was not simply bobbing happily atop the surface of the "water" but was bobbing *in* it with an up-and-down rhythm that matched that of the slight, pump-enhanced current. I knew that unless the Tekelians had some yet unseen, amazing amphibious ability to breathe underwater, this poor young thing was dead.

The smaller physiognomy, of course. The poison had done its job long before the colossal man killer behind me could even faint. I was never a particularly good liar.* Unsure and alarmed, I made the obvious mistake of freezing immediately, staring back to the deck where the gnarled-nosed gourmet clanked his head in the pans. No sooner did the creature catch my eye than I was exposed. Clearly, the beast could read my body language; my pause was the most easily decoded of mammalian reactions, I'm sure the average seal would react the same way. His mouth covered in wet brown, he darted his head to look beyond me to his young charge. Those crisp, ice blue eyes saw the scene and quickly recognized the horror for what it was.

Mr. Sausage Nose didn't bother with the deck's stairs, instead grabbing the railing with one hand and launching out into the air as if he could sustain that flight. For a moment there, as he hung

---

* A question not of willing but of able.

above me, he seemed impossibly powerful and graceful, and I knew that, regardless of how much poison he had eaten, my death must be destined to arrive before his did. When he landed, though, stumbling to a stop, I could already see that his invulnerability had left him, that he was diminished. Lurching forward, exposing an awkwardness I had never seen among these creatures, Sausage Nose still managed to get to the small corpse in less time than the fastest human could have. Watching him drag the delicate, now limp body from its sugar-water grave, for the moment, I was overcome with more grief and empathy than fear. Or maybe it was that by this point the fear had become so commonplace in my system that it no longer had the impact it should. Regardless, I couldn't deny the enormity of what we had done. No creature should have to know the loss of its young. Not even a worm. Not even an evil worm. But when the monster looked up to me, fixed me with those ice blue eyes and gave another scream, this sound beyond the range I knew any man was capable of, my knack for overwhelming fear returned, along with two other things: the enraged beast and his full attention.

It must have been shock that stopped me from running away immediately. I stood there staring at him, meeting his eyes as he tenderly laid the young victim down. Then the monster let out another roar equal to the first one. That was enough to get me moving. After he screamed, the creature grabbed his waist and bent over himself, vomiting violently right on the corpse. Looking over my shoulder as I struggled to run away, I saw him heave again and perfectly white bile spewed past his fangs, covering everything in front of him with a hellishly chunky chowder.

I took off. With every essence of my being, I ran.* Loopy and off

---

* For years I've had the common anxiety dream of running away from danger without being able to distance myself. In Thomas Karvel's heaven, even *my* dreams came true.

balance, Sausage Nose stumbled behind me as I attempted to get beyond him. Despite his sickness, he was moving so fast that on his first attempt to grab me he gave my side a good knock before hurtling past on his own momentum. Slamming into a boulder to my left, he hit it hard, headfirst. If this had been an actual boulder and not simply a hollow stereo speaker covered in papier-mâché rock, it might have actually knocked him out instead of just pissing him further off.

The house, I thought. Run to the house. This was the only coherent thought I could fix on. At least it seemed rational at the time, as if all I needed to do would be to lock behind me the door on my three-fifths homestead and all my troubles could be that easily kept out. Garth was in there brooding, and I screamed his name as I ran, as if he could help me in any conceivable way. Having been used to this minute commute, I knew exactly which rocks to jump on to cross the saccharine stream. This minor knowledge was in my favor, because the beast had to pause when he came to the water behind me.* As I kept moving with every muscle I could manage for the effort, I saw that the monster paced along the bank, back and forth like a great cat stuck in a cage, stopping only to vomit once more. I couldn't have been twenty yards from the cottage when I turned back to see that Sausage Nose was actually walking away, winded! A sense of relief—mild, but there nonetheless—flashed over me when I realized that this would not be my end, that my life might be spared. It was a feeling I needed and clung to, but it was ripped away when I realized that the monster was merely setting up his runway. Pivoting, robes spinning as he did, the creature ran with speed that made him almost a blur to my widening eyes. In one robust, two-legged spring, the white one

---

* For a creature used to the extreme cold of this polar climate, getting wet was probably the most sacred of taboos.

jumped across a dozen yards of the stream in a single bound. And it couldn't have taken him more than three steps to reach me.

I was gripped by my neck and lifted from the ground. He held me up before him and stared at me. I doubt those eyes had ever reflected so much hatred. The creature's bile reeked, I could smell it through his nose. And then another roar came, and I was covered in the unnatural coolness of his putrid breath, bathed in specks of his vomit and spittle. It was nearly impossible to get fresh air, caught as I was in his exhaust, and when it was over I realized his grip had made breathing impossible anyway. *"Guwk,"* I said to him. It was not the most eloquent final word, but it was all I could manage. There was a sound after that, dead and hollow like a pumpkin being kicked, I had no idea where it came from.

"Guwk," the Tekelian said back to me. And then, in a moment of vertigo I first attributed to my losing consciousness, the beast dropped me and fell on top of me. The weight was impossibly heavy, but I could already feel that it was a limp weight, devoid of all flex. Pushing desperately out from beneath him, I saw the metal tooth of the gardening hoe planted halfway into the creature's skull. And beyond that, my friend Garth Frierson standing in his work clothes, covered in dirt, staring down.

"Well, dog," Garth said, his gaze fixed anxiously on his own lethal handiwork. "That Negro island you keep talking about is sounding better and better to me."

CHAPTER XXIII

SAUSAGE Nose didn't even have the chance to grow colder before Garth and I devised a scheme to get the hell out of there. Our planning didn't take long. We didn't really have many options to consider. There was no negotiating with the monsters now. Even if the two beasts who had just died did so only because of the heat, how could we feign innocence at this point? How could we even stall for time? Soon the Tekelian Army above us would be wondering why its prominent citizen hadn't reemerged.

Our plan: we'd get the rest of the crew and the Karvels off the roof, then turn up the boiler as high as it would go. Then, while all of them were occupied with their pudding, we would sneak out the back, take the snowmobiles, supplies, and sailboat. And then we would sail to Tsalal!

"Or Argentina," Garth pushed. "Argentina would definitely be a good first choice. Matter of fact, if the others ask, just say Argentina, okay? That would be better."

We packed the food ourselves, placing a selection of the remaining canned goods and vacuum-sealed packets into the base of the fiberglass sailboat. Garth even wanted to take the microwave popcorn, but I wouldn't let him. I understood his motivation: the day's feast had seriously depleted the stocks of the kitchen's dry goods closet. Maybe there was more food hidden somewhere in the building's storage units, but even still, there had to be an end to how much food the Karvels had. Falling into a moment of clarity,

I realized that the instant the Creole crew had arrived at Karvel's utopia we had lost our chance for long-term survival here: there were simply too many mouths to feed.

But there was still the problem of what the Tekelians would do when they didn't see their lead warrior coming out with us to greet them. At first I gave this matter little thought, assuming they would take no notice. But already we had been gone so long. And what if they were starting to get sick upstairs as well? Maybe succumbing not quickly, like the child monster did in the heat of the dome, but slowly, comforted as they were by their normal temperature. They were expecting their massive, hooded, sausage-nosed thug to return, and anything less would send off warning signals. So this is what we decided to give them.

Since we couldn't just reanimate the corpse for the thirty or forty seconds we needed, we decided to improvise. If Sausage Nose couldn't appear and ease his fellow warriors' suspicions, then we would simply have to find an understudy for his role. I nominated myself for this—stripping the soiled cloak from the beast with no small amount of disgust. I was willing to take on the danger of trying to pass myself off as the monster, but unfortunately my frame was a poor match for the beast's jacket size. I even tried adding a line of broomstick to broaden the shoulders, but it was no use. So instead Garth Frierson went, his unique physique finally being applied to practical purpose. Garth's arms weren't close to as long as those of the character he hoped to play, but they were as thick. As long as no one got close enough to see that that circumference was simply fat, I hoped he might be convincing. The issue of skin tone, of course, had to be addressed. Any melanin at all would have revealed him to be an impostor. To camouflage him, we relied on teeth-whitening toothpaste, which the bright-smiling Karvels had in great supply. It took about two tubes each to cover Garth's hands and arms, another for his neck, and two more for his face. Not that we intended anything but his fingers to be seen, but in the wind of the upstairs it felt safer to cover up all that could possibly be revealed. The paste left the former bus driver a tad shiny, but fortunately I found an open box of baking soda in the back of the Karvels' Sub-Zero, and I blotted it onto Garth's skin like it was the finest talcum.

As soon as I stepped out onto the roof, I knew that we were right to have made our preparations. All of the creatures' heads turned on our arrival, and they clearly weren't just looking for the pudding. As I walked out with the pans in my hands, they saw behind me what looked like the arm of their leader slapping the back of my head to speed me up. Or at least they saw Sausage Nose's sleeve, wiped clean of bile. And from within this sleeve, they saw a white hand, even paler than their own, which I hoped they wouldn't notice. In my attempt to hide Garth's blackness, I'd been a little too eager, I realized once faced with the actual living Tekelian skin tone. In my mind it was white, but really it was flecked with tones of gray.

"You've got to come, and you've got to come now," I urged the Karvels as soon as I reached them. You have never seen two more relieved white folks.* In their brief time in the outdoors, their faces had become flushed and ruddy, their noses running and freezing at the same time. Mrs. Karvel was smoking right in front of her husband now, she didn't even care. I understood. They hadn't been living in the Antarctic like the rest of us, they'd simply been hiding within it. Pushed well beyond their comfort levels physically and socially, the two scuttled past me to the inside before I could even finish my request. My cousin, on the other hand, proved nowhere near as easy to convince.

"I don't want to have nothing to do with it, Christopher,"

---

* Or at least I haven't.

Booker Jaynes said as I came closer. "You see how well your dirty little trick went? You see that all that poison was for nothing? I could have told you that. If it was that simple, slavery would have been over by the seventeenth century." Jaynes moved past me to serve his mistress another plate of potatoes au gratin, a dish he had prepared himself. Hunka had come with the rest, looking for him, and Jaynes had found her. He had taken special care to ensure that she would receive food untainted by our deceit. None of her kin seemed to notice that her servant's efforts were a little too attentive. Even when he dabbed a smudge of cheese off the corner of her mouth, the other Tekelians apparently found this intimate gesture not the least bit out of the ordinary, the actions of a good slave and a good lover being more or less the same.

"Just get off the roof, okay? Promise me that. Take your lady and get her as far away from here as you can," I insisted, interpreting his shrugging nod as an ironclad contract.

"Well that's just insane," Nathaniel complained as he stepped in where he was not wanted, coming from behind me after listening to the substance of my little family spat. "There's simply nowhere to run to, don't you understand that? This is it. We need to get in with these people, make a place with them. Secure our positions. That's our reality now. Not some fantasy world."

Angela Latham stood beside him, so I spoke to her directly as she looked intently at her legal husband. "Angela, they're not just going to keel over instantly. They're going to get sick, and when they figure out why, they are going to get angry. And they are definitely going to figure out why." It was a simple argument, but it was all she needed to hear. Angela turned away from Nathaniel and started walking with me. Nathaniel didn't follow. And in this moment of my greatest heroics, Angela Latham grabbed my hand with the softness of hers when she reached me, and together we walked past that gaggle of goliaths and toward something I hoped would be our future.

"Angela!" I kept hearing Nathaniel yell from behind me. But no matter how demanding that voice was, it never got any closer. Nathaniel never made the simple effort to follow after all that he was losing. Angela walked through the exit door with me, and it was only Garth Frierson who seemed to have any reservation over Nathaniel's absence. As I came into the room, I saw past the costumed Garth to the Karvels, who were busy laying out rifles and ammunition before them in preparation for what was surely to come. Taking off his coat, Jeffree grabbed the largest rifle he could find in the pile, cocked it, and declared, "It's showtime!" as if Carlton Damon Carter hadn't been filming the whole time.

"Where the hell is Captain Jaynes?" Garth insisted, still not having opened the door wide enough for those behind to see that he was a fraud but unwilling to close it either with our two comrades on the other side. He'd taken his hood off, and given the smell, I couldn't blame him. Still, the patches of white toothpaste on his face made him look like he had a mutant strain of vitiligo.

"I told him, but he's not coming. He's with that woman. He thinks he can make it with her instead. What the hell can I do about that?"

"But where the hell is Nathaniel?" The question was addressed to me, but Garth was also looking to Latham's newly estranged wife.

"He's not trying to hear it," I told Garth. "It's on him now." Garth looked at my indifferent expression and replied to it with his own look of disbelief. He looked at Angela as well, and so did I, and I'd like to believe I saw a tinge of indifference from her too, but I can't deny that now she was crying.

"Screw this," Garth spat at me, and before I could stop him he leaned out the door and yelled, "Yo, dog! Nathaniel! It's time to get your black ass out of here!"

The command certainly got Nathaniel's attention. In fact, it seemed to get everyone's attention. All of the Tekelians on the roof looked up from the remainders of their feast to take notice of what had just been said. The now unhooded Garth, who had stepped just outside the door to make sure that he was heard, struck quite a figure before them. Even from the distance both physically and culturally, I could read the looks of shock on the creatures' faces. Never before had they seen a Tekelian with African features, that much was sure. Or a Tekelian warrior who, after stepping off of the two milk crates we had placed for him by the door, now stood at a mere five feet, six inches tall. The other thing I could tell was that the robe Sausage Nose always wore was a sacred object, a symbol of respect, earned right and privilege. It was clear from the chorus of angry howls that erupted from among them, rising first from the warriors and then from the females and even the children of Tekeli-li as they pushed back their chairs and flipped over the tables. Either we had broken some sort of snowman taboo or they just knew the truth: that the owner of that robe would not have parted with it willingly. Either way, the result was much the same and very immediate. Our reckoning would not be postponed a moment more.

• • •

The first one to die was my cousin. The man of my blood who at different times I had looked to as a leader, a boss, even as a friend. The reality of his death somehow eluded my consciousness in that moment of chaos and danger. And they didn't so much attack him as simply brush Booker Jaynes away.

"Ladies and gentlemen, brothers and sisters: I'm sure we can figure out what is going on here in a peaceable manner!" Booker bellowed. Years of practice at rallies and marches had given him a voice that truly boomed above the crowd. "Let's just all calm down, and get together in a circle," he pleaded. Alas, "Can't we all just form a circle?" was the last thing my cousin said before he was pushed to the side by the nearest of the creatures. The villain didn't even bother to acknowledge my cousin by looking in his direction. The monster just swung his simian arm out to the side and sent Jaynes off his feet and hurtling toward the BioDome's curved edge. Booker actually landed briefly, though not on his feet, skidding the remaining distance to where the angle of the roof became too steep to reconcile. And then he was simply gone. Dropped out of sight. It's a testament to my own capacity for denial that I didn't accept that the captain had fallen to his demise, instead clinging to a hasty notion that he had simply slid down the side and landed in the soft snow below. His Tekelian mistress harbored no such delusions. I have no idea what Hunka said, but the anguish in her garbled barking was undeniable. It must have been revealing as well, whatever language she used, because on hearing her harsh utterances the crowd of her brethren around her simply froze. Unaware of anything but her grief, the she-creature continued her lament. Those Tekelians kept listening as if taking in a confession, one that lasted until one of their number walked forward, put a hand on her shoulder, and then cut her neck wide open with an ivory dagger. When Hunka hit the ground, her assassin casually kicked her limp body off the side of the roof as well, in the direction her servant had been sent to his demise.

This is when Angela Latham screamed. I forgot that she was even beside me until I felt her hand stop me from closing the exit door. And before I could figure out what was going on, she screamed again, and this time I heard the name she was yelling. It wasn't mine.

Nathaniel Latham stood, bewildered, at the far end of the roof, separated from us by an army of monsters. All of Angela's disinterest of only moments before, whether feigned or simply delusional, was gone and replaced by a selfless passion I had long accepted she didn't have in her. They were closing in on him, having finally formed that circle that Captain Jaynes had begged for. Their horrible robes, packed in the fibers with ice and flapping heavily in a gust of polar wind, soon shrouded Nathaniel from our sight, but not before he could scream "Angela!" back to his wife and she could run out the door and after him. I tried to stop her. I tried to close the exit before Angela could escape to certain doom, but she was already too far out there. I tried to hold her wrists, tried yelling to her that it was hopeless, but years of step aerobics, spin classes, and Bikram Yoga made Angela too nimble for me. Ultimately, as those Tekelian warriors closest to us refocused on getting into the dome at the rest of us, it would take the strength of both Garth and Jeffree to remove me from the open door as well, as love overpowered my self-preservation. But they did.

The door was closed. When I turned around, the Karvels were armed and looking at me. Or at least looking past me, aiming their rifles at the demons that lay just beyond.

"Grab a gun and get ready to start shooting," Mrs. Karvel instructed me without taking her eyes off the closed metal door. Already it vibrated as the percussion of an unknowable number of frozen fists banged on the other side, enraged.

"The heat. We have to turn up the heat. That's what makes the poison work, that's what killed the big guy. They can't handle it, that's their weakness," Garth told them.

"You turn the heat up any higher and you're liable to blow us all straight to hell. The damn thing's broke, so just grab yourself a shotgun. I'm sure filling them with lead holes will kill them just as good."

"My wife has never spoken a truer word," the painter said, and he even put down the double-barrel in his hands for a moment to grab her face and kiss her.

"You fellas want to make yourselves useful?" Mrs. Karvel continued when he released her. "Then take the other exits and guard them too. Somebody cover the boiler room and somebody cover the garage door. Because they sure as hell are coming for us now. Just a matter of holding them long enough, right? As long as we keep firing these rifles, we're going to do us just fine." Mrs. Karvel gripped her Browning as she said this, giving it a little shake. Her husband did as well, massaging his hand along the hilt as he stared at the banging door. I wanted a gun too. I wanted to feel that strength, to have something to cling to. I wanted to know the texture of revenge, the weight of it. To at least feel powerful in this moment of complete doom. So loading up with arms and ammunition, Garth, the engineers, and I did just that. And it was as good to grab something within the tempest as I thought it would be.

But it was all illusion. The shooting began only moments after we left the room, the first gun blast coming as the Tekelians finally managed to burst open the exit door. I tried to count the shots as we made our way down the ladder to the main level, and the Karvels must have got off more than two dozen between them, stuttering their blast so that they could take turns reloading. Still, despite the impossibly long pauses between shots, the whole endeavor couldn't have taken more than forty-five seconds. By the time the four of us had climbed down to the main floor, the guns went silent. In their wake was the dull sound of meat being pounded and the short yelps that could have come only from human mouths. The inevitable had come to pass, the beasts had stormed the gates, with all their might. I didn't even bother looking to my compatriots to discern the moment. It was all so fast, but there was no question what was happening.

"Plan B! Plan B!" I began to yell to Garth, scuttling him toward the boiler room. I wanted it hot in there. I wanted it Texas hot. I wanted it hot like the very line of the equator. I didn't want to simply defend myself: I wanted to see those monsters melting. I wanted them to be like the tigers in "Little Black Sambo," pooled like butter on the floor. I didn't care what else firing up the boiler would do, I was going to turn that thermostat as high as it would go and burn those beasts to the ground.

"I'll do it." Jeffree, his hand on my wrist, stopped me. "You don't know nothing about anything mechanical, man. I'm not even trying to insult you. We'll manage the boiler, even fix it if we have to. Leave this to the professionals. Leave this to Jeff Free."

In that one moment, I believed Jeffree was every bit as heroic as he always told everyone he was. His jaw was so square, his forehead so shiny, the cowrie shells around his neck announcing a triumphant chorus as he spun around, possibly smelling his mechanical prey. I no longer saw a fool, an incompetent. This was a man. A silly man sometimes, sure, but a man nonetheless. Jeffree knew the dangers of his task, that if he was going to make a successful escape he would have to cross back through the BioDome to get to the snowmobiles. Jeffree knew this, and he took this nearly suicidal action anyway. Jeffree got to be the hero, and for my part, in that moment, I was actually happy to have him on our side. I would like to think that maybe I had never truly "gotten him" before this moment. Jeffree had simply stood outside the proper context. And Carlton Damon Carter caught him there in his element for digital posterity, both Jeffree's heroic speech and his impalalike bouncing away toward danger. After Jeffree disappeared down the storage corridor, Carlton Damon Carter put down his camcorder, closed the LCD display screen, and then handed it to me. He didn't say a word either, just pressed it into my hands, folded his own hands firmly around my own before giving them a squeeze. Carlton Damon Carter's eyes, his actions, imparted everything. He knew that most likely this would not be a task they would return from. That if he didn't give up his camera now, there was a good chance no one would get to see any of this.

"Film me too, as I run after him," Carlton Damon Carter whispered. And then, chasing after his husband, he was gone.

• • •

Arthur Gordon Pym lay in our sailboat, a bottle of bourbon in one hand and my bag of bones in the other. Whatever exploration he'd been making of the facility had been halted by his blood alcohol level. Fetal and clinging to the bag of the late Dirk Peters as if the remains were his to control, the man was completely oblivious to the coming storm. I didn't bother waking him to get my treasure back, just grabbed it and swung it over my own shoulder for good measure. The sailboat was already too heavy to lift off the ground without Pym in it, so Garth and I dragged the boat along with us on the way to the exit. With the screams of the beasts echoing behind us, we could see their long and violent shadows along the corridor walls, and we pulled faster. As we passed the piles of bulk snack treats and liquid refreshments, Garth and I simply knocked the boxes into the sailboat on and around Pym, who offered not a peep of complaint, not even opening his eyes.

At the garage, the Karvels' snowmobiles sat pristine and factory clean, looking as if they were virgins to the continent of powder that lay just outside the hatch door. As we tied the boat to the vehicles, a rope to each tow, we listened for sounds of an outside presence waiting for us when we opened the doors but heard none. No, all the sounds of intrusion were coming from inside the terrarium. The wailing, the aggravated howls, the metal clanging and glass breaking.

"We got to get the hell out of here, dog. We can leave the doors open, see if Jeffree and C-note make it out from a distance, but this sitting and shitting thing ain't going to work," Garth said, his eyes stuck on the door to the hallway behind us. And Garth was right. His face was covered in toothpaste, but he was right. Our gas tanks were full, the engines started. I was sitting on a bright pink bike with floral decals, but I didn't even care at this point. We hit the door opener and were out onto the snow at full speed the moment the gate had risen high enough for us to duck through.

Garth and I were about five hundred yards away, steering a path clear of the enemy camp, when the first explosion went off behind us. Such was the power of the blast and the sound it produced that I lost control of my speeding snowmobile from the vibrations. Still, it was nothing compared to the second explosion, which left my ears ringing to the point of deafness and knocked me completely over, my snowmobile skidding off beyond me.

I righted myself on the snow as soon I had gathered my senses. Behind me, a quarter of Karvel's amazing dome was now nothing more than fire and ruin, the section where the boiler was situated consumed by a fire that spread across the surface of the roof.

"Jeffree," I said aloud.

"It's not their fault," Garth said back at me, but my mind had not even gotten that far. The destruction of a quarter of the 3.2 Ultra BioDome, and the impending destruction of the rest of the building, paled in its catastrophic weight in comparison to the long line of ice caves that I could see were now imploding.

The ground turned from resolute to uncertain. It shook violently beneath us, until both of us were floored once more by the power and length of the quake. And even when our immediate ground grew less spastic, the roar of the landscape around us told of a destruction just beginning. Coffins of ice collapsing upon themselves where, only moments before, the still unbroken surface had sat placid. Yard by yard, the heat-weakened ice caves tumbled upon themselves, lines of jumbled ice succumbing like so many dominoes in a line of destruction I could see moving off into the sunset and toward the heart of the Tekelian empire.

Even Pym in his near-comatose state was momentarily awakened by the catastrophe, and had an opinion on the matter. Sitting up in the boat, staring left and right to see the surface collapsing into canals that stretched as far as I could witness, Pym seemed almost unfazed by the enormity of it.

"And so the heavens fell to earth," he yelled when the worst had subsided, taking another lethal swig straight from the bottle's neck before passing out again.

INTERLUDE

> The circumstances connected with the late sudden and distressing death of Mr. Pym are already well known to the public through the medium of the daily press. It is feared that the few remaining chapters which were to have completed his narrative, and which were retained by him, while the above were in type, for the purpose of revision, have been irrecoverably lost through the accident by which he perished himself. This, however, may prove not to be the case, and the papers, if ultimately found, will be given to the public. . . . Peters, from whom some information might be expected, is still alive, and a resident of Illinois, but cannot be met with at present. He may hereafter be found, and will, no doubt, afford material for a conclusion of Mr. Pym's account.
>
> —Note, *Narrative of Arthur Gordon Pym*

IT would seem that *The True and Interesting Narrative of Dirk Peters* was that promised material that would reveal the true end of Arthur Pym's *Narrative,* despite the fact that it was never delivered to the public during Peters's lifetime.* Of course, Dirk Peters did make the effort to construct those missing chapters, and his memory should not be impugned just because he (unlike Booker T. Washington) was unable to hire a ghostwriter who could sufficiently convey his story. Peters's attempt to secure the services of

---

* *Material* is an excellent word for Dirk Peters's collection; *debris* would be another less generous one.

Edgar Allan Poe to relay his story may have failed, but this was not to be the end of his ambitions in the matter.

In a folder at the bottom of the Dirk Peters papers sat an envelope somewhat different from the others in the collection. For one thing, this packet contained stubs from what appeared to be both train and ocean-liner tickets, both of which were dated in the spring of 1895. The note that accompanied them is even more difficult to decipher than the muddled script in the rest of the collection. Its lines are shaken, the curves large and slow—this would of course make sense if it was indeed written in 1895, by which time Peters would have at least been in his eighties, his poor penmanship having even further degraded. Here it is in its entirety:

Arrived in Amiens. The canals make it smell something horrible. I went to the writer's house, had a copy of 20,000 Leagues under [sic] Sea, going to tell him I like it, I want his help. I'm thinking that's a good one, on account of it's got an Indian in it, like me. That Nemo was a seafaring one two [sic], so if he can tell his story I don't see why the man can't tell mine. I speak a little of the Frenchy, so I plan on Parla vousing [sic] that to the man. Seems the book selling is behind him, and this Verne man he working at the politics. I ask the locals, they say just look for him. Then I see him like they say. It's easy to see because the man got a bad limp, in his left leg, like the kind you get after you been shot. Well, I start feeling sorry for him, being a cripple, then I'm walking up to him telling him who I was and what I'm wanting. But then, after he listens for a bit and I tell him how that Poe man took my story from me and now for the truth I want Jules Verne writing in stead, being as my writing boy, he hits me with his cane! I run off a bit and then I'm glad he got a gimp leg, because I do believe he was still trying to kick me.

While there is no other historical record of this interaction, this final effort on Peters's part to let his memoir be heard, it should be noted that *Le Sphinx des Glaces* emerged from Verne's publisher just two years later.* While the account that Verne gives bears little resemblance to the one Dirk Peters hastily relayed and is largely a hackneyed attempt to find closure to Poe's original tale, there are points of interest nonetheless. Verne's sequel has a black ship chef as well, much like Poe's novel. Describing this chef's reaction to being cast away on an iceberg, Verne wrote, "As a Negro, who cares little about the future, shallow and frivolous like all of his race, he resigned himself easily to his fate; and this is, perhaps, true philosophy."

* Or as this book is also known: *The Sphinx of the Ice Fields.*

CHAPTER XXIV

ON our return journey to the place where our saga began, we made "good time," although we did not have one. With rope tied from both of our vehicles to the boat, Garth and I plowed forward side by side while behind us, without clue or concern, Arthur Gordon Pym drunkenly continued sleeping. The journey back is often less labored than the trail blazed forward, and this was no different. We didn't stop unless we found ourselves cut off by one of the newly formed ravines created by a tunnel's collapse. We didn't talk, and in truth my ears were still ringing so much from the last explosion that I wouldn't have heard much anyway. We just followed our own tracks, and the tracks of the Tekelian war party that followed them, both of which were still frozen into the powder. The journey was so swift that I didn't realize we were even close when I first saw the billowing gray smoke rising in the distance. A half hour later, on our arrival at the scene, I barely recognized it to be the remains of the Creole base camp, our former home.

"They blew that shit up, dog," was the first thing Garth had said to me in hours. I don't even know when or how he'd managed to clean his face and arms off. The big man got off his snowmobile and walked over to the edge of the burning hole, sat down on its side, and let his legs dangle over. That was when I first realized that Garth was in shock, oddly enough. And I knew I must be in shock too, although this knowledge registered no further. I got off my snowmobile to see it, to look in the crater at the destruction that had been created. The only thing I recognized was the roof, the same one I'd climbed up to several times to adjust the satellite dish. That antenna was now gone, possibly blown free, and what remained of the wreckage was only black and smoking and sinking into the frozen ground, reeking of burnt rubber and unnameable plastics and pork rinds.

"Blew it to high hell," Garth repeated, pointing now at the massive, smoking crater that cut off our path to the ocean.

What I saw as I continued to look into the ruins was something far more horrific. Poking through the snow, I could see the charred gray limbs of the beasts in question as well, probably contributing to the pork smell.

This was not just a crater, this was a crevice, spreading a good fifty yards across. And then, lengthwise, it spread far, far beyond that. Leading back along the same line that Augustus's tunnel once had was a tunnel which had clearly become little more than debris and sunlight like the rest of them. I didn't know if every Tekelian tunnel had collapsed, but I knew that all those close to the surface must have, and that, even if the village still existed below, there was no way to return to it now.

We rode along the crevice's edge, following it back in the direction I knew Tekeli-li to be. Looking to my side as I drove, I waited for the massive crack in the ground to narrow and close, but it didn't. It just got wider. And then, it got so big that, had Garth not been focusing primarily on what lay in front of us, we might have driven directly into it.

At the sight of Tekeli-li, or at least where I estimated Tekeli-li to have once been carved, there was now only a space the size of a small village sunken into the ground. It looked as if a great and literal god had poked his hand from the sky and with one massive finger pushed the snow down. There was no sign of our vehicles, or the captors who held both. Just more broken fragments of ice that had once appeared to be solid ground.

Let me say here that I never saw the remains of any more of the species and so can't make concrete assertions about them. Nor do I have any information other than what I am currently presenting. But out of respect for all who must have fallen in the ice's collapse, regardless of race or species, Garth and I did say what words we could, and acknowledged the already present silence. After this, there was little more for us to do but move on. It was time to sail for Tsalal. Or to die in the noble effort of trying.

Following a groggy Pym's instructions, we rode to the southernmost point of what was once Tekeli-li, to the edge of the Ross Sea, and waited for the tide to begin its recession. Then, making our own room in the boat next to our semiconscious passenger, we pushed off into the water. Once we had sufficiently broken free from the mainland, Garth and I pulled our paddles in, letting faith and the surprisingly strong current pull us away.

The following I take from my written notes, composed during the journey. While I can't pretend strict accuracy in these dates, since we didn't have the battery power to run the electronic devices necessary for even figuring that out, I will note that they are accurate to the best of my knowledge. As was done before, they are given principally with a view to perspicuity of narration, and as set down in my pencil memorandum:

March 1

Although it is a region of novelty and wonder, I am glad to be leaving that world behind. When I think back to Thomas Karvel and his dome, I do not wonder about the last moments of his life, or of his art or even of Garth's lost collection—both of which are taboo subjects with the big man. No, despite all the free time, I find myself thinking about Karvel's pigeons. Or rather, why is the white dove so highly regarded because of its lack of pigmentation? How is it that something so minor as the color of a bird's feathers can make the difference between being regarded as the international symbol of peace and being the urban symbol of filth and nuisance? It might be argued that this disparity has to do not just with the vagaries of shade but rather with differences in breed, but since I can't tell the differences in species, that distinction would be lost on me. What then about the mice? my mind drifts to. Why are albino mice deemed worthy to be kept as pampered personal pets while their nearly identical darker brothers are viewed completely as pests? Does whiteness hold so much value for us that its presence is a wealth in itself?

Pym is awake. No, he has begun to wake, his consciousness rising in cycles, then sinking back into a stupor as the wealth of alcohol poison in his system works its way out again. In the last cycle, finding himself in a sailboat at sea, he weakly demanded to know where we were taking him, despite the fact that earlier he had mumbled to us the site we should depart from to find it. "Tsalal, dog," Garth said to him. *"Tsalal,"* Pym said back in a hissing sound that sizzled off his lips until he drifted to unconsciousness once more.

March 2

On the following morning, Arthur Pym woke up once again, this time more coherent than I had ever seen him, and extremely thirsty and complaining of nausea, a symptom that only got dramatically worse when we told him yet again where we were going.

March 3

True to his word, the instructions Pym had given earlier proved to be right. This is to his great luck, because his endless nonsensical discussion of coppering versus whaling in the New England maritime economy is annoying and, had he been wrong, I know I would have strangled him by now. Amazingly, around the three of us there stretched an expanse of broken ice which filled the water's surface like the foam atop a fountain soda. In front of as well as behind us on our stretch of roadlike path, the water was both improbably warm and ice free, the current shooting us forward, out of the frozen way, almost as if this hot spring poured from the center of the earth through a hole at the pole and now was rushing north to make the trip to the other pole and down once more.

Garth shivers all the time, wrapped in many blankets though he is. Still, he barely talks to me.

March 4

The highlight of our day was when, after a black blanket was laid over Arthur Pym's face in order to keep his hanging tongue from freezing, he woke with a horrific scream. "Tsalal. Tsalal," he kept murmuring in a drowsy stupor, falling back asleep without removing the thing.

March 5

The polar cold is retreating as the current pushes us on, squeezing us out and up. Garth, at the front of the boat, is inscrutable to me, as quiet as the waters we sit on. I don't know if he's mourning our lost compatriots or his life's art collection more, but I assume both weigh significantly on his thick shoulders. As it becomes warmer, the dread I have long been feeling begins to abandon me, along with the numbness I realize I had become so accustomed to. The closer we get to the heat, the more I feel my *existence*. The more I am ready to feel. To see color, to feel the dark earth, to be alive.

March 6

In the morning, I saw the darkest cloud I have ever witnessed coming from the distance. But it could not be a cloud, because it took up the whole sky, coming in a line and pulling over it like a blanket until it was directly above us. Then it started snowing. Except, this wasn't snow. It was not white, it was gray. It was not cold, rather it was warm to the touch. It was ash. Volcanic ash. We are near land, and land where there is a volcano that can produce this. Although for the moment this ash blocked the very sun, I was elated about this fact, and shared this across the boat with Garth Frierson. Garth just nodded, and asked me to pass the Cheetos, of which we still have many. Arthur Pym, for his part, threw himself on his face in the bottom of the boat, and no persuasions could induce him to get up.

March 7

To quiet his squealing, I offered Pym more food from our supply. The only thing I could reach at that moment, packed as it all was, happened to be a bag of Oreo cookies. These Pym accepted only after great protest, and then only eating the creme filling and dropping the cookies to the boat's bottom like they were feces. I found this extremely wasteful, and shared my thoughts with the man. When I did so, he screamed, "Your teeth!" cringing away from me in horror. Admittedly, my smile was darkened by my own Oreo indulgence, but I still found this further outburst very rude and told him that.

March 8

This afternoon I was woken by the screams of the lately mute Garth Frierson, who was yelling "Dog! Dog!" as he pointed off into the water. As it was his habit to preface much of what he had to say to me using the canine diminutive, I thought he was merely calling me. This, however, was not the case. Garth continued with "It's a dog, in the water." My first thought was that our journey was affecting the former bus driver's mental health. Following his finger, however, I did see something. What I at first took to be a log came closer to reveal a snout, eyes, and whiskers. It looked like a Labrador retriever, soaking and in search of dry land, just like the three of us were. But it wasn't bobbing in the water as it should, it was gliding, and within seconds I realized that it was in fact a seal of some kind, equally caught in this tepid current. For the next few minutes we watched the beautiful black creature circle our boat, inching closer with every cycle until he came close enough so that I could almost reach a hand out to pet his shining forehead. It was then that Arthur Pym, who had again drifted off, came back to consciousness. Turning listlessly to the side, Pym caught a glimpse of the black creature coming toward him, and this vision caused the man to begin a pattern of deep and grave sighing to the point of hyperventilation. This reminded me of a fact once read and long forgotten: in some segment of European folklore, there was a demon that came to earth in the form of a massive black dog, a monster seen along highways by those traveling by coach through the darkness. Although distinctly American, Pym did have the air of that continent about him, so maybe it was for this reason that continent's mythology now burdened him.

March 9

Another wave of ash now falls on us continually. It hangs on Garth's Afro, and over the straight greasy strands of Pym's raven mane as well. It sits on our clothes and our skin and our boat, and all of our possessions. Everything is the same color, under its volcanic weight. There is only gray.

March 21

Wherever we are going, we are going there fast, and shooting toward our conclusion. Although it is difficult to gauge the speed at which we're traveling, the increase of wind seems to indicate great movement, and the air now pushes forcefully past us. The food is gone; we are left now to revisit the bags and containers of past meals and scrape crumbs that were before beneath our notice. It's not Garth's fault; he barely eats in comparison to his normal appetite. Arthur Gordon Pym rarely rises up from the middle of the boat, and when he does it is to suggest that we pick straws. Garth and I have agreed to keep a watch on him, make sure his hunger doesn't compel him to try to dine on one of us once again.

For an hour this morning, I riffed on the Europeans' fascination with cannibalism, citing their use of the act in eighteenth- and nineteenth-century writings as the defining difference between savage and civilized man. All this despite the fact that their largest church practiced ritualized cannibalism daily in the form of a sacramental cracker and glass of wine. From there, I went off on a rant about how this unique cannibalistic nature was at the center of European American culture, citing their devouring of black culture and regurgitating it for sustenance. "So you telling me hip-hop culture is any better?" Garth asked me. It was the longest sentence I'd heard from him in over a week. To this I told him, "No." I hadn't realized I was not only being absurd but also talking out loud.

March 22

The largest black birds I have ever seen have begun circling our boat, calling out to us in lispy caws, almost joyous at our arrival. While I'm no ornithology expert, I think they are albatrosses, and on first spotting their dark wings I believed that this time this was truly, truly the sign that our rescue was imminent, that land was just beyond. Their song almost sounded like the name of our hoped for destination, "Tsalal, Tsalal," the gigantic things seemed to call from above, the sound building till, en masse, the flock retreated from our vision.

And there it was. Land, just beyond, and our boat rushed to embrace it. The stream we rode along aimed straight for a cave, in which it seemed the current met a river that traveled farther inland. In relief, in exhaustion, I let out a yell that was no rational word, just pure emotion. Excited beyond measure and too diminished physically to express this, I grabbed up the green canvas sack from beneath my seat and hugged the last remains of Dirk Peters to my chest in victory. Obviously the bones themselves were entirely less enthusiastic about their impending immigration than I was for them, but hadn't that been Garth's point all along? "I am placing you here," I said, taking ownership of that, and of the fact that this gesture would always be mine alone. It was then that Arthur Gordon Pym, prostrate, stirred in the bottom of the boat, rising to see what Garth and I were both now making a fuss about. As Pym slowly rose to take in the shore, he looked weak, he looked paler than I had ever seen him. Facing our destination, he trembled to take it in. And then, suddenly, Pym's eyes widened even further, and his finger shot up to point out something that clearly disturbed him. "Lord, help my poor soul," his dry throat managed. It was the next sound he made that disturbed me the most, a hollow sucking, immediately followed by his collapse to the base of the boat.

I reached out to his now stilled body. Despite the heat of the air around us, Pym's skin had grown disturbingly cold. Both Garth and I tried to resuscitate him, but his spirit had departed. Looking up to see what vision had mortified him, what there was beyond the tan sand and green palms that seemed so inviting, we could find no explanation. But we did see something, something that finally caught both sets of our eyes. Rising up in our pathway was a man. He was naked except for the cloth that covered his loins. He was of normal proportions, and he was shaking his hand in the air, waving it, and we, relieved, waved ours back at him. Past him, minutes later, we saw that he was joined in welcoming us by others, women, more men, and the offspring both had managed. Whether this was Tsalal or not, however, Garth and I could make no judgments. On the shore all I could discern was a collection of brown people, and this, of course, is a planet on which such are the majority.

ACKNOWLEDGMENTS

Special thanks to Gloria Loomis, for whom the title "agent" comes up short. For reading this book in several unfinished forms over eight years, for pushing me to realize it fully, for not letting me destroy the project six years in when I became hopeless, I will be eternally grateful.

Thanks to Geoffrey Sanborn for putting me in the place to get into this work and showing me the intellectual path to find my way out of it.

Thanks to the United States Artists Foundation for providing the support that further enabled this work to be produced.

ABOUT THE TYPE

This book was set in Dante, Giovanni
Mardersteig's last and most successful
design. Special care was taken with the
design of the serifs and top curves of
the lowercase to create a subtle
horizontal stress, which helps the eye
move smoothly across the page. Dante
is a beautiful book face that can also
be used to good effect in magazines
and periodicals.